MW00612337

"This first novel suggests the ambitious debuts of Joseph McElroy (*A Smuggler's Bible*) and Thomas Pynchon (*V.*), but author Evan Dara pushes the bar back upward to the height of William Gaddis' *The Recognitions*... It takes some work to look back at *The Lost Scrapbook* and say, 'Aha, so that's how all those parts fit together,' and then 'Aaah,' which signifies satisfaction or, with a different spelling, awe."

—*The Washington Post*

"The most formidable political novel of the 1990s."

—Jeremy Green, *Late Postmodernism: American Fiction at the Millennium*

"Monumental, cunning, heartfelt and unforgiving... Dara shows how a novel can be experimental, yet moral, rule-breaking but emotional, and post-humanist while remaining deeply human. A vast accomplishment."

—Richard Powers

"Evan Dara's magnificent novel [is crafted] as if James Joyce had widened the narrative ear of *Ulysses*... If this really is Mr. Dara's first novel, then he is either a young phenom or a well-practiced, reclusive treasure."

—*Chelsea Review*

"A radiant, innovative work filled with engaging characters...creating a complex world in which issues of personal liberty, private politics and public responsibility come into play."

—*Time Out New York*

"Dazzling...encyclopedic...a poignant meditation on isolation and community...encompassing the voices of America in a spirit of Whitmanesque accumulation that is brilliantly innovative and compassionate."

—*Rain Taxi*

"Wonderful...sensational...Dara's fiction is likely to prove enduring."

—*Confrontation*

"The most pure fiction I've ever read. I'm not kidding... The books behind the hot books exist, and if you give them chance enough, they scorch you. While fiction suffers elsewhere, Dara revolutionizes it."

—*Oculus*

"An extremely impressive work, Dara's sprawling epic deserves wider exposure."

—*The Modern Word*

"A dazzling novel. Dara is just a boon companion, whose startling technical brilliance never overwhelms or even impedes the whitewater rush of this hilarious and original narrative. A mind-blowingly fun book."

—*Popula Culture*

"A towering piece of American literature and one of the best three novels of the nineties."

—*The Fictional Woods*

"The best book you may not have heard of."

—*The Dust Congress*

The Lost Scrapbook

EVAN DARA

New York - Roma

This is a work of fiction. Names, characters, organizations, places, and incidents are the products of the author's imagination or are used fictitiously. Any resemblance to actual events, locales, institutions, or persons, living or dead, is entirely coincidental.

THE LOST SCRAPBOOK. Copyright © 1995 by Evan Dara. All rights reserved. Printed in The United States of America. No part of this book may be used or reproduced in any manner whatsoever without written permission, except in the case of brief quotations embodied in critical articles or reviews.

Published by Aurora, Inc., New York and Roma.

For information, address:
www.aurora148.com

Dara, Evan
The Lost Scrapbook: a novel

ISBN 978-0-9802266-1-4

First Aurora Edition

Jacket Design: Todd Michael Bushman

Evan Dara is an American writer living in France.

To honor every man, absolutely every man, is the truth.

—Kierkegaard

O let me teach you how to knit again
This scattered corn into one mutual sheaf,
These broken limbs again into one body;

—*Titus Andronicus*

— I am, yes; certainly;
— So how about medicine...?
— Listen to me: Yes; I am; *absolutely*...
— Or law—?
— Of course;
— Then forestry; does that—?
— Immeasurably;
— And—?
— Profoundly...
— Or—?
— *Passionately—!*

along with marine acoustics and quantum biography and psychogeology, not to mention their respective subdisciplines; but what I am *not* interested in, Ms. Clipboard—or Mr. Canker or Mrs. Murmur or Call-me-Carol, *all* of you—is your questions; even your pointing and tipping Enoch pencils have six sides, my dear definers: pay heed whereon you pinch!; I am interested, almost exclusively, in being interested, and your reductivist probings are only intended to cordon off wings of my mansion:

— Tell me what book has made the strongest impress— the tale of the suicidal *career counselor,* o Dr. Sphincter; it's a bizarre enterprise, this deciding what "to be": mostly it feels like negotiating what *not* to be; so spare me your solicitude, my dear diminishers, for I can already hear what you are going to say next: that before long I'll need to be realistic, and to acknowledge the inevitable, and that eventually I'll recognize the subtle majesty of moderation; after all, you'll tell me,

children can only make purposeful movements after they've learned to rein in their fitful, neonatal fluttering; learning to reach is actually a process of learning *not* to do everything *except* reaching; but let the watusi continue!, I say; think how we might move if all that innate waggling could be harnessed:
— But you know that isn't workable; now, if you'd just look at this pattern of crosshatched smudges—
and see the configuration of my future; no way, good sirrah; if I tell you, creviced Dr. Goatee, that I enjoy a good game of musical chairs, would you consign me to a lifetime on a loading dock?; if I mention that I had stubbed my toe on a rock in Hoppe Park on the way to your paneled offices, would that make me a born jack-hammerer?; save your TAT's and your Stanford-Binet's and your vocational aptitude tests for people who are born takers of TAT's and Stanford-Binet's and voc. ap. tests; do not ask me to choose classical philology over industrial catering when they *both* seem such powerful fun; I want to be a forensic epidemiologist *and* a floorwalker in men's hosiery—*look* at how those size 10-to-13's drape over their tiny 2-shaped hangers:
— All that is admirable, of course; but, you know—
— *But there is so little time...*;
So then, of course, it becomes a question of sequencing, of best organizing the delectable succession; and, in fact, I will admit to preferences on that count; there are things I would like to do first, undertakings that I am avid to attack even before all the others that I am agonizing to get at; for instance, I have always wanted to operate a centrifuge; now *that* would be deeply rewarding: separating milk from cream, reclaiming used motor oil, pulling blood platelets from plasma—it is an honorable calling; then, after having devoted myself to fathoming some small tittle of the centrifuge's irreducible depths, I would next like to work in anthropology; for here, if I may say so, I believe I have much to contribute—indeed, I believe I am on the verge of substantiating significant advances both theoretical and practical; yes, my inquisitors, I assure you this is true; for I have established, on my own, as an unaffiliated scholar, no less than a new definition of Man— yes, him—one that is easily more rigorous than any heretofore

proposed; forget opposable thumbs, disregard use of tools, lay down language capacity or abstract reasoning—those are clearly insufficient; my definition easily surpasses these provisional flouncings in accuracy, comprehensiveness, and elegance; and it is this: man is the animal who pisses where he shouldn't; and when this gets out, when this robust new paradigm is disseminated and attributed, I am sure that my modest Edwardsville will become as renowned in anthropological circles as the Olduvai Gorge!; that the Leakey family will be seen to have gotten closer to the truth with their name than with their 57 years of sun-scorched fieldwork!; that Billy Carter's ureter will seem more momentous than Lucy the hominid's mandible!, and this is what is called progress, this is considered advancement: putting one foot after another, putting one step after another; this is considered achievement, this is supposed to be movement...; but no: this is not progress, this is not achievement, it is much the opposite: I am a figure on a treadmill, and my steps are delivering me nowhere: I can displace nothing; going past Bennett Street, then past Seminole Street, then continuing past Sunset, storefront-glass gives way to rot-wood houses which give way to the green sweep of Meador Park; but nothing changes, nothing is removed: I am traveling nowhere; I am only simulating distance, shamming movement: action is only reinforcing stasis, effort establishing impotence...

...And all the while, accompanying my every step, The Photographer is sounding in my head, purling incessantly through my clamped-on Walkman; it's a good piece, Glass's homage to Muybridge, minimalism used to maximal effect: with its repeating rhythms, endlessly rechurning, the music resembles a wave that doesn't move, a standing wave; that's what you listen to, the change and unchange of the wave, not any emergent melody: listening not above, but within; nowadays, I sit in Meador Park for hours on end plumbing the piece, turning the cassette over and over to extend it indefinitely; and it goes, the music just goes, without faltering, without hesitation, not depleted through repetition, but enriched; and as it goes—without faltering, without hesitation—the rapid-rushing piece instantly becomes the soundtrack to what

I am looking at, regardless of what it may be: the varied tilts of oldsters' hats, wind-gusts corduroying the park's grass, the sparkling of pram wheels, children stepping onto the water fountain's access ledge and hunchbacking behind their button-pushing hand and jutting lips; the music suits it all perfectly, uncannily, as absolutely apt accompaniment, the spirit of vision converted into onflowing sound; further, it works just as well in the other direction: whatever I see also functions as a perfect illustration of The Photographer's ceaseless undulant nattering; every event and gesture in my visual field—bicycle-spokes fanning, pinkie balls trickling across the ruffling green—seems to spring from some hidden imperatives of this unheard music: sight and sound have adhesive properties of which I had never before dreamed...

...It's a question, really, of figure and ground, of learning to integrate the two: of linking the landscape to the flamelike cypress thrusting up within it, of considering the World along with Cristina: dissolving patterns into particles...; and I, for one, am perfectly positioned to make such investigations: I am either a bland assemblage of denim, sweatcloth, sneaks, connecting flesh and Walkman scudding through the streets of Springfield, barely perceptible in its random passages, or an indrawn 19-year-old with slightly stooped posture who has run away; it depends on whom you ask for the description: me, or anyone else in the world *but* me; figure and ground; figure or ground; but who, since Muybridge, even *looks* at the ground?; and Cristina was a cripple—

YIELD

Still, I cross Grand Street, then Catalpa Street, then Bennett, walking past unswept barbecue parlors, past unmanned parking lots, past the smudged and overcrowded display windows of heavy-metal collectibles stores, past Denn's Nip Inn and The Four Roses convenience grocery; and even though these streets and their shouting features have all but disappeared to me, the exhaust-stench from the passing Number 5 bus sluices through me, even if I hold my breath; there is no escaping you, civilization: you even trickle up pinched-closed nostrils;

when I could not countenance going to college, I got a job in Cinco de Mayo; when I could no longer abide dispensing microwaved prefab tacos I went to Sterne's Small Appliances; when I could no longer bring myself to peddle garage openers and 17-function four-blade blenders when exactly the same devices were available at invariably cheaper prices at DC Pritcher's around the corner, I found myself at Raiders' Pharmacy; when I could no longer endure Jim Raider's cruel commentaries about the customers, delivered the very moment the door had shut behind them, I went home and looked in one of my M.C. Escher print-books; heavy and covered in flashing cellophane, the book begins with a section about the history of tessellations, from Byzantine mosaics to Escher and his progeny; yes, I know that Escher is scorned and over-commercialized and pap, that he is non-art, that the arbiters have arbitrated against him, but as I sat and turned the pages the involuted lithographs began to draw me in; and as I was knotting more deeply into Escher's inlacings and refractions of dimension, I turned another page and knew that I had to come here: outside, beyond: in the midst, but also gone; finding invisibility through new presence; disappearing through assertion, through self-assertion: beyond, outside...

...So now I move about you, civilization, like an electron: amid your clamor and industry, your commonness and shared accords, I am a speck, whirling and circling, negatively charged; with no measurable existence save the statistical, I am everywhere, and therefore nowhere; I have now evaded notice for eight straight days: I walk through the Walnut Street district or stand on Glenstone Street pretending to be waiting for the bus, and I eat the wetfoam remains of dumpster buns and the gouged remnants of chocolate cake pulled from quit tables in the diners where I go to the bathroom, but I have not once been stopped by the police: there have been no sirens, no takings-in for questioning, no ID checks, no off-hand but edgy glances by serious men festooned with security equipment; in no way have they altered my orbit; in other words, they have entirely acknowledged my invisibility...; here, now, I have finally consummated my tendency towards non-existence, indeed I have pushed it to unforeseeable levels of accomplishment; now my sole function in this world is to serve as receptacle for the proof that I am inconsequential; every experience I accrete is only another stroke of an eraser; and experience is endless...

...For instance, five nights ago: it was five nights ago that I decided, after three full days outside, to go back—to investigate; I had an urge to see what had transpired at the point-center once known as *my house*; so after an early evening spent drifting through downtown—I played the game of asking people directions to non-existent streets—just past ten o'clock, I made the turn: moving rapidly, I took a twisty route of lesser-used sideblocks, and felt the granuly transition from urban-indifferent public domain to soft-massed *my neighborhood*; then I slowed considerably; finally arriving at my block, I rounded the dark corner almost as if tailing someone, edging forward in fractional steps, holding my breath forcibly back; and when I finally angled up to my two-story home, this is what my vortical eyes saw: no squad cars parked in front of the house, with no revolving roof-lights; no vigilant neighbors sitting in backlit windows; no newly-arrived relatives; there was only the customary leafy darkness shrouding the gray-green saltbox, swaddled by shifting suburban quietness; nothing had changed; nothing was different; nothing was at all unsettled; I had caught invisibility *in action*...

...For a few minutes, then, I remained outside, hidden behind a tree on the other side of the street, and just looked on; and then I decided that I had to go in: I needed to see if this was all just pretense and facade, to look for concrete signs of my own absence; so I approached the house gingerly, with slow, sidewalk-rasping steps, and then inched up the sheetrock entrance pathway; but the front-door lock unclutched easily to my key, as it always had, and the foyer was still flanked by the same familiar coat-closets; further on, in the living room, the rug was still abraded to stringy barrenness in front of the low-slung couch where my mother sits to watch TV, her everpresent ashtray ever poised on the plastic, metal-legged table beside her; in other words, nothing was different, nothing had changed: it was impossible to tell that I had been away for three full days; objects, furniture, all of it was still in place, and my non-presence had done nothing to alter that; there were no traces at all—of any kind—of my invisibility...

...But then the question came: why should there be?; why *would* there be?; my mother works as an assistant night-administrator at Lakeland Regional Hospital, and her job keeps her away six evenings a week, with heavy overtime; thus the situation in my home, that quiet night, was entirely within accepted tradition: over the last ten years my mother and I have regularly gone for days without seeing one another; locked into our complementary schedules, we push through opposite quadrants of a revolving door, in an ongoing pirouette that even Straussler might admire; of course there were occasional encounters, and every now and then I'd become conscious of one of her jackknifed cigarette butts in the ashtray, or of a sprawled magazine on the couch, and the refrigerator could always be counted on to be loaded up; but our orbits virtually never intersected; so that evening, that moment, when I was there, pelted by my house's unchanged sameness, I realized what I had to do: I took a carton of orange juice from the refrigerator and placed it on the kitchen counter, hard upon the metallic lip of the sink; I even made it hang out over the sink's basin; then I pulled one of the chairs from the kitchen table, whose plastic dahlia-patterned tablecloth was beautymarked with cigarette burns, and put it in the living room, just standing in room-center; these things, I suspected, would be noticed—they would certainly be noticed; and then I was off, clicking the door behind me, back into the night and the stroking wind, with its coolness and easy mobility, its dark lightness, among the silence that derives from depth and not from confinement; in other words, I was outside again: outside, in my achieved invisibility...

TOW-AWAY ZONE

I often wonder these days—when looking in the window of a record store, or when passing a jumbly newsstand—if I would respond if someone were to call out my name: if I would involuntarily whip toward the sound of self, or even feel the old esophageal shimmy of potential recognition; I doubt it: I feel as if that mode of particularity is lapsing away (and, accordingly, I can hardly care); but it doesn't stop there: I can barely align myself with generics any longer: it's difficult to feel like a runaway when no one has noticed that you're gone; being other-directed becomes problematic in the realm of no faces...

...It's like that time a few summers ago—I think I was 15—when I brought my bicycle into Andy's Getty station for air: I had a red, fenderless, 10-speed Raleigh then, with chrome-shiny Deraillieur-system gears, and I took good care of it (it had been given to me for an earlier birthday); all that summer, I spent afternoons riding up and down the hill to Ritter Springs Park, with its green slopes and abandoned gazebo; but by mid-season the bike had become harder to pedal, so one day after I had gotten to the park, I checked the wheels and found they had gone soft; accordingly, I stopped off at Andy's gasworks while on my way home; the station has a blood-red air pump across the tarmac from the garage, and though the sign above it says 10¢, this was more intimidation for the untutored than a real request; so, without disturbing anyone, I rode up to the pump, got off my sticky-seated bike, pushed the kickstand down, and began the pleasant ritual: I rotated each of the bike's wheels to bring its air nozzle to bottom, then went for the airhose; it hung in a looping circle from the bassety jowl of the pump's drooping metal cradle; with silent aplomb, I found the hose's bulbed tip, knelt on one knee, and pressed the chrome knob to the bicycle's front wheel; immediately, then, the wheel began plumping with the arriving 45 pounds of pressure, and the bicycle-frame edged perceptibly up; again, it was a pleasant process: I had effected a working linkage, the pump-head was huffing and clanging in a passion of airy output, when, from nowhere, someone grabbed my arm, pulled me up and jolted me around—so abruptly that I lost control of the airhose and it snaked away, hissing, on the ground; for a second I thought that Andy had decided to get mad because I hadn't paid the 10¢, but then a man's rough hand clamped over my face and crawled down over my mouth and chin; then the man pulled my throat up hard, making my throat-skin burn and sealing in my yelping; and then he wheeled me around toward the station, at which point I saw Andy, old and skinny Andy, come barreling out of his office beside the garage; Andy stopped dead, stared wildly in my direction, and faltered nervously; then, with his face grimaced and panicky, he slowly put his hands up...

...The man holding me had a pistol in his other hand; I saw it in the corner of my eye just before I felt its cold hardness crunch into my temple; pressed against my face, the pistol was hard in a way that seemed absolute, bone-smashing, beyond argument, and cold in a way that seemed perfect and permanent; the man then wrenched me directly between him and Andy, whose eyes were as wide open as his hands, and then there was silence and then I heard the air hose puffing and then there were words: *Hey* and *Come on* and *Leave him go*; the gunman then began towing me backwards by my throat and chin, and I saw that Andy was fretting and rubbing his reddened cheek; but then a red station wagon drove in off Route 44 and went up to the gas island, and the gunman hoisted my throat higher up against his hard-boned chest; Andy, all sweating and chomping, started looking back and forth from the gas island to us, and the gunman began exhaling *shit...shit...*, and my throat skin was burning, and my temple was erratically separating from and painfully banging back into the metal barrel of the pistol, and I was thinking this is really rather interesting: this feels like being in a movie and it is really rather interesting; there is something to be said for this; but then the driver of the red station wagon leaned from his window and called out *Hey Andy—*, whereupon Andy fretted some more and began backing towards his office without saying anything; and then, all of a sudden, the station wagon gunned its engine and tore backwards around the gas pumps, then shot forward and snorted away down Route 44; and as the car disappeared, I thought of the bullet in the man's pistol: before my eyes I saw the bullet in stunningly accurate cross-section, highly magnified but meticulously correct: the pointed projectile, gleamy within its snug chute, streaked and striped with reflected light; and then

I thought of how the bullet would be shoved through space—
how a slug, a bit, would explode out and Zeno forth and reach
pure continuousness before streaming directly into frayable
gut flesh; and I was thinking of what it would be like to have
such a wound, to lift up the bottom of my shirt at school and
have bandages to show, white brushstrokes on belly, when a
horrendous force *Huhhh* catapulted me forward and my neck
whipped back and I crumbled down to the pavement and my
entire face began to cry; and then, after an evanescent
interval, Andy was above me, just hovering there, splintering
the sunlight and sputtering *You OK?, you OK…?*; but he didn't
touch me; he didn't even bend down; and from my kinked
position on the tarmac I looked over my shoulder and saw the
gunman running towards a gray sedan waiting down the road;
then he scrambled into the passenger door and the car took
off; and then, with miraculous rapidity, that was it; that was
that; the whole thing was over, and things went back to
business as usual; Andy didn't even want to bother calling the
police—he said they aren't concerned about things like this;
he just helped me up, fluttered his hand over the front of my
pants to help brush away some gravel, and went back into his
office; I, of course, was all right: the gunman had only shoved
me, that was all; he had strong hands but there was no harm
done, and of course there hadn't been any bullets—of course
I hadn't been *shot…*; there was nothing like that at all; so I
just finished stuffing my bike with invisible air and went
home; and thus ended my career as a hostage—briefly,
inconclusively, with consummate inconsequentiality: a non-
event realizing its full potential, brave new currents in contemporary invisibility—

KEEP DOOR CLOSED

I am in an aisle, drifting…I am drifting down this shadowed
aisle, past shelves stacked with circus-colored cereal boxes,
canned corned beef, bread-loaves in ghost plastic, shiny Big
Jims, prim Pepperidge Farms, great excitements of carrots and
peas…such a small market, just a mid-street deli, but so
furious is the commerce…*grab me,* it all says, and *choose me,*

and *you must take me*...and I do...I do...for this now is my means...; so I move down the aisle, between these barricades of commerce, and I *use* my invisibility...through the trenches of commerce I move like a wave, propagating, a steady flow, perfectly invisible...inconsequential and invisible, I shoot my hand out and break off a piece of the barricade, I snag a unit of commerce...a Clark Bar...a Baby Ruth...a Drake's Cake...and slip each bit up my knuckle-length sleeve, or in the side-hole of my sweatshirt...and then I am out, out of the store...and looking...looking left and right, but never back...and perfectly calm, wherever I look...for such are the uses of invisibility...of invisibility affirmed...for how can invisibility be ruffled, how can inconsequentiality care...yes, now I can exploit my circumstances...I can achieve new mastery...I can serve as my own human shield...knowing that I cannot get caught...that I am, by definition, unnabbable...because I am everywhere...and therefore nowhere...

...In fact, such was the case last night...; for by last night, after nearly eight days out, eight days away, I could proceed with the certainty, the perfect certainty, that I would not be caught, that I would *never* be caught...; and so it was that, at ten o'clock, I was again moving through the road-rhythms of my familiar suburban sector; again I was propagating between the familiar ranks of one-family residences, past known shadow-masses and muting trees; and again the house—my house—was silent; again the streetlamp near the corner threw gradients of gray upon the house's planks and seams, the night wind stumbled among the overdraping branches; but the Welcome mat still lay flat upon the front step, and the stairway inside the house—my house—still led, in dissolving bands of shadow and black, up to the second floor; nevertheless, I looked around...: the carton of OJ that I had perched by the sink had been returned to the refrigerator, and was marginally lighter, and the chair that I had pulled into the living room had been fully retucked under the kitchen table—where, in its resumed normalness, it had become all but invisible...; in other words, the house was calm, orderly, ordinary; in other words, there had been no disruption of the domestic harmony; in other words, the house—my house—

was exhibiting an admirable continuity...

...So again I acted, again I took matters into my own hands—I could not stand apart and witness even my invisibility being erased; I looked around the living room, then took one of the couch's side-cushions and placed it on the floor, directly in front of where my mother sits beside her ashtray table; then, in the kitchen, I took a blue plasticene glass from the sinkside drying rack and put it on the counter—but tipped over, leaning on its side; and then I left, then I went away—though on the way out I grabbed a short stack of Euphrates crackers from the cupboard, as well as a couple of apples from the bowl; the apples drooped and swayed my sweatshirt, but I didn't mind; what I took, I knew, would never be noticed, would never be missed; no one, not even the police, would be able to tell that anything was gone...

...And then I was back, in Meador Park, where spaces can be seen, where the green is green even when it's black, where the night's dark breeze buzzed my ears...; while breaking from the house (my house) I had yearned for the park's sculpted expanses, for its possibilities of distance, I had needed its zoned openness—I had wanted to be there *instantaneously*; and so I walked quickly, bounderingly, past Sunshine Street and past Seminole, and then I picked up my pace still further when I saw a shifting figure—a man, out walking a dog, who had been a customer at Sterne's Appliances; in a dark-collared coat, he was trailing his charge on a taut, extendible leash; at one point, the man looked up and, quite certainly, saw me, as I was taking my boundering steps; but there was no hesitation, no recognition, no memory-flash leading to pleasant resolution; we both simply nodded at one another, in blind neighborly ritual, before quickly turning away...; and I wondered: had I known he lives near here?...

...And so I am outside again—beyond, distant—at home in my silent park; and I am quiet now; now I am sitting on the bench that I prefer, for from its boards, set in sways that graciously accommodate the human spine, I can see a full three sides of the park; I can see enough to know that it is a quiet night...; and it *is* quiet...; for a while there, I will admit, I had actually thought of sacking out in the house...my house...at least just for a few hours, just grabbing a few informal z's; I'm sure that the experience would have offered all kinds of softness—the stretching out, the gentling down...; it would have done so even on the stiff living-room couch; but then it was impossible; there was no way; to have become aware of myself there, to have become conscious of myself remaining in there beyond for purposes of surveillance, would have been untenable...; you see, in certain circumstances, it's better to be invisible even to yourself...; and so I am here again, outside, sitting with my knees bunched to my chin on my dark, preferred bench, nothing more than an incurled clot of denim and sweatcloth and sneakers; so I am, now, where I prefer to be, as part of the invisibility that is there, and not as part of the invisibility that isn't...; so I sit, and look out...; and from where I am, sitting, in the muted night, I see, constantly, other figures, I see an ever-replenishing succession of other figures...; walking down commercial passages, diminishing down unlit blocks, crossing streets after looking both ways, or after looking no way at all...; raked by the headlights of passing cars, or gauzed by the yellowish glow of overhead lamps, the figures are shadow-swept, various, self-involved, and as turbulent as waves, as standing waves...; and as I look at them, as I curl more tightly into shin-warmth on my preferred bench, I wonder which of these figures, too, are runaways, which of these scudding clumps are the moving forms of runaways...but runaways whom I don't recognize, whose rightfulness I don't acknowledge: which of these figures am *I* denying...; because it would take, I am sure, only a glance, only one shared eye-shudder, for all this to end, for their circumstances suddenly to reverse; it would only take one glance upon them...and one glance from them...; this, then, would be interpenetration, genuine interpenetration, a real refutation of figure and ground...; but this does not seem likely, it does not seem likely at all, so I clamp my Walkman onto my two good ears, and stand up at my dark park bench, and continue on, walking, just walking, one flung footfall after another, into deeper darkness, one foot after another, walking, just walking, forever walking, just continuing, walking and continuing, they continue, they continue, they just continue, the endless succession of rushing cars just continue on, one after another, entirely oblivious, entirely indifferent to my being late; but it's interesting, I then thought: that when you're waiting for something—when you're in line at the post office, say, or waiting, as I was, to get on the Interstate—and you're really in a hurry, I mean *really* hankering to get a move on, it doesn't matter how much you fret, and it doesn't matter how much your muscles gnash in vexation, and it doesn't matter how loud you yelp inside your head *Hey, come on!: can't you see I'm late?*, in other words, no matter what you do like that, it just doesn't make the slightest bit of difference, not at all; the world is sadly indifferent to silent appeal; no one ever cares how inconvenienced or anxious or miffed you are, if you keep it to yourself; sometimes you hope that wouldn't be the case, but it is; and so it was here: the cars just kept puffing by, one after another—the endless intent rush, innocent and oblivious; and I was thinking how disconcerting this can be, how these little situations of everyday delay can just get so hellish and debilitating, when, to my major surprise, a slight gap in the traffic appeared, and I seized the chance, accelerating huffily into the Interstate's flow...

And so I was finally on my way; the rendezvous had been set for 7:30, but when I looked down to the glowing black-on-gold numbers on my dash they already read 8:01; this was unfortunate: I was, in effect, imposing on the guy I was going to meet, and I really didn't want to put him out any further by being late; but the guy had sounded nice when I called him, in fact exceptionally easy-going; so I assumed he would wait, at least a bit longer: he had sounded like the sort who would even give a stranger the benefit of the doubt—an awfully good quality; still, I knew that I had to make time, so I pressed the gas and switched into the left lane, where I picked up speed, soon getting as high as 65 or 67—exceptionally dramatic, at least for me; then I hit the lights, both to deal with the dusk working its way down the hillsides and to cue the Nissan ahead of me to scoot out of the way—which, happily, he did; but just after my headlights lit, a brown sedan just about to pass me on the other side of the highway also turned on his lights; it was no more than a coincidence, I suppose, or a response to a unplanned act of suggestion, but I was tickled, because it reminded me of what are always my favorite moments in highway travel: I'm talking about those times when you're driving out on the Interstate at night, when the darkness is such that you feel as if you're sailing out into the void, through virtually coordinate-free space; of course there is *some* light—the milky secretions from the dash, your headlights' soft-edged forward thrusts—but those only serve to reinforce your sense of solitariness, of isolation; so you're out there on the road, coursing through the night's black canyon, when, seemingly from nowhere, some kind of glow starts to sparkle the distant sky—and then you see it's coming from behind a hitherto hidden butte, or the snaky coils of a curve; and then you realize, of course, that it's another car, it's other people, so you sit back and watch as the glow gradually brightens, slowly becoming a spuming cloud of orange-y granules, then a massing plume of radiant dust; and then, as you continue, the spume-cloud gets wider and brighter at the same time, it becomes more diffuse and more directed simultaneously, and it continues growing, and coming closer, and becoming much brighter, brighter to the point where it almost resembles a volcano on the verge of doing something *big*, when—*shlip*—the other car's headlights flip down to timorous low beam, to the safe and the normal and the rational; and then, of course, you duck your lights too, and wait for the other car to push by; and when the other car does pass, and is replaced by a *whup* of perfect night blackness, then you, with a relaxed wrist, click back to high beams, and continue to sail forth, seeing farther ahead; and that's it; but that's not entirely it—for throughout all this, even though every step of the transaction was virtually automatic, a part of you has been aware, if only subliminally, that an exchange has occurred, that communication has taken place, that some order of good something has happened; and you look forward, however unconsciously, to the next one...

My dash said 8:26 by the time I reached Exit 12; I followed the sign into Elbridge, as I had been instructed, but there didn't seem to be a diner anywhere along this nondescript strip, so after a few miles I doubled back and found the

aluminum-sided roadhouse—labeled *Tim's* in neon, as I had
been advised—just beyond the Interstate; the wrong turn had
only cost me seven or eight minutes, but I decided to keep this
misdirection ready if I needed to explain my lateness—
lateralling blame is always highly effective; I pulled into the
diner's lot and, amid the parked cars and RV's and trucks, saw
a guy leaning on a Toyota, three vehicles to the left of the
diner's smallish front door; he was tall and long-legged and
skinny-shouldered, and was holding his hands straddling his
hips in a way that could have served as a road emblem for
impatience; we were supposed to have met in the diner's
entryway, but I was sure this was him; after parking, I walked
directly over:
    — You Dave?, I said, from a few paces off;
    — Evenin', the guy said;
    — Yeah, I said: well put...
    He stood against the car, without moving:
    — Listen, I then said: sorry about the time, but I have this
landlord who likes to come by and—
    — Hey, he said, and smiled broadly: you see me com-
plaining...?
    And so we shook hands, and let smiles further the
bonding; Dave was not only fairer and taller than I had
anticipated, he also had an exceptionally unexpected pony-
tail, which was Creamsicle-colored and dribbled all the way
down the back of his plaid shirt; his jeans had seen better
days, and he wore a gold chain around his neck, bearing some
runic-seeming shape; I was so appreciative of Dave's good
humor that I immediately offered to buy him dinner—and
not necessarily at the slop house where we were standing, but
anywhere he liked; Dave thanked me for the offer, but said
that he had grabbed a sandwich and some home fries while
waiting, and that the home fries had been good, if I was ever
in the market for any; but then he said, with some difficulty,
that it had gotten so late that he already had to think about
getting somewhere else: he was due at a video shoot at 8:45;
Dave, I recalled, had described himself as a video maker:
    — Sorry about that, he said: but it's the kind of thing
where we have to be on location at a certain time, and

somebody's probably already there;

— Understood, I said, and nodded: listen—don't worry about it;

But then Dave did a nice thing: he explained that the shoot was going to be relatively short—probably lasting no more than an hour—and so he invited me to come along; we would be able to speak afterward; I agreed gladly, so we shook hands and piled into our respective cars—Dave's Toyota, I saw, had plastic sheeting and duct tape for a rear left window; I followed him back to I-51, where we headed north, towards Troy; by then nightfall was complete, and I drove by faith and Dave's brake lights for more than ten minutes; then Dave flipped on his turn signal—hundreds of yards before the exit, as it turned out, the guy really was thoughtful—and I followed him off the highway, down Route 21, and then through a sequence of swervy roads; this continued for several miles, and although the darkness was nearly total it was evident that we were passing through an area thick with trees, probably a corner of Reelfoot Lake State Park; then Dave's turn signal jumped on again and we slowed considerably, before I followed him off the road and into a smallish clearing; we both parked, and when I got out of my car I noticed that Dave had left his fog lights on; we walked along the throw of the fog lights deeper into the clearing, a good-sized semicircle of grass bordered by oak and tupelo trees and shrubs; these, in turn, dissolved into a backless expanse of pure night blackness; it was very still, and very quiet:

— Welcome to movieland, Dave said, and smiled again;

But this time his smile was more in awe than in irony; for as my eyes adjusted to the forest's deeper darkness, I witnessed the world slowly bloom into glittering; as if a visual volume-knob were gradually being turned up, a population of winks and speckles progressively came to the perimeter of the clearing, coursing about in currents of momentary blips: it was the highest concentration of fireflies I had ever seen:

— I know, said a voice coming from the darkness: it's like walking into Max Planck's wet dream;

This was Jurgen, Dave's partner; soon he emerged from

behind some trees and we shook hands; Jurgen, from what I could see, was like a riper version of Dave, with darker hair and a fuller frame but with the same plaid-shirted scraggliness; Dave provided a more formal introduction, after which Jurgen just said Welcome; then Dave said that it was time to get to work; on that cue, Jurgen went and obtained, from a corner of the clearing, two empty gallon-size bottles, which he held by means of jug-style glass circles near their necks, and a net on a stick, which looked like a slightly larger variant of the hobbyists' nets usually seen leaning on the sides of aquariums; he gave one bottle and the net to Dave, and then, with a smile, nodded his head:

— Ready to rip, Jurgen said;

But I was confused; I addressed myself to Dave:

— Hey, I said: I thought you said this was some kind of film thing;

— Video, he corrected;

— Ah, I said;

— Really—it *is*, Dave said, and chuckled slightly: we've been hired by an electronics shop up in Dyersburg to do some shooting;

— With a net?, I said;

— Starting with a net, Dave said, and smiled: it's all part of a promo thing they're doing;

— Hm, I said;

— Actually, it's kinda cool, Dave said: you remember how they used to have those Guess-the-Number-of-Jellybeans-in-the-Fishbowl contests at barber shops and such...?

— Mm;

— Well, Ribber, the guy who owns the electronics store, he wanted something like that;

— OK...

— So he thought about it and came up with Count the Fireflies;

— Hm, I said;

— Yeah, Dave said: Ribber's got one of those giant 60-inch Sony monitors in his front window, and we've been commissioned to make an eight-minute video of a cloud of these blinkers entirely filling up the frame; then he'll loop it on his playback machine so it'll run indefinitely; it'll be wild...

— Pure retinal overdrive, Jurgen said: when you're watching the swarm on the video and you see a chigger ignite, you won't know if it's one you saw before or if it's any of the others; makes the counting kinda fun...

— It's a good commercial idea, Dave said: Ribber's always got them; so we've been coming out here for a few nights to gather up the cast, then we go back to my place and shoot 'em; I've got a walk-in closet that we use as the flystage, then we just set up my Betacam and let 'er go;

— You know, I still think you should be careful when you do that, Jurgen said to Dave, though he looked over to me and smiled: I mean, lightning bugs' luminescence has been known to persist, like when frogs eat too many of the buggers and then *they* begin to glow; so think what all these nits could be doing to your camera;

— Really, Dave said: might throw off future exposures;

And with that, the hunters fanned out; Dave went to one corner of the clearing, while Jurgen penetrated a leafy overhang on the side opposite; then they got to work: in the glow from the fog lights of Dave's car, I could make out Jurgen lunging after flying blips with his fist and Dave whipping his net around; grunts and stepping sounds also issued forth, along with the glassy rasp of bottle caps being unscrewed and replaced; this continued for a few minutes; and although I assumed that some flies were being caught, it was, in fact, hard to be sure: from where I was standing I couldn't really tell if any of the sparklers were inside the transparent bottles or behind them:

— This is all part of a mating ritual, Jurgen said;

— Speak for yourself, said Dave;

— I *was*, said Jurgen, before swooping his closing fist downward: all the wafters you see here are males, which, as nature likes to remind us, are the more expendable members of any species; flying about is part of their process of getting together with their lady luminaries, who kind of have things easy: they get to hang out in relative safety near the ground, staying low in the grass; about every five-and-a-half seconds the guys give a wink that lasts about point-three seconds, and then the gals lay back for about two seconds before they torch up with their come-hither response; so, as always, it's a matter of timing: this light-flash rhythm is what brings the beasties together, and it's also what keeps different firebug species apart;

— Typical, Dave said, and made his net go *fwit*: the men go cruising and the ladies just put on the landing lights;

The two continued their pursuit; they stepped into shrub banks, crackled through unseen branches, and made scraping sounds with bottle caps; before long, Jurgen began providing vocal sound-effects—a cartoonish, nasalized *nyowp*—as he slapped at the night, while Dave whiffed more air; but as I continued watching, I came to find it, in a way, touching: at one point Jurgen thrashed after a speck of light that then blinked into nothingness, while Dave sped his net down on a perfect void that soon became a living scintilla; for these hunters, it seemed, presence and absence were, in a way, irrelevant, or at least folded into a larger continuity; Dave and Jurgen clearly understood that there was more to these mites than merely visual existence; it was both an admirable commitment to process and a reassuring act of faith:

— Jeez, these guys, with their on-again, off-again relationships, Jurgen said;

— Yeah, Dave said: now you see them, now you see them once more;

— They're virtual insects!, Jurgen said;

— Virtually in*num*erable, said Dave;

— I wonder, though, if we haven't got it wrong, Jurgen said: I mean, I wonder if maybe these guys' natural condition isn't to be lit up—if their ground state isn't actually when they're glowing;

— Hm, said Dave: so what they're actually doing is turning *off* their lights—

— Right: momentarily going under;

— Flashing darkness—

— Projecting their inner voids—

— Their repeating, periodic depressions...

— So then, I suppose, we should really call them douse bugs—

— Exactly...

— Or nature's faders—

— Flying extinguishers—

— Buzzing snuffers—!

— Or maybe—

— Or maybe, despite what it looks like, maybe they really *are* glowing constantly, Jurgen said: but, through some malign unknown mechanism, their everlasting light is periodically swallowed up by un-understood atmospheric forces;

— So then they're being occluded—

— *Rude*ly occluded—

— Denied their God-given right to shine...

— So that, I suppose, would make them—o horror— *victims*—

— Yeah: victims of predatory darkness—

— Of uncontrollable flares of night;

— So it isn't bioluminescence, but eco-eclipsis—

— Exactly: ambient effacement—

— Nature's station-identification—

— Ongoing lessons in humility...

— In fact, that might explain the nits' efficiency factor, Jurgen said: you know, these guys burn so cleanly that they produce what's known in the trade as *cold light*: they put together this real slow oxidation reaction within these little cell-structures called photocytes, using a really weird enzyme and substrate that're, like, named for the *devil*; and the result is virtually 100% efficient: almost no heat is lost at all...

— So, in fact, these folks should be our heroes—

— Exactly: our role models—

— Our ego ideals—

— Hosts of syndicated talk shows—

— Spokes-things for massive advertising campaigns—

— In fact, children should be forced to leave their families and go be *raised* by them—

— MacArthur winners, all...

Then, suddenly, I heard the sound of hastily approaching footsteps; in a moment, Dave strode into the clearing and

bounded past me; still carrying his bottle and net, he went
directly to his car, reached in the driver's window, and shut off
the fog lights; then he meandered back in my direction:

— Got to watch that, he said: just got that damn battery
three, four months ago;

— Hm, I said: funny, I didn't notice anything at all;

— Probably just your eyes further adapting to the dark,
said Jurgen, stepping from the bushes: probably compen-
sated;

— Mm, Dave said;

Dave and Jurgen then went to the center of the
clearing and checked their results; for the first time, perhaps
because the fog lights were off, I could see that both of their
bottles had conspicuous cumulative glows; they almost
resembled those ghostly radiant globes held by the faceless
monks in the Ave Maria section of Fantasia; it was nice, and
impressive:

— So how many did you get?, I said;

— Oh, I don't know, Dave said: maybe about what,
Jurg...

— Maybe about four, five dozen;

— Mm, about that;

— Yeah, Jurgen said: enough for a big old fry...

But I was confused:

— So then what, I said: you make your final tally later,
at home...?

A nightwind puffed the clearing; I watched it rattle the
tops of the sky-silhouetted trees; but then I looked back and
saw that Dave had turned somewhat sheepish: he was just
standing there, with his eyes trained towards the ground; and
then it took him another ten seconds to reply:

— Well..., he said: kind of...

From the twin glows emanating from the bottled flies, I
saw that Jurgen was also looking downwards; and then it
became obvious: he, like Dave, was avoiding my eyes; when
Dave started whisking the grass with his foot, I became even
more confused:

— I mean, you'll need an exact count at some point,
won't you?, I said;

Dave shot a glance at me, then dipped his eyes back down; Jurgen leaked a giggle, then sniffed it back:

— Hey, what's going on?, I said: I mean, don't you know how many you'll use—?

— *Yeah,* Jurgen let slide, from between clenched facial muscles: we *do*...

— *Sure* we know, Dave said, tittering, and still looking downward;

— So how many?; how many will you—

— One!, Dave let pop, amid gusts of released laughter from both he and Jurgen;

They continued snorting and kicking the ground for some time:

— Hey you *guys,* I finally said—

— Hey, man, you aren't going to enter this damn competition, are you?, Dave said, still giggling;

— Of course not, I said;

— Because we probably shouldn't say anything if you *are,* Dave said;

— We probably shouldn't say anything at *all,* Jurgen added, and sniggled;

— Hey...*guys*..., I said: what's going *on*?;

— You see, this guy Ribber is really, exceedingly *something,* Jurgen said;

— *Really,* Dave said, and finally looked up at me: you see, the Ribber decided early on that he wanted to make the contest a little *interesting*—

— *Really*, Jurgen said;

— And so, you know, he came up with an idea, Dave said, between broad grins: he had this idea that, as a kind of joke, we would kind of throw the folks a curveball and just shoot one firefly over and over again;

— So—

— So on the monitor they'll see this huge swarm of flickerers, and people'll be guessing numbers like 800, or 161, or 32 *million,* and it'll just be the blooming *one*—!

More laughter from Dave and Jurgen:

— And then, when the truth comes out, he'll use it to promote this new switcher system he got in that lets you marry, like, an infinite number of images, Dave said: it lets you simulate almost unlimited overdubbing;

— Yeah, Jurgen said: the Japanese originally developed it for HDTV, but now it's come out in a consumer model that's, like, *amazing...*

— And the whole deal'll be, like, *really* funny...

— *Really*, Jurgen said;

And again there was tittering from both Dave and Jurgen; it took them nearly a minute to subside, and after that they went back to staring at the grass, although both continued discarding giggle-fragments as needed; by then, Jurgen was holding both fly-bottles by their ears and had the net sticking out of his rear pocket, while Dave was fiddling with his car keys; for the first time, I became aware of the full moon nesting atop some nearby oaks:

— Sounds pretty good, I said;

— Yeah, Dave said, still looking down: I mean, I suppose...

Then we prepared to leave; Jurgen put the bottles and the net into his car—he had parked just past the clearing—while Dave told me to follow him back to his place, where we would be able to talk; as Dave coaxed up his sluggish engine, I climbed into my car and gave a brief farewell glance into the clearing; and now that my eyes were fully night-adjusted, I saw two things: one, that the scene's stippled blackness actually diffused into an area-wide aura, giving the place a generous overreaching glow; and, two, that, regardless of this, the clearing's churning activity seemed entirely unchanged, despite the removal of several watts' worth of inhabitants; we had done our business, scooping out our needed lode, but to the clearing itself, we had never even been there...

Dave and Jurgen's cars soon moved out, and I followed behind; with elegant linearity the three of us snaked through the twisty forest roads, communicating through brake lights and engine sounds and varying separations; the wind had grown still, and the sky was virtually cloudless, and the long unraveling of tree-lined road made the night feel hospitable and near; but as we progressed through the continuing turns, and I resisted the edgy instinct to turn on the radio, I found

that I was becoming concerned about something; for a fact had just become apparent to me: that each of our three cars seemed to have the highest likelihood of getting into an accident; Dave, up front, might collide with anything from a buck deer to a megabuck Impala, while Jurgen, in the middle, faced the peril of fallible, unpredictable automobiles both fore and aft; likewise, I had to contend with unforseeable rear exposure, as well as the additively greater risk of slamming into both Jurgen and/*or* Dave if something untoward happened; this seemed unjust; for a moment I thought of slowing down, to put some distance between myself and the others and thereby decrease the dangers of collision; but I then realized that being farther away would increasingly introduce some of the hazards associated with Dave's position as the forward member, while perhaps not appreciably lessening the risks of being last; it seemed, upon reflection, a tough trade-off; so, ultimately, I stayed put, last though nearby—although I was rather glad when we finally got to Dave's tucked-away house, after about a fifteen-minute ride:
— Home ho, Dave said after he had walked out to meet my car;
I parked on the street, and we walked across the modest lawn to Dave's front door; the place had a pleasant, disheveled feel, with two floors of clapboard flaking under a canopy of trees; up on the shallow wooden porch, the Welcome mat was fully four feet to the side of the front door, while cobwebs clouded many corners and interstices, most elaborately one between an empty earthenware planter and the windowsill it hung from, just beside the door; Dave unlocked the front-door bolt and flicked on lights both inside and out; stepping in behind him, I saw that his foyer was deep and narrow, with textured amber wallpaper and two low-slung benches, evidently handmade from varnished treelimbs, positioned along the walls; an assortment of video cables, light booms, and equipment cases was scattered throughout this entrance area, along with a few pairs of smudged yellow work-boots, whose tops flopped exhaustedly over; then Jurgen came in, with the shining jugs hanging from his index fingers down by his legs:
— Delivery from Chernobyl Dairy, he said;

At the rear of the foyer, Dave opened the door to the basement and turned on its light; he led Jurgen and me downstairs, and we all clumped thunderously on the tiled steps; the basement was a large-ish, low-ceilinged space smelling of dust and leaves, with tile floors, a few chairs, and a folded-up ping-pong table leaning against a side wall; in the middle of the basement, what seemed to be a small new room was under construction: an unfinished cagework of upright and transverse beams jutted from the rear wall, surrounded by several varieties of saws and drills and quite a population of lid-topped cans; most of them, I saw, were labeled as containing resins and shellacs and such; on the other side of the construction site was the walk-in closet slash soundstage; from the outside, it looked like nothing more than a nondescript corner door with a dirty knob-area, although, about eight feet away, a braid of electrical cables poured through a hole that had been punched near the base of the wall; Dave and Jurgen moved to the closet and spoke for half a minute about technical matters, then disappeared inside and began setting up; shiftings and squeaks came from the closet's hidden depths; I ducked my head in to investigate, but could see nothing within its near-total darkness beyond Jurgen, nearby, winding electrician's tape around a metal stand:
— I like this gig, he then said to me: all I have to say is Camera; Action;
After another brief technical discussion, it was decided that Jurgen would get a jump on the shoot while Dave and I talked; Dave then cordially invited me up to his room; after climbing out of the basement, we circled up onto the stairway that lead to the second floor, where Dave hit a few more lights; I then remembered something that I had been meaning to ask him:
— Hey, Dave?, I said, following him step for step;
— Yo, he said;
— You know, I'm kind of wondering something;
— What's up?, he said;
— Well, I said, reaching the top the stairs: I kind of find myself wondering why you guys catch so many fireflies, when you said you're only going to shoot one of them;

— Ah, Dave said: simple;

He opened the door to his room and flicked on its light; then, graciously, he waited for me to enter:

— Well, I suppose it's because the little fellers aren't exactly mediagenic, he said;

— Sorry?, I said, pausing in the doorway;

— They seem to have problems when they go in front of the camera, he said: we don't really know why, but before too long every one of them makes like a falling star;

— Yikes, I said;

— Really, Dave said: sometimes they go after only ten or twenty seconds, so as soon as we get one of them out of a bottle we really start hustling; we thought it might have something to do with electrical fields or some such like that, but we still really have no idea;

— Hm, I said;

— But don't worry, Dave said: we can always cut when they're blipped off, so it doesn't hurt the tape: there aren't any nasty verticals of light; the little guys are good that way;

— Mm, I said;

— And Jurg is pretty gentle with the broom;

— I see;

— But don't get me wrong, he said: I mean, we still shoot only one at a time;

Dave's room was an unkempt chamber, mostly filled by a bed whose unmade surface resembled a choppy lake; a mirrored bureau dumped with keys, coins, and paper scraps took up much of one wall, while a large wooden TV console took care of another; Dave gestured for me to sit in the corner behind the bed, in a beige upholstered armchair that was worn to raggedness at the wrists; once installed, I could see a photograph of a Slavic, vastly-foreheaded face captioned Sergei Eisenstein taped to the side of the bureau:

— OK, Dave then said: sorry this has taken so long;

— No problem, I said;

— So then, Dave said: what did he say about it...?

— Who's that?, I said;

— Your grandfather, Dave said, lighting a cigarette;

— Sorry?, I said;

— I mean why would he think—

— Oh, I said: no, *he* didn't...; I'm sorry; I probably wasn't clear on—

— So come on, man, put it right, he said;

He came over and sat on the bed, facing me; I rearranged myself in the chair, pushing a little forward:

— OK then, I said: well, to begin with, I was wondering if you were still working as a musicologist;

— Well, yes, he said: of course;

— Good; so—

— In fact, I am rather pleased to report that, after a somewhat longish fallow period, I have recently had an essay accepted by the Journal of the American Musicological Society;

— Well then: congratulations;

— Thank you, sir; it isn't at all a technical piece, but it's something I've been working on for quite some time;

— Then it *is* nice news;

— So it is, he said, folding his hands into his lap: I'm really rather pleased about it;

— Perhaps it's something pertinent?, I said;

— Not at all related, unfortunately, he said: but, for me, it does attempt to resolve something that's been a central preoccupation of mine for, oh, a good few years;

— Please, I said;

— Well, he said with a long exhalation, while rising from the bed to tap his cigarette ash into a slender standing ashtray: it has to do with that demon Beethoven; as you may know, Beethoven became, late in his career, obsessed with variations; more than fifty-two percent of his work after 1818 contains sets of variations or variation-like material—an astonishing figure for such a compulsive innovator; of course the best example is the Diabelli, which came in 1819, where Diabelli—but again, you probably know this—

— Not precisely;

— So: Diabelli was a music publisher of some prominence, and he was looking for new work to be issued by his firm; so he asked fifty composers to write a single variation on a simple waltz theme, with the intention of publishing all fifty as a set; it was a nice commercial gambit for the time; Schubert was among the contributors who wrote a variation, as did the 11-year-old Liszt; well, Beethoven produced 33; he sat down to write, and the monster just couldn't stop; he was almost uncon*troll*able—and so it was in almost all the work of his last years, where variations repeatedly form the very focus, the generative center, of an entire piece: there's the E Major piano sonata of Opus 109, and the arietta in Opus 111, and fully four of the five last quartets, including the ravishing Adagio in the E-flat Opus 127, and that thrilling, heartstopping Andante in the C-sharp minor; and there are reams of other examples throughout the music of the period...

He had begun to pace, walking from the end of the bed to a hutch standing along one of the long walls; the hutch held, upon its several shelves, a multi-component stereo system, splattered with dormant LED's:

— So I began to wonder why this would be: why Beethoven, the heroic conqueror of new musical territory, would all of a sudden show this radical turning inwards, this obsessive project of minutely reconsidering limited materials—or, to pick up current cant, why he would become so enamored of recycling, of telling his same story over and over again; and this, then, formed the basis for my paper;

— Mm, I said;

— And it *is* a riddle, he continued: why this Titan would purposefully invert the sustaining Western conception of progress as expansion—why he would challenge our central, Faustian myth of *more*—and turn so self-reflective, so damn indrawn, or, as I put it in my piece, so circumscribed: trying to generate infinity within a finite area; it's as if he had turned against the notion of history as progressive and so had set out to deny the workings of linear time...;

He pushed a rattan chair, strayed from the dining table in the middle of the room, back into position; it squeaked as it bobbled against the pinewood flooring:

— And so I set out to conjecture why, he said: at first I sought biographical or historical explanations; for the longest time, for instance, I thought it might have had something to do with the years of legal wrangles Beethoven went through when he was trying to gain custody of his nephew, Karl, to whom he was so deeply attached: all those torturous legal proceedings providing a model for change within stasis, of moving forward without going anywhere; then I thought the situation might be viewed as a consequence of Beethoven's growing deafness, which progressively cut him off from the world and drew him more into himself, into his own processes; or maybe it was a response to Europe's evolving sense of nationalism—of what it meant to pull impossibly divergent people into units based on imposed, and usually artificial, commonalities—which arose in response to the French Revolution and the Napoleonic Wars, which so disillusioned the composer; and later, when these approaches didn't prove adequate, I even thought in terms of attractors, those ideas coming out of physics; as I said, it isn't a technical paper;

— Of course, I said;

— But then, you know, after all this reflection—which took place over many, many months—something emerged, as it were, on the home front;   now, I don't remember if I mentioned that I have a son—

— No;

— Well, I do, despite what it might look like here; and he's a good and bright guy—a little lazy now and then—with an interest in electrical engineering and layman's Relativity and other such niceties; but up until about two years ago he never had much of an interest in music—at least no more than the inescapable marginal involvement that every teenager now has; but then, perhaps two years ago, as I said, Michael came home one day after school with his friend Ricky—they know each other from Little League—and it was clear that something was, as they say, up: the boys came in, and as they went into Michael's room over there, I heard them nattering about something in an especially giddy way; then, a few minutes later, I heard, muffled by Michael's shut door, that peculiar, pinched-bedsprings sound of an electric guitar being strummed acoustically—that is, unamplified; and then there was a chorus of gleeful squeals, and also a little comic, over-exuberant singing—a charming bit of something about rats and bedbugs, if I remember correctly;

Seemingly unaware of what he was doing, he stood at the end of the bed and slowly moved one finger back and forth over a segment of the footboard:

— By the next morning, Michael was asking me if he would be able to have a set of drums; But you've never played, I tried to get out, before he cut me off with But I can learn; And they're expensive and loud and, I said, before his quick That's OK; and this kind conversation went on for a few minutes; well, I assumed it was all a passing whim, to be forgotten with the arrival of the school bus, but his enthusiasm would not fade: that evening, Michael came home with a pair of plastic-tipped drumsticks and spent the whole night pattering about on his bed, tapping every whichaway to extract different tonalities from the mattress and the comforter and the pillows, and using the wall for accents—it's much more highly pitched; then, the next day, he came home with a few records—The Pretenders, Steely Dan, he has an ear—and by the following Wednesday he had started working at the local Sweet 'n Slim frozen-yogurt shop, with 80% of his earnings earmarked for a Walkman; well, all this ardor and discipline was rather nice to see, I must say, but I must *also* say that I viewed it with some ambivalence: he was interested in the drums, after all—not exactly Buxtehude's preferred vehicle; but, I consoled myself, it was music, and it had in some new sense galvanized him;

Standing at a small sink in the room's far corner, a dark forty feet away, he ran water over his hands; then he withdrew a white towel from a nearby rack and dried himself off:

— But eventually my resistance slackened, and I decided that it wouldn't be the worst thing for his new enthusiasm to receive some encouragement; so over dinner on a Tuesday night, I recall, I waited until just before dessert to tell him that on the following Saturday we could go to Soundmaster's music shop in St. Joseph and see what we could find; well, he squealed very nicely and took me around the shoulders and kissed my cheek, then he ran off and the mattress concerto didn't stop all night; well, I was pleased, I must say, and the loft was rather harmonious for all that week: Michael was cheerful and very bouncy, and he made sure to say Good night to me every evening before he turned in;

— Then Saturday finally arrived, and I used the car-trip to the music shop to lay out some ground rules: no practicing after 10 PM, no ignoring of schoolwork, robust gratitude till the end of his days; Michael snapped out his agreement to every one of them, and hugged me again; eventually we got to Soundmaster's, a big store up on Messanie Street, and for Michael, well, it was Disneyland: guitars hanging like ducks in a Chinese grocery, tiers of amplifiers large and small, drums in conic stacks or set up as full kits, exceedingly grimy white-tile floors; well, as soon as I opened the door into the place, Michael rushed to the drum department and its several set-up kits; and I must say, it was really rather something: at first Michael was almost afraid to touch the drums; he just got as close to the arrayed stands and cymbals and toms as he felt he could, and then simply gazed upon them, as if they were oracles, with radiant wonderment and a real sense of the sacral; never before had I seen his face so awed and expectant; it was terribly moving; but soon enough a salesman appeared—surprisingly, a middle-aged man—who introduced himself with impressive informality as Bob; and then Bob asked if he could help us—and I quote—with anything; seeing the sweetness in deference, I let Michael rip: he said, with just the most delightful eagerness, that he was in the market for a Tama five-piece kit—two rack-toms, one floor-tom, maybe three cymbals—and that he preferred it in a tiger finish; Bob said Sounds good, boy has good taste; he then showed us, rather nearby, a Tama five-piecer with two cymbals—though a third cymbal, a sizzle, could be negotiated for, he said; also, this kit was in pink champagne: to order the tiger finish would take eight to ten weeks—Don't worry!, Michael cut in, with an incongruence easily explicable by the absolutely astral radiance then emanating from his face; and as I looked on, I saw that Michael had begun gently fingering the edges of the kit's cymbals, and rubbing the lugs on the drums; and then he almost knocked the hi-hat over when he got caught up in a kind of slow, irresistible merging movement in towards the equipment; this, in short, was transfixion—which, in fact, I was sharing, right up to the point when gum-chewing Bob mentioned that the drum kit cost nearly nineteen hundred dollars;

He leaned against the nearer of the room's two support columns:

— My eyes dropped closed; I felt gloom; I could see anguish ahead; but it was impossible; my resources, as you might imagine, are somewhat limited; so it was with sadness and dread that I put my hand on Michael's shoulder, to begin gentling him away from the drums; Maybe we should..., I said, knowing full well that I didn't have to finish the sentence; and even as Michael turned to look at some of the other drum sets, his eyes slid down and drew inward; But that's, he said, that's exactly *it*—that's *exactly* the one; and then came But Daddy we can, and So I *prom*ise, and I'll work for the next two *years*...; and I asked the salesman to give us a moment, and I took Michael around the shoulders; then, with the gravity of the situation fully in mind, I found myself forced to articulate the horrid obvious: that nineteen hundred dollars was a lot of money for something he was just getting started on, and that he didn't know how long he'd stick with; and he said But Dad*deee*, putting a long heavy vibrato on the last syllable, and then he turned violently away from me and became darkly silent; but then the salesman stepped forward and asked if he might make a suggestion; he steered us a few paces towards the rear of the store and pointed to a black drum set that was stacked like a ziggurat on the floor, just in front of the keyboard department; he then explained that this kit, from its hardware to its heads, was exactly the same as the Tama; it was made by exactly the same people who made the Tama kit, in the very same factory, using all of the same materials; the only difference was that the second kit was distributed under the name of Power Plus; beyond that, the two drum sets were absolutely identical, except that the second kit would only run eight ninety-five; well, to tell you clearly, I was surprised and pleased and even touched by the salesman's suggestion—one usually doesn't expect such disclosures from the commercial sector; and I was about to ask the salesman for more details, when I turned and saw that Michael looked as if he had been poisoned: he was gray-faced, shut down, staring at the grimy tiles; so I told the salesman that we would have to think about it, and thanked him; then I took Michael's arm and began walking out;

He took another cigarette from his breast pocket; then he lit it with a cardboard match, torn from a book; a broad exhalation followed:

— On the way home, in the car, the fallout was non-stop: But Daddy, he said, *But Daddy*, followed by But what about what *I* want?, and Don't *I* have anything to say about it— they're supposed to be *my* drums; and then came But you don't see *anyone* playing Power Plus—no one's ever *heard* of Power Plus; Craig Norden plays *Tama,* and so does *Neil Curt,* and they can have whatever they *want...*; and after a final, blood-quickening *What I want is the Tama!* came the obscenities and the insults and the cantankerousness, and finally the silence that lasted past the slamming of the door into his room; and then there was no tapping on the mattress that night;

He looked down at the back of his right hand, in which the cigarette was working:

— Well, to speak freely, this eventuation, with all it implies, was all pretty difficult for me; further, from then on, life around here soured significantly: Michael was gruff, or he wouldn't talk at all; he ran out to school in the morning, then ran in at night, grabbed something to eat, and locked himself in his room; he no longer asked to get into the bathroom first and even stopped listening to his records; meanwhile, I was having a hard time concentrating on mine; I would sit there in the listening chair surrounded by Das Lied von der Erde and only be able to hear Why is this necessary?, Why is this necessary?, What is going *on...*?; and I would brood, I would brood, I would churn the situation over and over in my mind, just *end*lessly; and this went on for days: sometimes I would sit for hours in front of the silent stereo after records had shut off, twisting possible answers around; but I rejected all of them, I would find fault in every considered rationalization; and despite my constant efforts to soften Michael up—bringing in barbecue, letting him stay up late, in no way concealing that I wanted this to be resolved—the rift between us just grew sharper, and even wider; Michael even stopped flinching when he didn't respond to my questions; in this shared space, we had somehow begun living in different universes...

— Well, after about two weeks of this I had really had enough, and so I decided to end it, really just to put it behind us, and bring a little reason to the situation; so the following Friday, while Michael was in school, I went back to Soundmaster's and bought the drum kit, the Power Plus; I even went for the third cymbal, which was extra; I then spent all that afternoon setting the kit up, in best showroom style, polishing the chrome and the stands and putting two pairs of sticks on the bass drum; the kit was so damn impressive that I was sure it would melt Michael's resistance, especially since it was obvious that he, too, was tiring of the tension and would jump at an excuse for a thaw; so, that night, I waited in this chair right here for Michael to come home, trying to read Tovey on the passacaglia but incapable of concentrating on much of anything; and it was getting on towards eight o'clock when, finally, I heard Michael's keys chirp at the door; well, at that point my adrenaline leapt and my throat got dry, and then I became all expectant when the door suddenly stopped in the middle of its swing open, when Michael first caught sight of the set-up drums; and then he came in and walked right over to me, he just walked right straight across the loft over to where I was standing; and then he thanked me, in direct and unaffected words, and he hugged me across the chest, and held my back in his hands; then he went off to his room, saying that it was too late to play, which, in fact, it was; then he closed his door, and the next day he moved out;

— Moved out?, I said;

— To his mother, in South Carolina, after disappearing the next morning and giving me two days of the devil's hell before he called me; he used his Walkman savings for the ticket;

— Hm, I said;

He folded a stray scrag of hair behind one ear; his eyes remained on the gray window that gave, as best I could tell, onto a featureless airspace:

— Well, he said: dissonance is essential in any music of substance;

By then, his cigarette had burned back to his fingertips; he blotted it out on the rattly lid of a paint can that was sitting on the writing desk, just past the door:

— So, thereafter, when it was determined that Michael was in fact going to remain with his mother, I was left with, so to speak, a little more free time; and thus I found that I had ample opportunity to think all this unfortunateness over; well, I continued to be, shall we say, actively concerned with it for a rather extended period; and I stayed with it, I did—I thought about it incessantly, over and over, just all the time; but during this period, strangely, in the midst of all this, I found that my mind kept pulling towards thoughts of Beethoven; and eventually I came to think that there might be some kind of connection here, between my situation and my musicological concerns; and thus, over a few weeks, thoughts gradually came: that Beethoven's late interest in variations had less to do with exfoliating development or controlled tonal fields, as is traditionally taught, than with procedures in problem-solving; in other words, for Beethoven variations were a way, musically, of thinking something through, a kind of ongoing, Popperian method for testing a Thematic conjecture's aspects and implications and points of weakness from different angles; in other words, variations, much like my brooding, represent excursions towards some kind of higher understanding, repeated graspings-at and circlings-in towards some central truth; but variations also illustrate the cliché that the truth remains, ultimately, inde-terminable; that's why all the fancy footwork of variations is necessary: we never actually get to what we're after, to where all the gropings, all the variation-searching, would no longer be necessary, to that point where there would no longer be music—to which I say, All the better!; for late Beethoven, then, better the beauty of struggle and futility than the illusion of accomplishment; for as we struggle, he would seem to say, so are we beautiful;

— And this was the thesis of your article;

— Precisely; and, I am pleased to report, it was well-

received by the AMS journal; I even received a nice note back
from some kind of sub-editor;

— Bravo;

— Thank you; and, in fact, I do believe the piece has
some merit, especially since it deals with a technical subject in
non-technical terms—always the preferred approach;

— Mm, I said;

— Yes, he said, and exhaled: but, of course, it didn't
bring back my son...

He came and sat along the side of the bed, near me; it
huffed under his weight:

— But I assume that you and Michael are back in touch,
I said;

— Sporadically, he said: we call;

— Then have you ever thought about sending it to him?,
I said, gesturing towards the circles and cylinders of the drum
kit, standing in the middle of the room;

— Not really, he said: after all, it's hardly certain what
would happen; and I don't mind keeping it, actually, even
untouched: I think of it as a kind of commemorative sculp-
ture;

— Hm, I said;

— God *damn* God *damn* God *damn* God *damn,* he said;

— Sorry?, I said;

— You know, I've really got to establish something right
off, he said: and it's this: that there is one thing—only *one*
thing—that I want from this life; in the whole of creation,
there is only *one thing* that will do it for me...; but I yearn for
it, I *burn* for it, I desire and covet and *pine* for it; it is what
imparts substance and density to all other experience, it is the
source of *all* meaning—and it's for *this damn sprinkler* just to
turn around!...

He remained lying on the lawn, flat-out on his stomach,
fiddling with the tiny sprinkler head standing right in front of
his nose, whose bottom cartilage was almost certainly being
tickled by the scruffy lawn grass; the sprinkler consisted of a
small circular base and a single short pipeway rising to support
two upbent arms, like a minuscule weight-lifter flexing proud
biceps; from my point of view, there didn't seem to be much

anyone could do with the thing, but Nick just kept at it—
beanie-spinning the sprinkler's arms with his index finger,
picking the whole unit up and rattling it about, or compulsively unscrewing and retightening the hose:

— OK, he then said: OK...; now, just one last shot...

He hitched up into a semi-crouch, then scuttled along
the hoseway until he reached a small faucet jutting from the
side of the garage; after surveying the line once more, he took
a beat before giving the faucet a rugged twist:

— *Damn,* he said, when the sprinkler simply lobbed
water straight out to its sides, without moving at all; to me,
it looked as if the mini-muscleman's bi's had burst with
streams of excess testosterone;

I liked Nick: he had the kind of pattern baldness—a
honey-pink circle rising past the tree line on his pate—that
you don't see nearly often enough, and he had very skinny
arms, which he highlighted with baggy rolled-up sleeves; I
also liked the way he had missed the part just above his
Adam's apple when he had shaved, and the boniness of his
bare feet; he stood up, turned the water off and walked
towards the back door of his house:

— Let's go in, he said;

He held the screen door as I entered:

— So, he said: you were saying...

— Oh—yeah, I said, stepping into a shadowy hallway:
well, I think I was talking about how I got started...

— Yeah, he said;

— Mm, I said, and moved to the side of the hallway to
let Nick pass: well, as I think I was saying, when I was a kid,
maybe when I was about seven or eight, there happened to be
a period when my grandfather was living just a little ways
from us—no more than about an hour by car, if I remember
correctly; I don't think he rented that house because it was
near us, but my mother made the most of the opportunity, so
we would drive over there just about every other Saturday;

— Mm, Nick said;

— So we'd go there and just kind of hang out all
afternoon—my mother would talk or just work on her quilt-
ing—and before too long I'd more or less be left to myself; I'd

usually go out into the yard and play with whatever junk we'd brought over, because my grandfather didn't really have too much stuff to get into, but one afternoon I decided to stay inside and started to snoop around; and that's when I got up into his bedroom and found it;

— Hm, Nick said, pausing before the doorway to a room at the end of the corridor;

— Yeah, I said: my grandfather just left the book lying around, and I came across it on the floor in his closet, in among some old boots and cases and stuff; and I remember, that first time, that I was really kind of intrigued: it was this big, brown, scuffed thing, with stiff old-style leather covering, all smudged and scraped and weathered down, and it was held together by dirty black laces that ran through three little metal grommets on one side;

— Mm, Nick said;

— So I just saw it and, you know, became curious; so I laid it on top of an old traveler's trunk he had in his bedroom, over the slats and dusty leather, and began to go through it; and it was great, and really old, and old-smelling, and every time I turned a page and smelled the puffs of dust it seemed that little bits of yellow paper would break off from somewhere and splinter away;

Finally Nick turned and entered the room, which was deeper than it had seemed from the hallway; patchily lit by the afternoon window, the room turned out to be some kind of workplace or studio: several different filing cabinets and hutches lined parts of three walls, along with two bizarre-looking drafting tables; a couple of cork boards were tucked away into one corner, while two identical swivel-chairs floated in the middle of the white-tile floor; alongside one table, a wastepaper basket was being put to good use; Nick, after flicking on the overhead lights, offered me one of the chairs before plopping into the other:

— OK, he then said: you were saying;

— Yeah, I said, and settled into the sliding, squeaky chair: so, for some reason which I still don't understand, I kind of took a cotton to the thing, and so every time we'd go back to my grandfather's place I'd try to get upstairs and take a look;

and, you know, it *was* fun: the book just seemed to cover so much ground, and seemed so, I don't know, rife with life: even to an eight-year-old, all the photos and newsclips and such that he had stuck in there, with all their shapes and sizes and configurations, they all seemed to speak of a life that had had so much content, so much real activity, and not just the same old automatic going and getting; it all just seemed to *bristle*...;

— Mm, Nick said;

— And I also liked the fact that it would change—that it *could* change: at the time, my grandfather was still going off every now and then, and when he came back the book would have new pictures in it; the book seemed alive, just like he was, gathering experiences, it was evolving along with him in no obviously planned or predetermined way—but all of it was still a direct reflection of *him,* you know, of his essence; and there was a part of me that thought, you know, that the book, in some way, was keeping the old graybeard going—that as long as things kept appearing in the book he'd still be there, even forever...

— Mm, Nick said: yeah...

— And, well, that's about it, I said;

— Well good, Nick said: great; and thank you;

— You got it;

— Good, Nick said, and sat a little straighter up: well, I suppose I should begin by telling you, you know, that your call really got me going;

— Really, I said;

— Absolutely, he said: you know, I hung up and began thinking about the things you were saying—

— Great;

— Yeah: and you know the next day I just got out all the old boxes and all the things I have—which I haven't done for*ever*—and started digging through them; and I've gotta tell you it's been some heavy-duty fun;

— Great, I said;

— You know my father, if you think about it, was really a kind of archivist—

— I *know*—

— Saving and hoarding all this *stuff* that anyone else

would think was just kind of sub-trivial, but, if you really think about it, is really a kind of folklore, genuine folklore—

— Exactly;

— I mean, I found these wild old social columns from papers that not even the parakeets around here remember shitting on—talking about weddings and births and business openings, things like that—and, like, an entry for a sweepstakes to give away the last horse used by the hook-and-ladder company in Pryor Creek; and he even collected old jokes, bunches of them, which he'd scribble down on the backs of receipts from his pharmacy and then tie up in packs;

— Hm, I said;

— I mean, who would have thought this had any value?, Nick said: but *he* knew...

This was good: I had lit a fire in Nick; it could only help:

— Incidentally, Nick said: how do we know that Jesus was Jewish?;

— Sorry?, I said;

— How do we know that *Jesus* was *Jewish*?, Nick repeated, before brightening into a grin: it's one of the jokes I found;

— Ah, I said, and swiveled to one side: well...really couldn't tell you;

— His mother thought he was God, and he thought his mother was a virgin;

Nick laughed, while I swiveled in my chair to try and make my rather slighter reaction seem somewhat more; but while turned away, waiting for Nick to calm down, I became aware that the room we were sitting in contained an unusual abundance of shelves; virtually all of its wall space was hung with metal-armed brackets, even when there was room for only one or two crossplanks, while other shelves filled the room's cabinets and hutches, most of which were half-open; further, nearly all the shelving held shallow mounds of neatly stacked paper; it was apparent that Nick responded well to curiosity, so I figured I would move on this:

— So how about you?, I said: what do you do, if you don't mind my asking;

— Not at all, he said: I'm into mitosis;

— Aren't we all, I said;

— Indeed, Nick said, and smiled: actually I work in animation—animated films;

— Ah;

— Yeah; right now I'm working as an inbetweener;

— Sorry?, I said;

— I'm an inbetweener, he said: I make the drawings that go between the drawings made by the head animators;

— Didn't know there was such a position, I said;

— Sure, Nick said: it's existed since the silent years; you see, the studio bosses figured out pretty quickly that it isn't necessary for the chief animators, who pull down the biggest salaries, to do every single drawing in an animated film; by at least the '20s they knew that it's only what are called the extreme drawings that determine the feel of an action—like, for example, if you're animating a baseball pitcher, the drawing of the pitcher reared way back to throw, then the drawing of him with his arm shot all the way forward; those would be the extremes; so then underpaid lunkies like me come in and make all the bridging sketches needed to flesh out the movement;

— So you must produce a huge number of drawings;

— Not so much; there's a lot of work, but the sketches don't have to be all that close to reach continuity on screen; I mean, this isn't calculus; here—

He leapt up and grabbed an inch-high stack of paper from a nearby shelf; then he came behind me, bent over my shoulder, and dragged his thumb across the edge of the stack to flip its individual pages before my face; it turned out to be a sequence of pencil sketches of a cartoon gerbil, standing upright in a zoot suit and Panama hat—a rodent Cab Calloway, as it were; and as the sketches fanned by, I could see that the gerbil was dancing the meringue—rather contentedly, it seemed, with his eyes closed, his snout arcing upward, his fingers snapping, and little impact lines radiating from his fingertips as he twirled about the white page-surface; after he had finished flipping, Nick went back and showed me some of the drawings individually, going through several consecutive sheets very slowly so that I could see how the figures differed;

to my eye, at least, the leaps from one sketch to the next seemed drastically far apart, almost unbridgeably distant:

— It's a nice scene, Nick said, returning the drawings to their shelf and then sitting down: so you see what happens: once your brain registers sufficient similarities between the figures, it understands—it just *knows*—that they're the same character; then, with the help of good old persistence of vision, you blend together the movement and the sequence comes to life; what may seem like impossible differences in the individual images are submerged in the onrushing flow;

— Hm, I said;

— In fact, Chuck Jones tells a story about the old days back at Termite Terrace, when the guys used to pull a gag on the new inbetweeners who were being broken in—maybe someone like Benny Washam, who did all those great fingery things; they'd assign the new guy to inbetween a scene of, say, Bugs Bunny strumming a banjo, and then they'd film this sequence of sketches to show how the scene looked—they'd actually film the drawings, which is called doing a pencil test; but in the middle of the sequence, they'd throw in a drawing of, oh, Bugsy screwing a lovely lady bunny, without letting the new inbetweener know; then they'd actually project this pencil test for the new inbetweener, to let him see how his work looked on screen; and so everyone'd watch and the sabotaged spot would go by, and the guy wouldn't even be able to tell that the extra drawing was there; he'd just watch the scene calmly and never notice anything unusual, because it goes by so quick; and after it was over they would ask the new guy what he thought, and he would always say Great, you know, great, looked just fine; but then they'd play the film back and stop at the sketch of this raging rabbit carnality, and the guy would spook out;

— Ha, I said;

— So you see, even the wildest inbetweens don't disrupt the overflowing current;

I could see how Nick had been drawn to this work: the more he talked the more animated he became, the more widely spaced became *his* inbetweens, as he rocked back and forth in his swerving chair and scrambled his hands around;

I could almost imagine him producing, from a secret somewhere just behind him, a huge rubbery mallet of about six
times his body weight and clobbering me on the head with it,
just from excesses of enthusiasm; but it was an eagerness I
knew I should stay with:
  — In other words, you're saying that there may be reams
of subliminal raunch running all through Peter Pottamus;
  — Not quite, Nick said, and leaned back, smiling: we
have *some* professional ethics, and in case we decide to forget
that, the work is usually heavily supervised; every frame of
what I'm working on now is checked a minimum of twice; it's
a science film, so it has to be precise;
  — An animated *science* film?, I said;
  — Sure; they're always using animation to illustrate
things in science, because of the precision it can get; everyone
thinks that Snow White was the first full-length cartoon, but
way back in 1923 the Fleischers did an animated feature on
Relativity, and there's been lots more ever since;
  — Sylvester as Schrödinger's cat;
  — Exactly, Nick said;
  — So what are you working on now?, I said;
  — I got a gig freelancing for a small studio over in Tulsa,
he said: inbetweening on a nice three-minute film about cell
division;
  — Great;
  — Yeah; the studio scored this huge contract with the
Southern Education Foundation, so it's pretty big stakes—
educational films looping through kids' minds for the next 20
years; but so far it's looking good: I can hardly wait to get it
on the Oxberry;
  — Sounds good;
  — Mm, Nick said: and I must say it's been nice: I mean,
now we're doing the segment on mitosis, which is one of our
beeline links with the amoebae, so you *got* to get it right;
  — Absolutely;
  — Actually, it's kind of beautiful, Nick said: you know,
telling the story of this one little cell—how, in an ecstasy of
lifeforce and development, it surges forth and miraculously
divides up its nuclear material to form an exact replica of

itself, shivering into becoming two identical daughter nuclei...; it's amazing; it's *fantastic*...

— Mm, I said;

— I mean, I get the animator's sketches of these circles and wriggles and speckles, and they're the cell membranes and the chromosomes and the spindles—abstract shapes representing real particles of living tissue—of *livingness*...

— Mm...

— And then I get to help the process along!; with graphite and technique and technology I animate animation!; well, I tell you, as an inbetweener it's a thrill-and-three-quarters: to bridge the transition from identity to identity;

— I hear you—

— I mean, it's almost cheap theology: Lose yourself to find me—and then see that it's just yourself all over again...but more, *multiplied*...with sameness and difference subverted...and division refuted...and the fleshly terror of distance finally and definitively *denied*...; like yesterday, the studio sent over the stack of extremes for the mitotic stage known as anaphase, and this is *really* a wild time: you're just out of metaphase, and all the daughter chromosomes have come together at the very middle of the cell, preternaturally aligned along the equatorial plane; and then, just after this stunning conjunction, the chromosomes inexplicably begin to separate—to surge apart in magic synchrony, wrenching their world asunder in this miraculous passion of reconfiguration, this thrusting self-*re*assertion, harrowing the past to deliver the dream of the deathless future; and all around, the lifestuff is just furiously *selving*, instinctively manufacturing endless identity, perpetuating perpetuation, with the microtubules snatching free-floating molecules from the cytoplasmic pool in order to grow, or actually returning fragments of their substance *to* the pool in order to contract, assembling and disassembling in this constant transfusing flux, melding into their medium or emerging *from* it, enriched and enabled with every modulation, selflessly partaking of this great interpenetrative churn, dissolving the distinction between giving and taking and wo!...*Wo*, there—*wohhhh*—!, *go*—*grab*...*grab it*...and *get*...*get* it...I've *got*...I've...thank

God...back, and *safe...*in my...thank *God,* safe in my arms...and
back...fshew...*fshew...*; yow, it almost *fell,* that time; Jeez,
that was scary; that was *really* scary; you see, they never tell
you in the instructions how hard it is to install these things;
really, there's no indication at all of what to expect; they must
assume that people think Oh, an antenna: that's easy—just
put it up; but it's not, really, there are a lot of subtle
considerations: you have to figure in directionality, and
bracing, and wind forces, and things like that, and then you
have to find a place on the roof that's sturdy enough to hold
it; so it's much more difficult than it might seem at first; yet
despite my few little, shall we say, bobblings tonight, I still
think it's better to put the antenna over here, attached to the
chimney: I can anchor the antenna's entire lower mast, which
will make the mount more secure, and I should also be able to
squeeze out a few extra inches of elevation; and that's really
important: AM is easy—it bounces off the ionosphere or
moves in groundwaves, so you always get a good range of
reception; but FM—where the action is—is entirely line-of-
sight, so the higher the antenna the better, especially for what
I want; it's taken me eight months to save up for this guy
(including $60 just for the rotator—grrr...), but it's a good one
and I should be able to pull in more stuff; it's funny, in a way:
the taller you are the more distant your reach: height becomes
width; and I need whatever I can get: there's just so little *on*
these days that you've got to do anything you can to pull in
what's there: you have to wrest it from the skies; boy, I can't
even imagine what it was like back in the Golden Age, in the
'30s and the '40s, when radio was like a shower: you just
turned a knob and down came *splashes* of programming,
torrents of it, enough to douse yourself with, to drink in
through your skin; and it was available constantly, all the
time, there was *great* drama and comedy; it's true what they
sang in that song, that video killed the radio star—how in the
long war between the senses, the eye, in its unstoppable
scorched-earth campaign, has mobilized a kind of technological Gresham's Law against radio, and has almost entirely
sidelined it; but this is *radio,* I always want to say, *radio*—the
living medium, the medium of exchange!; I mean, how can

anyone resist this richness—you just turn it on, and curl back, and settle into softness, and then let yourself be transported, just by the power of the voice, by words and the instinct towards communication; with your eyes closed or with your eyes full-open, you can be taken far and wide; I mean, this richness even comes through on my reissue records, some of which have programs that are nearly fifty years old; think about that: half a century; and who, I wonder, will remember Inner Resources fifty years from now—that mini-series that my parents want me to watch tonight; they said I might be able to get something from it; I told them I'd rather be hit by a steam shovel; even the title—Inner Resources; I mean, it's unbelievable; this is not communication with, but communication at; if you want to know, I gladly ceded the den to my folks for the night; there was *no* problem on that count; besides, it gave me the opportunity to come up here, without unnecessary observation, in the darkening light—to get away from the eye, so stupid an organ; boy, the eye—stealer of sense; it tricks more than it transmits; you only have to recall the results of the polls taken after the '60 Nixon/Kennedy debate: who won—?

— Television viewers: Kennedy
— Radio people: Nixon

This may be a tainted example, from our vantage point, but still: every contemporary commentator said that Nixon gave the better answers, and that, of course, should be what counts; and there's that time when a British journalist, Sir Robin Day, found that radio listeners are nearly 50% more likely than TV viewers to know when someone is lying on the air; so it's true—no question about it: the ear sees what the eye is blind to, it penetrates Potemkin light; I really believe that to see a person is, somehow, to limit him, but to listen is to let a person bloom; just think of the great voice virtuosi of the radiowaves— Bea Benaderet, Ruby Dandridge, and, of course, Mel Blanc: those guys were performing in maybe six different shows a week, and then doing—who knows?—maybe eight different voices on each show; it was a time when a person could be a forest—and each branch, each leaf, each twig, communicated some untainted truth; Raymond understood this; we would go up to my room, and close the door, and keep the television and the stereo *off*; and then we would just relax, be fully at ease: I would lie down on my bed, and he would lie on his back on the floor, head supported on butterfly-folded arms; and there would be the Mallomars that I had brought up and, when we had them, the Scooter Pies, and most of the time some other stuff; in other words, we would achieve calm, real tranquillity, just munching on something good and resting our eyes on the ceiling, where there were no posters or photos; and we would talk about this and that from school, or be joking around about absolutely anything, and then, when the mood came upon him, but with great faked suddenness, Raymond would begin to imitate a kettledrum roll with his voice, all boomingly and dramatically—*rummm*...; and I, just as if I were responding to a preplanned cue—with no startlement, but relaxed and easy, and full-throated—I would go into my Ed Herlihy voice and:

— It's the Big Broadcast of June 6, 1987—!

And then there would be a swell in the oral kettledrums from Raymond, and then there would be me again:

— Coming to you live from the studios of KTGE in Oaklandon, with our special guests tonight of...well, could that be Artie Auerbach, as Mr. Kitzel—?

And now Raymond, doing a perfect imitation:

— Mmmmmm—it's a possibility—!

And back to me:

— And do I see Henry Morgan, from Mutual's "Here's Morgan"—?

And Raymond again, dead-on:

— Good evening, anybody...

Then me:

— And is that Henry Aldrich, portrayed by the great Ezra Stone—?

And Raymond again:

— Coming, Mother—!

It was so fun; we could keep it going for what seemed like hours on end, a couple of arboreal creatures lost in our vine-tangle of voices; I would laugh and giggle, because Raymond was a skillful mimic, and the Mallomars were good, and it was just us staring at the ceiling and letting our voices go; but, for me, I must say, there was something else about all this, there was another aspect to it all: for while we were in the middle of our radio-playing, all our acting and laughing and having so much fun, I would sometimes feel, then, at least at certain moments, that I had found timelessness, or at least a taste of it—if you don't mind my putting it that way; but honestly, those were moments of timelessness, when I just felt divorced from time, absolutely released, through our joyful suspension of care, our giddy snipping of the puppet-strings of time; and it was nice; and that's part of the reason why I find it just unthinkable that this tradition, this rich history of communications and exchange, has been allowed to wither, virtually to die; it smacks, to me, of some kind of tyranny—a tyranny that is never really addressed, and that we're supposed to accept as natural and inevitable; but, still, I can't say that I like it; neither did Raymond; neither of us liked it at all; of course, we couldn't really do too much about it, it was the kind of thing we both realized we had to live with, but one time Raymond and I actually tried to establish a defense against these tendencies, or at least tried to come up with a moderate counterweight; and it was this: the two of us, on our own, put together a plan that we hoped would, in some substantial way, resuscitate the medium of radio; we worked it out over the course of two long my-bedroom evenings, also spent in the company of a box of Vanilla Wafers; we decided that we were going to go to the networks and propose the creation of a new radio series, the first of its kind in decades, and we were going to *guarantee* that the project would fully regenerate the medium, with all the commercial opportunities that implies, although we would ask for no additional royalties; it was to be the return of weekly radio drama, a half-hour in length, set in a medium-size city, with a varying cast, and it was to be called World of Blondes; and each presentation would begin, even before the theme music, which had not yet been chosen, with a verbal attestation by one of the show's producers, either Raymond or myself, that every member of the cast was a blonde, or treated to be one; (Raymond had wanted to extend the guarantee to include crew members, but I said no:

it might have seemed like opportunism;) then, after that, the
drama would proceed; the stories, we reasoned, could be
figured out later, and, in fact, weren't all that important—this
didn't have to be Gang Busters; still, we were certain that the
series would mean radio's resurrection, and, more importantly, that it would be something that the networks would
snap up; we foresaw bidding wars among the networks and
the sponsors, and we also looked forward to taking cigaretty
meetings in sleek boardrooms with big guns in loosened ties;
I must tell you that we really worked up a head of steam on this
one, we really did, even going so far as to jot down ideas and
prepare the format for a proposal, although it was around this
time, about a year ago, that Raymond's condition began to
worsen, so we really couldn't continue to develop the plans;
and that was too bad; it really was; it would have made a
splendid series, a real rebirth for a scorned medium; but I
began to see Raymond less frequently around then—really no
more than once every couple of weeks, when he had some
time for himself—and by then I figured it was better to keep
silent on some subjects; so I just let the plan slip, even though,
at one point, Raymond said that he wouldn't mind if I did the
project solo; still, I think I did the right thing by not talking
about it any more, and also by continuing to go out and buy
reissue records—I was heavy into Fred Allen then—so we
would have something new to listen to; I'd try to have at least
one new album for each time he came over, because I knew it
was something he would enjoy—I'd go out and buy one the
day after every visit he paid to me, just to be sure; we would
go up to my room, and lie back, and even though the talking
between us was getting a little less lively at that point, the
record would give us something to listen to; it was something
to divert us, to counter any nudges of silence...

...I remember, soon afterwards, that I got a call from a
guy from school named Neville, who said he was another
friend of Raymond's; I assume he got my number from
Raymond's folks; still, he called and said he was planning a
get-together, and asked me if I wanted to come; so a group of
us ended up one night at Neville's house, parents gone; I was
the last to arrive, because I had had some other stuff to do; so

after I rang the bell, Neville came to the door and led me past a closet and a wall-mirror and into his living room; there were chips and Chocolate Towns and orange soda on a table in the corner, and six or seven other people on the sofas and chairs that lined the good-sized room—they could have put a pool table in there; I recognized most of the other people from school, including this one girl, Peggy Madden, whom I couldn't imagine ever talking to Raymond and who customarily wouldn't be caught dead saying a word to me; but she was there, and keeping quiet, sitting on a sofa with two guys I didn't know; Neville didn't perform any introductions (I suppose he forgot), so there was something of a cloudiness in the air as I settled into a sofa spot across the long direction of the room from Peggy Madden; the room wasn't terribly well lighted, and people weren't really saying too much, and at one point I became a little conscious of the fact that I might have been chewing loudly; but then two of the other guys began talking a little about some sneakers one of them had—or one of them *wanted* to have—then about something they saw on this TV program called Cheers, and then, kind of gradually, they turned to Raymond, and you could feel that people were relieved to get there; at that point the room grew quieter, and more still, as the words about him finally came seeping out; and little by little, you know, rather gradually, people began to conjure up memories, or funny things Raymond had said (and it was nice when someone finally allowed himself to laugh), or just little incidents and whatnot; and I noticed, as this was getting under way, that something interesting seemed to be happening: that whoever was speaking seemed just to be talking aloud—that is, just giving his or her words up to the darkish living room, and not addressing anyone or any audience in particular; the voices were just out there, suspended and alone, and, perhaps paradoxically, something about this solitary quality really made the voices draw you in; and so I settled back and listened: one guy, Alex, spoke about Raymond's plans to move to Nova Scotia after he went to college, and to start a small-animals farm there; then a girl, I think she was Susan, went on about a time she and Raymond had cut English and hid behind the handball wall at the far end of the school yard, and had smoked menthol cigarettes; then Peggy Madden spoke about some schematic diagrams of antique cars—Fords, Oldses and Reo Roadsters, she said—that Raymond had once given her to help her with a book report; and another guy, who had a grainy voice, he began talking about plans that Raymond had made to set up a horror house in his parent's garage, which he was going to charge admission to see, and how Raymond had shown him design sketches that he had made for it, sketches of stuffed costumes and spooky light machines and rubber insects on movable strings; and there were other recollections, and then still others...

...And, you know, I listened to this, I sat back and heard all of it; and, I will admit, I really appreciated what everyone was saying—the straightforwardness and directness of it, the way that, after we had finally begun speaking about Raymond, no one got funny or sarcastic or wise guy-ish, or tried to dodge the situation in any other way; but at the same time, I must admit, I found that I didn't quite know what to make of all the things I was hearing; in fact, I almost couldn't believe them— because, to tell you the truth, I had never heard about any of these events or interests before, or about anything even resembling them; and this was, if I may say so, somewhat strange; I mean, for me, I had always liked that Raymond seemed infinite—that his sense of humor and his voices just went on and on—but apparently he was infinite in more ways than I had known; and this was somewhat unsettling, I must say—although it was also a little comforting; in fact, while I was sitting there, listening to all the voices painting the quiet living room, the situation reminded me, somewhat, of a movie I once saw; it was called Rashomon, and at the end of it, for some reason, I cried; I remember that I didn't want the movie to end, to resolve itself in any way at all; I wanted the movie just to keep going, to keep coming up with more versions of its story, to keep producing more characters so they could add *their* takes on the tale; so I was really upset when the film felt the need to come to a conclusion and the lights came up; I remember walking home holding my fist to my mouth, to keep my crying from lathering out; so, that night at Neville's, I decided, while sitting on the sofa and hearing everyone else go on and on, I decided that I, alone among everyone there, wouldn't say anything—that I would hold my recollections back, and not talk about my experiences with Raymond; I would just listen, and participate in that way; because then, maybe, if I didn't say a word, maybe then the movie—the Raymond movie—wouldn't end; maybe then it *couldn't* end; and so I kept quiet, and just kept listening, all the while telling myself that I was probably making the most important contribution of the evening, by saying nothing at all; I mean, if I couldn't make any other contributions to Raymond, at least I could offer my silence— if my marrow wasn't the kind he needed, if it wasn't compatible, then I would contribute in the way I could; here was something that I could do, even if it just meant showing up, and being there, and then doing nothing; I mean, I would never be the one to finish him...

...I suppose, though, it's just another expression of the inherent sadness of sound, of sound's defective essence; after all, sound is so perishable: it's no more than a nudging of air, a fragile sequence of crests and troughs—soft, ripply, rounded like Mallomars, and perilously dependent on its medium; it's so different than light, which has hardness, and beaminess, and eternality; sound just dissolves, it radiates away into emptiness, resolving its curves into formlessness and passing through the atmosphere into directionless space; and this, too, is a sadness; for so much is lost; so much is lost; in fact, I can practically see the process happening right now, standing where I am—up here, on the roof; for up here, on my roof, looking towards the darkening sky, I can almost see the world's endless gusts of sound silently dispersing—all of them powerlessly unfurling against the distant clouds, dissolving into the leveling night...; and so, up here, with darkness descending, and with the breeze at my back, I plant my feet against the edges of a few sturdy slates, and get back to work, wondering what new things I'll be able to pull in, with my antenna, so well anchored:

— Mm...

— So then there was nothing—

— No, not at all: it's my first involvement with anything

like this;
　— So you had no previous inclination—
　— Oh, yeah...I suppose...; in my private thoughts...
　— So...please...; go ahead...
　— Well, I suppose there were always some doubts in there, mixed in among the littler voices; but I always managed to successfully ignore them;
　— Because, if I may say so, it isn't too often that—well, that political radicalism rises from the ranks of our substitute teachers—
　— But it wasn't radicalism at all—not at *all*; I mean, just because it involved some kind of concerted action, does that mean it's *radicalism*...?
　— No, not real—
　— Yeesh, that's funny...
　— Well, it's not that I—
　— In fact, I think what I did sprang from an instinct that is deeply conservative—
　— Oh...?
　— Absolutely: from something that lies near the center of what this country is supposed to mean: democracy—genuine democracy;
　— Whatever...;
　— That's how *I* see it...
　— OK...; *very* good...; but now—now I'd like to go back a bit, to how this all began, to give folks who didn't see the article in the Oklahoman a sense of what happened;
　— OK;
　— So: how did you get started, where did this...; tell us...
　— Oh, I suppose it's just a function of being alive, you know;
　— Mm;
　— But the first specific thing that kind of got me going, you might say, happened when I was at home, watching the 10 o'clock news, and seeing the campaign on television...
　— Mm—
　— I mean, night after night I would sit there watching what's happening with the campaign, what's going on and what the candidates are saying, and every day it's just more of

the same horrifying, degrading stupidity...; I mean, it's degrading even to watch that stuff, so I can't even *imagine* what it would be like to actually *do*...

— Yeah; so—

— So I'd be sitting on my couch, working a seam—I like to make my own clothes—or having my nightly dose of Breyer's coffee ice cream—but that's another story—and then from all over the country there'd be shots of this idiot spectacle playing itself out, all this footage of the candidates doing nothing but engaging in public relations; like when they're, you know, making these calculated, grandstanding speeches while surrounded by balloons, or visiting a factory where flags are made, or just gurgling out the usual transparent platitudes—or that time when one of them, the little mollusk, apparently believing he had been coming off as weak, scooted around in a tank—

— Whoo, yeah...; that was rough—

— And then all the ads, which are just *shameless* in their manipulativeness and stupidity and meanness, and all the posturing, and the sucking up, and the distorting—all of it, just *all* of it...; I mean, by now we're all well-versed in the inadequacy of language, so to speak, but I never feel this so forcefully as when I try to come up with some means of verbalizing the utter, total, and appalled revulsion and sub-disgust I feel at what has become of our political process...; I mean, watching this every night on television, I would just begin to get *sick,* I started developing physical symptoms—tensions, chest pains, actual *symptoms*; and I would sit there, you know, I'd sit there and I'd be thinking: this can't be it; this *can't* be what it's all about—I mean, *all* this unbearable shit—; oh...; sorry...; sorry about that; but it's kind of OK on cable, isn't it?...

— [Laughing] Go on...let 'er rip...

— OK...; so, that was it: I just couldn't believe what I was seeing; after eight years of monkey-movie man, now the election is just being treated as a massive con job, organized and controlled with almost unthinkable technique—a perversion of democracy and not its most important expression...; this is horribly naive, I know, I suppose this just seems a little silly, and I'm sure people have been thinking exactly these things since they shut down the circus maximus...; but I didn't know, you know, that I *could* feel these things—no one had ever told me...; and so maybe that's why it's just been so strong—now that, I don't know, I *have* begun to feel them...; I'm even getting a little sick right now, just by thinking about it—

— Just make sure you aim away from your microphone if—

— Yeah...; so that was the source—an un-understood physical response...

— But what then led...that is, everyone's disgusted by politics, but...but why did you get into this other thing—

— Mm—

— What led to your, as you call it, going around...

— Well, the more I sat in front of the tube just roiling about all this, the more it occurred to me that I just couldn't be alone in feeling this way—that there *had* to be other people who were reacting at least as strongly as I was; and then I remembered reading something a few years back, something about voting patterns; so the next morning I went to the library to see if I could research it, and I found the information very quickly, right in the Statistical Abstracts: it was plain as day, right there and obvious; and what it came down to was that Mr. Reagan, despite all the ballyhoo of landslide victories and bruited claims about having a mandate from the people— as it turns out, Reagan won, back in 1980, by taking only 26 percent of the electorate, and his results in '84 were only slightly better; so how could this be democracy, I began to wonder—the expression of the common will, the realization of our collective destiny—when such numbers—

— It's because no one votes;

— Exactly; this assemblage of hearing aids and contact lenses and Grecian Formula and shoulder pads won the election because very nearly half of his countrymen who could vote elected to stay away; rather than participating in the process they ran in the opposite direction; again, this is nothing new, but for some reason, as I said, I just began to feel what it means...; you know, it's a strange thing when that happens—I'm sure you know it—when some sense or feeling or idea just seems, for the first time, to work its way inside you, to penetrate all the fortifications, and then, when it's finally there, in the zone of vulnerability, to take root—to genuinely start to mean something, and *singe* you, and *make a difference*...

— Mm...

— So, that was it; I had, over the course of a few weeks, what I call my secular revelation—the veil was torn off, just torn away; and it's stayed like that, you know, it's still really with me—it's kind of lodged in my chest, this continuing force that, I don't know, seems to have jarred my compass; like one time, I remember, soon after this happened, I was at the supermarket, and I just started looking down the aisles at all the boxes and packages and colors, or once when I was driving down Reno Avenue, and I just saw all the houses with their lawns and paint jobs and numbers and...and all of a sudden the whole thing just seemed off, and different, and terribly sad...; and I just thought, you know, *Oh my God*...

— Hm—

— And then, you know, it also began to affect my work— it even got me there; I mostly teach history, and I remember about a month ago I had to go into a school in Minco for a few weeks, where they were going to cover the French Revolution; so I started mapping out my presentation and jotting down notes, things like that...but then, you know, I began to feel something nibbling at me, really nipping at my conscience; and I began to think that maybe there was, I don't know, another way into all this—that maybe I shouldn't be introducing the Revolution as this great moment for the common good, with the Social Contract and the Enlightenment and the triumph of equality over privilege, all that stuff, but that it should really be seen as the disastrous consequence of the financial problems resulting from the Seven Years' War and France's participation in the American Revolution, or that it should be interpreted as an act of auto-genocide committed by a people terrified of modernization—an upheaval whose real and lasting consequence was to establish Year One of rationalized mass wars and police states and the

idea that all opponents are traitors who therefore must die—
in other words, that it was no more than a speedbump along
a route that led from the Principia to the Gulag—

— *Whoa*, now—wait a...; whose—

— Oh...forget it...; but I was really taken over by that
kind of ridiculousness...

— So—

— I mean how can I be sure that what I'm teaching these
kids is right—I mean what, really, am I telling them—what am
I teaching them...?; it's become a real concern...

— And then this—this, then, fed into your going door to
door...making your rounds, I think you called it in the
article...

— Yeah, those were some of the things that led to it...;
I wanted, I suppose, to get in touch with some of the other
things, the other currents, that I knew were there, that *had* to
be there—to investigate them directly and find out for myself...

— And—

— And so I finally worked up the nerve to do it, just to
go and do it; and, you know, the resolve just came to me one
night, right before going to sleep; I was lying in bed thinking
about what I wanted to do, and all of a sudden the psychological resistance just dissolved...; and then I knew I could do it,
I just *knew* it...; so the next day, after coming home from
school, I just, you know, forged ahead: I put on a tan blouse
and a dark skirt, real neutral clothes so I wouldn't give anyone
the wrong signals, and I pinned my hair up in a good Victorian
bun, so it also wouldn't—you get it; and I also decided not to
go around in my building—most of us have hard enough a
time saying hello as it is, and those are the people I recognize;
so I went into Warr Acres, where I don't know anyone, to
avoid any problems with previous contacts or impressions;
and that's how I began, just over two weeks ago; I just went
around and rang people's bells, just before dinnertime, when
I figured most folks would be home;

— So what did you—*say*...; how did—I mean, at the
first—

— I simply asked whoever answered the door, assuming

it was an adult, if they were planning on voting in November; if they said yes, I'd thank them and move on; but if they said no, I'd ask if I might talk with them about it for a little while;

— But did you carry a—clipboard, or one of those little, I don't know, *badges* with your *pic*—

— Of course not; why would I?; I'm not part of any organization;

— So then why would they ever—how could you expect them...; in other words, you just wanted to talk;

— Exactly; why not; how else can you learn; and I got over the awkwardness of the situation pretty quickly, as a matter of fact; after about the second bell I was really perfectly at ease, and even enjoying myself: my throat wasn't dry, and my heart wasn't knocking, after the second one...; and it was kind of nice to get rid of all that communicative gunk for a while;

— But, of course, you did meet resistance...

— Not resistance to *me*—I don't see it that way at all; I mean, it's true that most of the nonvoters didn't want to talk, but most of them wouldn't even let the process get off the ground; time after time, at one house after the other, the people answered the bell and listened to my pitch very respectfully; but then they all simply said Sorry and closed their doors;

— But that isn't exactly the red-carpet treat—

— But I couldn't take it as a personal rejection, either: I hadn't begun to say anything, I hadn't even gotten beyond my first question; so what they were resisting—and maybe this is what you're talking about—what they were resisting was something else entirely; and this was exactly what I wanted to explore;

— So did you then—did *any*one—

— No; in my first seven tries, no one would talk to me— an amazing statistic, if you think about it; they all suddenly had something else that they had to see to...

— But then the last one—that was the one, yes?, where—

— Right: that was it, my eighth nonvoter; that was the one; and I tell you, there was absolutely no sign of anything unusual: I mean, it was a nice enough house, with trimmed hedges and a thermometer mounted on the little roof above the front door, and what looked like home-sewn curtains in the windows; and it was on a quiet, tree-lined street;

— But then—

— And when I rang the bell, in my sensible shoes, a middle-aged man and his son, who must have been about twenty, came to answer the door together—they both had identical eyes, milky-gray and set very close; and then they listened to my pitch very politely, without saying more than about two words between them, just looking out and listening; and then, you know, I was kind of pleased when the father just pushed open the screen door and invited me in— he said we could talk better inside; and I must tell you I was really kind of excited as I stepped in the house, because this was the first real contact that I had made—the first positive feedback at all; so they led me in and offered me a chair in a little eating nook they had between the foyer and the kitchen; and it was nice: the father sat on one of the built-in benches that formed three sides of the nook, and was looking at me with these intense, lamplike, ash-gray eyes; and then he started asking me questions about why I was speaking to people, and who I was, and who I was with, and where I came from—things like that; so I started telling him about the kinds of things I had been thinking about, and why I was going around, and the man was listening attentively, and it was all kind of nice, when the son came up and, all of a sudden, wrapped a section of lawn hose around my chest and tied me to my chair with it; then he tied me up completely, all the way from my chest to my legs, as the father just sat there looking at me, or occasionally leaning over and staring straight into my face with these big gray eyes; and when the green hose was squeaking all around me—around my arms and legs and chest—the father went and called the police;

— Hm...

— Yeah...

— So then...then what were you—*thinking* when...when all this—

— Actually, I was just thinking *Hm*...: now *this* is interesting...; this is really something I hadn't anticipated...

— But weren't you—*scared*, didn't you struggle when—

—Not really; after all, he had called the police, so by that point I just wanted to see what would happen;

— But all the charges they filed—

— No, there were no charges—by the father, the son, *or* the police; as best I can tell that was entirely made up by the Oklahoman; there was nothing *to* charge: I hadn't made any false representations or anything like that, or committed unlawful entry—heavens!; and I'll have you know that I said virtually none of the things that the article attributed to me; those weren't my words at all...

— Wouldn't be the first time;

— There weren't even grounds for detaining me; the police just asked me a few questions, then they gave me a cup of coffee and sent me off; though one cop did suggest that I think twice about doing this kind of thing again, as he put it;

— Mm; and just a quick reminder here that we are *live* in the studio here, where you can reach us at (405) 295-4355 with comments or questions...; so, then, what I'm still wondering—to come back to this...; I think, for me, the question still is *why*—what you had really hoped to learn from...from...

—Mm...; I mean, I'm still not entirely sure, myself...; but I suspect I just wanted to prove something—something that I've really come to suspect for quite some time;

— Please...

— Well, you know, over the past couple of months, as I've watched the just repulsive and really disheartening charade of our political process playing itself out, it's occurred to me that there has to be a reason for this—that with all the candidates' advisors and consultants, this horrifying spectacle just can not be accidental; and so it came to me that the parties had realized, maybe unconsciously, that it wasn't enough just to attract the faithful; they also had to put off the infidels—to neutralize, to demobilize the opposition; and so, in effect, this is a rare instance of the parties working together—of silently agreeing to work to keep the greatest segment of the electorate from joining in;

— But certainly you don't think—

— Sure I do; why not? —that's the *result*...

— But—

— Come on, there's barely a whiff of difference between the Democrats and the Republicans; that's absolutely obvious, while all their furious competition would make you believe that these two parties represent the absolute limits of possible options—that there are no real choices beyond them, when, in fact, they're only offering the slightest variations on the same political theme; but to me it's interesting that one of the few things that the Republicans and the Democrats agree upon is that nonvoters should be disregarded—that the people who decide not to participate in the formal activity of voting are as voices who have fallen off the edge of the earth;

— But that—I'd think—comes from the Constitution—

— And has been perpetuated by those with an interest in doing so ever since, playing off the assumption, it's clear, that these people—virtually the majority of the country—are either indifferent to the decisions of their collective life or incapable of dealing with them; that's clearly the reasoning; but this is something that, while doing my rounds, I immediately found *not* to be true: shutting the door on me, or walking away, or all that other stuff—marshaling all that rudeness, which isn't easy—this was an expression of real political *passion*, of a willful choice *not* to be drawn in; but this is a kind of passion that we do not acknowledge and have been trained to discount;

— Mm...

— Politically, it's as if we're living before Faraday—still believing that our human fields are vacant, rather than filled to fullness with invisible lines of force, just boiling with activity;

— Hm;

— It also reminds me, you know, of a Rubin vase—you know, those drawings of a silhouetted vase, or what *looks* like a vase until you come to see that it's also two faces in profile, moving in for a smooch; and this second reading of the picture is absolutely there, you know—there's no way around it; and then, once you see the future smooch, you can never *stop* seeing it: it lunges out at you, you can't believe you ever *didn't* see it; so that's what the political situation seems like to me...; I mean, who needs a vase, anyway: I prefer to spend my time, any day, with the smooch...

— So...if I'm not getting you wrong...you're saying, you're saying that—

— That for me, our minimalist voting situation presents a problem not of minds but of measurement; you see, it seems to me that not to vote *is* a decision, not the absence of one— that not-voting is closer to negative one than to zero, and so has the same absolute value as a tabulated vote; in fact, I've even come to see not-voting as exercising a basic American freedom—the Fifth Freedom, it may be; in its way it's deeply traditional, maybe even patriotic; think of the Puritans...

— But surely you're—

— I know someone, I'll have you know, who says that not-voting is actually voting in another dimension, in an alternate world, but one that we've lost the ability to perceive...

— Well...and—

— For me, though, it's all part of something else: of learning to hear the roar in the quietude, of learning to distinguish between the silence that is there and the silence that isn't; to be able to see no, in certain circumstances, as an affirmation;

— Indeed; but tell me, then—once again, our number here is (405) 295-4355—so tell me: I'm still interested in...sources; why is it—why do you think you've come to feel this way...as you do...

— Oh, just common sense, I suppose...; once you step outside the circle it becomes kind of obvious;

— But...OK; OK...; but why would—is that a call?; yes...?; oh...; OK...; so...so then, tell me: maybe was there some, I don't know, some previous expression—some earlier...I don't know...

— Well, you know, I've kind of been wondering about that myself, because, as I mentioned earlier on, I never really had any direct or obvious preparation; I've never worked in politics, or on political campaigns, or even really cared that much, for that matter, not even when I was in college;

— So this, then...

— But what did occur to me, recently, one night last week—I was sitting at my kitchen table, thinking about how that sticky green hose felt wrapped around my arms—for some reason it occurred to me then that, you know, my grandfather was kind of an interesting guy, a real character, and maybe, you know, *he*...

— Mm hm...

— Yeah...; that's what I was thinking...; he was a great old coot, my grandfather; he was this tough, spiky old Welshman, with this unkempt sweep of hair coming down from the crown of his head and this big, broad nose...; and he had his own way of doing things, that's for sure...; he lived his way with such fullness and, well, naturalness that he made you think there was no other choice, at least for him...

— So...

— He was a musician, you know, though when he was young he started out by running some kind of textile factory in Scotland, and apparently he made quite a bit of money from it; and I also think he earned some small measure of renown from this factory, because apparently he instituted some fairly humane labor and living conditions for the employees—that kind of thing was unknown then, so he was really blazing the trail; he improved the housing for his workers, and gave them better sanitation, and shorter hours, and he made sure all their children were educated; he even opened up a general store where the prices were kept to just above cost; and the operation became pretty well-known: ambassadors would come to visit it, and there were Austrian princes, and bishops, and all kinds of others;

— So there we go;

— Mm...; but apparently he later gave this all up—something must have happened—and then he came over to the United States to help set up some kind of experimental, progressive community, which eventually became some kind of model for enlightened reform—

— Hm;

— Yeah; it was somewhere in the Mid-West, I think; he didn't like to talk about it too much, because apparently it

didn't work out; the whole thing shut down after just a few years, with, apparently, a bunch of bitter feelings all around; and all he would say about it, afterwards, when someone still knew enough about it to bring it up, was that it didn't remain true to its fundamental principles...; I can still hear him saying that, in that amazing, cadenced, Welsh-country voice: *fundamental principles...*
— Mm...;
— Even so, the town instituted, I think, the first free library in the United States, and the first kindergarten, and the first community-supported public school, so it was something...; but I think the experience was a little difficult for him—disillusioning—the way his plans couldn't sustain themselves; and he came, I think, just to prefer his independence...
— Sure;
— Eventually, though, he reinvented himself once again, and started traveling around as a musician, actually earning his keep by going around the country singing and playing; he played really fine classical violin, but at that point in his life, after the shutdown of the township, he preferred playing the dobro, strumming it like a folk guitar; I think he liked its metal body, and the twanginess it got when he played it acoustically; so after things didn't work out with his town in the Mid-West he mostly lived on the road, living off his dobro, going from town to town, singing...
— But how...what would—
— Oh, he'd make up songs, most of which were actually put together from bits of local news, so he was actually communicating events from town to town; he'd sing about how Hilda and Frank over in Grand Junction were getting married, or how barley prices had taken a dip, or that a fire in Steelville had left a family with a new daughter without a home; much of this, you understand, was during the dust-bowl days, so lots of the scattered people didn't have many other sources of information; and so he was welcomed—this inter-town crier, an American griot; he would be away for months on end, although once, I understand, he traveled for over two straight years;
— And he would go to different—

— Yeah: he would just wander around the country; he'd pull up in, you know, sun-baked prairie towns, or mountain villages folded away behind shutters, or he'd show up in a run of riverside hamlets that had more fishing boats than children; and once he'd get into any of these spots, he'd find a good-sized public place, open up his dobro case and just start to play; he told me he usually sang for twenty or thirty minutes, then took twenty minutes down and then started up again; and when he came home, you know, after a trip, back to wherever he was living at the time, he'd have all these pictures of himself, sometimes torn from local papers or sometimes just snapshots taken on the spot, which people had later given to him; and these pictures, you know, were just *so* great: he'd be there with his beard and his floppy shirt, and the taut cord from the dobro would be spanning his shoulders and holding the instrument high up against his chest; and his listeners would be standing in a semicircle in front of him, intently looking on—just totally imbued with what he was doing; it was touching; I remember one shot where he was singing to a group of people standing near a gazebo in a town commons—and another with him next to a pharmacy's window filled with bottles and beakers, and also a smaller picture with him planted in the worn-away grass beside a game booth at a fair...; and there might be two people listening or there might be sixty, but still—he'd be there, with his eyes closed, and his face bent up to the sun, and that great scraggy throat thrust way out...

— Sounds like a wild old git;

— Yeah; I'm sorry I never really got to know him all that well; I was just a little too young, you know, although I do think I got a good sense of him; but by that time he was older, and kind of quiet, and he moved more slowly, although he was still very energetic; and he was bulky, too, really solid— but ashlar, not marble—and quite tall...; I still miss him...;

— And so you see him, you think, as a possible—

— Oh...; yeah...; maybe...; I don't know...; you know, it's funny, because I never really thought about him too much until relatively recently;

— So where...do we have a call—?; hello—?; hello—?;

no; OK, that's a no...; so...so then what do you see...do you have any other plans for—for activities along the lines that—
— In fact, I do; I really would like to continue with what I'm doing, if I can...
— In any particular—
— Oh sure, in several ways; I mean, with the passion I I'd like to do is get all these people—the Silenced Majority, as I call them—somehow recognized, and therefore bring them into the debate; I'm looking into forming some kind of new political group, or union, where nonvoters would be counted, at least in some way—somewhat along the lines of the original Maverick, if you're looking for a model; and I was thinking, incidentally, that we could call this group the Negative Ones, although you have to be careful where you put the emphasis when you pronounce that—
— OK...; OK, now I'm told—I see we have a caller now— *yes*...?; OK...; so hello; hello...; he*llo*—are you there...?; no...?; yes...?; *no*...?, is there someone there...?; *no*...?

...Well, in fact, *yes*...

...yes, there is someone there...

...yes, in*deed*...

...There is someone here...

...*I* am here...

...I am *right* here...

...and so are you...

...But are you here?...

...*are* you?...

...are you listening?...

...are you *there?*...

...Yes, you...

...That's right, *you*...

...Are you listening?...

...Are you *there*?...

...Yes, you are listening...

...You are *there*...

...And I am here....

...And that, for you, is the problem...

...that is *precisely* the problem...

...Because now you are confused...

...confused and perplexed...

...and now, even, a little frightened...

...Yes—*fright*ened...

...*What is he doing inside my headset?*...

...But don't bother looking at your machine, hanging from your belt...

...and don't waste your time pushing buttons...

...Pause, or Stop...

...or even Eject...

...Because I will still be here...

...And you will still be there...

...There—where, by now, you have stopped what you were doing...

...what you were trying to *absent* yourself from...

...walking to the magazine shop...

...sitting in the curved, cheek-friendly chair in the Trailways waiting room...

...collating photocopies...

...skimming an undernourishing book...

...Because, you see, wherever you are...

...wherever...

...I am there...

...*I have rooted you out*...

...It is what you feared...

...what you have feared all along...

...And it is this:...

...Someone has gotten to you...

...Someone has finally reached you...

...reached you *where you live*...

...It is, in short, what you feared...

...So by now, you have stopped what you were doing, and are *looking around*...

...Somewhat wildly...

...And now you are staring at your player, and thumbing its buttons...

...Somewhat feverishly...

...And you are thinking Who *is* this?...

...What is going *on?*...

...*What is he doing inside my head?*...

...But, dear listener, I am here with a purpose...

...I have come with a cause in mind...

...I have penetrated your fortress for a reason...

...Yes: I have smashed your private portcullis...

...I am already behind your personal parapets...

...And what I have come to say is: *here is our chance*...

...Our only chance...

...It's said that the first thing radio announcers are told in broadcasting school...

...is to pretend, when on the air, to be speaking to only one person...

...only one...

...to achieve the preferred delivery...

...And this I do...

...I pretend to be speaking to only one person...

...and that one person is you...

...The dictum is also true, one assumes, for pirate radio...

...So let's pretend...

...But this is not pirate radio...

...No, not at all...

...This freebooter is made for Walkmen...

...And that's just what is true...

...Yes, it is made for a concatenation of heads...

...Yours...

...Mine...

...Its...

...For, this is nonprofit, listener-transported broadcasting...

...Your own private piracy network...

...Coming to you through your Walkman...

...Just head to head...

...to head...

...Why, are you skeptical?...

...No, don't let's be skeptical...

...Or is it inconceivable to you...

...that there could be a leak in the loop...

...No, it is not inconceivable...

...It's just a question of effecting an interface—a linkage, if you will—between waves and granules...

...That's all...

...Between sound waves, brain waves, and the granules of magnetic material affixed to recording tape...

...iron oxides, chromium dioxides, cobalt-absorbed ferric oxides...

...in perfectly even dispersal...

...which, when they *whirr* across the playback head of your portable entertainment center, with the head's 50-microinch gap...

...deposit a residue that, to an almost astonishing degree, approximates the receptor sequence of—...

...but perhaps it isn't the wisest thing to say more...

...No, not at all: not one word more...

...After all, someone might consider our activity as breaking and entering...

...psychoacoustic edition...

...and while this is not outlawed by any domestic or international conventions or treaties...

...one never knows...

...Because there has been resistance...

...There has been opposition...

...Remember: we can break down the entirety of our

transmitting equipment in just over four minutes...

...and fold it such that it becomes indistinguishable from a normal ham radio...

...no larger than a weekender's suitcase...

...and in no way conspicuous...

...to anyone, or anything, at all...

...It was designed that way...

...So don't try anything...

...again...

...We will not be silenced...

...We intend to continue frequenting this frequency...

...And to do this for one simple reason:...

...Because this frequency is *your* frequency...

...That's all...

...Because just when you thought you had finally found...

...a means of avoidance...

...a method of escape...

...I have tracked you...

...I have reached you...

...Where no one else can get you...

...can get *to* you...

...in your internal exile...

...I have rooted you out!...

...And now the news...

...In Washington today...

...Oh—but let me turn on the teletype...

...For we all know how important that is...

...for full credibility...

...Ticka-ticka-ticka-ticka-ticka...

...In Washington today, an announcement came from the Centers for Disease Control...

...that advertising has been found to cause cancer...

...Although innocuous in small doses, the announcement said...

...advertising, when consumed at levels of over 80,000 suggestion-units per day...

...a quantity that falls well within exposure rates common to most industrialized nations...

...has been found to be highly carcinogenic...

...Most often, the document continued, exposure leads to a highly virulent cancer of the conscience...

...which metastasizes into an atypical form of cancer of the sense of dignity...

...in roughly 78% of cases...

...All are known to be entirely inoperable...

...In response, the Advertising Council of America today announced a $68 million campaign to combat what it described as, quote, These unfounded and totally unproven findings...

...before subsequently announcing, some four hours later, that it was withdrawing from this same campaign...

...Their reasons were undisclosed...

...At a press conference held later in the day, a spokesman for the National Institute of Persuasive Diseases commended the move...

...Ticka-ticka-ticka-ticka-ticka...

...In Rochester, New York, a privately-funded communications institute associated with the Xerox Corporation, which has a base in that city...

...has announced a project to produce energy from flows of language...

...The project, called SemanTechs 2000, will be based on geothermal models, Xerox spokesman Vernon Duke told reporters...

...According to a preliminary outline released today, the project will explore means of extracting units of energy from language as it passes from its producer to its consumer...

...The technique, the outline said, will utilize the differential between the amount of meaning invested in the language by its originator and the invariably lesser amount of meaning withdrawn from the language by its recipient...

...As Duke told reporters: For the first time we will be able to put inattention, incomprehension, and indifference to productive use...

...For instance, Duke continued, we envision a time when a brief chat about car-pooling will power a window-style exhaust fan for as long as four hours...

...Xerox spokesmen added, moreover, that they saw project applicability growing, quote, at least exponentially in the future...

...Ticka...

...Thus, the news...

...the next edition of which will be at...

...whenever I want it...

...of course...

...a time that I alone will select to fall at...

...when *you* least expect it...

...Of course...

...So pity me, with my determined autonomy...

...And now the news...

...Although this is *other* news...

...News of a local variety...

...In other words, news that cannot be sold...

...and thus which may not actually qualify as news...

...but for which we, somehow, have managed to retain some affection...

...despite its evident valuelessness...

...And it goes like this:...

...You may recall...

...that's right...

...*you*...

...you may recall, some three weeks ago...

...how your favorite pirate personality, in the middle of a particularly memorable Walkman-cast, suddenly had to...

...go silent for an unannounced interval...

...Go silent, and thus leave you alone...

...all alone...

...That is, forlorn...

...adrift...

...bereft of your sustaining input...

...denied your necessary rations...

...for a full, long day...

...until emissions could be safely resumed...

...This was a situation, management here decided, that would not be allowed to recur...

...For we know how fragile you are...

...how needy...

...how perilously dependent...

...That much is known...

...Thus, we decided, after lengthy internal debate, to relocate...

...to pack up and move...

...to where no one could find us...

...No one...

...Not even—...

...you know who...

...But the move brought considerations...

...significant considerations...

...It brought modifications of operations...

...shifts in demographics...

...all kinds of such things...

...In particular, we were no longer certain of...

...our target audience...

...that happy elect into whose ears we...

...inescapably creep...

...So a mission was assembled...

...a reconnaissance mission...

...to determine the extent of our...

...market penetration...

...Appropriately, I was chosen...

...to carry the mission out...

...After several days of high-level conferences and collo-
quies here, I was the one chosen to see...

...how far our signal carried...

...to investigate our—if you will—depth of field...

...(and I'm sure you will)...

...Ultimately, the mission took place just last Tuesday...

...which happened to be, if you recall, a sunny, shiny-aired, unwindy day...

...in other words, a day that offered the precise combination of atmospheric conditions that lend themselves to...

...the farthest throw of our signal...

...I began, here, in our studio...

...our *undetectable* studio...

...by preparing the test signal...

...I read the contents of an arbitrary document into our Revox 3180 tape recorder...

...a four-head, broadcast-quality instrument, which comes equipped with an infinite-repeat function...

...Arbitrarily, I chose to read a brief manual of instructions, one that details how to assemble a Kronkit & Company mobile wet-bar...

...a handsome item that boasts, among other fine features, four coaster-style wheels, a built-in sunken nut-cup, and an access hose adaptable to any household faucet...

...and which the studio here had recently purchased...

...for its own purposes...

...Sitting at the same microphone where I am sitting just now...

...entertaining you...

...I read the contents of the manual into the Revox tape recorder...

...Then, I programmed the tape machine to play my test message back forever...

...But don't be impressed...

...I only had to hit the Repeat button twice...

...Such is the nature of...

...electronic infinity...

...I then sent the signal out over the airwaves...

...the very airwaves that are now so delighting you...

...and prepared to go...

...I grabbed my Walkman, shut down the studio's idle consoles, monitors, and stray lights, locked the doors, and left the premises...

...Then, out back, I boarded the studio Toyota, adjusted its reassuringly resistant rearview mirror, sparked its engine, and headed out...

...First, I drove up—...

...Ah...

...Hm...

...You thought you had me there...

...Didn't you...

...But it will not be so easy...

...No, not at all...

...So, then, let us just say: after an indeterminate amount of driving...

...in my indeterminate car...

...proceeding in an indeterminate direction...

...I found myself on I-80...

...somewhere between Lincoln and Aurora...

...*very* somewhere...

...From this point, I headed west...

...in the direction of the flattest rural expanses...

...a scheme that was selected, after extensive management excogitation...

...to minimize interference with the signal...

...Thus, I was, how shall we put it...

...on my way...

...I passed a small farm...

...field-filled with sunflowers...

...then an unused pastureland, tracking towards an unattainable horizon...

...Thereafter came a greensward dotted with clumps of roan horses...

...the majority of which were standing in parallel configurations:...

...swatting tail to fly-tormented muzzle...

...fly-tormented muzzle to swatting tail...

...And so forth...

...Then I passed...

...some other stuff...

...stuff known, in the trade, as scenery...

...such scenery as tall-grass prairie...

...and more tall-grass prairie...

...and more tall-grass prairie...

...and more...

...There is a lot of tall-grass prairie out here...

...as you well know...

...While sailing down these first stretches of the Interstate...

...I was pleased to hear that my voice...

...purling in my ears...

...through my snug, electro-ardent Walkman...

...was showing no falling-off of fidelity...

...(Attach dowel B to ligature joint 2)...

...(Slide panel C between the two longer struts)...

...No falling-off at all...

...In other words, I was still within...

...audible range...

...My signal was loud and clear...

...and expressive...

...*Excep*tionally expressive...

...In fact, if I may make the admission...

...the sound of my signal was proving...

...rather alluring...

...This is something that I suspect you understand...

...that you understand very well...

...But this time...

...my signal was proving rather alluring...

...to *me*...

...The signal's owner and author...

...its forger and fabricator...

...who was then hearing his own signal, for the first time...

...at a distance...

...and while in automotive movement...

...For it must be said that the experience proffered, in its own subtle ways, considerable pleasures...

...considerable pleasures indeed...

...All of the pleasures that can be had from hearing...

...the plosive crispness of a well-articulated k...

...the wisping sibilance of a well-phrased s...

...the impish titillation of a...

...well-crafted t...

...Even my furtive, fine-whistling nose-breaths, when closely attended to...

...provided their share of...

...aural gratification...

...If you know what I mean...

....and I trust you do...

...So, then, we had an additional impetus for the mission:...

...To see for how deep a distance this fine voice...

...my voice...

...would provide its considerable esthetic satisfactions...

...If you'll permit me...

...and I trust you will...

...Thus, I carried on...

...maintaining my progression down I-80 at a modest 50 mph...

...and keeping my windows wide-open (screw faucet onto threaded connector)...

...The landscape unfurled before me...

...I coursed by an immense and newly seeded field...

...its loamy brown earth tumbled up in furrows that ran off to distant blurriness...

...Soon thereafter, a long, spindly metalwork arcade rose up beside the Interstate, drizzling water onto the field from suspended nozzles (Fasten wingnut 4 to sheath C)...

...A few miles on, something incongruous caught my eye:...

...Amid a small group of houses, barns, and storage structures huddling in the middle of a vast swath of farmland...

...and shaded by tall, slender trees...

...a horse seemed to be feeding on the contents of a windowbox, hanging from the main farmhouse...

...Driving further, and thereby making the horse's corpus twist...

...I saw that he was actually just pressing his snout against the windowglass...

...in an effort to achieve slaking coolness...

...Still, it was an engaging episode (insert round bolt B into *smaller* bolt-hole)...

...By then we were some forty-five minutes into excursion-time...

...The sun was high in the cobalt sky...

...and I found that I was becoming a bit thirsty (clamp clamp 2 onto inner ridge)...

...But I remembered, just then, having spied a road sign admonitorily proclaiming 18 miles until the next services-bearing township...

...but that had been at least 10 minutes previously...

...So I licked my lips...

...and continued on...

...Before long, I pulled into tiny Henderson...

...a placid burg...

...with two gas stations, an unneeded motel, a Church of Christ meetinghouse, and...

...and etcetera...

...Eventually, though, we found what we wanted...

...what we needed...

...in the dusky booths of smoke-strewn Carmelina's...

...and a tall bottle of cool wet Coke (to sheath C, beside the bolt-hole)...

...To Carmelina's—my thanks...

...For we needed you...

...to resume our mission...

...our *important* mission...

...Later, back on the Interstate, I Walkman-confirmed that my voice was evincing admirable tenacity...

...stunning tenacity...

....After nearly two hours of driving, down the endless I-80, my signal was still as strong...

...as when I had set out...

...All of my articulations (panel C), even the troublesome m's and the evanescent soft th's, had maintained their clarity, their expressiveness...

...their subtle expressiveness...

...It was as if, at 100 miles out, I was still as close to my signal as when I had been sitting in the studio, adjacent to its source...

...It was still a perfect, proximate whisper, into my own ear...

...(long screw 2)...

...Indeed, as I continued driving on...

...settling into my signal's rhythms...

...its delicate cadences...

...the signal progressively seemed to become...

...particularly well-suited to its context...

...Indeed, my signal came to resemble, more and more, a narration for what I was seeing...

...an apt and clarifying narration...

...somewhat like those portable cassette-playing guides for whose use museums charge a square four dollars...

...A tumbledown gate at the end of a wirefenced horse pasture (slide rubber bump-guard into lower bump-guard holder)...

...The Mondrian quadrangles of corn and barley fields incompletely harvested (wingnut 4)...

...Indeed, it even worked when I stopped, several miles later, at a 7-Eleven...

...Clark Bar (big bolts)...

...But that was not all...

...For, not very long thereafter...

...after perhaps an additional hour of glissading down the Interstate...

...and putting several more tiny, rattletrap towns past me...

...I found that, to my slight surprise...

...I had, at some point...

...begun to talk along with my signal...

...That is, actually to recite, from memory, what I was hearing...

...in perfect mimetic synchronization...

...regardless of what I was seeing through my open windows...

...Snap two top fasteners into metal sleeves...

...beside the bolt-hole, and tamp tabs down...

...Often, then, soon thereafter...

...it arrived that I could not tell...

...that I could not tell at all...

...if I was hearing myself talking...

...or my signal whispering...

...In other words, it became difficult to distinguish between...

...internalizing...

...and externalizing...

...inflow...

...and outgo...

...Or, in still other words, they became...

...the same...

...virtually the same...

...with lips and ears...

...working as one...

...flowing as one...

...harnessed together...

...jointly providing accurate, evocative narration...

...narration that perfectly fit the landscape it was describing...

...Big bolt-holes

...Indeed, the narration was always apt...

...magically apt...

...Although I did begin to wonder...

...perhaps eight miles further on...

...why nothing was getting built...

...At four hours out, my signal was still crystalline...

...though nuanced and warm...

...Of course, I was...

...pleased...

...Wouldn't you be?...

...But then, about twenty miles further along...

...while maintaining my felicitous 50 per...

...I began to wonder...

...about something...

...I began to have doubts...

...Concerns, unsettlements, began to creep into consciousness...

...In fact, I began to bristle...

...a bit...

...To chafe...

...somewhat...

...For I began to wonder...

...to wonder earnestly...

...if, perhaps, the Interstate's insistent linearity might be contributing to...

...my signal's impressive performance...

...For I-80 is, in fact, exceptionally straight during that long stretch of...

...wherever...

...Perhaps, then, the long, unimpeded Interstate was

serving as a channel, or furrow, for my signal...

...and freakishly interfering with the findings...

...freakishly *non*interfering...

...It has always been policy here, as you well know, to seek out, indeed to insist on...

...reliable information...

...The possibility, then, of unnatural highway non-blockage proved rather distressing...

...For myself as a broadcaster...

...And for myself as a listener...

...So, there—then *and* there—we decided to run a test...

...an efficacious test...

...to rule out confuting variables....

...And it went like this:...

...I drove some few miles further on...

...until I came upon the latest in a series of wooded patches that had recently begun extending towards the side of the Interstate...

...I believe they were corners of several State Recreational Areas...

...Regardless...

...for the upcoming extension was thick with trees, all in leaf...

...Fearing nothing, I drove off the Interstate and entered directly into the fragrant forest...

...where there were no roads...

...indeed, no other vehicles...

...Indeed, there was nothing at all beyond...

...the woodland primeval...

...For many long minutes I threaded my way through stands of upsplaying trees...

...and past clusters of bushes, and carpets of leaves, and many fallen, fragmented branches...

...In so doing, I penetrated deeper...

...ever deeper...

...into the forest...

...And as I continued, the afternoon's errant sunspray became splintered...

...ever more splintered...

...Daylight, progressively, left me...

...while my car, forever forced to new slowness...

...by an ever-increasing density of obstructing forest-features...

...began, somewhat incongruously, rocking back and forth ever more fitfully, ever more heavily...

...due to the growing number of hummocks and earth-burrs along my route...

...a route that had never before known...

...human tread...

...But still...

...Press second insulator sheath under clamp ridge...

...just as loud as always...

...My signal was showing no signs of letting up...

...of letting go...

...even this far off the road...

...So I plunged on...

...deeper into the forest...

...deeper...

...into massing millings of shadow-streams and earth-scent...

...slipping between tree trunks entirely unaccustomed to automotive incursion...

...banking around impenetrable copses...

...thrusting further into verdure...

...traveling, and traveling some more, for many long minutes...

...And then...

...then...

...perhaps sixty feet in front of me...

...after I had swerved to conserve a cottonwood...

...I saw...

...in a hollow of deep green...

...and played upon by shifting leaf-light...

...a man...

...a man kneeling...

...a man on his knees, sitting back on his heels...

...with his face angled up to receive the cool air...

...and his eyes closed...

...gently closed...

...Seeing him, I immediately pressed my brakes...

...and, after a moment, turned off my car...

...for, of all things, I did not want to disturb him...

...For he seemed to be, though sitting motionlessly, in the midst of some sort of...

...devotions...

...The man looked to be in his mid-'50s...

...with a graying fringe of ragged hair...

...curling around an oblong of skull-skin...

...He had a roundish, red-tinged face, with a small, can-opener nose...

...and was dressed in a patched dark shirt and patched functional-green pants...

...And as I watched him...

...as I sat in my car and looked on...

...with fascinated attention...

...though remaining silent...

...I saw that, in fact, he *was* doing something...

...something subtle...

...but something...

...For, as I looked longer, and closer, I saw that the man...

...who was sitting with his left forearm crossed diagonally up and over his chest...

...somewhat like Leonardo's Saint John...

...and with his left hand laid flat upon his breast, near to his neck...

...I saw that the man was tapping his first two fingers, in tandem, upon his collar bone...

...in a steady rhythm of two rapid taps followed by a pause of about one second...

...two taps...

...then one second...

...two taps...

...then etcetera...

...This continued for several full minutes...

...as I, some sixty feet away...

...continued watching...

...while becoming, gradually, intrigued...

...Deeply intrigued...

...And after this deep intrigue pitched up to a crest, I slowly opened my door, left my Walkman in the car, and got out...

...making every effort not to disturb the forest kneeler...

...Happily, as I gently closed my door, the rubicund man remained motionless...

...and calm...

...except for his two drumming fingers...

...while the wind somersaulted leaves around him...

...and tossed rags of sunlight upon him, and around him...

...And then the man said Can there be majesty without immoderacy?...

...Well, I was startled...

...surprised and startled...

...for the man hadn't moved at all...

...He hadn't even opened his eyes...

...So I took a few steps closer...

...just a few...

...and delicately, almost frightfully, said *Sorry?*...

...And then the man said Good...

...He said That's good...

...and then he opened his eyes, and stood up...

...and relaxedly stretched his arms...

...And then, after brushing off his pants-tops with one brisk downward whisking...

...the man turned and walked into the forest...

...And as he diminished into the misty distance...

...he said...

...without turning around...

...You can come along...

...So I followed him...

...I bumped from my spot and followed him...

...That's what I did...

...For what else was I to do?...

...At first I moved briskly, trying to catch up...

...but then, having drawn closer, I decided to keep pace from a few steps back...

...The man, as it turned out, was significantly shorter than I would have guessed...

...and as ruddy as dark peach flesh...

...with broad thick shoulders...

...and massive hands...

...His steps were bounding...

...lively and bounding...

...although nudged by little sidewise torques...

...and his breathing was marked by noticeable sibilance...

...I've been looking for several weeks now, the man then

said...

    ...while continuing his vigorous strides...

    ...between tangles of treelimbs...

    ...Oh yes?, I said...

    ...Indeed, he said, pushing past a horizontal branch...

    ...then doubling back and peering at the tree trunk from which it hung...

    ...Although it's equally valid to say that I've been look-ing for three or four years, he said...

    ...still examining the tree...

    ...I see, I said...

    ...while becoming aware...

    ...that there was a certain gruffness to the man's voice...

    ...That's when I first came upon it, the man said...

    ...gruffly...

...Indeed, I said...

...And, I must say, it was very gratifying, the man said...

...Very gratifying indeed...

...One doesn't often run across white tree fungus that so closely resembles the face of John Cage...

...I wouldn't think so, I said...

...No, the man said...

...It should be inspected again, he said...

...whereupon he, with a spurt of speed, started to walk away...

...deeper into the forest...

...Well, I followed along...

...For what else was one to do?...

...We threaded through the sparsely-lit woods...

...First he, then I, eased past boughs and thorns...

...and looked right and left...

...and made fallen leaves snicker under our feet...

...And whenever we saw a pale, gnarled growth upon a tree...

...we stopped...

...to investigate...

...This happened regularly...

...even frequently...

...Apparently, white tree fungus is well adapted...

...to these gentle climes...

...One such whitish growth, chanced upon after but a few minutes of forest-searching, proved pleasing...

...With its little whorls and setbacks...

...it recalled a tiny ledge of terraced hillside cropland...

...long after its topsoil had been washed away...

...It's very, very interesting, the man then said...

...while tight-eyeing the growth...

...Certain edible forms of tree fungus are, I understand, edible...

...Ah, I said...

...and nodded my head...

...But my source may not have been entirely reliable, the man said...

...I see, I said...

...at which point the man again took off...

...Without signaling, the man then led me through the shallows of a pebbly brook...

...My sneakers got wet...

...then got warm...

...Thereafter we veered towards a slight clearing, no more than forty feet in diameter...

...At the edge of the clearing, the man scanned the shanks of a few trees...

...bending his torso around them, to take in their full girths...

...And then he again moved on...

...striding off to our right, into denser growths...

...And so continued our activity, for some twenty aromatic minutes...

...pushing deeper, ever deeper, into the forest...

...Once, after maneuvering beneath a branch of spiky something, I turned and looked back, to comprehend our progress...

...At which point I grew intrigued...

...Or, shall I say, intrigued and concerned...

...For it was becoming clear that the man's intent endeavoring was evincing little in the way of method, or pattern...

...precious little...

...Indeed, there was manifestly no method or pattern to it at all...

...The man was simply stamping about the brush...

...going left...

...then right...

...and then continuing straight on...

...making no apparent attempt to attack his objective...

...systematically...

...In fact, the man was proceeding through entirely random movement...

...making no markers...

...taking no mappings...

...The man, evidently, was not disturbed by this...

...But as we continued on...

...I noticed that I...

...I...

...was, in fact, becoming somewhat concerned...

...somewhat concerned, indeed...

...And so, after some six more minutes of suchlike wandering...

...and fungus-investigating...

...I worked up the nerve...

...to speak...

...If you don't mind my asking, I said, as the man peered around an elm trunk...

...Do you have any idea...

...where we are?...

...Certainly, the man said...

...while inspecting the tree...

...Certainly...

...We're right here...

...Ah, I said...

...Where else could we be?, the man said...

...and then trod towards a willow stand some sixty feet to our left...

...I continued to follow behind...

...largely because...

...at this point...

...this *very* point...

...I was somewhat unsure...

...where else to go...

...The man then stopped in the middle of the willows,

and put one hand to his waist...

    ...and then started to scan the nearby trunks from this vantage...

    ...And it was then, it was just then...

    ...that I summoned up the nerve...

    ...Do...

    ...you...

    ...live...

    ...out...

    ...here?...

    ...I said...

    ...*In* here, the man replied...

    ...*In*...

    ...Ah, I said...

    ...and nodded my head...

...Yes, this is my shelter, he said...

...looking up towards the tops of the trees...

...Your shelter?, I said...

...Precisely, the man said...

...It is the one structure that keeps me safe...

...The only structure that keeps out the monotheists!, he said, still gazing upwards...

...Who?, I said...

...Your com*pat*riots, the man said, now with a slight, snarled rasp...

...Ah, I said...

...Enemies of immanence!, he cried...

...Authors of the orphan-people!...

...Sires of one-way time!...

...They will never penetrate here!, he said...

...It is one of the great advantages of being *coordinate-free*, he said...

...his mouth parting into a semi-smile that revealed two ranks of misshapen teeth...

...before he paced off into another part of the forest...

...I followed behind...

...passing more, ever more, trees...

...and all the while...

...hearing my erratic footsteps syncopate the man's more vigorous rhythms...

...So what's the matter with monotheism?, I then said, approaching the man from behind...

...*What's the matter?*, the man screeched...

...and then stopped and winced at me...

...Better to ask what's so *smashing* about...

...bureaucracy...

...the cosmetics industry...

...the *concept album*...

...*Yeesh*, he said...

...Axes and hierarchies, that's all it assembles!, the man bellowed...

...Killer verticalities!...

...Unhealthful alignments of persona and structure...

...Fetishes of feeling and desire...

...Historically, monotheism means one thing, the man went on...

...only one...

...*Empire,* he said...

...The creed, in the form we know it, derives principally from the legacy of Akhenaton, son of Amenhotep III, of the 18th Dynasty...

...and was developed during Egypt's New Kingdom, when the country was for the first time unified under a native ruler, and its conquests expanded all the way from the Fourth Cataract of the Nile to the Upper Euphrates...

...Appropriately, then, Akhenaton proclaimed himself, during his reign—which took place in the fourteenth century before our quote-unquote *common* era—as the sole son and manifestation of the first universal, all-uniting god...

...*Aton,* the man said...

...formerly a sun god, but now the *only* god...

...Thereafter, Akhenaton set out to obliterate all other cults, at the same time as he proclaimed that all human truth must be made to accord with *his own* preferences...

...Indeed, Akhenaton also established that his own physiognomy would serve as the unbending norm for all pictorial representations of people—not only royals, but also commoners...

...As a result of this, and more, the Egyptologist James Henry Breasted called Akhenaton, quote, the first individual in human history...

...The first individual...

...But there was one thing, beyond doubt, that Akhenaton realized very early on...

...the man said...

...Akhenaton realized that it would be useful for all of Egypt's myriad subjects to worship *exclu*sively the man to whom they were shipping their tributes and taxes...

...It would be *very* useful...

...But it has no truck here!, the man said...

...I will *never* be colonized by this cauchemar...

...That is one thing you can *bank* on!...

...And then the man marched away...

...directly toward a clump of trees some forty feet to our left...

...I soon caught up...

...and saw the man running his hands over the bark of a tall elm...

...just gliding and gentling his hands...

...up and down the rough, resistant bark...

...Remember Einstein, the man then said, while still rubbing the tree...

...Remember...

...Remember what Einstein said at the University of Berlin...

...at a colloquium in Spring 1926...

...It is the theory which decides what we can observe...

...The theory...

...That's what he said...

...Remember Einstein, the man said, and moved to the next tree...

...which he also began languidly handling...

...Remember and dream, he then said...

...Dream as I dream, he continued...

...A dream not at all too wild...

...Dream of a game of musical chairs, he said...

...and then he went to investigate another tree...

...Dream of a game of musical chairs that begins with one person sitting in a chair, in a comfortable room...

...just one person, sitting in a room...

...And then the music starts...

...and it sounds and plays...

...And when it stops another person puts his chair beside the first person's chair, and sits down...

...And then the music starts again...

...And when the music stops again, another person brings up a chair, and sits...

...and then there are three people sitting side by side...

...in the room...

...And then the music starts *again*...

...And then the game goes on, like this...

...just like this...

...until everyone is sitting in the room...

...sitting together...

...All of them together...

...And all of them are smiling...

...And the music is playing...

...And all of them are winners...

...And what are they listening to?, the man continued...

...You heard it here first...

...Oversoul music...

...And then the man moved to another tree...

...Well, I stopped where I was...

...and stood quietly, in the shady quietness...

...pushing leaves and fallen tree pieces with my foot...

...stirring them about...

...making them crackle...

...And when I looked up, I saw the man going off, to my right...

...So I scrambled after him...

...I scrambled after, and when I caught up, I said But Sir—...

...*Who?*, the man spat at me, wheeling around, glowering, his eyes afire...

...And then he turned and continued walking away...

...Sorry, I said, from where I was...

...Sorry...

...Still, I started walking once more...

...until I caught up with him again...

...But what about the ancient Greeks?, I said...

....and how about the Romans and the Hindus, and Shinto and Mithraism and Taoism and Vaisnavism—in fact, virtually every religion besides Christianity, Judaism and Islam, the three religions of the book...

...at which point the man spat frothily...

...None of them limit themselves to just one deity, I continued, and they've hardly been models of morality or conduct...

...They've had militarism and slavery and impassable caste systems, and corruption and favoritism and expansionism and abuse of women and—...

...I know, the man said quietly, while walking...

...I know...

....And it's common knowledge, I went on, that Akhenaton's religion and innovations were entirely trashed almost immediately upon his death—...

...I *know*, the man said...

...I know...

...and he slowed to a halt...

...Well, the man then said, it's one idea...

...and he marched off, briskly, towards another group of trees...

...swishing the forest floor as he went...

...I hung back...

...and heard his sound dissipate into the forest's absorptive growth...

...I did not follow him...

...for he seemed to want to be on his own...

...at least for the moment...

...So I hung back...

...and mused...

...and tacitly certified the countless flashing surfaces of the forest's innumerable leaves and branches and trees...

...But then something occurred to me...

...Something rather unsettling...

...It occurred to me, then, that I was, in some real sense...

...lost...

...In other words, entirely lost...

...For, from where I was...

...in the forest...

...I had no idea how to find my way back...

...That is, back to my car...

...I had entirely lost the trail...

...I had no points of orientation of any sort that I could reasonably call my own...

...In other words, I would have to wait...

...I would have to wait and hope that the man would—...

...that the man would—...

...In other words, this was a predicament...

...It was unsettling...

...It was even...

...a little scary...

...Thus, faced with this scary unsettlement, I reasoned that there was only one thing to do...

...only one...

...and that was to try and help the process along...

...In the hope that going further *in* would eventually lead to...

...getting definitively out...

...And so, from where I was, I scanned the area nearest me...

...and took a breath...

...and then took another...

...and then plunged in...

...On my own...

...my very own...

...I started by investigating a congregation of trees some twenty yards to my right...

...a nice, crisp-scented congregation...

...with many handsome limbs...

...Now moving among them, I surveyed their varied barks...

...one by one...

...circling and searching...

...and then circling some more...

...Yet, after no more than a few minutes of this, something occurred to me...

...something else with an aspect that could be considered...

...unsettling...

...For I realized that I was unsure...

...utterly unsure...

...if the trees I was then inspecting...

...were new to me...

...or if they were among the million-sprouting multitude that we had already canvassed...

...In other words, I was not at all convinced...

...that we had moved at all...

...That is, if we had made any progress...

...of any kind...

...Because the trees all looked different...

...and, simultaneously, the same...

...In other words, this was a predicament...

...Still, seeing few options, I continued on...

...passing from one trunk to the next...

...and to the next...

...survey-searching for pale, lumpy growths...

...for what else was there to do?...

...And then something unexpected happened...

...something extremely unexpected...

...While investigating a chipped-away knot on one thick perhaps-fir...

...I spied, in the corner of my awareness, a blob of blanched color protruding from an adjacent willow...

...just a few feet to my left...

...So I went to it...

...I went right over to it...

...And then I was surprised...

...Deeply surprised...

...For it was, indeed, a clump of white tree-fungus...

...hanging like a frozen froth from the bark...

...And its ripples and indentures, arrayed around its oval shape...

...made it, indeed, resemble...

...a human face...

...There was a bulbous nose, and hollows for eyes, and a wavery shadow-line of a mouth...

...while other undulations in the spongy matter evoked wrinkles...

...etched into the fungus cheeks and the fungus forehead...

...Well, it goes without saying...

...that I was pleased...

...surprised and pleased...

...Indeed, I was all but incredulous...

...*This was it!*...

...With the one possible hitch that...

...to me, the fungus looked like the actor William Demarest, and not like John Cage...

...Nevertheless, I straightened up...

...and leaned my hand on the host tree...

...and felt myself fill with uplift and expectancy...

...Then I looked for the man...

...And when I saw him, bent around another tree, some eighty feet away...

...I called to him...

...Hey!, I called...

...Ho!, I called to the man...

...Hey, I think I may *have* something here!...

...And he looked up and replied: *What's that?*...

...And so I called out: I think I found your fungus!...

...I think I found your fungus on this tree!...

...You did *what?*, he replied...

...I found your fungus!, I cried...

...And the man then said Oh, *please:*...

...Just let me know if you come upon bark textures that recall the erosion patterns of human hope...

...And then he disappeared behind a tree...

...and the forest fell into silence...

...For a moment, then...

...for a worrisome moment...

...as the salient syllable *Ayy!* chimed in my mind...

...I couldn't see the man at all...

...In other words, he was gone...

...invisible and gone...

...Until, perhaps half a minute later...

...I saw two pale hands emerge from the sides of a distant elm...

...and begin to crawl over its dark bark...

...Though at that point...

...all I was concerned about...

...all I could *be* concerned about...

...was finding my way...

...the hell out of there...

...I mean, I had done my piece...

...I had performed my function...

...and for *what?*, I wondered...

...For *what?*...

...All that I had accomplished...

...it occurred to me...

...was to lose my car...

...utterly and totally to lose my car...

...And I thought: *I have given my time to this man...*

...I have given it *will*ingly...

...without expectation of gratitude...

...or recompense...

...And in return...

...I have been forsaken, left hamstrung, in a deciduous abyss...

...surrounded by endless densities of trees...

...in every direction...

...*If* direction still meant anything...

...for, at that point...

...to me...

...it didn't...

...For, at that point, in the forest...

...direction was something that could only make tenuous claims to existence...

...For all there was...

...for me...

...was undifferentiation...

...trees and undifferentiation...

...with a lump of anxiety in its midst...

...In other words...

...for me...

...the forest had a direction in...

...but not a direction out...

...an everywhere-center...

...and a nowhere-circumference...

...*It might take hours*...

...I heard myself thinking...

...between craggy leaps of adrenaline...

...When, without forewarning...

...I heard something else...

...something coming from outside of me:...

...*It's over there*...

...I heard...

...in a familiar, unstrained voice...

...And I looked in the direction of the voice...

...and saw, peeking from behind a cottonwood...

...a hand...

...one pale hand...

...pointing towards my left...

...So I looked in the direction indicated by the pointing hand...

...At first, my gaze raked across a stand of tall, columnlike trees...

...before I came upon a slight indentation in the woods...

...It was no more than a forest alcove...

...And then I saw...

...sitting in a leaf-strewn swatch of shade...

...all by itself...

...Toyota...

...my own Toyota...

...my very own...

...Well, of course...

...I was pleased...

...relieved and pleased...

...Sense, compass, significance—all immediately returned...

...And so I went to my car, I bundled myself right over to it...

...and rubbed the lipped edge of the roof, by the driver's window...

...and let my hand alight upon the jutting, purposeful sideview mirror...

...and heard the happy jangle of liberated keys, handsprung from my muting right-front pocket...

...And so I called a quick Farewell! to the man...

...who was now entirely invisible within the community of trees...

...But I did not wait for an answer...

...No, I did not...

...For I was already in my car...

...sitting comfortably within it, with the door closed...

...and settling into the sculpted hug of my bucket seat...

...and putting my hands high on the ridged steering wheel...

...and smiling to the lone twig nesting in the tendons of my windshield wiper...

...I put the key into the ignition...

...and the familiar gesture of slip-inserting the key, and feeling it click...

...was a pleasure...

...And I twisted the key, and splashed some gas, and kicked on the engine...

...and it was a pleasure...

...And even turning my torso, to look out the rear window...

...was a pleasure...

...Muscular and a pleasure...

...For the car was rumbling beneath me...

...rumbling, humming...

...and it was powerful, and brimming, and ready to go...

...So I put on my Walkman, and looked up to check the rearview mirror...

...and put my hand on the gear box...

...and then I stopped...

...I stopped dead in my seat...

...Quickly, I turned my engine off...

...and waited for the car's huffing to fully subside...

...And then I waited a bit longer...

...And then I listened...

...I listened hard...

...and then I shook my machine...

...But it was true:...

...There was nothing...

...There was nothing there...

...My signal had stopped...

...My signal had gone away...

...All that was coming from the Walkman was silence...

...Silence, ear-abradings, and forest-mutings...

...But, most conspicuously...

...silence...

...And I was stunned...

...startled and stunned...

...For this was not something that I had anticipated...

...So I sat in my car, amid the outside's buzzings, and siftings, and chirpings...

...And wondered where I had gone...

...The Walkman was still working...

...every diode-light and rotor-movement and solenoid-button was functional...

...all of this I checked...

...But I had gone to silence...

...So I sat in my bucket seat, and listened to my silence, and did not know what to make of it...

...did not know at all...

...Though, before long...

...I found that I was becoming...

...impressed...

...deeply impressed...

...Yes: deeply impressed by the hidden capacities of my tape machine...

...Apparently, the engineers at Revox were even cleverer than we had thought...

...than we had *dreamed*...

...For, evidently, they had foreseen situations like this one...

...evidently...

...Evidently, they had built some kind of shutdown function into the tape recorder...

...into its playback mode...

...to prevent excesses, forgetfulness, or abuse...

...to save heads...

...Indeed, this was the only way to explain...

...my situation...

...This automatic shutdown function, I reasoned, must have been located...

...way down deep in the Revox's workings...

...real deep...

...at a depth entirely hidden from consumer awareness...

...Obviously, the Revox engineers had understood that no one ever really wants a program to repeat *infinitely*...

...to go on *forever*...

...That is advertising, they understood, and not application...

...And so they constructed a limiting circuit...

...in the machine...

...for the machine...

...without sharing such information with us...

...to let us keep our little illusions...

...In other words, they had designed something...

...something artful and hidden...

...in the entrails of the equipment...

...to protect ourselves...

...from ourselves...

...for which, of course, we can only be grateful...

...although I suspected it was leaving the Walkman a little hungry...

...Thus, I headed home...

...in silence...

...in self-silence...

...That is, free...

...free to prepare...

...this program for you...

...Free to work on this rousing entertainment...

...for you...

...For, as you well understand...

...we do it all...

...for you...

...To bring people together...

...to share simple pleasures...

...through the magic of communication...

...For here, now, it *is* magic...

...and, for the first time...

...real communication...

...For this broadcast...

...its every syllable and sigh...

...is being savored...

...as you well know...

...by every Walkman-wearer in your vicinity...

...Just think, o listeners, just think of this miracle union...

...Think and rejoice...

...Yes, rejoice...

...For such is the power...

...the puissance...

...of pirate communications...

...It penetrates...

...then unifies...

...Smashes...

...then lashes...

...Inescapably...

...Unarguably...

...In fact, go ahead...

...go ahead and look around you...

...Yes look, o listeners, look at all your Walkman-colleagues...

...wherever you may be...

...On the weighing line...

...on the end of the bus-shelter bench...

...in the laundromat...

...wherever...

...See all the Walkman-folk around you...

...And then...

...and then shiver...

...yes, shiver...

...For you know, finally you know...

...that all of you...

...*all* of you...

...ensheathed in your Walkmen...

...have achieved linkage...

...solidarity and linkage...

...Know that you are all listening, solitarily, *together*...

...*Yes!*...

...But wait—...

...*Wait*...

...What is that I am picking up?...

...What is that I hear?...

...That is to say, do I hear...

...Do I hear *doubt?*...

...Do I hear doubt that this linkage *can* be achieved?...

...that it is, by definition, *impossible?*...

...Very well, then...

...Very well, then, *indeed*...

...We will offer...

...confirmation...

...Iron confirmation of the solidarity of your environing

Walkman-folk...

...All it takes...

...is a gesture...

...a simple, solitary gesture...

...a slight and secret show...

...to dispel all doubt...

...*all* doubt...

...that the Walkman-folk are, finally, together...

...invincibly together...

...crosslink-listening to the same pirate signal...

...silent, but together...

...So look around...

...and search out your Walkman-kin:...

...on the escalator...

...by the cigarette machine...

...wherever they may be...

...And now *assert* the truth that you are together...

...pirate-together...

...through sharing The Universal Walkman Gesture:...

...Lay your left hand high on the right side of your chest...

...flat against your warm, ripply self...

...and tap your first two fingers against your collarbone...

...Two taps...

...then pause...

...Two taps...

...then etcetera...

...Then wait for the signal to be returned...

...No one need ever know...

...that you are together...

...No one...

...Ever...

...But you will know...

...*all* of you will know...

...finally...

...conclusively...

...that it is so...

...You will know, through the means of what we shall henceforth call...

...the Pharaoh's Tap...

...Now go ahead...

...Do it...

...Go ahead and do it...

...Go ahead and give your Pharaoh's Tap...

...Assert your secret, silent network...

...There...

...*There*...

...Well done...

...It is done...

...It is well done...

...But...

...But what is this?...

...What is this you're seeing?...

...That gentleman...

...over there...

...that gentleman in the Walkman, over by the magazine stand...

...clad in the blue serge suit...

...He hasn't returned your Pharaoh's Tap...

...In fact, he has turned away...

...turned away without even *acknowledging* your gesture...

...not even acknowledging it *at all*...

...So then what...

...*What?*...

...How to explain it?...

...How to explain his silence?...

...Why no collaborator's communication?...

...Will his training not permit it?...

...Do his standards denounce it?...

...Could *that* be it?...

...*Could it?*...

...Or could it be...

...Could it be that he is *not* part of our pirate confederacy...

...that his Walkman is *not* whispering secret frequencies to him...

...in fact, that he isn't hearing anything unusual *at all*?...

...So then wait...

...Wait!...

...Could it also be true...

...could it *also* be—...

...Is it any way conceivable that *you, too,* can*not* hear me?...

...that you are *not* hearing me right now?...

...In other words, that your headset has *not* been over-run...

...that I can*not* kick down your portcullis...

...that something here is fundamentally *wrong?*...

...Perhaps even *impossible?*...

...Could *that* be it?...

...*Could it?*...

...So then disprove it...

...Go on, disprove it...

...*Try* to disprove it...

...I mean, do you think this voice going inside your head is *not* being put there by someone else?...

...Do you think that?...

...So then try to stop it...

...That's right, stop it...

...Try to stop it...

...Try to get away from it...

...Try...

...Just try...

...Try to get away...

...Try to run away from it...

...That's right, run...

...Run...

...Don't walk, *run*...

...You, who are listening to this...

...That's right, *you*...

...You, who are listening...

...*Try* to run...

...Try to run away from what you know you can not

hear...

...Try to run away from what you *know* can not be true...

...Run...

...*Run*...

...That's it—*run*...

...*Try* to run...

...*You miserable motherfuckers!*...but no...; wait...; please, just wait...; now you listen...; now you wait and listen...; because there is something that I want to say just now, there is something that *I* have to say, and in the midst of this incessant self-suffused hurt-rant where is there room for such consideration...; faced with your endless incantations and propositions, where can I—where can anyone—talk of things, where can anyone really talk of anything...: of past and present; of tenderness; of yieldingness; of the infinite fragile things; of Ravel—yes, of Ravel, because I want to tell you, it does something to you to work on a hit; it really does; even while driving in from Parma Heights, where I live, I feel it: my foot just seems edgier on the gas pedal, and my ribs feel, I don't know, kind of giddy, and I just want to get there, to *get to* the theater; even my *car* seems to go faster—even the *Toyota*'s picked up the buzz, it just seems to *sail*; and then, when I finally get on 85th Street, and then turn the corner on to Euclid and see the theater, the good old Athanasian, even before there's anybody there—when there aren't any lines, and no limos, and no scalpers, and no people happy and, like, expectantly dressed—even then, you feel that something's in the air; you can even see it in the uninvolved people just walking down the street, just happening to pass underneath the unlit marquee, but in some way reacting to all the draped, dark-lettered banners:

HARROWING AND HILARIOUS:
GET UP AND GO!

and

A JOYRIDE THROUGH THE BACK
ALLEYS OF THE MODERN
MINDSCAPE...DEVASTATING!

next to

KENNING FLACK'S FINEST HOUR (AND A HALF)...
WHITE HOT AND PITCH BLACK!

and about half-a-dozen more; even Ken, who's gotten used to these kinds of reviews, was a little unprepared for the reaction this time: two extensions of the run, and both of them entirely sold out, and folks allegedly *flying in* just to see the fucker; even though—if anyone wants to know *my* opinion— I think the last show, which he put together about two years ago, was a little better: it was a little funnier, and a little more varied, some of his characters don't seem as fresh this time— but that's to *me*, y'see; so maybe, it occurred to me, maybe all this hoopla is just a reaction to Ken's declaration that this is his last go-round for this kind of show—although none of us working on the crew, of course, believe his usual Time-to-pack-it-in incantations anymore; well, maybe *Ken* believes it—until, of course, he tries his luck out in Movieland again, and gets his usual fucking *nowhere*: Hey man, you're too dark for us, your shit's too Out There, it'll work in the theater but never on screen, it's un*think*able on screen, but thanks anyway, now take a walk...; and so he does—right back here, to where it all came from...

...Still, I don't think too many people were expecting him to do another one-manner...; I mean *shit*, for Ken it's a shit-load of work: writing the stuff, then really honing it, then having to make every line sing, all by himself, with no one to fall back on even for a second, and no one to work off of during rehearsals except the director...; it's a chore and more; so I suppose Ken was right in trying to put a buzz on this gig by announcing it was his last show ever—let's put a capital E on this Event; I mean, why not: he's learned, despite his anti-bullshit image, that the first character he has to play for *any* of his performances is The Publicist...

...In fact, that would be kinda funny, if he would add a segment like that to the show: a segment about a guy, a struggling actor or something, who's so poor that he uses a different name and acts as his own publicist; and so then we see him on the phone speaking to a casting agent, feverishly pitching this other name that happens to be himself—and then, afterwards, having to drop himself as a client when he fails the audition...; it could work...; I could light it from underneath, with reds and purples, and it would go really well between The Shrieker and The Double Dribbler—it would go *really* well in there...; in fact, I'm going to propose it to him, I *am*...; although I wonder if Ken'd accept any story sugges-tions that weren't his own, no matter how good they are; I mean, you have to doubt it; I don't think he's ever done it, even though, I must say, he *has* been loosening up on a couple of things recently, relaxing this fucking illusion he keeps up about himself of, like, hot-soldered control; like on Wednes-day night, in fact, there was an example, all of us were kind of surprised by Ken's, shall we say, liberalness...: Ken had arrived on time—as usual—for the pre-game in the Blue Room, and I was there and also Billy the soundman and Natalie, who does Ken's make-up (Mario, our fearless director, is long gone to his next gig); Ken was still in his street clothes, wearing his usual denims and boots, although he had already gotten made up, and we're all just talking about this 'n' that—Natalie's landlord hell was, I think, the overriding focus—when Ken, apropos of nada, produces from his denim jacket pocket a sucking-candy tin just filled with blow;   well, y'know, at that point Natalie's landlord-spiel just peters out, it spontaneously dissolves, not only because of our new sacral presence but also because it's such a *surprise*: I mean, Ken has a policy of never taking even a one-granule snort when he's doing a show, and, though he's never said anything, it's assumed he expects the same from us; but there it is, God's terrestrial goodness, in exceedingly admirable quantity, and all of us just start giggling because, well, we just can't *believe* it...; and we're all just standing there with our brains salivating, and then Kenny, y'know, while kind of looking down at the ground, Kenny hauls off and says:

— Aw, what th' fuck...; it's our last week, i'n' it...?

and he heads to the table in the corner and sits down; well, y'know, we're all just soldiers in this army, no dissension *here*, so Billy and Natalie and I just go over and pull up chairs and join him in the preparation, display and ingestion of some industrial-strength shit; and y'know, as we're doing it, and we're getting into it, we all look up and see, in the glittering smilingness of each other's eyes, such phrases as *Well, we are* near the end of what Kenny says is our last-ever collaboration, and *Well, after all, Kenny* wants to do it, and *Shit*, this does taste *sweet*...; and after nostrilling a good couple of lines apiece, and also, I might add, looking into the bottle of Absolut that Billy has somehow produced—I mean, why not?—we're all sitting around putting together a good giggle when Eric, the stage manager, calls out the fifteen minutes to places; so Kenny scrambles off and the rest of us break and head to our battle stations, and before too long I'm at my lighting console, checking the first cues; well by then, y'know, I'm getting acquainted with some pretty serious chemical transportation, and as it happens my buzz is being pretty well matched by that of the crowd, who's now dribbling down the aisles and horizontaling over to their seats, all jittery-jumpy because, well, they're going to see a performance by the great Kenning *Flack!*; and gradually, y'know, the hall fills to seated human fullness, and it takes on its usual sense of breathy expectancy, the nice clothes combined with the give-it-to-me receptivity, the crisp air-conditioned understated anticipation, when all of a sudden my headset feeds me the cue: so I bring down the house lights just as Billy the sound monster triggers the snarling guitar riff that snaps the audience to eyebrows-up silence; then Billy hits the drum intro, all the crashing and stamping, and it gets me on guard, and then I splash a shell-shape of luminous green across the upstage wall just as the music's churning fury finds the pocket and slams into its chugging, super-rapid four-four funk...

...And then Kenny comes on, unlit and ominous, taking precisely six panther-strides in silhouette until he hits his mark at center stage and freezes, his back to the crowd; and then he stays there, y'know, he just stays there—immobile, though rinsed in invisible imminence—until his blackness suddenly begins to bop up and down on the balls of his feet, four, five, six times; and then I douse him with a spot of astral amber light and he scissor-kicks into his guitar-moves, thrashing and weaving like the heavy-metaler on Billy's soundtrack; and then, after writhing some more along with the music's huffing audible overdrive, he does his Springsteen leap and lands in sudden silence and full ambient light, mostly oranges and yellows: a wiry little guy in his trademark black jeans and T-shirt...

...And then, instantaneously, he's into the first segment, barely moving at all and talking timidly in an adenoidal voice about how the Xerox machine in the supply room keeps breaking down—how he's had to keep opening the machine up and tearing gnarled papers from its entrails; and he's had to do this four times already, he says, to wrest smudged pages from warm metal; and every time it's the same fucking thing, he says: he has to clear out the machine's paper-path, then close the dismembered monster up, then wait for it to reset, then replace the stack of feed pages, then watch impotently as the whole process gums up again; but now, he says, he's become really jumpy, because 100 copies of bossman Jake's two-page inter-office memorandum have got to get done quickly, just im*med*iately, because they're already four hours overdue; and he explains that he's new to this job at Equitable Insurance, and he's super-happy to have the job because he hunted for seven months to find something after he was let go with two weeks' severance by Phillip Morris, two days after his mother was diagnosed as having uterine cancer; and so, then, he decides, after the fourth Xerox-machine shutdown, to take Jake's memorandum to the commercial copy center on the corner, just to take it out to a professional place himself, to make sure it gets done, and just absorb the cost himself; so he steals a ride down his building's service elevator, the one that's hung with bump-absorbing insulation fabric, and he slips out the back of the place; then he curves past the refuse bins around to the street, then rounds the corner onto Kinsman Road and begins hustling past the front of the Equitable building in the afternoon sun, not wanting to be seen by any of his bosses; and he's approaching the copy center, he's just two doors away, when he feels something down by his feet and then, suddenly, he jolts to a stop; so he looks down and sees that a street bum has grabbed his ankle—that the bum's just reached out from the cardboard and debris on which he's coiled and has locked onto Ken's foot with one hand; and Ken, then, y'know, tries to shake the guy off, he wrenches and pulls his leg around and yells down at the guy—*Hey*, y'know, *Hey*—but the inert body just won't let go; and there Ken is, just alone and late and horribly embarrassed on the street, carrying the original of Jake's memorandum, which is getting all creased and dented up, and he's freaking out because it looks as if this bag man's last human gesture was to put a death grip on Kenny's argyle sock; and so on—and so Kenny's home free, into his act; and, as usual, the audience is with him, immediately and entirely with him, heart-and-breath into it, responding like a single crosslinked neural network with explosive laughter, then nervous laughter, then throat-throttles of a kind of shame and horror, then *real* nervousness, and then laughter all over again...; and so, in other words, we're all feeling good, it's a good time, the audience is just about as gone as I am...

...So then, after that, Kenny continues leading the people on, moving through the segments: next is The Recycler—which requires a bit of attention from me: I've got to follow Ken with a yellow-mauve blend at the same time as I'm bracketing off the dark space of the dumpsters he's supposed to be climbing into—and then he goes into The Ameliorator, which is a good one; and all in all it's beginning to feel like it'll be a nice night, a good, punchy show: the laughs are breaking where they should, as are the collective chokings-back, and then the audience *really* bites into the failsafe, which happens in Hell's Laundromat, when Kenny chugalugs the back-to-back Coors 16-ouncers: by about 10 ounces into the first can the audience is wildly whistling and whooping it up, and when he incisors onto the second column of brew and tilts it—real slow—*way* up, well, they all be goin' *nuts*...; after that, The Skin Doctor comes off well, as does Biodiversity, then I get a bit of a break in Robert Wilson, which is just a stationary cylinder of azure in penumbra, with no moves or fades at all; but it's during this bit, right in here, that I begin to notice that, for no reason I can think of, something kinda weird seems to be going on: as I said, Kenny's doing Robert Wilson—his mistiness, his calculated childlikeness, his tacit egomania—but then, in the midst of the Wilson moves and mannerisms, it begins to seem as if parts of The Ameliorator have begun creeping back into Ken's performance—that is, into Robert Wilson; I mean, at first, Ken, from out of nowhere, does one of The Ameliorator's jaw-wrenching movements, which slightly derails the Wilson-spiel, and then he pulls out one of The Ameliorator's big full-face blinks; well, no one in the audience notices this, of course, but to me it's plain as day, it's obvious as hell; and I must say, it strikes me as a bit bizarre: it couldn't just be a device, especially an unannounced one—Kenny's far too disciplined for that; but when he moves on to the next segment, Mammon, there they are again: in the middle of Mammon's downstage groveling, which is really kind of a funny bit, conserved parts of The Ameliorator again begin to reappear; but now they're even stronger—there are a few jaw-wrenchings and big blinks again, along with one of those moves where The Ameliorator violently scratches the side of his head, and there's even a trace of The Ameliorator's gun-runner's gravel voice; and I'm sitting there at my console thinking, y'know, *hunh?*...; this is *not* typical Kenny, to blur the boundaries like this; usually his characters are as well-etched as woodcarvings—but there it is again, an Ameliorator big blink, and this shit just seems to be getting more and more pronounced; The Ameliorator, of course, is the character that's been mentioned most by the critics, and, I suppose inevitably, it's the one that the audience almost always gives its biggest reaction to, although they still don't even seem to be noticing what's going on—and whoops, there goes The Ameliorator *again*, this time in The Troglodyte, and now *again*, but even more forcefully, in The Boneyard; so tell me: what the fuck is The Ameliorator doing in The Boneyard?; well, for me, I must say, the whole deal is getting a little funny, seeing The Ameliorator beginning to mash into all of Kenny's other characters—especially The Boneyard, whose rap on organic soap definitely should *not* be wracked by those jaw-jumpings or delivered in that goon voice; but Kenny, I mean, is just going on with the show, just continuing from segment to segment, and he doesn't seem to be aware of what he's doing, or to care, and I've got to say that I'm still feeling pretty good, I'm not bad at all, so I figure *What the hell?*, *Go with it*, and so I begin laying some Ameliorator light cues into The Freedom Fighter, which is where we are now: gradually, I fade up The Ameliorator's diffusion of gold at upstage left, and throw on the downstage spot where the lawn chair had been; and the effect, I must say, is really pretty hilarious, witnessing the stage beginning to decompose visually as well; and then, y'know, I'm sitting there enjoying all this, when I notice that Billy, that swifty, has picked up what's going on and has begun to join in at the soundboard, adding the sound of The Ameliorator's massed jackboot marching and uncued jay chirping to the mix—and, hearing this, y'know, I can almost see Billy boy doubled up at his soundboard, just writhing with gut laughter that he's got to clamp in; still, no one in the audience seems to be noticing anything wrong, their responses are as per usual, laughing and grimacing in all the right places, the trance is unpuncturable, so as the segments proceed Billy and I just continue dropping in our appropriated Ameliorator sounds and visions, while by now Kenny has become virtually one character, almost entirely conserving The Ameliorator's erratic movements, tics, stance and delivery over all the succeeding characters and dialogue; and well shit, by now I'm almost on the *floor*, a ridge in my stomach is just clenching with suppressed laughter, and I can't *imagine* how Billy's holding on, when all of a sudden some kind of howl or bellow comes from the audience, this huge, roaring throat-disgorgement that seems to be issuing from somewhere in the orchestra:

> *BUT I DO NOT*
> *I DO NOT*

Immediately, then, I snap to attention, and stand up at my console, because that howl was *loud*; and I look around and it's obvious that something, somewhere, has gone wrong— that something has *really* gone wrong; and I see that Kenny too has stopped what he was doing on stage, he's straightened up and come out of character; so I run downstage to the front of the wing and take a peek past the proscenium, and then I see, about seven or eight rows away from the stage, this guy, maybe in his late thirties, sort of big-boned and wearing a beige suit, but with his shirt collar open and his tie skewed to one side; and he's standing way over in the orchestra's extreme right aisle, with his arms extended all the way out to his sides, and he's smashing his back and neck against the wall of the theater, just smashing himself into it over and over again; and, I mean, he's all goggle-eyed and showing teeth, and he's howling, he's just howling at the top of his voice:

> *AND WHAT DO YOU KNOW OF*
> *OF*
> *AND WHAT DO YOU*
> *DO YOU*

At first the audience seems to think that this is part of the show: they're in their seats, laughing, turned towards the man, or smilingly sharing the moment with their neighbors; but soon enough it becomes apparent that this is real, that this is not rehearsed, so then everyone jumps up and scrambles to get away from the raver; and there are shouts and terror, and a surge toward the opposite wall, and the crowd just starts shoving itself as far away from the guy as it can get; and then everyone just starts stumbling over one another, just ramming and pressing, I mean there goes everybody frantically jostling down the narrow rows or clotting up the aisles; and in the middle of the confusion security is trying to get through, but the guards are caught amid all the bodies surging the other way, the blue uniforms are flailing their arms trying to push through the repulsed audience:

AND THERE WILL BE NO SECOND CHAN

Then I feel Kevin, one of the stage hands, breathing behind my right shoulder: he's also come forward to take a look; and we just stand there and watch the guy, the poor fuckin' guy, just smashing his neck against the wall and raving away, just raving away, with his arms and jacket and tie-end waggling, and everything dithering—the poor guy, entirely taken by brain-chaos:

AND THERE WILL BE NO ETERNAL RE

Kevin then mentions, in a respectful voice, that he's read about things like this, about how a guy can all of a sudden snap—about how some folks are just machined too close to tolerance, then one day this early weakness is somehow accessed, and the twist-tie comes loose:

BECAUSE WHAT IS LOST
NOT TO BE RE

Finally, then, a black security guard from the Athanasian manages to push his way through the crowd, and he plops into the hollow in front of the raver, a hollow created by the whole audience having offed the other way; then the guard, holding both palms up to the poor loser, approaches him real slowly, *real* slowly, trying to talk him down, but the raver just lunges from his position at the wall and makes to attack the guard, who leaps back into the seats and stumbles; and the people are really getting edgy now, everyone is *seriously* tense, even though the raver has hurtled himself back against

the wall—and then there's Kenny, slowly walking over to the raver from the direction of the stage, approaching him with his hands held up in front of his chest; and he's trying to reassure the guy, to calm him down, inching towards him and saying slowly and gently:
    — OK, now, man...: just calm down...just be cool...

> *BECAUSE IT IS BURIED*
> *IT IS BURIED IN MY BLOOD*

— OK, man, you can do it...; yeah, you can...

> *AND I WILL BURY*
> *I WILL BURY YOU IN MY BLOOD*

And Ken approaches, and stays real calm, and wipes his forehead when he gets close, and talks, he just calmly talks:
    — Because the shore is stony, and steps jostle and pinch, but do not sink, I am stumbling toward a seam in time, here where sky swallows sea: Let me come close enough to see that you are unreachable; tell me that this arrested falling, my progress, is movement toward tendency, so that I may reach evanescence and transparency—impermeable transparency; show me that my suffering grows because it is constant, while I diminish; make me see the tenderness in this terror—the permanence of my fragility; allow me to draw force from this endlessness, where step blurs into slide, and difference becomes commonness; enable my inexhaustibility; show me that I am the template to corroborate time, moving so quickly that I cannot see the change: You are the shadow on the inconceivable edge of me: be attainable, but impossible; prove my finitude, extended infinitely; make me see that as I suffer, I continue; make of my evanescence something everlasting...
    — So, yup — can you believe it? — I'm back planting trees again, but this time they're made of language — it's always a question of roots, you know (hoe, hoe, hoe) — (er...) — but 'tis true: I know I must seem so fickle to you, so crackpot-inconstant, but the guy I was living with turned out

to be a bit of a flippo — wouldn't yer know it? — so it was time for a change, again, away from the maniac and his music — and Chomsky is soso much the contrary: passionate but understated, endlessly right-minded yet e'er open to debate and divergence (—cy?) — so I've come to work/study/learn/ evolve with him — fun among the phonemes! — and 'tis true: Chomsky was about the first (I tink) to posit the notion of universal grammar (as opposed to Paramount or 20th Century-Fox) (sorry) (and then some) — that 'tis, inborn language capacity, that is, linguistic ability as part of our big bad biological endowment — and now, maybe 30 years on, it's still dicey, some people still don't want to believe it — but I do, I be-leave it, here pruning my language trees—

— Dear Robin, I adore her, I do, and her breathless letters; I'll finish this one later: it's too good to go through in just one gulp—too plentiful, too rich in nutrients; we think so similarly, though she's the one who's always jumping around, while I sit here in Huntsville pretending the clocks' ticks are prison bars, or crosshatches in an etching denoting shadow, or void; I wonder, sometimes, if her flightiness springs from inner turbulence or from inner confidence, if it's an expression of strength or of weakness; regardless—I am susceptible to her, before explanation; she reaches me through unexpected places, finding access roads that are otherwise never used...

...It has always been like this: when we would go for our afternoon-long walks, back during high school, she would always choose the route, and I wouldn't mind; for me it would always be the right one, the most fortunate one, for Robin was always a few steps ahead on it; and when she would fling herself on the ground near Byrd Spring Lake, amid the Bouncing-Bet and Queen Anne's Lace, and stretch her limbs out starfish-wide—surrendering to the sun, she called it—I would lie down and spread out too, despite the dirtiness, which I knew I would hear about; I found that, with her, I could spend an entire afternoon talking and gabbling and still be at the beginning of what I had to say, whereas with other girls—at lunch, or waiting for the sink in the bathroom—all conversation on the universe and its contents would be exhausted in a matter of minutes; I thought of Robin, her smile and her spirit, as a roller coaster, joyously flowing over hurdles and high obstacles, and making all the swerves and ascents and swoop-downs breath-wresting fun; there was, then, this ferocious closeness, this unique sense that explanations weren't necessary, and her going off to Oberlin hardly put an end to it: she rarely came back after that, but we would write, and the details of her constant displacements—to an Adlerian institute in Seattle, to archeological digs in New Mexico and the Yucatan, to a bikers' dive in Eugene, and through all the boyfriends—only strengthened my sense of similarity, of congruence; the differences in our experience only underscored the fact that we thought about things in exactly the same ways: Robin would describe the sensation of soft-brushing the sand of centuries off a Mayan rain-god mask, and I would know just how she had felt; she would write of finding her live-in taking a shower with another woman—and using Robin's hypoallergenic soap—and I would be right there with her, all clutched and taut in my throat and chest; our surface divergences only confirm our deep identity, by showing how our solidarity can never be shaken; for distance and difference are, between us, as nothing...

...This, then, is kinship; yet, perhaps ironically, amid this boundless openness and easy communication, our closeness has always been the one thing we never talk about; for years, since our first meeting in junior high, I've wanted to tell Robin about this, about how I feel—about how I feel with her and how I feel about her; but I've always held back: I've always been afraid that doing this would bring unintended consequences—in fact, I'm certain that would be the case; I'm afraid that my putting into words what I'm sure we both exhaustively understand might in some way alter the tonality of our togetherness, and this would be a heavy cost; for, from that point on, I'm sure, things between us would lose a certain unreflective innocence, or at least a measure of spontaneity; certain kinds of contact would only kill what I cherish most in my relation with Robin—its easiness and unexplicitness, its unforced airiness; and I'm sure that these qualities could never be regained: as we had shared effortlessness, so we would swarm with self-consciousness; reversing this would be as easy as regaining virginity; I grieve to think that closeness requires some measure of distance as its preserver, if only as a safety measure, because it certainly seems as if connection, in any deeper sense, introduces a specter of estrangement; for to come into contact with someone is to change her—there is that certainty; it reminds me of a game that Robin told me about one day after school, as we were walking down Anatta Road certainly twenty years ago: find a word, a familiar word, on a page, and then stare at it for a while, just let your eyes linger upon it; and soon enough, sometimes after no more than a few seconds, the word comes to look as if it's misspelled, or badly transcribed, or as if there are other things wrong with it; so I tried it once, with the most familiar word there is: love, first verb in the Latin primer, the word known to all men; and after no more than five seconds I could swear that it wasn't the same word that I had always known: it looked odd, misshapen, and as if it had all kinds of different pronunciations, except the one I had always believed was correct, and had always used; and so there was dissonance...

...In fact, I had thought about this situation again just last week, when something oddly similar happened in my office; it was Thursday, and we were packing for our long-dreaded move across town—last month Henry won regional distribution for Sun Microsystems, which also clinched his yearlong deliberations about getting more office space, so there were cartons and large, rolling refuse barrels scattered among our desks; Joan, Jess, Madeline, and I were pulling out our old files, memos, message slips, and the like, and either tossing them into a garbage barrel or stacking them in the cartons; at one point—it was about half-past three—Jess took a trip to the coffee room, and when she came back, the conversation turned to a television miniseries that had concluded the night before:

— God was that sad, said Madeline;

— Cried my *eyes* out at the end there, said Joan;

I knew what they meant: the series had indeed been an incorrigible tear-jerker, one of those malady-of-the-month offerings that, somehow, over three evenings, had gathered real force; it had centered on a priceless little moon-faced girl named Hillary, who had been stricken with leukemia at age six; true to form, the story looked into many corners of that sad world, visiting special hospitals and children's clinics and portraying other afflicted families; perhaps predictably, I grew susceptible to the tale, so when, after the last program in the series had concluded, the screen showed the 800 number of a referral network for marrow donors, I bundled up my Kleenex and ran to the telephone table for a pad and pencil; I also jotted down the information, delivered verbally, that financial contributions were welcome; in fact, I had had ideas along these lines while watching the series, beginning during the second night: I had thought that I would like to do something for these unfortunate people, for donors, they made clear, were in short supply; here was something that I could contribute to, I had thought: it was a means of giving of myself where it was genuinely needed, and where it might make a real difference; here, finally, was something that I could do—that I would love to do; and so I was pleased when they provided that information at the end of the show, and I slept very well that night; but when, the next day, Jess and Maddie started talking about the miniseries, and then just began prattling on and on about its details, while pulling scrap paper from their desks—

— And do you remember that scene in the kitchen—

— What a face on her—

— Do you know I think I would someday like to—

—I felt my ardor curdle; my instinct evaporated, and the whole possibility of my contributing turned burdensome and sour; this was not, in any way, elitism—I was glad, of course, that the series would likely lead to an increase in donors—but my urge had been pushed to the periphery; and by the end of that afternoon, with its continuing exposure of words, my participating in what I still acknowledged to be an inordinately worthwhile effort, even though I have an unusual blood-type, had become frankly inconceivable...

...In fact, this happens often—when I feel as if words, others' words, have crowded mine out, and have left me no place; I do not know why, through what mechanism, this occurs, but when it does, and it is often, I find that I develop a need, an earnest yearning, for words that have not become sour and strange—that is, for words that are my own, words that are uniquely mine amid this foreign wash; and yet I find, when I look for such words—my words—none seem to be there: all of my words, upon the slightest inspection, seem so foreign to me, so much the work of others; and so I wonder how I can claim that anything that occurs in my consciousness is mine, and not the product of some otherness; often I feel that I am not thinking so much as eavesdropping on my own thoughts, listening in on a narrative being told between othernesses—that it is the otherness thinking me; because none of it, in truth, seems to issue from me; even my unplanned cries, my most heartfelt exclamations, have been determined by others: I have noticed that it is precisely at times of highest emotion—when I am going to the deepest regions of my responses, to the deepest particularity of me—that my words, which would then seem to be at their most personal and spontaneous, are in fact at their most derivative, just pure banal cliché: O my God!, Will you look at that!, I don't believe it!; but where are *my* words, I wonder, *my* own thoughts?; it seems, sometimes, that I am a conduit and not a content—a transfer point, a capacitor, a pattern in waves; or, at most, I am a bricklayer, combining chunks of accepted solidity to wall out fresh perception; is this adolescent thinking?—I don't know, but I wonder where the suggestion came from that it *is* adolescent thinking; at best, I see my self, that coal-stone, as some kind of irritant, as something that makes flows of culture coagulate, pearl-like, in my consciousness: I am not expressed, but accrued; lopped off from my sources, submerged in received history, I feel myself only as an offputting unknown: I do not know why I never wear the same shoes two days in a row; I do not know why I tell people that I don't like to travel; I do not know why I keep so little food in the apartment; I do not know why I fret so when I have to wait in line; I do not know why I surge when I see Masaccio's Expulsion from the Garden, while Michelangelo's version of the very same tale leaves me utterly cold; I do not

know how I ended up in the work that I do; I do not know why
I work on presenting an appearance of unrufflable affability;
I do not know why I even pay attention to myself; but I do
know that these concerns, and the words that compose these
concerns, sound, as well, as if they had been taken from
others—lifted wholesale; even my words for articulating my
sadness are only an embodiment of the otherness expressing
sadness, are part of its system, this Möbius culture, and so
further confirmation of its dominion; others' words have
even determined the content of my suffering, and what I
want, above all, is to find my own means to suffer, to be able
to express myself in sadness; this, then, will be my project,
my creative enterprise: to find an absolutely personal mode of
sadness; it is, perhaps, the most significant work left me; yet
I shouldn't even say *me, my, myself,* when speaking about this,
for doing so represents too bold an assertion; it would be
better, more accurate, certainly more discerning, to use the
third person, *she,* to best capture the situation—or even *he,*
the masculine, the form that is even more generic: I should
really say He wakes up; He sloshes to the bathroom; He
winces and big-blinks for the mirror—yes, that is better; that
certainly is right: He twists the handle that flushes the blue-
bowled Standard toilet; He skims His eyes, He brushes His
teeth; He takes lather from a nozzled canister and shaves with
a razor of orange plastic; He taps on aftershave, and feels its
cedar-y acerbity frost His nose; He paints Ban under His left
arm, His right arm; He holds His arms outward-elevated until
the pit-chill abates, until He has received the all-dry; from His
armoire He withdraws a pastel blue Lauren shirt, then unclosets
a deep blue Paul Smith suit, with silvery pinstripes; He breaks
the cleaner's paper band from His shirt, then feels His shirt's
textured stiffness wrap around His shoulders, His triceps, His
belly, Him; He buttons and smoothes, He collars, He feels the
heft of His suit; it rectangles at His shoulders, it slopes at His
waist; He sits and bends to soft socks and smooth, scuffless
shoes; He combs His hair-layers to their destined fallings,
which they seek out, regardless, on their own; He checks and
inverts His black plastic comb, then uses its milkteeth to align
His eyebrows; He takes up the tiny, trim envelope from the

surface of His bureau, and is reminded of what it promises: Rostropovitch, Dvořák, Beethoven; He gathers unto Him jewelry, analog watch, coins, keys, wallet, then seals them upon His person with the tightening knot of His tie; He waggles His neckskin to final snug comfortableness, then breaks open His wood door, transiting to the crisper flatness of His hallway carpet...

...downstairs, He sits to a short glass of Florida juice, before His houseboy, whom He greets amiably, though glancelessly, presents a plate of warm beef sausages, A-framing unrunny eggs, plus a potful of coffee, piping-hot; He crosses His legs and permits His left hand passage from the well-positioned toast rack to the edge of His upheld Post; He consumes; He tosses His cloth napkin, folded labially, onto His stained, vacated plate; His chair legs grumble over His white tile floor; He secures His burgundy attache case, its ostrich-leather handle grippy in His fist; He opens a selection of doors, to differing sounds; He is face-warmed, chest-warmed, by the day...

...His seatbelt hugs Him, bottom and across; He backs out with gentleness, looking this way, that, at the sidewalk, this way, that, after the slump into the street; He drives in smooth silence, steering with but one of His hands; fender reflections torment Him; He considers, decides against, sunglasses; He turns off the highway, He turns on the street, He turns the corner; He finds, and turns into, the hotel lot; He leaves His engine on, His keys in His car, His door open, for the attendant; He receives His receipt; He walks directly, wordlessly, inside; He proceeds to the elevator-bank, and experiences slight thoracic lifting when the bell sounds, the light flares, the doors glide , the moving chamber accepts His feet...

...upstairs, He negotiates the hallway, through narrow neo-Rococo stucco and trim, in peach; He knocks, once, a door of previously accreted sentimental associations, then enters, unto people, milling, light bulbs, tables strewn with documents; He is greeted; He clasps human shoulders, clasps human hands; He joins, silently, a triplet of persons sitting in lively discussion, around a nickled coffee table unfavored by physical coffee; silently, He rises from this colloquy, then joins a sextet of persons engaged in lively discussion in a flanking bedroom; He is asked questions, calmly; He responds to questions, calmly; between calm questions, He regards Himself, His shoulders, in an adjacent mirror, enjoying light from a nearby bivalve-shaped sconce; He sits, in an upholstered chair; He cracks open His attache case, leafs through paginated documents, skims their capital letters; He considers coffee and Danish, considers against them; He stands when tapped on the shoulder; He squares and buttons His creaseless jacket; He twists His wrists twice, in quest of extremity-freedom; He is led by some down the hallway, leads others; He takes the first elevator; after waiting, downstairs, for the spill from the second elevator, He walks first—He is first, the others follow; nevertheless, He is steered down halls, around corners; He is steered through a kitchen, then unused and dark, and out through swinging doors; immediately, He hears undertones, He hears undertones hushing under; He pivots His wrists once; He rocks back on His heels; He climbs three shallow steps; He lays His documents on His lectern; He sees the bouquet of microphones before Him:

— Welcome; our statement will be brief; the two Federal Appeals Court rulings this week, Palmer versus Liggett & Myers, as adjudicated in Boston, and Stephen versus American Brands, adjudicated in Atlanta, are merely the latest in a historically unbroken series of judicial decisions proclaiming the right of a law-abiding business to provide a service desired by the American people; within four days of each other, two of our nation's highest courts have asserted a victory for reason over prejudice, for correct business practice over spurious litigation, indeed for the ideals of America over those who would deny them; in determining that the warning labels that cigarette manufacturers place on every package of their products, federally mandated since January 1966, take precedence over state product-liability laws, on which the two denied suits were based, the two courts, we believe, have affirmed their confidence in the intelligence of American consumers and their belief in the right of every American to make his or her own choices;   cigarettes have now unchallengeably earned their just position in the free market-place, while the warning labels, it has been demonstrated abundantly, will henceforth obviate all further litigation of this kind;   and now, if there are any questions...

—

— No; we do not;

—

— No; not at all;

—

— We believe these decisions significantly limit the scope of claims that plaintiffs can bring;

—

— Of course: the stock market's response, which was virtually immediate, naturally reflects the widespread cer-tainty that the threat to the financial integrity of the cigarette companies has been cut;

—

— No; never;

—

— No; of course not: studies which conclude that smoking causes disease have regularly ignored significant evidence to the contrary;

—

— The authors of reports such as those signed by the Surgeon General have selected favorable evidence to review and ignored the results of studies contrary to their conclu-sions;

—

— Eminent doctors and research scientists have ques-tioned the claimed significance of these experiments;

—

— We believe it was well put by Doctor Eysenck, an esteemed independent researcher at the University of Lon-don, who said that the major problem with the existing evidence is that it concerns correlation, not causality;

—

— The causal theory is just that: a theory;

—

— No; the statistics do not provide us with a cause-and-effect relationship; that is simply the fact; epidemiological surveys can only point out a statistical association between factors, such as smoking and disease, but cannot determine whether the relationship is causal;

— Yes, and smoking has been found to be correlated with drinking, with womanizing, with changing jobs, and with many other behaviors; does that mean that smoking causes these things?; we cannot imagine that anyone would agree;

— Not at all: the public has been heavily propagandized along one definite theory of causation by those convinced by one level of information; some of us demand a different order and level of knowledge before we accept causation or condone presentation of conclusions to the public;

— Compelling doubts have been raised about the statistics and their interpretations involving smoking and health;

— Science does not know what role, if any, smoking may play in the production of disease;

— Smoking may cause illness; it may not; we don't know and we don't think anybody knows;

— It is not known whether smoking has a role in the development of various diseases;

— There is little evidence—and certainly nothing that proves scientifically—that cigarette smoking causes disease in nonsmokers;

— While smoking has increased among Swiss women in the last quarter century, the rate of heart disease in women there has declined significantly in the same period;

— Whole-smoke animal inhalation studies have failed

to reproduce the heart and lung diseases in question; indeed, some smoking animals lived longer than nonsmoking animals;

—

— The excess of perinatal mortality reported in mothers who smoke is not found in higher income families but only in poorer families;

—

— No: statistics do not provide us with a concrete relationship; as Claude Bernard, the great French physiologist, once said: I do not reject the use of statistics, but I condemn not trying to go beyond them;

—

— Although both lungs of the cigarette smoker are exposed equally to smoke, lung cancer rarely occurs in both simultaneously;

—

— No...no; we have read all those numbers, too; but they represent an opinion, a judgment; but not scientific fact;

—

— Hardly: cigarettes are only one of many causes of smokers having more illnesses—that is, getting sick; people who smoke tend to differ importantly from people who do not—in their heredity, in constitutional make-up, in patterns of life, in the pressure under which they live; cigarette smoking may not be the health hazard that the anti-smoking people say it is because other alternatives are at least as probable;

—

— Again, we quote Doctor Eysenck: There seems to be little doubt about the existence of some genetic predisposition to lung cancer and coronary heart disease, and equally about the existence of some quite strong relationships between susceptibility to the diseases in question and personality; thus, smoking may not be the causal factor;

—

— As our scientific understanding advances, more and more factors come under suspicion as contributing to the

Evan Dara

illnesses for which smoking is blamed; these include air pollution, viruses, food additives, occupational hazards, and stress; when this is viewed in conjunction with any allowance for a constitutional hypothesis, it suggests that style of life may be a more important variable than smoking by itself;

—

— No; we are not creating doubt about the health charge without actually denying it; we merely claim the right to pursue knowledge through scientific research, the right to hold our own point of view, and the right of the public to be aware of it;

—

— Claims that cigarettes are addictive contradict common sense;

—

— We simply believe in the ideal of personal accountability; we don't encourage smoking and we think it is a matter of personal choice;

—

— We think that there is still something left to the idea of someone being responsible for his own conduct;

—

— The cigarette industry does not want young people to smoke;

—

— People want choices; they don't want to be told what to do;

—

— Smoking is truly a personal choice that can be stopped if and when a person decides to do so;

—

— No, we are not advocating the public's right to smoke without actually urging them to take up the practice; we simply believe that until the answers are found about smoking, everyone needs to make up his own minds about it;

—

— Of course we have heard Doctor Koop's description of cigarettes as—what version do you have?—far and away the leading health-care crisis facing this country; we simply find it a flagrant distortion; for us, looking for an objective assessment, we wonder how large a problem it can be when it has never, as far as we know, been mentioned by any of the candidates in the current Presidential contest;

— Not at all: the Surgeon General has clearly abused his position, placing his political agenda above scientific integrity; indeed, he has exploited his office in a blatantly propagandistic manner;

— Through past centuries, there have been many such one-sided attacks on tobacco, and they too were based on anti-smoking bias rather than on fact;

— In our opinion, he is simply subverting science to politics; it is a matter of scientific fact that in our present state of knowledge, no one knows the answers;

— The proof of harm remains as wispy as cigarette smoke itself;

— Many animal inhalation experiments with cigarette smoke have failed to produce emphysema in animals;

— No, we are not engaging in variations on the theme that the case is not proved; like any controversy, this one has more than one side; we simply hope the debate will be an open one;

— Much more research is needed if the causes of these diseases are to be known;

— Far more research is needed to find the cause or causes of lung cancer and the mechanisms of the disease;

— Only through much more research can causes and mechanisms be established and the cigarette controversy resolved;

— Honestly, I have not seen one piece of medical evidence that has been presented by anyone, anywhere, that absolutely, totally said that smoking caused the disease or created it; I believe this; I'm standing here talking to you with an extremely clear conscience; if I saw or thought that there was any evidence whatsoever that conclusively proved that, in some way, tobacco was harmful to people, and I believed it in my heart and my soul, then I would get out of the business and I wouldn't be involved in it—

— Well hello...hello there; come on in;

— Not at all: now is just fine—the regular hours are just a convenience; I'm glad you caught me...

— Good; so come on—come in; sit down over here; I'll just get these out of your way...

— There...

— Good; good; it's good to see you; welcome back;

— Yeah;

— Don't worry about it; it shouldn't be a problem; I'll photocopy my lecture notes for the...what was—?

— For all six classes; don't worry—you'll get them; and if you ever want to discuss them, to talk about—

— Exactly; I'll be glad to;

— Yeah; I'm sure;

— I can imagine; well, did you ever...I don't know... maybe think of taking some time off, taking a semester away...?

— Good; yeah, it isn't necessary; this way you can have

a distraction; you can lose yourself in your work;

— Yeah;

— Were you very close to...that is—

— Sure;

— Mm; he must have been a relatively young man;

— Mm; and your mother, is she still—

— Mm;

— Yeah;

— Well, you know, if I can—

— Mm;

— Great; so then—what's...what can I...?

— I see;

— Mm hm;

— No: *sure*...

— Definitely...

— Of course;

— Remind me what your topic was...; I don't—

— OK...

— But why would—I mean, have you—?

— But it's a terribly exciting subject just now—

—

— So have you gotten into some of the things that Metz has written, The Imaginary Signifier, or anything by Noel Carroll—?

—

— You should hunt them down; there are good things all throughout the journals—

—

— So check over in Reta E. King—I think they have most of them in the periodicals room;

—

— So if they don't, I can lend you my copies;

—

— Still, I hope you'll think about it again before you—

—

— But there's tremendously exciting work coming out of France just now, all kinds of interesting applications of Freud to film, and I think it could make a wonderful—

—

— Exactly: notions of the mechanisms of narcissism at work in looking at films—

—

— Precisely: of only seeing ourselves on screen...re-enacting a primal symbolic rapport....

—

— Right: and Metz's whole concept of the mirror relationship—

—

— Right: this is all distinctly Freudian—

—

— OK...

—

— OK...

—

— But then there's Todorov's criticism of this kind of approach...

—

— Sure: Todorov has written powerfully about this...

—

— Not so much on that as about—

—

— But more specifically about the parallels between the practices of Medieval exegesis, in which all stories were interpreted to harbor the same fundamental theme—man's fall and his eventual salvation through the sacrifice of Christ—and the psychoanalytic tendency to see all stories as retellings of the Oedipal drama—

—

— Exactly, with everything from Hamlet to Parsifal to North by Northwest viewed as differently elaborated versions of the same basic tale;

—

— Right: Todorov saw the theological project underlying this kind of criticism;

—

— Exactly;

—

— But still, you see, Todorov himself was working within a Freudian conception;

—

— But it's still a very powerful handling of the means through which we look at movies—

—

— Still, the Freudian framework—

—

— But if you'll let me, for a second, go back to Metz—
— But I no longer think I'm interested, that's all;

—

— Really, I'm just not all that—

—

— Of course; but the subject isn't really, I don't know, engaging me as much as I—

—

— Of course;

—

— Mm;

—

— No...not really;

—

— Oh, I suppose it has something to do with...

—

— Yeah...

—

— Maybe...

—

— Well, the thing is...I've been reading Eisenstein a bit recently—the Notes, you know, and—

—

— Yeah: and it really seems that, you know, his whole deal about montage, about the productivity of the collision of images—

—

— Right: the—

—

— Yeah; all his bit about the viewer's participation in creating meaning;

—

—Right; it's like: Ask not what your narrative can do for you, ask what you can do for your narrative...

—

— Yeah...kinda patriotic...

—

— Also kinda Nils Bohr...

—

— But what I've been thinking is that there's a better way of looking at Eisenstein's devotion to montage, at least better than the usual ways—

—

— Right—not at all in terms of his work with the Constructivists, or haiku, or Marxist dialectics, or even of his parents arguing so much when he was a kid—*none* of those—

—

— Right; but what I think is that it should be in terms of Piaget;

—

— Exactly; where Eisenstein saw the creation of cinematic meaning in the cut, in two shots juxtaposed—

—

— So I thought I might be able to do something comparing that to Piaget...

—

— Right, who, you know, did those studies with children, and their disregard, or discounting, of intermediate-
ness...

—

— Right: that thing with the water in the short fat glass
being poured into the tall thin glass, and the kids always
thinking there's more water in the second one—

—

— Mm; and so compare that to certain kinds of montage, and their dramatic effects;

—

— Exactly; or like in Superman—the Tommy Carr
Superman, not the Donner—which I just saw again on television: when Krypton is about to blow up, and first you see Jor-
El's face kind of normally, then there's a cut to him looking
alarmed, and then there's a cut to him really freaking out—
it's much more dramatic, *really* more so than just a gradual...

—

— And this, I think, is very Piagettian, and accords with
Eisenstein's sense of film actually creating its own language
by crashing perceptions together through montage, fabricat-
ing a bridge...

—

— Exactly: bringing meaning into virtual being, through
montage—
— But of course there's an even more fundamental link
between film theory and Piaget...

—

— *Oh* yes;

—

— Going way back...; of *course*;

—

— It has to do with the whole notion of a cut, of adding
any kind of discontinuity on screen, and how radical a

departure that was;

—

— Oh yes, at the very beginning: even before Griffith, going back to Porter and even as far back as Méliès;

—

— Sure; because audiences weren't used to anything like that; the first movie audiences had only seen continuous takes, or onflowing plays, and then filmed transcriptions of plays, the early photoplays...

—

— Precisely: it's related to Piaget's work with neonates, or newborns—how they aren't born with a sense of the permanence of objects, how they have to learn this;

—

— Exactly: you show a child a ball, then you put a screen between the child and the ball, then the child no longer thinks the ball is there;

—

— Mm: but to the child the ball hasn't only disappeared, it doesn't even *exist* any longer; the child withdraws his hand, and doesn't even attempt to push aside the screen; the ball has literally ceased to exist for him—or, as Piaget said, the child has not achieved object constancy...

—

— Exactly;

—

— And so the first producers and promoters were worried about the effects of a cut: at one moment, something—even a character—is on-screen, then the next second it isn't: they were afraid this was going to disorient audiences, that the viewers wouldn't understand it and get roiled, then charge out and never come back...

—

— Exactly: where do things go when they go 'away'—that was it, the big question;

—

— And that's Piaget, it's all Piaget; so if you are intent on changing your subject, you might well consider extending your paper to include a consideration of—

—

— But I really think it would make the discussion much more—

—

— Really—*really*: so why don't you consider—

—

— Sure; and I've got—*some*where—some journal articles that I'll Xerox for you, and—

—

— No no: don't bother: I'll give them to you, so you can get started right away, and it was about this time, at the arrival of the Cranberry-Corns, that I began to think: I wish this would happen every night; I just *wish* something like this would happen each and every night: let the saran-wrap machine go down—and *stay* down—every night if it's going to deliver me here; because I loved getting in on the action like this, I just *loved* it: rolling up my sleeves, scraping my nails against the bottom edge of my belt to clean them up a bit, taking a position along the line, and then just getting *in* there, in the trenches, working in the wrapping area alongside Tom and Bobby and whoever else was free: with all the efficiency, and the synchronized movement, and the entire plant pitching in and participating flawlessly, regularly, with im*mense* productivity, elbow to elbow...; and the smells, you know, the *smells*—I mean, if only our customers *knew*; they haven't got a *clue* about the greatness of these things when they buy them the next morning; you see, when the muffins come down the conveyor belt, and they're thrown from their pockets in the rack pans as the belt turns down—well, this paddlewheel action, if you're standing right there, flings this absolutely a*maz*ing hot aroma right into your face—from the Oat Brans, from the Banana-Rhubarbs, es*pe*cially from the Double Double Chocolates; and then the muffins themselves are so warm and nice-shaped, like these great little trumpet mutes of cakelike texture, and you're feeling this kind of glistening inside your cheeks, this liquidy glowing, and you're thinking that these muffins would, you know, just fit *so well* right in your fist, where you could take them and shove them sugar-warm right into your *face*—just fill up your mouth and chew and chomp, densely, sweet-texturedly, liquidly...; and then, you know, while you're sweet-chomping, it would be like you could smell them with your entire mouth, with your entire sinuses, with your *pores*...; but all this is gone by the time the muffins are distributed to the delis and diners in the morning, all dead and cold and dry; in fact, no one out there even has the *beginning* of a clue how good this shit is; and that's why, for a little while there, I got a little sad when I realized how I was cutting the muffins' greatness even further by wrapping them up—pulling the saran from the sticky rolls, then tearing it, then grabbing the muffin with it, then scrunching the plastic all around, absolutely deadening this baked greatness inside wrinkled shiny sheaths...; but I suppose I had to do it—the wrapping machine *had* gone down—so it had to be done, and so it was better for me just to forget about it and be glad I had been given a chance to get in on the action...

...Not that I don't like my usual gig; hardly: I take to it just fine; I love it, in fact; normally, I do odd jobs—handimannery, I call it—down in inventory and shipping, during the graveyard shift; it's OK-enough work—I just do it, forget it, and go home, boosted by a Coors or six—but basically I spend my eight hours in my department, and don't move through the building much; and that's why I didn't think twice when I first saw the guy in the corner workstation that night, far off behind the wrapping area: I figured he's probably always up there, and that I just hadn't seen him before; maybe his hours were different than mine, or he worked part-time—*I* don't know; they're not too, shall we say, dogmatic around here; but when I was swinging back down to my section, after the saran system had been fixed—thank you Ronnie and your enchanted wrench-set—that's when the guy kinda caught my eye; and so I took a moment, because, you know, it became obvious pretty quick that this feller was into some zony shit; so after stopping in my tracks and staring at him for a second, and his not looking up, I tucked myself into the shadows behind the elevator cage about twenty feet in front of his station, to get a better bead; but even then, I still couldn't really make out what was going down: I mean, this guy had, like, debris—genuine junk and debris—scattered all over the workstation; there were just piles and drifts of it on the floor, on the central worktable, on the shelves behind him, strewn over the larger assembly table to his left, leaning against the legs of the oven to his right—and the guy just seemed to be searching through it all, moving among it and, like, *look*ing for something...; and the whole scene was, like, quasi-infernal: this scraggly guy, bone-skinny under a lank black jacket, with greasy black hair and a singe of beard, scavenging among these mounds of muck in a tent of dusty amber light from the fixture hanging above the central worktable...; well, the guy himself seemed out to lunch, and what he was doing hadn't even come in to dinner, so I decided just to leave him with my best blessing and get on back to work, where I should have been anyway, and not concern myself with things that didn't pertain to me; but of course, later that night, when I saw Lonno—as in Section Manager Lonno—it was Hey man, what is the *story* with...?

...And the word was this: the guy's a friend of Huey's [AKA Mr. Big], they've worked out some kind of deal, so whatever's going on just let it go: the dictum from on high is not to bother the bizarro bloke; apparently the guy had been showing up most nights for about a week, week and a half, putting together his slophouse and then just kind of shifting the stuff around; well, OK, sure, I can live with that, I've got my invoices to collate here so I won't pay any attention to the *shithole* being assembled in the corner of the plant...; live and let live, I etc.; but the guy, though, the guy was like this real *zoner*—so sue me if, later that night, I decided to go to the men's room upstairs, near the guy's junk-garden, and if I lingered in the area, in the shadows...; because the guy was oblivious, anyway, he was so *into* what he was doing: rooting through the ranks of rubbish, sorting it out, putting some on the central worktable, then moving some of that selected shit around, stacking it, arraying it, then circulating around the table and sizing the shitpile up, from different angles, with incendiary eyes...; and then, the next evening, I saw there was *more* shit, the guy must have been *bringing it in*...

...Such shit as *what?*—such shit as bicycle fenders, bent blades from Venetian blinds, a seated smiling rubberized

Buddha with a good gash taken from his side, newspaper pages, spent batteries, beer bottles, kiddie Camaros made of tin, fence sections, photographs, crack vials, crushed cigarette packs, electrical cables, amputated table legs, plastic sleeves for guitar strings, laceless boots, forests of fast-food wrappings, tire sections, hemorrhaging audio cassettes, coverless paperbacks, unknobbed bureau drawers, a lobotomized clipboard, dragaways from the umbrella holocaust, single socks, a walkie-talkie doubled over into a sit-up...

...Such shit as *that*, and *then* some; and he would handle all this debris delicately, with care and attention, as if it was all something *precious*—the result of which was that I began going to the water cooler more frequently, to give myself an excuse to trot back up to the second-floor men's room more often, and so check in on Mr. Inexplicable; not that *he* ever noticed *me*, of course: his obliviousness was epic; I mean, like, listen to what happened after my third trip to the excretorium that second evening: I had finished my kidney-contribution and had tucked myself into my behind-the-elevator-cage shadowland, in order to cop a view; and I saw that the guy was deep into his patented dance: he was stalking around the scattered refuse, picking things from the rubble, then meticulously configuring them on the central worktable, eyes ignited...when suddenly—check this out—he *slams* his fist on the table, freezes, cranks his eyes up to high-beam, and growls out at the pile of selected shit:
— You *fuck*...you fucking—*fuck!*
without ever *once* considering that someone might hear him...; in other words, this was weirdness, this was a trip to the zone—and then it got better, it even got better than that: right after he finishes screaming at the shit, the guy then takes a sheet of gray, rubbery material from a stack of it on a rear shelf, lays the sheet on top of the screamed-at shit-heap on the table, grabs a scissors, then proceeds to cut the rubbery sheet down so it just fits over the pile of junk, which is about three by four feet big—and then he picks the entire deal up and shoves it right into the fucking oven!; shit, I hadn't even seen that he had been arranging his debris in one of our large baking pans; but when the guy starts adjusting the tempera-

ture knobs on the oven, and then just kind of paces around the work station as the shit cooks—well, I got out of there real quick and slalomed back to my section and just had to get it straight with Lonno:

— So *what?*, I said: I mean, *what* is the story with—

— Listen, that oven's got one of the high-suction exhaust systems; don't worry;

— But that's not—I mean, this *guy*...

— Listen: Huey says he does it, so he does it; and Huey doesn't want no inter*fer*ence, neither;

All of which only served to send me *directly* back to the water cooler...; still, though, I decided I should get back to work for a while—I mean, the guy's garbage had to cook, *right?*—so I went back downstairs, and got busy moving several barrels of glucose syrup that had just come into the processing area—you know how you rock those big barrels back and forth to get them going; and I was down there, along with the rest of the first-floor crew, getting the job done, it was real pleasant accomplishment—although at first, I should say, I was kind of having a hard time concentrating on the work, because the guy—his image, that is—kept flashing into my head and just de*rail*ing me; but soon enough, maybe 35 minutes later, I was back in my shadowsphere behind the elevator cage—by then I wanted to give my kidneys a ticker-tape parade—and I could see zone-man again; and, lo and behold, he was still at it: checking his watch, jotting things into a schoolboy's marbled-cover notebook, standing against the worktable and gnawing on the first two cuticles of his disgustingly smudged left hand; but then—*then*—after checking his watch again, he took a breath, grabbed a pair of cloth towels, flung open the oven, pulled the shitpan out and then quickly slid it onto the worktable; immediately, then, he became serious-looking, or, how shall I say it, *contemplative*, holding a hand to his chin and a dark fixity in his eyes as he slowly circled the worktable and stared down what he had produced...; but what *had* he produced, was what I wanted to know, this ugly lumpen mass of diarrheic grayness, the rubber layer having melted and totally covered the junk that the guy had so carefully orchestrated underneath it; and to me, I'll tell you, the thing resembled nothing so much as a boulder, but a semi-shiny one, a magmatic chunk dislodged from the hawking earth...; in other words, this guy was *deep* in the zone, he was way blooming *out* there, making his garbage parmigiana...

...But he continued at it over the next several nights, this lone denizen of his own deep space, he who was locked in the realm of the hyperweird; and when I would pass by, at least five or six times a night, the shitmaster would *always* be doing his bit: scanning and heaping, or psychotically micro-repositioning, or pencil-writing in his notebook; sometimes, though, I'd get lucky, and I'd catch him when he was hissing-sputtering:

— Fuck you, fuckwad—fuck *you*—!

or

— You miserable...you miserable *fuck*—!

right before he shoved the shit into the oven and slammed the gate closed; and gradually, you know, over the next four or five days, the shelves of his work station began to fill with his magnificent offspring, his cooked children, all of them looking exactly alike, like giant tumorous TV dinners that the world had decided it was afraid to unfoil; and it seemed as if the word had gone out to leave the loon alone, because no one else in the plant ever seemed to come over or to notice him, and no one seemed particularly interested in talking about him when I brought him up, which at first was constantly but then screeched down to never; not that I had lost interest, of course—in fact, it kind of ruffled me that I had signed up to take my vacation right about then, because I would have liked to have kept up with the guy, to see what was going to happen with his cookfest; but the vacation was coming on too quickly to find anybody to swap days with, and, despite my slight residual curiosity, I couldn't really see showing up at the plant during my time off just to check out zone-man's progress—I mean, come on...; so I ended up taking my two weeks, only nine days of which counted because one was Labor Day; and it was a good old time, all right: I righted my schedule pretty quick and started keeping human hours, so the sun could get a look at me, and I caught up on some daytime tube, and didn't shave, and drove out to the stock-car races with Rodge, and hung out, and hunted some field rabbits, and saw the bottom of a couple of bottles, and chased the skirts, and got a little older and a lot uglier, and hung out...

...And was not entirely prepared for my disappointment to find, when I got back to the plant, that Ye Royal Zone King had apparently picked up stakes while I had been away; that is, some of his street-shit was still lying around the work station, but the dry roasts were gone, and so was he, and all Lonno would tell me was that the deal was over and that I should just forget about it; well *fuck*, y'know...; that is, I know about the value of mystery, but every now and then...— put it this way: it would have been nice to have just a little, what d'you call it, *resolution*...; but I also realized that my downness on this was probably just part of my first-day-back grumbles, so I put it from my mind and got back into the swing of things; and it was nice to be back, you know, with Tom and Julian and Snifter, real good guys, and, after some understandable initial resistance, it felt good to climb back into the clockwork of the plant's operations, just fitting right in: putting things that were out of place into place...helping unload suppliers' trucks...restocking inventory...distributing purchase orders...sweeping out Jeff's office...checking invoices...signing invoices...

...And, in fact, all this felt so good that when, that Thursday, four days after the Big Return, Bob from Sales asked me if I'd make a delivery on my way home in the morning, a special order, I chippered out:

— You got it;

And even though it wasn't as exactly *on* my way home as Bob had advertised, I still didn't mind; the order consisted of a couple trayfuls of our best, Banana Walnuts and Blueberry Gingers, and they were ready for me on Bob's desk as I was leaving; granted, they were sadly smell-less, but they fit just fine on my back seat, and, in fact, they were rather handsome sitting there in our industrial-brown cardboard trays; I made sure, as Bob had told me, to go to the back door of the place where I was delivering, which was a converted school building over on Forsyth, and there I found, again as Bob had

said, a little slanted-letter sign, *NEXUS*, which seemed seriously out of place against the building's unfinished brick
rear wall; I parked right near the sign, then was kind of
pleased that I managed to knock on the hollow-sounding
door while holding the shifty cardboard trays and not spilling
a one of our factory's fine fruit; I soon heard some approaching scuffling and what sounded like wastebaskets being
kicked away, and then let sound:
— Delivery from Mindee's Muffins;
The door opened abruptly, and a guy in a blueberry-
blue, narrow-lapelled jacket led me through some eerily
abandoned but bizarrely familiar-seeming school hallways
into an unlit, almost unfurnished office, where he had me put
the muffin trays on what looked like an old assistant-principal's
gray-metal desk; he then said he'd come back with the
check, and disappeared out another door; well, when he took
his time getting back, I drifted out into the building's barren
hallways and looked around;   a few folks were buzzing
about, entirely oblivious to me, and I waited for a while pretending not to be looking at any of them; then I began
enjoying the old schoolhouse smell—dusty, and vaguely
sneakery—and the sight of the half-windowed doors extending down the scuffed hall, and all the Scotch-tape residue on
the yellowish walls, before I noticed that there seemed to be
a brighter room towards the front of the building;   so I
wandered in that direction, down the unscrubbably grimy
hallway, when *Say HUH...?*
...It was the zonester's fry-babies! —but this time they
were sitting on pedestals, and the pedestals were positioned
all around the immaculately painted orange-beige walls of
this large sleek-ish room, and each one was lit by an individual
narrow-beamed arc lamp attached to the ceiling above; and
the oven-baked boulder that was right near me—though I
couldn't tell you how it was any different from any of the
bloomin' *others* in there—that one had a little white card
attached to its pedestal that said:

The Invention of Solitude
(475°: 40 minutes)

and on the last line was the figure $2,500!; so this bakeoff shit was...? —*it was*...?

...Still, regardless of *what* it was, I found that I didn't have to actually *look* at the pedestalled shit-rock for very long, because there was nothing at all to *see*, so I moved down the wall to the next one, and its lumpy grayness was very prim on its pedestal, and remember now what I said about identical, and:

Critical Mass
(400°: 50 minutes)
$3,500

Thirty-five...! —but what was...I mean, who did they think...?

...But such was the deal with *all* this embalmed lava, one after the other, an entire *room* of it; and I checked out one called The Good Earth, and another labeled The Blues and the Abstract Truth, which I think had a couple of touches of rouge smudged on it, and another one called History is Written By the Winners, and I don't have to tell you what I *thought* of this macadamized but still eminently qualifying shit, when:

— Nice to see you;

I stopped dead—I mean *really* dead...; it was *him!* —and he was wearing a very, *very* skinny tie—!

— Hey, I said;

— I mean, I still think they should have made the walls darker, he then said: you know, for the luminousness, to bump it a bit...; but fucking Frederick here: *Oh, no...*

Fucking *say what?* —he think he was talking to someone *else?*...; and it was all I could do to hold myself back from hitting him with Yo, man, do us all a favor and go inject yourself back into the *zone* you seeped out of, with your little skinny sateeny suit, when:

— You be able to make it to the opening tonight? — people'll be getting here about six, six-thirty;

Another floorer; but a guy's gotta answer, so:

— Really like to...but, mm, probably not gonna work; that cuts into some pretty prime sleep-time for me;

— Yeah, he said, and kind of laughed, semi-snortingly: gotta keep them fuckers cookin';

Could have knocked me over with a piece of saran...; *arro*gant, too, or so it sounded to me, even quasi-*snide*...; I mean, who the fuck does he think he...?; I mean, *really*...

...In fact, it was the spindly guy's *att*itude—and that's what it was: *att*itude—that kinda stayed with me, and that kept me up for a while when I tried to get to sleep that afternoon; I mean, it wasn't only that the loon was as obnoxious as all get-out, which he was, but that the attitude he was emanating seemed, like, entirely at odds with what he was doing—especially considering the kind of *shit* he was producing; I mean, where do you develop an *att*itude from *that?*...; still, you could feel this fucking attitude underlying, like, everything the guy did; in fact, once you got to think about it, this attitude business seemed like the source for his whole deal, for the guy *and* for his shitworks, as if he had somehow let attitude substitute for inspiration; so rather than receptivity coming from his stuff, all you felt was closure, fixity...; and I thought about what that kind of attitude would do to my line of work, which would be to gum it up entirely; you see, in my gig you couldn't be all suffused with attitude, because then you couldn't do what you were there for, which was to move things along—just to get in there and do your bit, open to any and all demands, receptive to what must be done...; and it was nice, sometimes, to see yourself as plugged into the sequence that way, multiplying your energy by adding it to the current already charging through the circuitry, being productive in ways that you couldn't possibly be on your own, deriving your strength from the onflowing force of its requirements, and so just flexing with it, shoving the ball along—or, as I once told some joker, being the bouncer *and* the bounced...; like when I had my unloading to do, or my loading up, or my inventory checks, or even when I was noodling some paperwork, and I was all varied and flexible, and I just felt like I was liquid—adaptable, dimensionless, flowing over to where something needed to be done, providing the necessary lube, then flowing on to the next needful situation...; but if you ever stirred any *att*itude into the scheme, then it would all seize up, it wouldn't work at all, it would smother its own functioning as thoroughly as the melted over-rubber had suffocated the zoneworks I had seen that morning...

...So I put the guy out of my mind, seeing him as counterproductive to what I was all about—good riddance to bad shit, as the sage put it—until maybe a week later, when I had to fetch a handtruck for Freddie from rear storage; so I was cruising through up there, tucking my invoice pad into my back pocket, when I happened to look into the far corner and then, you know, I couldn't *believe* it: the area's ceiling fixture was illuminated in a familiar way; and, I mean, *really*: I just thought it *could*n't be...; so after I dropped off the handtruck with Freddie's assistant, I hustled on back up there—*fuck* the kidney system—and there he was again, back at it, circling around his work area, which had been richly replenished with street-shit; and once again, he's doing his dogshow, demonically placing junk into the baking pan, then staring at it, and then hissing out, while glaring at his opus:

— So what—*what?*...what the fuck do you *want*...?

In other words, the same old shit-fit bit—until, all of a sudden, rather than shoving his masterpiece into the browner, he slowly looks up and stares at *me*:

— Oh, I say to the guy: no, I don't—

— Don't you know it isn't safe to interfere with the *process*, he then splutters: the sacrosanct *process*...

— Well, sorry; I—

— Because it's *revenge*, that's what it is; art is *revenge*... So what did I say before: a *zoner*, right?, a total *loon*...

— Well, sorry to disturb—

— Aw, what the fuck, he says, and then drops a lens cap onto the crumbling pile and comes around the table toward me: so, Maruta: what's up...?

— Uh, nothing, really, I say: I mean, I thought you were finished—

—You know, I give so much, I give so much, I give so much, I give so *much*...; and what do I hear back? —nothing, null set, voido, *niente*...

— Sorry to hear th—

— No one cares, man: no one sees, no one knows, no one *feels*...; the urge presupposes the presence of the counter-urge, but when the urge is blocked it turns into a talon, and grows inward, and dips itself in *poison*...

OK...? *OK*...? this guy is *out* there, *right*...?

— Man, I deliver groceries all day so I can deliver myself up here all night to do *this*...; and do you think I *want* to come up here...?, do you think I *love* it...?

— I, uh—

— Because I don't; so that's why I pick this shit up while I'm making my rounds, just throw it in the back of the truck: clunk, crash—*reclamation*...; so I get my show, my pinprick, big shit deal, but where does it go—the barred flow, my sterile immensity, totally untended...

— Mm...

— The connoisseurs at the opening were more inter-ested in your *muffins* than in my work—that's what they *came* for; you should *see* them all giggling and friendly by that table—all small talk and champagne laughter...; and I put so much into it...*so much*...

— I, uh, know...

— Of course *you* know...; but can *they* see it, feel it, perceive it? —it's not that they don't *like*, it's that they don't *see*...they don't *want* to...they refuse to take that first step; and fat chance for anything else: if you're not in New York or L.A. you don't *exist*...whoosh—the phantom!; just try to get Art fucking News, no matter *how* many capital letters they got in their title, to do something on a show in Atlanta—just *try* to!; an avalanche of overdesigned press releases won't lure them...; and I tell you this more-than-hurts, it more-than-stunts: it auto-*defames*...

— Hm—

— I mean, even the *monkeys* die, the little baby *monkeys*, if they aren't touched enough—the experiments *prove* it; in the laboratory, where they test these things, if you don't touch the baby monkeys a sufficient amount they literally ex*pire*...they cloud over and wither, and then just fade into unfeeling...

— Wow...

— So, huh, back to deliveries, back to shirtlessness, back to my shithole two rooms...

— Hm...

— Yeah...; after the first death, you know...

In other words, the guy was inhabiting a more distant zone than even *I* had imagined—for right after this, immediately after, he leapt back to his crackpot cookfest—picking through, distributing upon, staring down—as if I weren't even *there*; and I just figured *Later*, you know, *enough* of *this*: just leave the guy to his loonland and for*get* about it; and this was in spite of the fact that a part of me, in truth, wouldn't have minded trying to help the guy a bit, if that could have been done, maybe put him out of his misery a little, perhaps even go so far as to buy one of his pedestal crispies, if we could talk about the price...; but then I caught myself, I just reined myself in, and thought What—*that* shit?; c'mon now—it's better *not* to encourage him, that's the *best* service I could provide for the raver; I mean, who *needs* that shit—especially since it wouldn't be all that different from what's already lying around my apartment with*out* the assistance of old friend Fahrenheit; so I figured OK, that's it, just do what you were telling yourself to do before: just put the looner behind you, get him out of your mind once and for all, and just stay the fuck away...; because all of a sudden, I must say, the fascination with the guy was just over, all the intrigue was gone, and he just seemed sad...; listen to the world about this guy, I caught myself thinking; the world was right in this case, it had wisdom...; there was a reason that no one else in the plant gave two shits about him, *like*wise the folks at the gallery: they knew something that I didn't...; just forget him...put him past you...

...If only I *could*, if only it was that *simple*...; because after I had happily ignored the shit-chef for about a week, not even looking for his work station's glow in the upstairs rear corner, I tooled into Carl's the next Thursday night and, kick me in the soft spots, *there he was*...; same gangly black jacket as always, same angly posture, standing alone at the bar and tilting a glass into his up-angled lips; and he seemed, at least to me, entirely out of place, a black smudge amid the smoky conviviality, and:

— Monsieur...Mon*sieur*...!

Shit; he had seen me;

— Welcome, my good Monsieur—*bien*venue; and now, though, you must—you *must*—join us for...La Fete de la Reclamation...!

Oh, Jeez...

— So just step right up here and try your tonsils on the official unguent of La Grande Fete...

And he called out to Rudy for another glass, then poured me a drink from a blender pitcher he was guarding:

— Thanks, I said: but what's—

— A local specialty, my friend; a memorable blend that I call—ta *da*—Teamsters' Early Grave: one part Pernod, one part Robitussin...

Give me a fuckin' *break*...; still, the shit was pretty good:

— Thanks, man, I said: but I've got to...I'm waiting for—

— *But*, my good Monsieur, don't tell me you aren't going to congratulate me...

— Sorry...?

— Yes: con*gra*tulate me—on my recla*ma*tion...

— Well sure, man, I—

— Because it's true, my dear Tzaddik, it's veracious, it is *affirmed*—I have been ex*on*erated!...; I have been elevated *above* the graspings and meanderings of the heathen horde...

— Great, man, that's—

— I have earned *riches*—ten thousand dollars of convertible United States currency; I have earned re*wards*—camera equipment, sporting wear, household goods, a *shoulder bag*; I have earned—*recognition*...

And if this guy didn't let me off the hook he would earn—

— All because I—not you, but *I*—all because *I* took the photograph, the very photograph, that was destined to become—ta da!—the 100 millionth picture developed by the W.W. Berkeley Corporation in its distinguished 29-year history...

At which point he whiplashed down what remained in his glass; then he cackled once with demon glee and filled his glass again; sitting on a stool beside him, a bearded guy I didn't recognize was obviously doing his best to ignore the spectacle:

— So that sounds like good news, I said: a contest, right—?

— The *best* news, my adjutant, the *best*...; because without even making an attempt, without in the slightest way capitulating to conventional connivances, I have made, now hold on tight, my first sale! —it's of im*mense* careerological importance...

— But I don't—

— On the contrary, my interlocutor, it is *better* than a sale, because the selection process utilized by the honorable W. W. Berkeley Corporation validates my very own methods; it affirms my techniques of retrieval and random selection: they're buying something I hadn't even put *up* for sale! —it's *perfect*, it plays *right in*: they're doing *my gig*...!

— How about that—

— You see, all they have to do is put a piece of wood covered with carpet in the laboratory, for the monkeys to rub against...that's all that's needed, just wood and carpet, for the baby monkeys to survive...

And he banged down another hit; and, you know, I looked over at the guy—this assemblage of knobs and cords hung with lank rags, smiling behind a greasepencil beard and holding up a filmy glass—and all I could think was: Get the fuck away; really, get some displacement going; just close the account, and sell it all for scrap...; and as he swigged another dose, it just kind of came clear to me that the guy was nothing but sadness, really nothing but that, the weakest link in the Great Chain of Being, and that if when raging he was pathetic then in triumph he was tragic; and it also seemed as if, at some level, the guy *knew* this, that he also was aware that the whole package he had put together for himself had been misconceived, and that any effort to refashion it would just reconfirm its faultiness; and that the zone he inhabited was one that he himself had built, but as a barrier, of course to prevent the world from getting too close but also to forestall any seepage of self, whose effects on other folks he could too easily foresee;

and that the poor loonster had become addicted to the language of communication because he knew that each word showed just how hopeless he was—and that people would sense this, and so would stay even further away...; the guy, in short, had built himself a quicksand situation, a real no-winner, and I just figured OK: give him what he wants and keep the fuck away; don't only ignore him, but force yourself to forget; acknowledge his desire and leave him to his internal exile...

...So I managed to break away and got out of Carl's real quick, and rather than heading over to work I buzzed on home; I then called in and, citing toxic faijitas, got the night off; immediately, then, I headed out and drove around near Harp's Lake almost all night; then I came home and collapsed; Friday night I spent in Willie Z.'s, playing foosball and consulting Dr. Coors, before spending Saturday day eating deli-bread sandwiches and watching sports-roundup hosts talk and smile, from inside snug suits; then Saturday night I again headed out and drove all the way to Oconee Forest, pouring myself into the back seat to sleep when I got tired, before taking the long route home, all the way through Eatonton, and landing at my place in time to nosedive into a couple of additional hours of unconsciousness before delivering myself to Mindee's; and then, that evening, work was good, the gang was there, all was as it should be—highly involving and productive: we received a large shipment of frozen raspberries that had to be processed quickly, and that went well; and so things continued through Tuesday, then Wednesday, and everything was OK—going to work, coming home—and on Thursday I had to bring some cartons to the dumpsters out back when:

— Know any good jokes...?

I whipped around and, well...of course; of course; he was leaning against the blotched brick wall, near the refuse receptacles, as mottled and smudgy as the dumpsters themselves...of course:

— Because I do; like, How do you know that Jesus was Jewish...?

— Uh—

— His mother thought he was God, and he went into his father's business;

At which point the guy coughed, but didn't laugh; then he looked up, turned away, then looked at me, insistently:

— Why, he said: don't you like it...?

— Well, I...I think I heard something like it once...

— So in that case, Dudley, I know another one, the guy said, and began tapping his right heel against the bottom of the brick wall: and I guaran*tee* you that this one is funny; and it's novel, too, though it may not be altogether new;

— OK...

— But to make *sure* it's effective—that is, more in*vol*ving, more *immediate*—I tell you what I'll do: I'm going to tell it in first person, so you'll really feel you're there, in the action—*OK?*...

— Fine by me;

— Good, he said: so, it goes like this...: one day, I go up to the spangled offices of W.W. Berkeley, Inc., photographers to the queen—and, just for the sake of throwing in some of those what you call 'em?—oh year, *luminous details,* let's say it was 10:30 AM on Tuesday, because that's when some kind of magic letter said I *should* show up; so, y'know, I go up there, and it's this nice, aseptic office tower, and I park my car over in a corner of the lot, where it won't be too conspicuous, and the tower's lobby is proud of its wood paneling, and I'm wearing my suit—because, of course, one *understands* these things; so I'm met, and greeted, but all the main men are on the eighth floor, sitting around a corner office that has no walls but only windows, and a silvered water pitcher on a glass desk, and there are lots of *signs* all around featuring the large number 100,000,000; and the men are smiling, and they all introduce themselves one by one, and they all want to shake my hand, and two of them are named Bob; and then the blue-suit guy who will subsequently do all the talking whips out one of my pictures and says So what's this?; and I reply That's The Blues and the Abstract Truth, and he says That's nice, that's what we thought, and here's why it's not gonna work; and so he begins this rap about promotional campaigns—massive, ubiquitous, already budgeted at six million two—and how they work, but in order to make sure that they *do* work, with all that's at stake, management requires anticipating various contingencies, and that's why you—that is, me—never saw any pre-publicity about the contest, because, you understand, the winning picture could have been *porno*, or de*file*ment, or *who knows* what—

— Hm—

— But it's no problem, no problem at all, the blue suit says, just give us any other picture, any other picture you have—that is, that *I* have—and we can move ahead, our rules permit that manner of harmless substitution; and I say But that's all I do have, I just took pictures of my shit in case of the off-fucking-chance that I made a sale, you see, those *are* the only shots I have, and they said We know; and then they asked if maybe I would care to submit a picture from another roll of film, taken anytime, and I said But I don't even own a fucking camera, I just borrowed this one from the gallery: I *hunt* for pictures, I re*claim* them, I don't slice off new ones; and they said Well, this presents certain problems, problems and disappointments, as we are by law locked into the findings of the independent monitoring organization that we engaged to verify the selection process; and then some of the men starting looking at one another, and I thought to propose that maybe, to salvage something, they could see fit to use the picture of the piece of mine that has the John Cougar Mellencamp button pinned to it, but they were already saying But of course you can have the prize money, and the lovely gifts, we are good to our word, although, of course, we cannot—but by then I was already screaming Hey man, you can *keep* your fucking money, and your fucking *gifts*, and your fucking *word*, and you can *go* and you can *fuck* and you can *die* and boy do they know how to stand up quick, but I wouldn't let them touch, and I wouldn't let them steer, and then I was in the hall and then I was out—

He looked down to his foot, still tapping against the brick wall; he had his palms against the bricks as well, for additional leverage; I wanted to say something, but couldn't:

— So, Dudley, he said, fully a minute later: pretty funny, huh...?

— Not too bad, I said;

— Mm, he said: tough times for the piano man, eh...?

— Mm;

— Well, he said, and tapped his fingers against the brick: at least I have some new things to put into my next piece...

Still pressing his shoulders into the bricks, he looked up into the distance, then looked down; it occurred to me that I should be getting back in...

— But you know, what really gets me, he then said: a hundred million pictures, and from just *one* company...; I mean, where's a guy supposed to *begin*...?

He exhaled heavily, then pushed himself away from the bricks, without giving me a glance; then, after stretching his arms up to the sky, he walked into the plant; I followed behind; we passed the offices and the cold storage areas, and when I saw that the guy was proceeding up to his work space, I just stayed with him, from several feet back; soon enough, he arrived at his station, and I ensconced myself behind my elevator cage, nearby, deep in shadow; then the guy settled back into his patented bit, surveying what was in front of him and beginning, as per usual, to sift through the drifts of junk; but then, in the middle of picking an extension cord out from the debris, he stopped, turned towards his worktable, and put his hands down on it; then he just looked around for a moment, taking in the entire work station, before letting his gaze sink down to the table; after a moment of this silence, he suddenly lifted his glance and broke from the area, and then he walked over to the men's room—*my* men's room— and disappeared into it; and when he emerged, a few moments later, I saw that his face was noticeably rosier and his hair had been wetted and combed back; well, I got on my guard, and then followed the guy as he slowly walked down to the office area and waited for Lonno to get off the phone; and then he actually started talking to Lonno; and although from where I was standing it was hard to make out what was going down, and I had a hard time believing what little I was hearing, I actually think he was asking Lonno about a job; I mean, the guy was saying how he already knew some of the people here, and how he already knew how to handle some of

the plant's equipment, that he had the skills—he was saying
things like that; and sure enough he got it, he got the job,
Lonno took him on; in other words, Lonno understood, and
so here I am, and I have never been happier...but no...; please,
no...; please, just let it go...; please put an end to these dreams
and defeats, so that—for an interval, just for one evanescent
interval—I can have my say...; for there is something that I
want to say, that, in truth, I *need* to say, so please...please just
listen...; for here, especially here, especially in the midst of
all this, I would like to talk about Ravel, to tell you about
Ravel—not about the music, but about the life, specifically
about the life...; so let me, then, talk of Ravel—please let me
talk, just for an interval, about Ravel, and I am standing here
thinking Please, lady, please, you who are slowing up this
checkout line, please, sweet Madam, please find your check-
book quickly, *please hurry up!*; dear lady can't you feel how my
tongue is tensing and arching within my mouth, don't my
little fretting steps and fidgets communicate something to
you, can't you hear the blue seawaves swelling under my
heart?; sweet Madam, can't you be quicker in finding your
driver's license, and end the endless froths of miscellany
coming from your bag, so I can be on my way—because I am
ready to pay in cash!; and then quickness, quickly, I will be
off: I will be moving toward him: my legs will press, and so my
feet, I will rush up against the electric door quicker than it can
open, because I will be propelled, inner winds will loft me, I
will sprout scarves to flutter behind me, to lift me from
beneath my arms and make of coarse movement something
windswept and free; yet now, still, I am stuck here on line,
behind others, before others, and none of my silent proddings
are accelerating this mulish process in any way whatever; my
urgent surging of muscles counts for nothing out there, where
the cashier is copying down identifying numbers and the
ignorant purchases are still sprawled about the counter, er-
rantly unbagged; and so I look at the glass door, and its touch-
sensitive mat, and the sales signs posted on the long window
leading up to it, and my tongue tenses, and my radiance
wakes...

...and now, finally, the world is streaming behind me—

the curve-top lamps, the dashlike lane-lines, the hummocky slower cars, the divider's clumpy shrubs—I am making all of them hurtle past me; and the way is clear and the sun a comfort, and to get where I must go I only need follow this plucking at my chest—to continue tracing the transparent string tugging at my solar plexus, and almost lifting me from my seat, and leading me there; but now, though, because I have still not gotten there, I feel as if distance—as if distance itself—has developed a density, a viscosity, and that I am pushing against it, that I am fighting distance's density; so I press the pedal, and the car surges, and I attempt to push to the terminus of distance, and when this does not happen and I am still not there I feel as if the tenacity of time will smother me—that I will be smothered by the atrocity of distance, by the painful failure of simultaneity; and I struggle to keep the gas pedal within civilized limits, and I go astride cars and around cars, and I am doused in the unthought thought: Please let me get to him quickly; please; because the car might stall or I might smudge my skirt or ordinary air may no longer be able to sustain me; but I do not think these things because I know I will soon be with him, in his presence, I will be present and there, in rich existence—my hair tips and my fingertips streaming colors, dispersing lantern light...

...and after the door opens I am snugwarm within him, with his arms a bracing glistening across my back, and his kisses sprinkling delicious spiders on my neck, and I am clutched, and I am sustained, and I can only think Finally my Diaspora is ended; and without a word, without untangling, we move, as one, a colt-walk on four legs, through the foyer to his living room; and I see that the blinds have been lowered and the coffee table moved, and I put my hand to his warm temple; then I glisten, I shimmer, as he gentles me to the carpet, that soft seabed, and he stays with me, warmly with me, landing on his elbows, and he nuzzles his face into my neck, and I feel the gracing of his lashes, and he exhales hissily, and I thank God for his ardor; low with me, present and dense, but not burdensome—he knows how to counterpoise his weight—he is a sultry shadow, eclipsing care, as he inches down to suck and lick beneath my shirt top; he cools my collarbone in little pieces, then swallows them in hot breath, and his hand, rumbling at my side, is a powerful firmness, an unstoppable exploration; but this strength turns into hard delicacy as his hand begins to crawl, in little stops and inexorable starts, to my breast; lightening his pressure, he rustles atop my shirtcloth, using the fabric to make his fingertip-touch into a whisper, and soon he is slow-circling my nipple with little fabricked lightning shocks; then, thankfully, he introduces the tips of his fingers underneath my shirt, warm and firm and solitary, and they are followed by the rest of his hand, and its hard heel comes to anchor on my chest; and then he finds my nipple, and he cups it, and trails his fingertips atop it, delicately floating above my nipple's sparking; and when his other hand magically appears to undo my shirt buttons, his first hand does not give up my breast: it clutches to it, taking all of it, and his hand becomes firmer, and it does not want to leave; but when it does, when it must, to pull my shirttail from the top of my skirt, his other hand is already upon my breast, and it is rougher, it is scratchy-crisp, its graspings are harder and deeper, and more fluid in movement; and his pressings and cuppings reach down into me, eliciting me, deep-shivering me, before his lips drop and sip at my other breast, my left, with my shirt wisped away, and open, and off...

...and so my softness flows through him and returns to me as yearning, and I am arching and flexing as his tiger-tongue curls to catch the underside of my nipple; and it is gently abrading, reaching and withdrawing, inventing texture; his licks beneath my nipple distribute treble-tones of feeling, before he circles with kisses to the top of my breast and sounds its lower notes; then he starts sucking, just little lippy pullings, crimping my nipple into him, and I am with him, I am within him, my little, total penetration; and he just continues—he nips at my hard soft pellet, my pinkness, all pliancy, all givingness, and I wish I could thrust fully within him, to insert myself in him, my softness so willing; but his touch is a tension as it slips down my ribcage, and it merges to shimmeriness as his hand crosses to my belly, to its slopings; and I am tingling as he grazes and circles and ladles

my middle, the lines of his movements all leading to conclusion, to certainty; and I am calling and halting and calling and
halting in language I know he can hear, our breath wet
thunder between pressings and kissings, when he dips the
tips of two firm fingers beneath the top of my skirt, at the
yielding hollow of my hip, where it is warm, and just lets
them sit there, and just lets them sit there...

...and I press and splay my hand across his strong warm
back until I feel his entirety, and we are one system, we are
continuous, sharing long glissandos of feeling that are lacing
between us, stitching us; I hear his heartbeats as my own, I
feel his urgency as my own, our covalent union making of us
both a new, charged, unknown substance; so too my skin, my
liquidy skin, is both our separation and our merger, it is our
shared, evanescent frontier; yet when he kisses the valley of
my belly so long and so shiver-warm I realize that I am also
beyond his skin's extremity, I am past the barrier of his skin,
I am also living *within* him, for the juncture is no longer clear:
utterly, entirely, I feel his response to me, I feel his churning
when I surge; and it is sublime circuitry, this overlap, this
confusion, giving me new contours, new periphery, expanding me into added dimensions, and so unlike the present I
bought for him, the magic square of letters, which slide about
their small tray in endless shifts of senselessness, and whose
plastic hardness I feel pressing against my leg from inside my
skirt pocket; for here, now, with him, every configuration
accords, every arrangement speaks, our bodies are multipliers
of meaning, our every move and gesture is a new expression
of a limitless significance; finally, engagement does not require strategizing, and all I must do is welcome his kisses, the
plashing of his kisses upon my face, my lips, around the ridges
of my eyes, and up into the top of my throat, into my
gibbering pulse...

...and as I grab a fistful of his hair I feel he is descending
again, his kisses are crossing the speedbump of my collarbone, and now he is licking and savoring my skin, my chest
skin; and I feel with my tongue and lips the sweet saline
textures he is drawing from me, the astonishment of my warm
skin; and now, again, he is climbing to my breast, sidling up

with silvered tongue-trails and halting nibble-kisses, until he comes again upon my nipple, lapping it with firm lickings, and taking it, supporting it, with his hard, gentle hand; and the two move in gentle synchrony, his hand stirring and his lips flicking, as he slips his other hand behind my back to brace me, to hold me wholly, to pull me impossibly into him as he laps more and more of my breast into his lips, his open mouth, this pressing of soft firmness to softness; densing his tongue, he deliciously caresses the full expanse of my nipple, and I want to be entirely inside him, where he is gnawing and tonguing to bring me...

...but I make him pull his mouth away, and then I unbutton my skirt, and I lift out of my skirt and panties and push them away, onto the carpet; and as I lie back his dark hair fills my vision as he descends and kisses the crevice between my breasts, then litters kisses this way and that, like shifts in wind, up the slopes of my breasts, then down to their bottoms; and as he slides down and across the curvature of my ribs his kisses feel like asterisks: imprinted, prickly, referring to some fuller explanation, some deeper meaning, at levels below; then, when his licking dips to the soft of my stomach I get little screeches of feeling, and I shudder, I shimmer, just a bit, as he starts licking left, then licking back, but always notching lower; I have my hands in the rough hair of his head when he slowly starts licking up my sides, and across my belly, and again over my breasts, and his tongue, as it traces, is the sealant that knits my fissures, that pieces me back together, rejoining my broken shell; and then, finally, he puts his hand down upon me, and he lets it hover there, large and hard and powerful, before he slowly, gently, dips one finger, and then he is in me, finally in me, a firmness dipping into me, into my liquidity...

...and he is stirring me, and he is slipping me, and I am swarming with yearning, and I thrust up to take his face to kiss, to slather; but then suddenly he breaks away from me, and leans back on his knees, between my legs, looking at me; and he stays, and looks, for just a moment, his wonderful strong-boned face earnest and yearning, before he draws up my knees and, in fluid movement, puts my legs atop his shoulders; he then starts stroking my legs, upward and down, firmly-roughly, gliding his hands from my knees to my buttocks, along my legs' insides; then he holds my right leg with one hand and begins kissing, almost slurping, large lipping kisses where I am softest, at my leg's inseam; then, slowly, he begins to descend, hand and kiss-lips slowly coming unto me, and I am inviting, and I am urging, so wordlessly, so breathlessly; and when he is just beside my center, my legs now spread full-widely, flared totally, my skinscape and fur all for him, entirely for him, his kisses jump to my other side, to my other leg, he ignores me completely, and he again starts tonguing, bringing long warm lappings to my left thigh; and he is still near me, but he has not touched me, he is only longly tonguing up in my thigh, when suddenly he is right upon me, he lands within me, his tongue stroking the inside of my cunt and ladling, and lapping; and as I welcome this shimmering surge he extends his long body full out, to lie straight out on the carpet; from far across the living room he is a runway rushing up to me, so his tongue can nudge and circle my cunt, probing and stroking and sampling its seeping; and I am pushing towards him, against him, yearning to open up against his entire face, to cunt him entirely, to feel the full warm liquid merging; and his tongue is tilling me, it is rummaging me, he just goes on and on with his arduous, pointless, lapping searching; and I am pressing into him, I too am searching to achieve our impossible transpenetration, with the drawbridge of his tongue crossing my murky moat, or like a Soyuz mission docking in space, with two weightless craft meeting in the empty blackness of orbit, like it was, like I saw, in a magazine that had that, a shot just like that, pictures of the two halves of the space mission intersecting and fusing into a single ship, their electrical systems interconnecting and their two distinct atmospheres miraculously merging; and so this is our coming-together, our seamless mingling, like it was yesterday, in the newsstand, just like that in the newsstand over on 19th Street, when I had stopped to pick up the Avalanche-Journal, and the small, shadowed shop was overrun with magazines, garish maga- zines: I was there yesterday, and the magazines were filling a long wall from ceiling to shin-level in ranks of open shelves, and they were stacked on counters, and they were strewn over a series of horizontal shelves towards the back; and as I was reaching down to pick up the Avalanche-Journal, my eye was lured by the colors and faces on the magazine covers; so, automatically, without thinking, I picked up a copy of Rolling Stone that happened to be there, an issue that had Van Halen on the cover, with their eyes all colored to resemble cat's eyes, and I began leafing through the magazine's large pages; and without warning, as I was looking at the type designs and the splashy graphics, and at the pictures of Belinda Carlisle and Paul Stanley, I felt—suddenly, with a sudden shudder—a foretaste of my own death; but still, I continued to flick through the magazine, past the preenings and the glowerings and the rushing hair, and as I went through the innocent pages a kind of claw-grip suffused over my chest and throat, a clutching fist of heat and shame; and at that point I came upon a photograph of a hardhat eating strawberry yogurt, and I suddenly heard myself begin to think This is not innocent, this is not unknowing, every angle and facet and posture in this has been mapped out and calculated for maximal effect; and I heard myself think That these people have spent fortunes to do this, to hire peak professionals, monumental scholars of deception, to determine precisely how to achieve their invisible, irresistible manipulations; and when I turned, by chance, to an advertisement for Virginia Slims, featuring a radiant girl-child in a summery blue dress, a flare of shame ran through me, flashing in my neck and face, shame for the smiling abuse foisted upon a trusting public; and I heard myself think This cannot be the purpose of our putative freedom, to be able to engage in cruel deceptions with smiling faces, to conduct this inconceivable squandering of resources and effort and ingenuity solely for the purpose of hoodwinking the trusting, and producing uselessness, and nothing of what is so desperately needed—this can not be what freedom was supposed to serve; and now, when it is universally accepted that these deceptions are natural, or necessary, or inevitable—now I am dead; I have perished; I am no longer part of this world; But it's only an ad, another

voice sounded within me: it's nothing but a flicker of ambition in a two-dollar tatter, which will achieve its greatest
significance as landfill; But if so, still another voice responded, then the discrepancy has become too great: the
discrepancy between what the signals are saying and how I
hear them; in other words, it has become total, this discrepancy, and I am lost, I am disappeared into this rift: the
disjuncture between seeming and being has become too vast,
too painful, for me, and I am disappeared; so, torn by new
sadness, I put the Rolling Stone back on its stack and readied
myself to move on; but inexplicably, rather than moving
away, I picked up a nearby copy of Vanity Fair, somehow
snagged by the cover of Sigourney Weaver in a low-cut, blood-
red, leopard-spotted dress; and I again turned through the
magazine's first few pages, past the Guess Jeans ads and
Eternity by Calvin Klein ads and pitches for Crisca clothes,
filled with beautiful people imitating suffering; and then
words came to me, words arrived in my mind, quickly and
insistently, words representing the real sound of my feeling:
The shot has been lost; the experiment has not been worth it;
the species does not deserve to continue; it is much too late...;
so, dark-flooded, I slipped the magazine back into its wall-rack
slot and gathered myself together; then I took a single step,
and suddenly wanted to weep: before me, in tiers and on
shelves, spread out in endless, assertive array, were dozens,
hundreds, of these magazines, preposterous numbers of them;
and all of them, it then came to me, were further indoctrina-
tions into fraudulence, into sham existence; despite their
seeming diversity and uncontrollable multiplicity, it was clear
that virtually all of them were saying the same things, precisely the same things: *come into the world of lies, of distortions
and inessentialities; learn to feel inadequate, and to be ashamed
of what you are; accept the power of others to form, to shape, to
determine your preferences, your thoughts, your hidden enclaves;
internalize the master myth, specifically in order to feel excluded
from it; realize that you are a nothing—a cipher, a target, a
marketing opportunity, a connable and dupable marketing opportunity, but ultimately a nothing, entirely a nothing; learn to hate
yourself, while always remembering that the hater is a nothing;*

and this was being conveyed with a quantity and consistency so overwhelming that doubt or resistance had become all but impossible, a disfiguring futility experienced not as genuine opposition but as confirmation on one's total impotence; and thus the magazines, too, were a magic square, but one whose shifting, gripping letters only served to produce unending combinations of disfigurement, limitless small mutilations; and yet, even though I knew that what I had seen was right, that it was the bottom truth, I immediately felt bad that I had thought this, that it was somehow *my fault* that I had found the death-messages in the motley light, that it was a disease in *me*; for light is not sad: or should not be; and it hurt, it was just a soul-scourge, to be punished for being right, to be scorched for seeing through and seeing right; in other words, no longer was I a daughter of light: I had become, definitively, the product of shadows, finding darkness where human eyes only registered brightness; this could not have been what was intended, it could not have been part of anyone's plan—to have the shadows speak through me, and not the light; I have never known which photograph my parents were looking at when they met, but it was, of course, an interplay of shadow and light, the product of granules speaking and silent; otherwise, my grandfather would not have saved it, and made a place for it in his book; but clearly I have sprung only from its shadows, and have worked, and suffered, to kill its light; no, this could not have been part of anybody's plan, to produce a sick-seeker, a selfsick-maker, an enemy of the light; no one could have wanted this: this could not have been part of any man's plan; nor did I foresee that I would lose my left hand: I had just graduated from college then, perhaps 12 or 13 years ago, and was still trim of midriff and possessed of a masterly smile; but, one evening, I was sitting and chatting with an acquaintance in Mother's Laundromat, over on West Belt Line Boulevard, when I noticed that his gaze was repeatedly drifting down to my left hand, which I had casually draped over my crossed leg; so I subtly modulated my posture to be able to glance in that direction, and saw that the hand contained some nibbled fingernails, with a few excelsior cuticles; I was not entirely certain what to do about this, so I decided to get rid of it, the hand, and put it in my head; and this was good;

Some time thereafter, I observed a bank teller, a young woman of perhaps 20, interrupting her activity of sliding nickels into a red-colored roll by looking up at me, whereupon she glanced at my widow's peak; so I got rid of my widow's peak, and put it in my head; later that week, a swarthy immigrant tailor turned away somewhat rapidly after he had measured my shoulders for a suit of clothing, so I got rid of my shoulders, and put them in my head; then I got rid of my right ear, putting it in my head, after a young woman of perhaps 18, standing in front of me in line at the butcher's, turned to see if her car had been ticketed and noticed that my right ear's lobe was not detached; that left me with one remaining ear, but I got rid of it when the shampooer at Shear Perfection asked me to sit back into the dousing sink and saw the three darkish hairs curling from its pinna; I put it, along with the three curling, darkish hairs, in my head;

Approximately seven months further on, a young woman of perhaps 21 noticed the thinness, and perhaps the paleness, of my calves as I sat on a towel by the side of Carys Lake, so I got rid of them, putting them in my head; at the Calhoun County Fair some four months further along, a caricaturist, who works in charcoal, attempted to solicit employment by making an amusing pulling gesture in front of his face as I strolled by, prompting me to get rid of my nose, by putting it in my head; no more than two or three days later, I believe it was, I observed that Mick Jagger's scrotum, as espied amid the energetic cutting in a film entitled Performance, was a different color than mine—darker, and more purplish; so I got rid of my scrotum, and put it in my head; then the hostess at Tronco's Ristorante, a woman of perhaps 38, seemed to see, as I was waiting behind the cordon to enter, the small scrape of eczema above my left elbow, even though I had my arms crossed in the way that usually renders the white patch invisible; nevertheless, I got rid of the elbow, the entire joint, and put it inside my head;

Soon thereafter, while thinking of approaching a young woman of perhaps 22 who was standing near a planter on

Gervais Street, perhaps to essay some spirited conversation, it occurred to me that the pigmented mole on my right arm, some four centimeters from the wrist, was somewhat raised, so I got rid of it, by putting it in my head; then, an estimated four months past that date, the thought came, while I was unsheathing the cassette player/FM radio unit from the dashboard of my parked Honda Civic, so as to be able to lock it in the fine security of the trunk, that my right foot, by its own inclination, turned somewhat inward—that is, off-parallel—so I got rid of it, and put it in my head;

Now, I am not one to belabor details, or to diverge unnecessarily, so I will just point out that, subsequent to that event, I have, for various, meticulously observed reasons, gotten rid of my triceps, the folds at the back of my neck, my toe fur, my penis, the white stipples swimming in the pinky nail of my right hand, my veins, the angle of intersection between my back and my hips, the remaining entirety of my right hand, the sense of tension radiated by my lips at certain moments of repose, and my eyelids, and put them in my head; accordingly, now, when I look in a body-mirror I can not see them at all: when I am fully clothed, partially dressed, in shower-wear, or nude, they are no longer present; they are invisible; they are nowhere; yet even though they are all safely put away, and are fully gone, I suppose I should add that at occasional moments—when I am walking through parking lots, or when I step onto escalators, or at other times, in fact, rather regularly—at occasional moments I still feel as if they are there, still precisely in place, where they had been; in other words, at those moments I regenerate a false completeness, a phantom entirety, which I perceive as a tactile sense of all my disappeared features hovering unto me, and glistening prickily, almost as an aura, although certainly, definitively, they are gone; and I might also add that my head, in general, seems to have become, how to characterize it, somewhat heavier, and larger, and harder to balance upon the pool cue of my neck; so, in general, my head now tends to list somewhat forward, tensing the muscles at the base of my skull, and along my shoulders; this occurs both during moments of activity and during periods of calm—both; so the question then becomes what to do with my large and heavy head, how to accommodate myself to it, and, in fact, it to me, leaving me to suspect that I will, some day, perhaps soon, perhaps momentarily, observe that this is information, this most definitely is information...empirical, corroborable, independently verifiable information...coming from somewhere, going to somewhere...but now, here, for just an interval, this is information that is receiving expression, that is bursting into articulation, through me...that is pooling, momentarily, and then living, eternally, via me...because I heard...(sounds become meanings, outside becomes inside)...(psychology becomes biology becomes chemistry becomes physics)...because I heard the story...the informational story...that virtually without exception, the suicides from the Golden Gate Bridge jump not from the side that faces the ocean, but from the side that faces land, that faces humans...this is true, this is verifiable, this is information... but is it a leap away, or a leap towards?...no: not a pertinent inquiry...but it is a leap...yes: a plunge, a leap...a leap into information...into signification...into increasing the signal-to-noise ratio, *though they do not know it*...(but Thompson knew it, he *did*: our different music doesn't sound different, it sounds the *same*)...thus, the leapers find a concealed continuity, a hidden determinism, although one that is terribly refracted by time, and uncapturable without time-lapse photography—*if* the pictures could ever be assembled...yes: drop by drop the leapers seek to become a current, to become like water, a waterfall of man...to go from sundered, suffering flesh to massed and unshameable information...to the realm of hard data: cogent...certifiable...dimension-denying...*meatless*...courting the single sorrowful chance that might fleece the feared frontier...thus one must commemorate their ignorant assertion...their unknowing, determined merging...their blind *insistence* on informational meaning— their desperate exchange of substance for significance...and so, elsewhere, in other circumstances...and so, at other times...when they have guns...loaded and ready, when they have guns, stuck in their mouths...what, then, are the guns pointing towards?...what is their orientation?...toward what center, what figure, what concentration?...this is important to know...this is *essential* to know: what the guns shoved in their mouths are pointing towards...because I was right at that juncture when, every day, I turn selfish: blindly selfish, shamelessly selfish, *will*fully self-pampering; I do this not only because I believe it good, and salutary—I endorse the notion of applied self-indulgence—but also, at bottom, because I believe that I deserve it; after all, it had been a good and productive day; in the long quietness of the afternoon, as the shadows from my yard's birches slowly slipped off the corner of my desk, I had finished line-editing three long chapters of an odd, repetitious book on massively parallel processing systems, written by a UC Santa Cruz professor who seemed to have read a little too much Raymond Queneau; the manuscript had been typed on a manual, which, as usual, had left the text somewhat dodgy, but the writing was relatively clean and, blissfully, triple-spaced; distractions had been few, and I had emptied my coffee cup only twice; so it was the kind of afternoon in which I had taken real satisfaction from my wriggling red pencil, performing its poky arabesques among the crawly rows of black type; tightening the good professor's readable text had been a fine first outing for my luminous new birthday pencil—a birthday gift that I had bought for myself despite the fact that yesterday, which was when I purchased the proud number 1 3/4, was not my birthday; mine, in fact, is in October; but I had reasoned that it isn't just every day that my daughter, Rebecca, turns 5 1/2 months old, and so the day certainly warranted considerable commemoration; further, why not appropriate the day's goodness for myself, I reasoned; as I have said, I subscribe to the doctrine of concerted selfishness; yet whether it had been more selfish for me to buy the pencil-present or to receive it, I had not yet determined...

...So there I was, at 5:30 PM, pampering myself preposterously: pouring a deep cup of apricot-flavored decaf, plopping down at the kitchen table, stretching my feet onto the adjacent chair, and flipping open my Redbook—best arts coverage of all the monthlies, no doubt about it; then, to cap things off, I took the walkie-talkie from my skirt pocket and placed it on the table, in front of the napkin rack; now *this* is indulgence, I thought, this is what is called for; it was pleasant to feel the walkie-talkie physically removed from me—its tug-weight in my pocket often grew tiresome; and it was just as pleasant to see it stretched out on the table before me: the constancy of its dense gray hum meant that Rebecca was sleeping peacefully; and so, too, I could be at ease; Rebecca was a difficult sleeper, fitful and cranky during her passage out, but, thankfully, almost unflappable when she was under; and that was nice: I cherished her company when she had achieved her quietness, perhaps feeling—again selfishly—that I had helped provide her with this ardent repose; occa-sionally, in fact, I would read to her while she was asleep: I would sit by her crib in her low-lit room and, taking my time, share one-way words with her; this tenuous act of communi-cation was, of course, no more than a sanction for my remaining with my daughter a little longer; but I adored the experience, principally because Rebecca's silent response was, to me, incomparably expressive and moving; when I read to her, her quietness, her peacefulness, was what I sought to hear, and it echoed in me as if in an expanding cavern, and often left me trembling with love; and so, then and there, after taking a final gulp of my decaf, I decided to indulge in even more self-pampering: I lifted my legs down from the chair, and, with lightness and celerity, stole upstairs...

— Darling, I said, in my low dusk voice: we got a letter;

...I approached the crib and saw her apple face and voluptuary's lashes; she seemed warm within her bulky bedclothes; her breathing was regular, and her lips gnashing; gently I pulled the brown corduroy chair closer to the crib and settled into it; being closer meant that I had to speak even more quietly—precisely what I was after:

— Yes, we did, I said: in fact, *we* didn't get a letter—*you* did; look—she even addressed it to you....

...Amidst the dense quietness I showed her the enve-lope, where Rebecca's name, and only her name, was written above the address; I had been thrilled to pull it from the letterbox that afternoon; it was just like Robin to do some-thing like that:

— You see?; so, here's your letter;

...I withdrew the envelope's several pages and unfolded them, careful, though, not to make too much rattling noise; as always, the letter was handwritten, in Robin's angled script; I cleared my throat, quietly, and settled in to read:

— So, here we have it...Dear Rebecca—Hey, how do you like that?—so...Dear Rebecca...O tiny tykelette, o noble neonate, let us now talk of transformations...not grammatical, of course, no clause for alarm *here*, but personal, ezymatical, sociobiological...for your faithful correspondent, your penning epistler, AKA your Auntie Robin—she spells it a, n, t, i— has found something that makes anti—spelled a, *u*, n— matter!...O 'tis true, 'tis true!—and, my darlin', I'd better take a break already!—

...In fact, I had forgotten how rollercoastery the gal could get; I put the pages in my lap and, in the tenebrous quietness, stretched my arms and shoulders, readying myself to dig back in; flighty Robin, how busily she worked to achieve the expressivity that came inevitably, inescapably, to Rebecca, just sleeping and warm; the counterpoint could not have been more telling; and yet, I thought, looking over towards my system's second walkie-talkie, which was taped to the railing of the crib, it would only be Robin's expressivity, as I read it, that would be conducted by the walkie-talkie to its sibling in the kitchen; only her words would be burbling to the shiny appliances downstairs, while Rebecca's infant eloquence would not come through; the instrumental world, it occurred to me, inhibits certain kinds of communication; absent the right kind of listener, all sorts of essential signals are lost; still, it seemed funny, as I envisioned the scene downstairs: the stillness, the walkie-talkie, the words; and I wondered, perhaps, what a burglar might think, coming in upon the chattering room:

— OK, then, here we go again...; so: 'tis true!—*so*—And what would so newly enthrall your pen-y Auntie?—oh, just figure it out—Nothing but a regenerative slap of worthwhile work...Yes, 'tis a project, projecting me into modes of research, modes of inquiry, modes of understanding, and modes and modes of fun...sorry...but really, as the latest of his delvings beneath the frozen sea of official reality, Chomsky, my ongoing guidewire, my lifely thrillmaster, has asked me prepare a report on events at Al Yarmouk University, in *your* favorite city, Irbid, Jordan, where, several muddled months ago, the Government slipped the pink slip to more than a dozen professors and half as many U administrators just, make that unjustly, because they came out in support of some student protesters...in other dicta, 'twas a nasty bit a business, squelching students and their academic inspirers, who would believe anything like that ever happens...ne'ertheless, for me, it's a hugely engaging and galvanizing gig, though for Chomsky, of course, it's just anti-business as usual, as he continues writing and talking and generally crusadering about all his other unstoppable passions...abuses of democracy in bosom-ally Costa Rica, America's backing of Indonesia's invasion-cum-massacre in East Timor, the selective blindnesses and biases of the allegedly free press...I've started calling that ragged institution the *de*press...the sorry circumstances of the pal-less Palestinians, and many Chomskian moral more...and he continues with all his work and support despite all the fat-catcalls and obloquy, great word, that Chomsky should hie back to noun-town, as in Things'll be great when you're...where all the blights are right—Oh, God—that is, that the little academic linguist should stick to tending his grammatical garden, where he has some expertise, and not if, and, or but into affairs that he can not possibly comprehend...but such is the genuineness of Chomsky's greatness that he can not help speaking out when the world requires the word, when wrongness has become the only surface structure in sight...Tha 'tis, the Chomp's deep, universal concernedness excludes nothing but indifference, and his totally generous essence springs from a democratic instinct so passionate that, hearthlike, it warms you, it incites you, if you be around...I know that I have certainly stolen my fire from him...even though, a course, the fire was freely given...

...And *whew*: time for another intermission; there was only so much of this my poor tongue could handle in one take; I then rose and stretched and went to the dresser behind me, where I pulled the cord on the little lamp, whose burlap shade was decorated with a big clown face; as I had been reading, I had been racing, somewhat, against the room's increasing darkness; then, while settling back into my chair, I thought of the Oxbridge don who, night after night, would read Herodotus to his sleeping son, to see if the child would have an especial facility for learning classical Greek later in life; it had been an interesting experiment—although I wondered what skills Rebecca might acquire after but one evening of Robin-exposure:

— So, my dear: Round three; so...But the connection, a course, between Chomsky's linguistic researches and his political activism is as plain as pre-petrochemicalized day...Tha 'tis, as you must recall from when yo mamma slipped this into your chest pressé—Thanks, Rob—that it was Chomsky who, in the supple Sixties, reached back to the linguistic tradition of hardy old Professor Humboldt and championed the necessity of distinguishing between linguistic *performance* and linguistic *competence*, and then chose to climb up the latter...Tha 'tis, Chomsky said that linguists should devote the utter most of their attention not to faulty, fractured, floozied speech, but to the cerebral structures that *enable* language activity...because he saw, you see, that everywhere, every time, everyhow, everywhen, people develop astonishingly complex and versatile language capabilities, capabilities that allow them to produce and understand a literal infinity of perfect sentences, even though they have only been exposed to limited and usually imperfect linguistic input...and that what he be meanin' about innate competence...Tha 'tis, in Chomsky's perfect words, the subtlety of our understanding transcends by far what is presented in experience...or, once agin, in my imperfect rewording, from shattered shards we reconstruct the crystal...*how* did we learn to do it?...I mean, *I* didn't go to shard-school, did you?...and Chomsky *marvels* at this, at our miraculous linguistic competence, he *glories* in it, rather than rifty-fixating on the shortcomings of corrupt, imprecise, wheezy speech...and what's more, my diapered dreamboat, this is also true at the level of phonetics, of physically producing speech-sound, where we also exhibit what can only be considered a kind of miraculous

competence...Tha 'tis, just *think* about the glories you are
growing into, my pre-verbal princess, just take a moment to
consider the accomplishments that await you when you
arrive unto the Age of Articulation....effortlessly producing
endless streams of luscious sounds...affricates, fricatives, glot-
tal stops...all those saucy snippets of sound and meaning,
each of whose physical production represents no less than an
astonishment of movement and coordination...performed
on a microscale so exquisite that, if you think about it, it
should leave you speechless...but 'tis true, 'tis true: even the
process of articulating so simple a phrase as "I am not worthy
of your consideration" entails a dexterity and physical finesse
that outstrips Irina Kolpakova's entire career at the Kirov, and
Ivan Lendl's every move at the net...and this Chomsky saw,
and felt, and was moved by, and was overtaken by, and has
now, also, articulated in me...and it's been so fun, so
transportive, so remaking, my good gurgler, to have found
within myself so rich a palate of possibilities...sorry...real, real
bad...

    ...In fact, I was rather glad that the phone had begun to
ring: by that point, I welcomed an external prompt to jump
off the joyride of the letter; so, hearing the second ring, I
nudged my chair away from the crib, put the letter down on
the seat, and pivoted to leave, lightly bunking my foot on one
of the crib's legs as I turned; then I slipped out, after
confirming that Rebecca was still asleep; I crossed the hallway into my bedroom; there, I sensed the dense, silencing
presence of the mattress and linens almost as an atmospheric
change; this was evidently a site of repose; I decided to keep
the lights off:

    — Hello, I said, picking up the phone;

    — Hello, said a masculine, somewhat metallic-sounding
voice, before the line lapsed into silence:

    — Hello?, I tried again: hell—?

    — Now in your neighborhood, the voice cut in, before
the line again settled into scratchy silence:

    — I'm sorry; who is—?

    — A service new to your community, and now avail-
able—

...Ah, I thought, pulling the phone from my ear and hearing the bright voice continuing on: it's one of those machines that electronically dial phone numbers and make solicitations; I had read about these devices—in fact, more than once—and had wondered if I would ever receive such a call; curious, I decided to listen for a bit; but I already suspected that this wasn't the kind of thing that I would welcome regularly:

— Difficult-to-get-at eaves and overhangs, without exception, without risk; statistics show that 70% of all homeowners overlook the necessity of adequate gutter maintenance, even though clogged or insufficiently cleaned gutters can be breeding grounds for unwanted pests, while the slow corrosion of gutter metals can—

...And enough, I thought, placing the handpiece down: more than enough; the call was funny, and ironic just now, but it was also kind of eerie: the call had been made at random, but the pitch held such purposefulness; it was an odd combination; thus I was glad to return to Rebecca's room, where the calm and the muted lights were unperturbed; I bent over the crib and saw that she was there—just beautiful and there, sleeping peacefully; but then, while looking down at her, my selfishness flared volcanically and I could not resist picking her up—just for a moment, to feel her warmth and solidity; and so, for a second, I luxuriated in the tactile sense of her, her warm, articulated physicality; then I put her back and tucked her in, and laughed once to myself when she hiccuped slightly: such small, unexpected eruptions I always found heart-rending, thrilling, the littleness of their urgency; I stroked her once on the chest and watched warmth and peacefulness retake her:

— So, then, where were we?, I said;

...I settled back into the chair; the letter's several pages had been disheveled in the move, but I found my place with little rattling, little difficulty:

—OK; so—right here; so—And there is much much more to be gotten from all this, my little listener, once you come over to applying a competence criterion, as you do already, I might add, for a lily, or a tabby, or a child—good ole

Rob, still at it—Thus, in short, in sum, in all, it was but a baby-step for Chomsky, graced with this understanding of the ineffable richness of our bio-abilities, to become the universalist that he be, to extend his understanding to the political realm...and to leap, by bio-necessity, into his political work—

But enough: that had been Rebecca's third hiccup; the rest of the letter, and there wasn't much, could wait; placing it on the chair, I rose, found the pacifier in the crib, and gave it to Rebecca, who was by then awake: her arms and legs had already taken on the waggly insistency of wakefulness; this transition remained, for me, a pleasure—to see how she changed gears, from sublime quietude to flappy agitation; but for some reason she did not take the pacifier, plopping it out in a froth of saliva; I tried again, but again it came tumbling over her cheek; so OK, I thought: we'll just wait this one out; I got close, and smiled broadly, and kissed her cheek; then I pulled away and, with one finger, started stroking her chest; such little disturbances, I thought, yet so total, so automatic, are our responses; we were made large and strong to come to the service of smallness; I continued stroking and smiling, then started humming—a tuneless something, in lower tones, that just passed through me and limned the air; it would help her, I sensed; and, in fact, before long, Rebecca became calm, and settled back into drowsiness; then she hiccuped again; I picked her up:

— Yes, dear one...you just took in too much of Robin's letter, now, didn't you?, I said;

I placed Rebecca's quilted warmth against my shoulder and again applied the pacifier; but still it was not taken: Rebecca twisted her head to keep it away; so then I simply held her and stroked her back, and this, thankfully, seemed to work; her left hand crawled relaxedly down my chin, and her breathing became fine and regular; then she hiccuped again; but it occurred to me, this time, that what I had heard had not been an ordinary hiccup: coming close to my ear, it seemed deeper than usual, closer to a full cough; and she seemed to linger with it for a little longer: it took greater possession of her system than was customary, and didn't finish as decidedly as

did other such bursts; I began to walk around the room with
her, slowly:

— Yes, my darling, yes; we'll get this one out of you one,
two, three;

I strolled her about the room and heard, before long,
that her breathing was settling into its usual huffy sibilance:
evidently, she was slipping back into sleep; There, I thought:
that's what was necessary; then her hand relaxed at my jaw,
and she exhaled deeply; it was working; but when she
spurted into wakefulness again, with a thundery cough, I
then sensed, clearly, that something was a little off; there had
been something in that cough—it wasn't a hiccup, but a
cough—that was not right; there had been an extra presence
of wrenching, of chokingfulness; and as I began to bobble her
at my shoulder, she began to cry—or to attempt to cry, for at
intervals a cough would rush up and dislodge the crying, cut
it off and supplant it; so I concentrated my attention on her
breathing, and heard that she seemed syncopated, out of
rhythm with herself; I put her back down in the crib:

— OK, now, sweetness; just let this pass; just leave it go;

I reached to the washstand for her bottle of apple juice,
but found it empty; so I gave her the knuckle of my index
finger, because it seemed right, as if it would work—perhaps
it would open her up to some air; but she could not take it;
she was, by then, crying and coughing rather fitfully, diffi-
cultly alternating between the two: her crying would reach up
in volume until it was knocked back down by a spluttering
cough; and while standing above her, and looking down,
holding her small shoulders with my hands but feeling very
far away, suddenly something within me began to feel a little
decentered, or confused and lost; I began to get the sense that
I was out of my depth, that some sort of unknown threshold
had been crossed, beyond which I, as a mother, despite all my
reading and preparations, would not be at my best; her crying
was not normal crying, everyday crying, which I knew how to
minister to; her coughing was also uncustomary, an invasion
from somewhere else; there might be, it occurred to me,
something genuinely wrong; and then I became aware of a
voice, a low, dull voice, drilling within me: Please, Rebecca,

please; please stop coughing; please just *stop*; but then, right then, she coughed again, and I, unthinkingly, pulled my hands away from her; I didn't know if I should move her, if I should even touch her at all; I became afraid of the possibility that the slightest jostling might compound the problem, interfere with the natural processes of self-correction; but I had to, I had to touch her, and I did: I picked her up, and heard her breathy struggling, and felt her jumping, and took her downstairs...

In the kitchen I placed Rebecca on the table, softened by a placemat; then I smoothed my skirt with the flat of my hands and went to the refrigerator for some apple juice; I got one of Rebecca's bottles from the cupboard and, after nervously spilling cold juice over my hands and the counter, filled the bottle to the half-way point; but Rebecca would not take it: she shook her head from underneath the nipple, she could not organize herself to suck; I put the bottle aside and, brushing my hair from my face, noticed that the child's crying had grown somewhat subdued; but at the same time her coughing seemed to have worsened—to be coming from more deeply within her, to be happening more frequently, and to be jackknifing her belly slightly up with each one; and now, after each cough, she would lather or gurgle for a moment, then wrench her chin up, which tensed her neck; at the same time, the hot-and-cold drafts that were then coursing through me, and the flashing stiffness besetting my arms and forehead, all left me stuck—immobilized, lost, uncertain of what to do; and again I became aware of the voice drilling within me: Please, no; Rebecca, please; please stop coughing; yet my inability to act on these pleadings, to do anything to help her, splashed through me like a wet fire, an inward bludgeoning of doubt, of panic, of fearful complicity: my daughter was suffering, possibly grievously—I could feel the difficulty that her body could not specifically express—but I had hit the end of my capacity to effectively respond; I saw her distress, I was in the very presence of her ordeal, of her little body jolting, but I did not know what was happening within her, I did not know what to do, and was terrified of doing the wrong thing; all I could do was grab and release the cloth of my skirt; all that was delivered to me was Please, Rebecca; please stop coughing; and dark clouds, fire-clouds, like the black clouds of an oil fire—wind-tumbled and billowing—gathered in my peripheral vision, fire-clouds of disbelief, of impotence and rage; fearing to be consumed by the clouds, I pulled away, hitting my hand on the sharp corner of the counter; but from that distance, the phone mounted on the wall by the refrigerator came into view; I rushed to it, picked up the handpiece and dialed Clovis High Plains Hospital, whose emergency number I had taped to the fridge...

Quickly, immediately, there was someone on the line; but I could not wait: I rushed past the formalities, the technicalities:

— Hello, I said: *hello*; please, as quickly as you can, an ambulance over to—

But they were still talking, they were insisting on talking first; so I stopped; if I had to, I would listen, I would hear out their formalities:

— And while the strength and durability of copper will guarantee many long years of use, the lighter and more economical Teflon gutters allow for decorative touches that—

And with a sudden *whump* the fire-clouds swelled and eddied around me: this could not be true, I thought, this could not be happening; this is a movie; and then I stumbled, almost falling, against the kitchen wall; but I immediately regained myself, and rushed back to the phone and crashed the handpiece back into place, making sure that the connection was severed, that I had hung up; then I brought the handpiece to my ear again:

— For instance, our new Palm Beach Green, in scalloped trim—

Again I crashed the phone back down; and not knowing whether to leave or to stay—but what could I do in the kitchen, with my heart drumming, my heart blithering—I bounded past Rebecca and mounted the stairs, taking two at a time; running into my bedroom I clicked on the light and saw, with horror, that the other phone was also hung up; but still I ran and picked it up, to double check, and when I heard the same metallic man-voice I pressed and pressed the disconnect button, down to its bottom, forcing my fingertip into the button's little sharp hole, and then I held the rounded button down for an unendurable five, six, ten seconds; but still the crawling voice was there—every time, unstoppably, cutting through the fire-clouds continuing to engulf me, and I screamed Damn you *Damn you* as I ran out and back down the stairs; but back in the kitchen, before I could get to the phone again, I saw, ecstatically, that Rebecca was coughing much more slightly, and was hardly crying at all, and had diminished in movement; but when I came closer, I saw that her face was brownish and strained, and that her lips seemed coated with phosphorescent-seeming off-white; and then the fire-clouds tumbled in on me, enveloped me, leaving me thinking No; no; this can not be; things like this just do not happen—this is impossible in a million ways; and I bent down and grabbed Rebecca and brought her to my shoulder, and I pumped the small of her back with the heel of my hand, over and over, then harder and harder; but she was not responding, she was barely moving, her hand was a chill against the top of my neck; and I could not strike her any more, I could not hit her again, so I put her back on the table and petted her temple, and felt a frightful, scalding flame flare within my shoulders and face and chest; and I knelt down beside her, and made myself promise that I would not faint, and I thought No, this is impossible, it could not, it could never happen so quickly; then I heard myself begin to intone, to say:

— Please, Rebecca; please; *please...*

And I leapt up and ran to the kitchen phone:

— *Hello—!*

— So why not take advantage of—

— Hello—*hello!*, I continued, repeatedly pressing and punching the disconnect with the flesh of my hurting index finger, making the plastic clatter and the bell ding:

— Hello!, please...*someonr!, please*, pick up the phone!; *hello—please—this is an emergency—!*

— New to your community, and now available—

And I crashed the phone down and returned to Rebecca, and again knelt by her side; and as the fire-clouds swarmed across me, and crested above me, to unsensingness, to closure, I again started stroking her chest, her shoulders, her cold and unmoving hand; and I felt a surge of liquid crying rushing up within me, and overrunning me, and my knees were hurting, and it was becoming difficult for me, too, to breathe; the fire-clouds were eclipsing me, invading my access to air, I was struggling to keep a sip of breath coming through the clouds' blackness; but I knew that I had to fight back, that I had to fight them off; so with my elbows and arms I forced them away, I buffeted the fire-clouds from me, pushing them, I was jostling and shoving, feeling their massy billowiness resisting my arms; and in the clearing, past the clouds that I was struggling to force away, through the slight remaining aperture of light and air, I saw, behind Rebecca, on the table, in front of the napkin rack, the walkie-talkie, lying on its side, perfectly quiet...; but I still have my marquetry, oh yes, there is still that; in fact, I just finished some nice palisander patterning—octagons and pen-tip shapes, things like that— for the sides of a stereo-hutch I made, a real nice one, too; and before too long I'll put the hutch up in the living room, oh yes, so then maybe I'll get around to replacing my old Marantz amp, maybe get something with an equalizer, something good; and that'll be real nice; and I'm still fishing, of course, that goes without saying, usually from the dock over in Kiwanis Park, they've got good rainbow trout and brown trout in there to work with, the Roaring Fork is good for that; and productivity on that has been good, I must say: I've been using lures I make from sucking-candy wrappers, which I get from stuff they sell over at the Peanut Shack over on Highway 6; they're real bright-colored, and the trout seem to have a thing for Cadbury lemon, that's for sure; so do I, for that matter, so it works out; it all works out, in fact, always does...

...Although I couldn't have known, you see, I really couldn't have known too much at all when Angelo came over that first time; I mean, no one could have known it; now this was, oh, two winters ago, right in there, in the middle of snow season, maybe, oh, four months after the Forresters, who used to be next door, took that job with the prep school back East; of course I had seen the semi and the boxes and the moving men, but I hadn't really met Angelo yet; in fact, first time I did meet him I realized that I had seen him during the move, but that I had thought he was part of the crew; regardless: at first he stayed away for a few days, and I didn't quite know what to make of that—there's only our two houses on the block, so you'd figure; so I was real glad, then, when he came over on that second Saturday, a real bright day all bright with snow; he rang on the bell, you see, and introduced himself straight away, saying real nicely that he was 804's new owner, and that he had taken a job teaching mathematics over at the St. John Middle School; how about that, I thought; and he had a nice bright smile and seemed relatively clean, so I shook his hand and thanked him for his courtesy and told him he was welcome whenever; and we talked a little bit about the neighborhood—I told him about that cashier at Geno's Market who gets funny with the change—and I asked him to let me know if he needed any decorative woodworking done, that I was real reasonable; and he said he'd be sure to let me know, oh yes; but then, you know, rather than maybe telling me a bit more about himself, like maybe about his family, he simply said that he was glad that he had come over; and then, you know, he took this little step aside and gave this big arm-gesture towards the street and said:

— And I do not come alone;

Well, in fact, he hadn't; for when I looked past his extended arm I saw, sitting at curbside, a brand new snow-blower, all red and gleaming, like a scaled-down National Harvester tractor; well, it sure was a sight, I'll give him that, so I took it in and said:

— Looks real nice;

And I let him bask in it for a moment, you know, because he seemed to be looking for it, with his big smile; and I tell you my doing this seemed to pay off, for just then he offered something real nice, just real nice indeed: without once breaking his smile, he asked me if he might clean my sidewalk and driveway with his new snowblower, just as a neighbor, no charge of course; and then he said he'd also make a path over the flagstones that lead to the front door; well, hearing this, I thanked him kindly; after all, it was real nice; he had his blower and cared to share it in a nice, neighborly way; no problem with that; so we smiled and shook hands again, and I waved as he went toward the machine, still smiling; and I watched through my screen door for a while as he started her up, and as he went back and forth a few times on the sidewalk, winging the powder up from where it wasn't wanted to where you could live with; and he did a good job, oh yes; it took a good forty minutes, but before he finished I brought him out a coffee and half a cellophane sleeve of Lorna Doones, and he ate everything right on the spot, from his seat, with the engine shut off; in other words, with the sun and the mouth-vapor and the nice clean paths, it was a real pleasant episode, no question on that; no question at all...

...Still, though, if I can say it, I didn't mind not seeing him for a few days after that; you know how that is, a good neighbor knows how to be friendly, the best neighbor knows how to keep to himself, that kind of thing; beyond which, I understand that a new arrival has his load to tend to, he has his portion of chores, so I didn't actually expect to see him around too much; so when I tooled home after work one night about eight, nine days later—I've got a little pest-control business up on Grand Avenue, usually keeps me out 'til five or six—and saw my sidewalk and driveway again visible between cliffs of pushed-back snow, well, I was a bit surprised that he had thought of me again; sure I was; but still, I was pleased—got to say it—and all the more so when I saw that he had also done the flagstone walkway up to the door again; after all, it was a real nice job; the guy didn't have to do it again, but I supposed he thought that as long as he had his machine out for his own property, why not bolster that first good impression; and I thought it was kind, I'll tell you that, very kind indeed; so without even looking in at home I went right over to Angelo's door and hit the bell, intending to thank him; when no one answered I hit the bell again, waiting on the step; but he wasn't in; which was too bad, of course: I wouldn't have minded seeing what he had done with the house...

...But soon the snow thinned and left and the sun changed—I did see Angelo a few days afterwards, incidentally, in his driveway with packages in his arms, and I made sure to thank him, to a big bright grin—and so I went about my business, I did my thing; life doesn't stop, of course, at no time; and I didn't really give much thought to any of this 'n' that, you know, I had something of a grippe around then, that was about it; until one day, around the dinner hour, the door rang and I got it and it was Angelo; and he said his hello and we shook hands and were friendly, talking about the warm new spring; and then, though, he told me that the day before he had been in town and had ended up buying a little too much lawn seed, that he had made a miscalculation; and so now he was wondering if I'd like to have the excess; perishable, he said; so I replied:

— That's very, very kind;

because I thought it was; and then he smiled real broadly and said:

— OK;

with his voice ringing out like a chime; and then, with me just standing there right behind my screen door, Angelo turned and waved at me, and then he began to scatter the seed from the little sack in his arms, tossing it like chicken feed throughout my yard; up and down the lawn he went, walking around like a real professional, like he knew just where the seed went; and when he turned to me with a big smile I said:

— But you don't have to—

— Hey, he cut me off: it's my pleasure;

And then he gave a wave that said Just you forget about it, and he turned away from me and went back to work, tossing and scattering; and, you know, at that point I felt my eyebrows lift and I made a little face; and then I heard myself figuring Well, OK, let him do it, if he wants to; those were my thoughts; so I just closed the door and decided to try to forget about it, to think about it no further; it's just a little eccentricity, I thought, that's all; fellow has his own way of going about things; I did feel a little funny, though, going back and heating up my packet of soup while he was out there working; I mean, maybe I was getting a little beholden to him: maybe he would ask for something; and I wondered if I should invite him in; but the thought came that there was

something in the nature of the unpredictable to this guy, so
it was better just to let it go...

...And it went, it went, oh yes, very peaceably, but then
it came back: maybe a week later, Angelo—I swear he must
have been hiding behind the bushes, just waiting for me to
come home—one evening Angelo came bounding over to me
as I was getting out of the car, and out of nowhere he up and
offered to *fertilize* my lawn; well, I just looked at him in his
jeans and blue windbreaker jacket, and then I looked into his
big smile, and I said:

— But what you...what you want to be doin' with—

— Because I *like* it, he said, his voice just pealing: I like
this sort of work, and as long as I have my yard to do, it's just
as easy to move over to your—

— But you're not going to be asking for any money or
nothing, later on down the—

— *Aw*, c'mon, Angelo said, in a smiling, confidential
way;

So I looked over my property, and over to his, which was
essentially the same tract of grass, though separated by the
azalea bushes and his driveway; and then I looked back at our
respective homes, which had been built at the same time in
mostly the same two-story suburban style with layered-pine
finishing; in other words, I was reminded that, take away
some of the details and ours are just two identical houses on
one big lawn; and so I looked into the distance and said:

— But if you're ever intending to do more such like this,
just do it, and don't ask me; don't even ask me;

And I went indoors; I don't think I was rude, and I don't
know why I was huffed, but I wasn't altogether comfortable
until Angelo had quit my then-fertilized lawn, maybe thirty
minutes later; in the meantime, I had spent the thirty minutes
sitting in the high-back armchair in my living room with the
lights dead off, imagining that I was hearing Angelo's footsteps popping across my property, which I usually couldn't;
and then I could hardly make up my mind about what to fix
for dinner; I'm unsure why I got so disgruntled, except that
maybe a man, you see, resents being put in a situation where
he has a false illusion of choice, and Angelo knew that it would

be discourteous for me to say no to his request, because it was a service for my benefit; even a kindness can become unwanted when you don't have options, oh yes; something new always brings considerations, you see; so just let it be done and don't *tell* me about it...

...Which is just what happened; over the next few months, along no particular schedule, Angelo started taking me up on my offer; I never saw him at it—in fact, I rarely saw him at all—but one evening, when I came home from the shop, I saw that both of our lawns had been mowed, cropped real cleanly all the way to their edges; they looked smooth as water; then, one afternoon several weeks later, I found that he had done our herbaceous borders, clipping them until they were nice and straight—in fact, he even did the shrubs on the opposite side of my house from his, which were nothing to him at all; and, I must say, that touch made my whole front-yard look real nice, no doubt about it; then, some time later, maybe a month past, he lined trails of small white stones, decorative kinds, along the sides of the flagstone walkways that lead up to our houses, setting them off in brightness; and I must say that also looked nice, yes it did; I had never thought of that effect, but it added a nice color-contrast, oh yes; it was a real decorator touch; in other words, for me, you see, despite my early resistance, this whole thing had turned into something of a sweet deal, and quite a nice reason for coming home every night...

...So about a week later I decided just to go over and thank him, to pay Angelo a call; his car was in the driveway, and I thought he'd like to see that my sour feelings hadn't stayed:

— Well thank you, he said, standing within his opened screen door after I had said my piece: very kind of you to come over;

— Well sure, I said, and nodded my head: really appreciate what you've been doing; it's worked out real nice;

— As I said, it's my pleasure, he said, and then that smile came out again: I like to help out;

— Yeah, I said;

— I mean, what's the big deal that I can only work on one

side of the shrubs, he said brightly: when I get home from school it's still early, and I like to be doing something, so...

— Hm, I said thoughtfully: yeah...

I turned away, and looked over our two nice-sized yards; and they looked good, that's for sure, green and clean and trim, as if they had been through some kind of basic training; but what Angelo used to justify all this was his business, I thought; I don't have to agree, or even to see it; I'm just living next door; the fact that he was doing it for me was kind of irrelevant, I realized; the guy has his own considerations, so let him follow them: these principled sorts have their own ways, and that's it; they've got to do what they're going to; there was even a tradition of something like this in my family, couple of generations back, so I know you should just let them go; that's the way they operate; besides, you can't even see a gift horse's mouth, once you're riding it...

...And so my property received a real makeover, yes it did; next up, about two, three weeks later—it became more difficult, you see, to keep track of the dates—nice little birdbaths appeared on our lawns, standing near the left-hand shrubs; and the baths' white stone was real pleasing among the green, I'll tell you that; made the green look deeper; then, kind of near the birdbaths but closer to the houses, Angelo planted two of those spindly little Japanese trees, the ones that are real delicate-looking; and throughout, maybe every ten, twelve days, the lawns would be mowed again, giving them a sheen, and seemingly done by some real top-of-the-line equipment; well, for me, I must tell you, it made coming home each night real pleasant, really something of an adventure: you never knew when Angelo was going to hit next; driving up, I would scan the place and look for any differences, all ready for a surprise; but I decided that I would never let myself get disappointed when nothing had changed: that could have queered the whole deal; besides, sometimes they were a little hard to notice: one time, for instance, I saw that Angelo had cleaned the outsides of my windows, and that was real nice; but then, I'll mention, I realized that I wasn't really sure when he had done it—it could have been weeks earlier; further, to this day I'm not certain if he replaced the cracked tiles up on the roof; by the time I noticed that there might have been a change, other tiles, it seemed to me, were already rotted, so you never know; you see, I also decided early on to, well, kind of keep my distance from the guy; of course I was cordial if I saw Angelo on the street—I would wave and say friendly greetings and such—but I just thought that it was the wiser tack not to interfere too much with the run of events; Angelo didn't seem to want any more from me than a good wave and a ready smile, and I certainly didn't mind limiting it to that; so the thing went on without too many words circulating between us—though I did have a notion to ask him about his choice of colors when he did the painting; but as it went up, and as I lived with it, the rusty brown did become more and more attractive; it was real rustic-looking, so I let it go at that...

...All in all, then, the house was looking beautifully— even such, let's say, pedestrian details as the nice new green-plastic garbage cans by the kitchen door, out back; in fact, the place gave me a sort of glow in my gut, so much so that, one day early last autumn, I finally got around to asking that Cathy Watkins—a customer, a divorcée—if she'd care to come out with me for dinner some evening, maybe over to La Casita; she's always got a smile ready, that Cathy, I've always found her real nice; so when the evening came and I picked her up, I made sure to have forgotten my credit cards back at the place; we passed by and I suggested that she just wait in the car, and she did; and the evening was nice; Cathy ordered one of those chimichangas, then I dropped her home; she didn't say anything about the house, but we still had a good time; then I asked another customer, a Vicky, if she would care to go out, and that evening I just went ahead and drove right by the house on the way to eat; I even stopped at the curb out front, and told her that was where I live; and she seemed to like it; after about three or four minutes, though, I sensed that Vicky was ready to move on, and besides, from her position in the passenger seat she had to turn in opposite directions to look at the place or to look at me, so by talking I risked distracting her attention; when we left, I just backed right into my driveway, to turn around, which gave her another good look; and also, this way, we wouldn't have to pass Angelo's place; then we had some Chinese that was real nice...

...By then, though, we were getting into autumn, which is traditionally the beginning of my slow season; so, as usual, I was able to close up a little earlier each day, and I noticed that my winter paunch was working itself into place; with my longer evenings I would sit at home and, as usual, worry if I'd be able to lose my seasonal gut again, and, as if that weren't enough, I also began having my traditional autumn-time thoughts, real naggy ones, about maybe getting out of my business, just closing up and moving on to something else that I might like a little better; and as I was sitting in my living room early one evening thinking that maybe this time I would do it, that I would use the quietness of the winter to start to put something together that was more my speed, I heard a loud skittling, followed by a metallic crash, come from the street; then there was silence; well, I jumped up to the front door, opened it wide and saw, on the opposite side of the street, just past Angelo's place, a motorcycle slid up against a tree at the side of the road, and the bike's driver stretched out on the pavement right in front of it; I got there as quick as I could:

— Hey—you OK?, I said, bending to the guy, who was lying in his leather jacket among some leaves;

— Shit—aw *shit*, was all he could say;

When he took off his helmet I could see he was in pain; past his scraggly hair I saw that he must have been about 26 or 27, no more than six, seven years younger than me:

— Can you get up—can I give you—

— My fuckin' *leg*, man, he hissed through a grimace, and bent over to grab his knee;

— I'll get an ambulance, I said, and was off;

I high-tailed it back indoors and called the emergency medical service, then scooted back outside; the first thing I did was pick up the bike and lean it against the tree, but by then there were already some other people around: a middle-aged couple who had been driving by and had stopped, along with some retirees who lived around the corner; everyone offered assistance, but I let them know that the ambulance was on its way, and so it was decided just to wait; the biker stayed lying on the street—we decided not to move him—kind of whimpering every now and then and also tensing his face...

...The ambulance showed up a few minutes later and stretchered the biker away, and as the other onlookers were saying goodbye and going off, I offered to hang back and wait for the police: the EMTs said they were coming and would have to fill out a report, that kind of a thing; so I made time with the bike and the leaves, making sure not to kick any of them, in case the police wanted to see what the scene had been like; and my thoughts passed to what had just happened so quickly, and that had so quickly ended, and how things were like that; but then, while waiting, I began to notice something—and I continued noticing it all during the time I was telling the police what I knew, such as the biker's name and the hospital he had been taken to; in fact, what I was noticing made it a little difficult for me to talk to the police at all, with my eye constantly being pulled away like that; because from my vantage point at that moment it became obvious that there *were* differences—small differences, but differences nonetheless: *defi*nite differences; I mean, I was standing there trying to keep talking about skidding noises and I just couldn't believe what I was seeing: there were differences in the herbaceous borders, and in the paint job, and even in so recent a thing as the raking that had been done just a few days back; in fact, there were differences every-where, consistently so; and then I noticed something else: after comparing the two houses real closely, sending my eye back and forth between them, then doing it over and over again, it became clear, as well, that in every instance Angelo had favored his own property; there was no question about it, it was plain as day: the guy had always done a little better for himself; his shrubs were slightly—but noticeably—larger, and more regularly trimmed, while the white stones alongside the path to his doorway were definitely straighter—*definitely*; the painting on his house was real clean, just regular and nice, without any of the rougher patches that showed up on mine—

especially above the bedroom window—and without even one of the splotches that appeared on my rain pipes; his Japanese tree was just better, it was just bigger and better— bushier, wider, better—and his birdbath wasn't standing at that little angle that I had always wondered about with mine; and I could have gone on, I tell you, I really could have, because differences were there practically across the board; and they were noticeable: all of them, no matter how minor they might have been, were definitely noticeable, each and every one of them; well, this just hit me like a moving van, I must say, oh yes; so after the police left I stayed outside comparing the two houses for a few minutes more, with my pulse racing and my ankles sometimes being tickled by drifting leaves, and then I just barreled right into my place and pushed the door closed, hard...

...It was dark in the kitchen, where I was sitting; I must have been there so long I had brought on the dusk; but I wasn't of a mind to have anything to eat, oh no, I had no appetite at all; so I just fiddled with a couple of apples that I had taken from the birchwood bowl on the counter, rolling them in my hands, and between my hands; you see, I didn't want to stay in, but I didn't want to go out, either; I mean, I had no plans for the evening; of course, I could have always just gone over to The Black Nugget and knocked down a few Molsens, there was always that; but I wasn't too inclined to do that: the place was smoky, and sometimes you had to park a block away; and it was getting a little chilly out, too: it was nearly winter; also, I didn't really care to run into Angelo just at that moment, if you must know; he might have been in his driveway—who knows; then again, maybe he would, for some Godforsaken reason, stop by here; who knows; *I* didn't know; so I got up from the kitchen table, intending to do something, or maybe go somewhere, but then I bobbled one of the apples I had been passing through my hands, and it fell, *flatch*, on the linoleum flooring before rolling right under the Partchean system of tonality, the site of something new, where sound was healed, it was restored to rationality, to physical correctness, it was made healthy and balanced again after 300 years of mangling and musical scoliosis—

— Sir, would you please—

— Listen: a gumball manufacturer makes millions for introducing a new flavor to the marketplace—there is a hunger for new experience, for expansion, for life-augmentation; but Partch introduced new sounds, new *notes*, new dia*pas*ons of auditory possibility, experiences that were incom*par*ably richer—

— Sir...

— We had a great, a genuinely great composer in our midst, a great *American* composer, conjuring astonishing sounds, thrilling the air with innovation; so how can anyone—how can I not do my *ut*most to help spread this richness—

— Again, sir, we do not see what bearing this has on—

— So then wait, just wait, and listen; that's what it's all about here—listening; you see, through his work, Partch sought to make music more physical, or, as he called it, *corporeal*, which can be seen most directly in his devotion to the human voice, sounding singly, the lone cry; accordingly, Partch felt that he too had to find his own voice, a process that made it necessary for him to shake off the shackles of the Western musical tradition, its centuries of hermetic dominance of our musical thinking; just fine for Pergolesi or Rachmaninoff, the Western tradition functioned as a deadening set of limitations for Harry Partch; in particular, Partch sought to open music to what he called a new fusion of the sensual and the intellectual, and during his life he created lush, lavish musical-theatrical spectacles to accomplish just this; Partch himself likened his methods to those of, quote, primitive man, who, he said, quote, found sound-magic in the common materials around him, and who then built visually beautiful instruments with which to actualize it; then primitive man, quote, involved the sound-magic and the visual beauty in his everyday words and experiences, his ritual and drama, in order to lend great meaning to his life...unquote...

— *Sir*...

— Just *listen—will you?*...; accordingly, Partch spun out into his own flight path, to where the air was clear: he assembled his own performing ensemble, and trained them in

his own musical techniques, teaching his singers and instru-
mentalists to liberate themselves from conventional musical
strictures, to stalk something genuinely *new*; and then he—
Partch himself—built the vehicles for their musical emancipa-
tion: he actually created and constructed entirely new instruments for his musicians to play; at first Partch only length-
ened the fingerboards of conventional violas and guitars, but
later on he built all kinds of new instruments, entirely new
portals into musical possibility, instruments that he gave
names like the Gourd Tree and the Blue Rainbow, or the
Diamond Marimba or the Kithara—that's K-I-T-H-A-R-A—
each of which, decades before the advent of synthesizers,
accessed stunning new languages of sound; and the instruments themselves, the ones that Partch built, were often so
beautiful—some of them, you should see, are these great
monumental altars of wood and bowls and suspended glass—
some are so damn beautiful that they were exhibited in
museums, as if they were sculptures: museums in San Fran-
cisco and New York: the Whitney—
 — Yes, but what—
 — *Please*, sir—*sirs*: you said you wanted a statement!...;
so this is it: this is my statement...
 — ...OK...OK; go ahead; but briefly, though; please try
and be brief; OK, Pete, take it down...
 — Thank you...; so: Partch's was a magisterial musical
mind: he envisioned things, he *heard* things that no one else
had beforehand—and nowhere more so than within the very
substrate of music: *tonality*; for here was the greatest efflores-
cence of Partch's genius; the Western scale, of course,
contains twelve semitones, running, for example, from C to B
natural; commonly it's assumed that this segmentation of the
scale into twelve parts is somehow mandated by nature, or
reflects some absolute physical imperative; but, in fact, it is an
arbitrary convention settled upon just a few centuries ago and
rigidly perpetuated ever since; twelve tones to the scale: that
is *nothing*, especially when you know there is so much more
available; indeed, music history shows that there have been
all kinds of other approaches to tonality, systems that work
with greater numbers of tones to the octave; in the 16th

Century, for example, the Venetian monk Zarlino—that's Z-A-R-L-I-N-O—proposed two keyboards of 17 and 19 tones to the octave; and elsewhere in the world, even today, traditions exist that are more musically generous: the Indian intonational system, for example, boasts 22 srutis—S-R-U-T-I-S—to the equivalent occidental octave; but even this is nowhere near the limit of our potential; indeed, in his book Psychology of Music, the great Carl E. Seashore—as it sounds—avers that the human ear can distinguish some *300 separate pitches* within the confines of the octave, using the Fechnerian model of the JND, or just noticeable difference; so then *think* of all the music denied us by the coarse stepway of Western diatonicism; and, by the way, we *sense* this, we know *instinctively* that there is more than what the Western musical monoculture permits: consider, for example, how we express emotion in music most directly, most ana*log*ically: through *vibrato*; but what is vibrato if not a breaking down of the rigid divisions between pitches, a temporary ending of our sundered musical segmentation; we evoke the deepest and richest of our feelings by bending tones *between* the line spectrum of the Western scale, by ending its divisiveness; we locate what is most human in between, where we are no longer quantized, constrained—

— Sir—

— And Partch intuited this, he *heard* it, and thus he went ahead and created a scale of *43 pitches* to serve as the basis for all his great compositions, starting in 1930; because Partch heard *more* than what our crazy Kroneckerian tradition told him was available, he heard his way *past* what he called the esthetic censors of what he called, quote, our one system; moreover, the scale that Partch created was in Equal Temperament: it was a *just* scale, without the mutilations of tones that the Western scale demands in order to maintain the illusion of their harmonious coexistence—

— Sir...*sir*...OK; now, we've listened to you, to what you're—

— Why: are you *tired* of hearing about Partch—is this, perhaps, not holding your *interest*...?

— Sir, look—this is *not*—

— Isn't Partch *famous* enough to sustain your—isn't he enough of a *VIP*?...

— Look, sir—it has nothing to do with—this is *not*—

— Because *that's* why I do it, why I give my lectures...; OK?: here it is; this is what you want; you can calm yourselves...; you see, I lecture because Partch hasn't even got an entry in the Encyclopedia Americana while Burt Bacharach *does*...; but even *Bach* fell into total, benighted oblivion until Mendelssohn conducted a concert of the Saint Matthew Passion at the Singakademie and regenerated his reputation, fully *100 years* after the piece's premiere—

— *Fuck it—sir!*...will you *get* to—

— *OK*...OK; please—control yourselves; just con*trol* yourselves—*please*...; I will begin again; so, today I gave my lecture, to commemorate the 11th anniversary of Partch's death; I've been giving Partch lectures over in Campbell Library for seven years now, in the hope, of course, of doing a little more for the cause, something more direct than just writing to concert societies and musicological journals and then waiting for nothing to happen—because Partch, you see, a visionary far outstripping Ives, gave concerts all over the country for 40 years and...well...OK...OK...just calm yourselves...; but don't you see, you need to get some kind of critical mass together, to get things rolling...; but there's always, every year, just the same five or six people there, in the whole hall, two of whom just happened to wander in and another two who go to everything presented in the place, indiscriminately; and then, today, you see, when I began speaking of Partch as our Timotheus—that's T-I-M...oh, forget about it—when I began speaking of Partch as our equivalent to the ancient Greek who was driven from Sparta because he sought to add four new tones to the scale then in use—just when I was using that to describe our magnificent mugwump, it was then, *then*, that a couple of young people—*young people*—got up and left, making a lot of noise with their feet...

— And...

— And there you have it;

— So—so what about your statement, your—

— You have just received it;

— Sir, listen...what the *fuck* are you trying—sir, we have been very patient...we have—so before I *cite* you for obstruction will you *please* tell us the facts about—speci*f*ically why you—

— But I just *did* that...; why—isn't that sufficient for—

— *Sir*—

— OK...; OK...; if you insist...; if the one system requires it so, so be it; so: after I had concluded my lecture—OK?, is this what you want?—after playing a few snippets of Partch's recordings and then fielding questions, of which there were maybe two or three all told, I just said thank you and packed up my notes and records; and after watching two old *ladies* leave, I stopped in to thank the Campbell administrators, and then started home; I go on foot, so I crossed New Bern Avenue and Martin Street on route to my place, and then, over on Garner, where it intersects Martin, I saw that there was some kind of movie production going on, some kind of location work—

— Correct; they were shooting a commercial;

— Of course; and as you know, I stopped for a moment to watch; and as I was looking around—at all the technicians and the open vans, and at the parked trucks and the light diffusers and, *I* don't know, all the cables—it was just then, as I was standing there, waiting for this to burst into mythic significance, just then this young man walked in front of me; he was maybe 22 or 23—a skinny thing, in a blue T-shirt—and he had a clipboard under his arm; and as he passed I saw that he—this nondescript boy, obliviously moving by me—I saw that he had this little smile on his face, just this little hovering facial presence of self-satisfaction, of self-contentedness; and then something tore in me, and I was upon him—

— Oh, *please!* —would you just cut this shit *out*...?

— I'm sorry...what—what's that? —who—?

— Come *on*, now—*enough*...*enough* of this insufferable shit...

— ...Hey Pete, did you say—?

— No, I—I, uh—

— So who—what's—?

— Just *can* it, will you?, fucking *can* this simpleton

shit...; *put it the fuck away—!*
 — But—
 — Yo Pete—what *is*...I mean—
 — *Would you please just shut the fuck up!*...I mean *Jesus,*
how much of this can anyone be expected to *take?*...I would
get out *right now* if I were you, after a lame fucking payoff
like that...fucking imbecility...fucking boring insipidity...*all*
this stupid neo-Pythagorean shit-rant...I mean, it's *enough*
already—*that will do!*...*enough* of these diversions...enough of
all these fucking distractions...enough of even *asymptotes* to
truth—or is that too arrogant an assertion, queasy
relativist...because *I* don't think so...because even if there are
no more positive absolutes, there are still negative ones...or is
that too straightforward a statement, have I been insufficiently *artful* in encoding my *sentiments*...in camouflaging
them for *esthetic effect*...well, too fucking bad...my life has
convinced me of few things, but the absoluteness of the
negative is one of them...light bends, it diffracts, it scatters,
but darkness fucking endures...it is what remains when the
strayed-in rays and scintillas have long disappeared...it is the
fundament, the ground...and I am one who can tell you this:
behold my blackbody...
 ...so what remains?...where does that leave me?...only,
then, to tell of Ravel, of the composer himself, his life, his
story, his suffering, to tell you what I know...to pass on the
story of Ravel, the miracle-worker...Ravel: conjurer of incom-
parable sounds, elicitor of amazing washes of feeling,
summoner of living music that defies, that shatters
analysis...irrefutable Ravel, how amused he would be to know
that I am speaking through him...the news would have made
him raise up his voice in *song*...it would amuse him, no doubt,
almost as much as hearing that the Bolero, the work that he
abjured, that he denied, has become his emblem...his very
signature...the one thing he is known for...and so it is: one
man, one piece—end of consideration...thus the man is
muzzled anew...a tragedy is compounded...and this with a
piece that argues for continuance, for inclusiveness and
indeterminacy...if I could, I would tell Ravel, I would tell him
of my dream, my long-dead dream to study composing, so

that in the same way that others have "completed" the Mozart Requiem or the Mahler Tenth, I would be able to complete the Bolero...that is, to extend it, to continue it...to continue it indefinitely...into unexplored new combinations of instruments...into brilliant orchestrations that were left untried...because they *are* there...they *exist...it could still go on...*

...but no: I will not take up this Millenarian tango...for I have not studied composing...I have no music in my head...I am not among the major players...though I am told I am the substance of history, I wonder why I have to be told this...so, at last, I can not complete the Bolero, I can only live the piece...measure by measure, bar by bar...I go by the rules...I play by the book...I orchestrate my time...I show up every morning at the print shop and I pay my Visa and I keep up on the news...I do what is expected of me...I play my part...differently and identically, I tell my story with each day...and the result, for all this, for all my stolid sticking-to-it, the principal result is variations on disappointment...unrewardings of my implicit trust...and I can already hear your thoughts: so what else is new?...yes, I know...but so much for radical recognition...

...so then listen: recently, I pulled together my diaries, taking them down from shelves, and out of boxes, and off of stacks...(I have never been able to keep them together)...and over 17 years' worth of closely-written pages, since the time I reached my majority, I count the names of 66 men...boys and men...66 of them...it is a preposterous procession...an unthinkable sequence...endlessly chiming on...and I remember them all...*66 of them*...I am told I have a sought-after shape...so the trigger was automatic, the program imperative...they understood their interests...they knew what they were after...and I chose to believe that it was me...but the structures of trust proved asymmetric...my self-generosity proved the simplest thing to betray...I gave them the bouquet, and...*these were not rehearsals, but each one an act of faith*...with every encounter there was exposure...exposure, alas, without development...yes, I can tell you this...for I carry the proofs within me...so I can tell you of Bill, with the generous eyes and the talk of endurance, who took me to jazz cafes, and snacked on carrot sticks, and then just stopped calling...and of Vernon, the locksmith at Lovelace Medical Center, who said that before I thought it, he understood it, and who would take me out for sunset drives, but who said I was leaning on him when I wanted to see him more than once a week...and there was Jimmy, the hugger, big lathe-operators' hands skimming, nesting among my shoulder blades, who struck my forearm when I reached to take one of his French fries...and Mason, who would have continued telling me for the next ten years that he was going to leave his girlfriend...and Tommy J., whose nightlong rap on reciprocity and our commandment, our shared *commandment* to climb to the towers became a pitch to lend him $350...

...and also there was Morris, whom I trusted, whose leisurely stride and immaculate apartment translated into someone whom I implicitly trusted, but who then called up and, from out of the blue, said he was getting remarried to his ex, but that I should feel free to call him any time...and he was followed by Melvin, who was returning to school, who wanted to study electrical engineering; and I heard his entreaties and I felt his approaches and I laughed at his slyness and hesitancy; and then I gave in, twining my arms around him and pulling him close, so that he would know, and then there was no other night...and Maurice, working at the newsstand for all those years, friendly and folding the Tribune as he handed it to me every morning, then finally, timidly, proposing that we meet for a coffee, with his eyes never coming up from the counter to meet mine; well, I laughed with surprise; but he didn't show up, and then never said a word about it afterwards, never making the slightest reference as he sat at the newsstand with the ring on his finger that I had never before seen...and Nelson, who, while I was telling him my dream of studying in El Paso to become a midwife, reached for his Sports Illustrated...and I can tell you of Manny, who once called while I was in the middle of a long, slow bath—and when I rang him back, and said that I only permitted post-hygienic communication, he faltered, then fell silent, then chortled out, with a little laugh: Oh, I get it...and there was Billy, who said he was in marketing but who actually did telephone sales for a carpet-washing company, and who told me in a restaurant *never* to cut him off when he was in the middle of a sentence...and I wrote about The Jammer, as he called himself, with the beam-bright smile and the broad, broad shoulders, who, once, at his cousins' place, sprinkled sugar on my hair to show just how sweet I was...and I can tell of Troy, behind whose beard resided a Judith Jameson fan, and who, despite his campaigning for affirmative action, never once let me inside his heart...and Mac, running deliveries for the dry cleaners by day so he could play trombone at night, forever telling me that his home phone was out of order, or had been wrongly disconnected, despite the woman's voice that answered it when I found the number in the directory...and also Junior, who, when I asked if he, too, thought that women don't hold theories, but tell stories, smiled and replied that that sounded OK, if I said so...and I can tell of Michael, the whisperer—but isn't this enough, isn't this entirely enough, how many must there be before one of them does the trick—before one gets close enough to your own experience to effect some sudden sparking, some mobilization of empathy and response—in other words, some sad narcissistic shimmy—which is the only thing you'll pay attention to...and which is exactly, which is precisely what I am after...

...but no: I do not want that any longer...not at *all*...that is part of the past...the unworkable past...for I will no longer settle for merely exchanging emblems, for working surrogate linkages...those are the failed strategies of the past...the techniques that, simply by virtue of being techniques, had always guaranteed my disappointment...because I know that there is more than that...that there *are* unencoded connections, unmediated contacts—I *know* that they exist...they must exist, I must believe this to be so...and this is what I want—what, in truth, I have always been after...an end to emblems and strategies...finally, an *end* to those things that, in truth, were only frantic compensations for the felt absence of genuine conjunction...

...but how long it has taken to see this...how astonishing that I realized this only recently, that it only came to me a few months ago...after half a lifetime of inconsequential little sufferings—you see, I can read your mind—it was only recently that I put this together...during a regrettable little episode—the details of which I won't bore you with—featuring someone called Stephen...but when the realization did come, it came decisively, definitively...the realization that my failed strategies and frantic compensations had to be done away with...that once and for all I had to get *beyond* them...for my tendencies had taken on, I realized, a self-perpetuating force, the force of a narrative, one whose irresistible, onrushing self-determinism led every time, every time, to disappointment...and so I realized that I had to break out of my narrative, to smash it entirely, this ordering of codes that always betrays its content...in other words, the time was ripe when Raymond came into view...because Raymond, it was evident, it was immediately evident, was someone for whom my making such efforts was warranted...yes, it was perfectly clear that he was someone who demanded it, who would under-stand...Raymond—the tall man, the good man, the one whose fineness could not be advertised or asserted...the man who took my hand when we went down stairways, who weighed *my* words, a person who listened...the man who said that the hallmark of an evolved soul is compassion, and only compassion—that intelligence is not the ability to make connections between ideas or things, but between people...the man who knew...he was a high-school teacher, an educator, teaching twelfth-grade elective courses in sociology and a subject that he had introduced to the curriculum, urban studies...an admirer of Lewis Mumford and of Durkheim— remember the social market, he would say, the social market—he hoped to go back to school so he could teach at the university level...he had ambition...and he had a density of being, a warming presentfulness that washed over you when you were in his company, a sense of personal solidity that arose more from his thoughtful self-command than from his full frame and bulky shoulders...he had been raised by his mother and his three sisters, and so carried a comfort with women, a delicious relaxation of barriered strangeness and gender antagonism...he hated rudeness in all its forms—he called it the most offensive four-letter word—and kept his guard up against such abuses...there was some sensitivity there...and though it did not happen often, when he laughed you knew that it had been earned, that some surprising discovery had come his way...we met at a gas station on Lomas Boulevard, in line at the inside cashier, waiting to pay before pumping...there were few words, but he left with my number...I thought about him all that day, his warm-burgundy voice and his unfussing directness...when he called, the next evening, we talked endlessly, effortlessly, about spontaneous everything, as if propelled by some mutual automatic pilot...it was as if we were already old friends, easy confederates, our ceremonies were straightforward and simple...and I could tell you more, because there was more, and it was good...and I was determined to preserve the good, to keep it from dissipating, to prevent our relations from turning too mannerist...for he was worth it, how clearly he was worth it...and how clearly he would understand...

...we went to an Italian restaurant one Thursday night soon thereafter, our first time out...then, two evenings later, we went to a movie, followed by a trip to a neo-Deco diner...and we talked, and talked, and touched fingers, and we held off making love, because we understood...because I understood that I did not want my narrative to take over, I did not want to surrender to its undeniable determinism...so the next day, after work, I went out for a walk and thought things through...I spent 45 minutes walking around Old Town and its passionate two-story sham, going up 12th Street and all the way past and around I-40...then I sat out in the square in front of San Felipe...from a bench facing the amber Franciscan relic, I hooked my thumb on a whorl of iron rising from the baroque black armrest and looked over to the tourists' Mexican restaurant on the east side of the square...and to its verandah, which had been white-line divided into parking spots for the native peddlers to sit in...and by the time I returned home I had seen what I had to do...for I had been given an opportunity, I had been given my chance...clearly it was time...finally, I had been presented with someone who would understand, someone through whom I would be able to put an end to my past patterns, to free myself from myself, once and for all to smash my narrative...indeed, Raymond would want nothing else, he would demand it, the man who listened would accept nothing but the ending of my punitive self-incarceration—he would lend me the energy to achieve my own escape velocity!...for he would understand...you see, with Raymond I could not bear the thought of remaining mired in patterns that would keep me mostly absent, that would make me hold my essential center back...no, with Raymond I wanted to be, for the first time, fully present...and he, too, I was certain, would welcome an end to division and distraction, an escape from emblems and strategies...and after the first words there would need be very few more, for we both would understand...so I decided to speak with him the following Thursday night, when we had informal plans to go to the Caravan East, a cowboy haunt that still manages to be tolerable...and I decided not to plan what I was going to say too much, to overly package things, because I felt that presentation and salesmanship would be inappropriate, even opposite to what I had to say...and I decided not to strive for effect, or to do anything more than just say what I wanted to say straight out, simply and directly...for style is sickness, and cleverness is the enemy of content...and then, that evening, wearing nothing special, I opened the door...

...Ray came in, and we quickly embraced...his warmth and big-boned huskiness, solid beneath his Harris Tweed blazer, comforted me...he smelled, as always, very good... lacquery, grainy...I steered him to the divan in the living room, and offered him something to drink...but I did not have the cranberry juice he requested, so he said he would wait...and we caught up on some day-to-day this and that, and then, not really intending to start just yet, it came...and now that it was coming, I let it go...I did not want the pointillist discourse of everyday, I loosed myself in waves...for minutes in a row, I felt what it felt like to eddy...to empty...and I attempted, above all, to get at the truth, not the masquerade that declares itself as genuineness when, habitually, the truth is invoked, but a wholesale leveling of the artifices of personality, a selfless plunge into...into what I had thought must remain forever hidden, to the substance of what I had always kept in shadow...to that point where self becomes sorrow...to my fear that I was so essentially distanced from all other people that I had been consigned to a lifetime of solitude...to my sense that something within me sought to poison all good times with awareness and analysis, while leaving all bad times undiluted and pure, and therefore miraculously potent...to my certainty that awareness had made me incapable of marshaling the ambition and the cruelty necessary to excel, or even to survive, in this world...and I told him of my fear that I could never let my thoughts out, to share them with others, because anyone who heard them would become infected by them, would become infected by *me*, by my disease...for I was a virulent agent...and I told him of my even greater fear that my listeners would *not* become infected, that they would *not* understand, because the rift was so great that nothing could get across...and I told him of my inability to participate in the simple rituals of life, the talking and transacting, the dressing and greeting and circulating, the blisses of the commonplace, because I was always denying and denigrating...and how I felt as if I was being punished for the sin of understanding, that my virtue was my undoing...but also how I took a secret pride in the thoughts that were my scourge...and how I have never felt, never once in my life, as if I were a part of anything...that I have never once felt as if I was in a context that made sense for me, and in which I belonged...in other words, that I had never felt there was a place for me, a genuine place, anywhere—but rather that I had been torn from my time and left flapping and tumbling in history's slipstream...and I talked of my certainty that there were other people who felt as I did, very much the same, but that even if we found each other it wouldn't matter, it wouldn't make a difference...for it was too late...and I told him of my horrible fear that my struggle had rendered me incapable of achieving my struggle's objectives, that the process was irremediably undermining the goal...that my spine was being progressively mangled by my efforts to stand up straight...and I talked of hating this quicksand consciousness...but of the fear that my self-definition derived, to a terrifying degree, from it...from its pure destructiveness...and I talked...and I talked...

...and when there was no more to say, he already had his arms around me...at first, when I was talking, he had reached over and taken my hand, and stroked its fingers...and then he knelt by my upholstered couch, looking up...then he sat on the armrest...and when I was through talking he was beside me, hugging me to his shoulder, strongly, and kissing my temple, and the side of my face...at first he said nothing, and that was preferable, for I felt naked and scared and hollow and fearful of what words might do...I was short of breath, my heart was knocking, as if I had just run to jump on a departing bus...but, still, he held me...and at one point, just for a moment, I thought I felt him tremble, too...and then he talked, for I could say no more...so he talked, he whispered...and his words, delivered from close, shimmered in my ear: Bless your wounds...

...in time, we assembled ourselves and, in silence and inconsequentialities, prepared to leave...outside, going to his car, we walked arm in arm...I realized that I had forgotten my purse, but decided to leave it behind...for at that point I did not need money, I did not need identification...the Caravan was relatively quiet that night, with only a few rowdies...but the music was nice, some local boots-'n'-guitars originals band that wasn't too loud, and Raymond and I smiled and small-talked while sipping bourbons...we embraced fiercely when we said good night, underneath the yellow lamp at my door; Raymond's hard kisses pressed the bones behind my face...later, my bath, long and very hot, proved generous and worthwhile, despite the lateness of the hour—it was past 1 AM before I was able to get to sleep...and I was grateful that Raymond had understood that the time still hadn't been right to make love...when the call came, at 8 PM two days later, I knew instantly...the usually articulate Raymond began with silence, then faltered over his words, and I knew instantly...instantly...almost as if I had been expecting it...still, I had to fight to prevent myself from putting the phone down, from simply hanging up...but I listened, and I continued listening, as he talked, slowly and with difficulty, of how touched he had been by what I had said, how it had stirred him, how he had been so moved and had felt so for-tunate...honored, he said, chosen...and then, when he said, in a lower tone, that he had been thinking, though, that he had been neglecting his work, that he really should be spend-ing more time with it, all I did was jump in and say I understood...and after a slight pause, he just said thank you...and I replied, again in calm voice, That's all right...you see, there were no harsh words...no harsh words at all...why should there be discord?...because, you see, I accepted the call well...in fact, I accepted it as confirmation...as confirmation that I had been correct about Raymond all along...that my instincts had been exactly right...that I had accurately sensed, at our first meeting, that he, too, was a creature of solitariness, and that this was what I had responded to in him from the first moment, from the first words...and so I understood, and still understand, that Raymond's call was, in fact, his means of bringing us together...certainly, together...for he, clearly, had understood that we could be together only by remaining unbridgeably distant...because solitude, he understood, is our shared condition...our defining mutuality, our mode of access...the only means available to us...and so, alone, we would be together...in the community of isolates, we would achieve our link through separation...our dividedness would be the proof of our bond...as I have said, I understood...so I let him go, to welcome him to me...to confirm our alliance...

...I stayed indoors for three days afterwards, over the entire weekend...I clipped coupons, and left off area lights, and got down to the seemingly permanent presences in my refrigerator, those musty, forlorn backshelf derelicts, so I would not have to call anyone, to emerge, to make contact with otherness...and I looked at a lot of TV...but I did not miss him...I did not know him well enough to miss him...a fact that I had counted on...after all, the narrative has to be good for something...if only to help console the loss that it had guaranteed...and, of course, during those three indoor days, I found myself reflecting, and reflecting over and over again, as we all could have foreseen, on my father...the father that

I still find myself thinking, and genuinely believing, that I never had...for that is how it feels...how it feels to me...after all, my father left, as I was told, even before my mother knew she was pregnant...so then what he did, on one level, wouldn't even qualify as leaving...for there was nothing there to leave...my parents were very young...he, I tell myself, was an adventurist...in fact, he was just a boy...a boy who took a shot...I was told that he had widely-spaced, beacon-bright eyes...and that he liked strong coffee...that he would fling his hands around when he talked, and would stamp his feet from excesses of energy when he laughed...he was introduced to my mother at her father's place, when both happened to be visiting...my mother later said that she had never met any-body like him...his puppy's spirit was infectious, she said...he was interested in everything, she said, and would talk with anyone who he thought could tell him something...which he seemed to believe was just about everyone, she said...one time, my mother recalled, he stopped the car and climbed on its roof to look at the moon, hanging huge against the night horizon...he went on about it for minutes, she said, why it looked so big, how it was an optical illusion due to the proximity of the landscape...and he would talk about his dream to see every single state in the country, and to have a friend in every one...but since he didn't have the money to travel, he liked to look at travel pictures, even personal ones stuck in an old beat-up book...he had written to, and received a few letters back from, Edward R. Murrow, that was a big thing...and although he didn't have a profession yet, he was ambitious, my mother said...and she also said he wore natty shoes...and...and you see, I'm still a sucker for this...a total sucker for this shit...for all of it...for nothing but a dream, a dream that forever returns, the desperate dream that aligns me with my time: the dream of the absent father...

...but where has it taken me?...unto what have I been delivered?...unto nothing but exile, internal exile...exile and neo-Pythagorean silence...where I carry my own censor within me...and crush my own insurrections...alas for the egg!...for I have read about oceanic feelings, but I know about dying of thirst in the middle of the ocean...and I have heard about the thousand points of light, but I have seen that they provide no warmth, no canopying glow...but such is the program, our great cultural project, the perceptual imperative laid down by the whole Democritus/Descartes/Leibniz slice-'n'-dice cartel...by dividing, by reducing, that is how we understand...making the atoms and particles ever smaller, ever further subdivided, that is how we know them...and so with us...we are each of us an experiment...we are each of us a problem that needs to be worked out...to be thrust into isolated focus, to be understood...and you can read all about it in De Particulier à Particulier...but after a while, don't you remember, after a certain point the particles cannot again be divided...before long there is just nothing there...nothing beyond spontaneously assembling forces...which then spontaneously break down, and instantly decay...rot, decay...in other words, after sufficient reduction the situation becomes inherently unstable...it becomes both self-creating *and* self-destroying...it endlessly consumes itself, and can only be fixed, can only be calmed, by an observer *outside*...don't you remember?: one of the few things that Relativity and Quantum Theory agree upon is the necessity of the observer...in other words, events, their very *existence*, requires two agents...but if existence is a meeting, then how can I...

...and thus I search...thus I hunt among you other poor neo-Pythagoreans to find a means of ending my ceaseless dissolution...thus I spend my life hunting for an actualizing gaze, for a certifying touch...for a true and certifying touch that will put an end to metalife...to existence as compensation...thus I hunt for the intent touch that will turn particles into waves...but, you see, my search is faulty...my efforts are evidently amiss...for though I labor to achieve this reunion, though I suffered to summon my actualizer with truth, it did not work...so, clearly, what I was offering was not it, was not the truth...even then I could not get at it...even then I had only come up with, a disruption, of truth...because I, too, am a lie...*I am a lie*...a false appropriation of reasons and resources—*even the resource of sympathy*...and so my tainted undertaking could not span the gap...

...and so I send myself back into deep cover, I slip behind my screen...a rare foray aborted...while reciting the saw that comforts as it cuts: if a rock falls on an egg, alas for the egg; but if an egg falls on a rock—alas for the egg...and thus appeased by confirmation...precisely assured in what I know...rather than shouting out *motherfuckers—fuck you!*, I curl into the silence of confirmation...the final consolation that there *is* a pattern...that events, even at their most isolated, conform to a larger flow...to the flow that proves that Darwin got it wrong...that both Darwin and Spencer, the great competitivists, turned things on their head...that the two of them, our favorite imperial porte-parole, were infected by a middle-Victorian conqueror's optimism that entirely corrupted their findings...I mean, just look at the statistics...natural selection, the survival of the fittest—that can*not* be the case...it *can't* be...those laws speak of a teleology that can*not* be supported...*just look at the evidence*...the impetus for the life-processes cannot be for the One, or the One Group, to survive...for the One Group would then be stranded in a world that is unvariegated and unworthy and infinitely lonely...and then its members would set upon annihilating themselves due to unendurable boredom, unslakeable guilt and a residual instinct to struggle...until there was truly only One...altogether alone, pathetic and pitiable...no: it's just a matter of looking at the numbers...at the weight of evidence...of switching perspective...by any measure, the survival of the One is teleologically worthless in comparison with the endless and harried struggles of the indeterminable fucking trillions that didn't make the grade...it's only blind optimism to say that the survival of the One is what counts, that this is what is driving the system, while the incomprehensibly vast and unending ordeals of the numberless trillions is insignificant...this position is indefensible...so the purpose all along was *to bring these ordeals about*...that was the *goal*...that was what the structure was set up to accomplish...thus, amidst the world's ceaseless struggle and inevitable death, it's clear that the final purpose of life, of biological existence, is to create *the maximum possible suffering*...that is what the experiment of life is for...that has always been the plan...and that is the scheme into which we fit...indeed, it is the scheme through which all our actions finally make sense...perfect sense...and the vision through which the world, and the entire human enterprise, is gloriously, extravagantly, superabundantly successful...yes: we are worthy in proportion to the quantity of our suffering...it is our metric...our final adjudicator...our judgment...our indisputable reason...

...but no: there is no evolution: there is only serial ecology...Darwin was only an advertising man, an egomaniac...while the vision will only come from an egomaniac without an ego...so good luck...still, evolution remains the model through which we create...it provides the inspiration, and the incentive...yes: Man, the Creator...the activity through which everyone must make his contribution...even I, who am otherwise feckless...I, who otherwise sits in my living room, impotent, barely breathing...it is here that I can pitch in...that I can make my meaningful contribution...for I, too, am given over to imaginings...to idealizations...I, too, confect scenarios...I see playings-out of imaginary though inevitable destinies...I am possessed by sightings and dramas...dramas cast in gray tones...and hard surfaces...dramas of ashen people lying side by side on an office-tile floor...in a gray room, cold with air-conditioning...and the feeling of a cold, hard floor pressing against bellies and knees, a cold floor unyielding against outstretched elbows and chins...and there are pulses pounding, and bleary sweating, and choked-in whimpering...and erratic, gaspy breathing...from all of the terrified people, stretched out in a line on the unyielding floor...only capable of seeing table legs and dust motes, and the bottoms of wastepaper baskets and the squared-off bottoms of desks...while sweating and whimpering...and then there is a boot, a crashing boot...slapping the linoleum floor, a boot—*no, two of them*—high and laced and black...and the boots are striding through the room, thunderously...big boots smacking the linoleum, in thunderous steps, scattering dust clouds and paper clips among the bottoms of metallic table legs and the short square stumps beneath bulky desks...then from overhead there is shoving and crashing, and pens and staplers and curls of paper spraying down to the linoleum...the cold hard lined linoleum upon which they are splayed...and then more thunderous steps...and the sound of slamming drawers, and shoved chairs, and shoved chairs crashing to the ground...then knocking and settling...and the rattling of cabinet metal and the kicking of file drawers...and more shoving and scattering...and wondering why there is no siren sounding...and a boot loudly kicking a wastepaper basket, sending it crashing into a metal desk...and the ground-smash of a desk lamp and the further spray of pens and memo pads and paper clips...some of which land against arms and cheeks, and on the smalls of backs—though they cannot be removed—*they dare not be removed*...and then there is bursting and further kicking, then further stepping, then the stepping's slapping growing faster and louder and then going silent and then there is whimpering and screaming and whimpering and then silence and then the horrific clicking and—

— God no God no God no God no God *no* God *no* God *no God no God no no*—

— and please and please do not do *not* and please do please do not *do not*—

— my planting my seedling my planting the window view porch window and Helen and Helen and never I never *I never*—

— but not like this *like this* on the ground like animals like skins like animals *on the ground*—

— take just take me I give take me I rape me take me take just leave the just *leave them*—

— and God oh Len dear Len at end oh God oh God poor Len but Len but Len was it I can't was it Len was it *God*—

— maybe pity he'll pity he'll think or pity pathetic pity pathetic in vomit God vomit look look at pathetic look pathetic look *look*—

— and grab and grab quick ankle down shoulder and fall climb grab smack and everyone then everyone on top on so *go* so go *so*—

— in my head in my skull through my hands *in my skull* through my hands this can not I can not this can not *this can not*—

— *shit* on me on my side wet his fucking shit *shit* on me

on his *him* on me *on me shit him*—
    — to the end of seeming and the end of urgency, to the pristine re-sipping of sovereignty, of light, with supple sounds rising and twining, with—
    — though they stood by the ditches just waiting and thinking just standing and looking down in the ditches silent and looking horribly waiting not fleeing not fighting not fleeing *not fleeing because alone where could where could they go*—
    — so tell me now tell me I have waited so tell me a lifetime of waiting and seeing a succession of seeing the barque at the dockside poised and waiting for loading so tell me now tell me now *now tell me*—

Hi ho—

    — Just thought you'd like to know that a chaffinch is singing by my window — chortling out cheep trills and chirp cadenzas — perched tall upon a rounded bough...
    — Although the song, if you really listen, actually sounds more screechy than anything else...
    — Just thought you'd like to know that...
    — In other words, 'tis another letter, yes 'tis, I may be

forgotten but, alas, I'm not gone — so letter rip — letter ride — oh, letter *rest* — but 'tis true, here we be, back again, right in yo hot little hands — and it's good, it's very good to be back, just now, in what passes for touch...

— But if the chaffinch lore seems, unlike me, unlikely, then let me swiftly aver: 'tis true — for I seem, somehow, to have moved again — yes, I now find myself decidedly living *somewhere* — in fact, yo's truly is now a dweller in a rented house (and, if that doesn't sufficiently floor you, I will add that I actually only rent the upstairs) in the decidedly unbumptious burg of Emporia — yes, there — there where the postmen and the pharmacists still smile, where a kid pedaling a bike recently received a speeding ticket, and where time itself seems to have slept in — in other words, there's enough good stuff here to sustain *anyone* — including, among such stuff, I might add, and so I will, a willow, all moody and mighty, out by the Meherrin River, a lone wood that looks as if it had been co-produced by Arthur Rackham...

— But why such moval and removal, you may wonder — well, it all began a few months ago, when a good buddy — who's also named Robin, wouldn't yer know it — rang up and, in the course of carousing, happened to mention that a nifty-sounding small business out thisaways was looking for some administrative help — and she said that the business was called Apeiron, and that they're a bite-size but growing distributor of nontoxic art supplies — well, of course, all that seemed like sufficient incentive for me to zip up my zip code and exchange identities yet again — for self and sameness, you see, are not the selfsame thing — one's sighs can't always fit *all*, after all — and so here I am, outfitted with a roomy new me — though this latest me, I might add, is one that I think I can learn to be comfortable with, one that I would like to get to know a bit — and so I think I will do just that, here in the o'erabundant calm of Emporia, where I can richly participate in all its furious inactivity — woman is an island, of course, but at the moment I genuinely seem to be in the market for some time for myself — or, rather, for developing a species of self that knows how to negotiate with that ole tyranny of time...

— Not that my time with Chomsky wasn't big-time boffo, of course — for it was, it certainly was — and it will continue to be for as long as I have morphemes in me to describe it — after all, the man is one of our national treasures — a ferocious fighter for pure right — although most of the folks he's fighting for will never know it — though now, I must say, what lingers with me about Chomsky, even more than his passionate championing of the most enlightened ideals, is his essential gentleness, his reasoned and resolute calm — his steadfast insistence on maintaining a stance of honorable humility — in fact, he himself once articulated it, one time maybe four months ago, at one of our colloquia at the Institute — it was just one of our weekly set-togethers — as usual, there were about eight of us present, sitting around a circular table in a backstairs seminar room — laureled in smoke, jotting in opened notebooks, hanging onto his every word — that day, we were talking about Nancy Dorian's book Language Death, and I remember that, at one point, Chomsky's low, cultured, melodious voice offered the words We must recognize that our comprehension of nontrivial phenomena is extremely limited — yes, that was what I heard — and then he went on to say We understand only fragments of reality, and we can be sure that every interesting and significant theory is at best only partially true — you see, I've memorized it — his antidote for arrogance — and I remember sitting there listening to him, and being awed by his powerful sense of humility — and being inspired to think that the only qualities worth feeling proud of are those that lead to a total sense of humility — well, coming from such a headstrong man, Chomsky's words moved me as much as if I had been listening to the Juilliard Quartet, performing late Schubert — and if you'll just hold on a second I'll go dig out my notebook to make sure I've got this right, and thereby do the good Chomsky justice...

— OK — so — I've got it — it was right under the lamp in the back room — so — so then, if I can read my own hand-writing, the class then went on to something interesting — something really pertinent and interesting — a discussion of what Chomsky called "counterevidence," which is his term

for facts or findings that just don't fit in with whatever
research or experiment one happens to be doing — y'know,
all the things that just don't accord with your theory — a
situation that crops up virtually all the time — so then
Chomsky went on to say, as I see it here, that When conduct-
ing real research, serious questions usually arise concerning
the attitude one should take toward apparent counterexamples
— At what point, he continued, must they be taken seriously
— and then he said In the natural sciences, apparent
counterevidence is often ignored, on the assumption that it
will be somehow taken care of later — whereupon there was
considerable debate among the class — debate about such
things as factuality and reliability — and about what good ol'
Tommy Kuhn would make of all this — but Chomsky then
went on to add, if I'm reading correctly, that Such a stance
regarding counterevidence is quite a sane attitude, within
reasonable limits, because it is a precondition for any significant progress — that is, if I understand the Chomps correctly,
we've got to learn to live with a bit of counterevidence, and
even just to forget about it, or else we'll never get anything
done at *all* — because there'll *always* be a few things that are
a little off, and we just shouldn't let them hang us up — but
at that point, alas, my day's notes end — and such sad sad
whiteness it is, at the bitter bottom of my notebook's page...
   — Chomsky's attitude about counterevidence, I might
add, without getting *too* counter about it, is a handy one for
him to uphold, because he can use it to justify some of his own
more speculative linguistic work — it builds a little breathing
room, y'see, into his theorizing — but Chomsky, bless him,
also applies this idea elsewhere, outside the realm of science
and into all sorts of situations — one thing you can count on
with this guy is a sense of principled consistency — and, in
fact, some time after the colloquium, Chomsky published a
piece in the Phoenix (natch: the Globe never touches him)
that dovetailed with precisely these issues — it was, as gloriously predictable, an excoriation of Iran-Contra, and how
its prosecution was being across-the-board botched — for
while the whole Iran-Contra deal was obviously a dangerous
perversion of justice and democracy and public trust, as

Chomsky described it, the country was losing that sense by getting bogged down in the counterevidence — which, by the by, 'tis all too true — the counterevidence of the meretricious patriotism being flaunted by a photogenic criminal — and of the mythic unaccountability of bureaucracy — and of the untouchable amiability of the hairmaster — scusi — just felt me blood boil — and I tell you it was an effective piece, altogether pungent, and we all congratulated Chomsky, after it came out, in the certified way — with our patented few-syllable deadpan appreciations, all of them along the lines of a mumbled Nice work, Professor — acclaim, you see, is not something Chomsky's terribly comfortable with — must be counterevidential to his identity by now...

— As it happens, though, something happened with the piece — something kinda interesting, in fact — because someone, it seems, in the local bureau of CBS seemed to have read it, and to have seen something of merit within it — because a few days later a phone call came — check it out: a phone call! — a phone call inquiring if the good Professor might be interested in making an appearance on no less than Face the Nation, to discuss what he had written — now sit back, if you will, and think about what this means — for twenty years, since haute Vietnam, Chomsky has been a mainstream-media pariah — fully as absent on American television as Ceausescu has been present on Rumanian tube — in other words, Chomsky's was a voice virtually entirely silenced, all but denied on the channels that count in this country, despite his continual and strenuous efforts for that, shall we say, not to be so — he was the alternative negated — by the cries of freedom of speech made by those with chokeholds on the microphones — so when the phone call came it was, shall we say, more than a curio — after all, this was one of the *networks* beckoning, proffering a national broadcast — and a widely-respected national broadcast, at that, with a prime perch on Sunday morning — so Chomsky just went and holed up in his office after receiving the offer, making notes — for if they wanted him on Face the Nation he was going to be prepared — and although word of the offer spread through the department almost instantaneously,

Chomsky took things in stride, letting some of us know casually, almost inadvertently — in fact, he told me about it when we crossed paths on an Institute stairwell, after mentioning a thought that he had had concerning a paper I'd written on freedom of word order in Walbiri...

— But then, a few days later, I had a surprise — a real surprise — when Chomsky, to my adrenaline-y delight, called me into his office and asked me—yep, me—if I would accompany him to the interview — *well*, now, I thought — but then he explained — he sat at his desk and explained that the interview had been scheduled for the following Sunday, and that he had decided to travel to Washington to do it, rather than being beamed in from Beantown — quite calmly he said that he wanted to sit down with the program's host, that he wanted to be in the same room with him — for some reason, that seemed to make a difference — and he had also thought, he said, that he would like to have an ally along for the journey, perhaps to assist him if something came up — well, that sounded plausible enough to me, I thought — though I wasn't about to deny him anything even if it *hadn't* sounded plausible — so, of course, I immediately up and agreed...

— CBS flew us in on the following Saturday afternoon, and put us up in the Ambassador Hotel — separate rooms, of course — no embedding of *these* dependent clauses — and I found myself very happily adapting to the place's lovely, understated class — and especially to its wonderful shower — *mmm...* — that evening, we took in an OK Italian restaurant down the block — Chomsky isn't one for making reservations at Sfuzzi — and walked as far as Thomas Circle, talking phonology — but then we made it an early night, for the limo, you understand, was due at 8:00 the next morning — we met in the lobby, come the big day, and were met in turn by a driver who was miraculously punctual — Chomsky was wearing an everyday jacket and tie, both of them beige-ish and altogether unmatching, while I tried to be nondescript — the ride to the studio was brief, through streets that, except for some straggling taxis, were largely deserted — and *boy*, rich folks like their leg room — at CBS, smack downtown at 2000 M Street, we were escorted into the lobby by the driver, where we were met by a big-smiled, handshake-happy guy named Chuck — Chuck then conducted us through some large doors into the long-corridored building, and led us straightaway to the guests' waiting room — whereupon Chuck said that we should, quote, just hang out for a while, and then he scooted off...

— The room was a moderate-size rectangle, with upholstered chairs touching much of its perimeter — along one wall, a table offered muffins, bagels, a coffee pot, styrofoam cups, and the like, while another table in an opposite corner tendered the Sunday Post, the New York Times and a telephone with many buttons running up one side — meanwhile, a large television set, mounted on a massive black metal arm that jutted from high on one of the long walls, doused us with real-time CBS — and thus we settled in to wait — as I did, Chomsky looked through various sections of the Times — and largely kept to himself — though after a ten-minute buffer interval, I did venture forth and hesitantly establish a rapprochement with one of the table's blueberry muffins — which had nice crumbly stuff on top — beyond that, the room was quiet, though there was a good measure of to-ing and fro-ing in the corridor outside — at one point I got up and ambled out of the room, and then took a small look around — surprisingly, no one seemed to mind — probably because there wasn't too much to see, beyond the hallways and a few darkened studios — so I ambled back in, and we waited — and we read — and we waited — and we read some more — and once I saw Chomsky look at his watch — and, in fact, he was right — it was getting somewhat close to air time — *very* close, in fact — but then I reasoned that his kind of interview doesn't require too much in the way of preparation — so I just sat back and, p'haps inevitably, surrendered to the tube — though Chomsky continued to read the paper, or just to look into the distance, consulting his own thoughts — and then a young guy, who was not the Chuck who had led us in, bopped into the room — he was nicely muscled, and was carrying a clipboard, and seemed a little pasty — and he began by saying Uh, Mr. Chomsky? — Pardon me, Mr. Chomsky? — and then he said, after clearing his throat, that there had been a change — a decision had come, he said, and he lowered his eyes — a decision had come to go with another guest who, unforeseeably, had just become available, right at the last minute — the decision was that it'll make for a timelier show, he said, and then he coughed — newsier, he said — and then he got to it, yes, he got to the big word — sorry, he said — I shot up from my chair, but before I could sputter too much Chomsky cleared his throat and said, with perfect calm, that it was entirely all right — and he hardly moved at all — he just sat there with his hands on his knees — then not-Chuck exhaled and said thanks, thanks for your understanding — thanks a lot, he said — we appreciate it, he said — we're sorry to put you to all this inconvenience, he said, but things like this happen all the time — it's built into the nature of the news business, he said — understood, Chomsky said — again, it happens all the time, anti-Chuck said — understood, Chomsky said — and finally he got up...

— Looking down at the carpet, unChuck told us that the car would be ready whenever we were, then apologized again for, quote, any inconvenience — Chomsky reassured him that it was no problem, no problem at all — and then he asked to visit the men's room before leaving — and so he was led away — leaving me in the presence of the burbling tube, and just shaking with conflicting feelings — with feelings of rage doing battle with feelings of confirmation, along with a sorry tincture of shame — I mean, I could not believe it, I just couldn't believe what had happened — the brazenness of it, the shamelessness — and as I stood with one hand on the waiting room's banquet table, I was shaking, I was just shaking — my body was expressing what I would not allow myself to say — and so, before too long, I too had to look for a bathroom — in other words, I just had to get out of that place — so I drifted down the corridor in search of someplace else to go, and passed a sequence of darkened, dormant studios — and when I slowed and looked through their thick, gray-tinted, acoustically-reinforced glass, I could make out glints and sheens on the studios' inactive consoles — and all kinds of knobs and cables and screens — and it all seemed so mysterious, so computery, so intriguing and alluring and powerful — in other words, the studios were exactly the kinds of places you always wanted to be — but still, I continued on, looking for the bathroom — passing doors, and swatches of wall, and a mail chute — then walking still further — yet I couldn't seem to find it, the bathroom — I wasn't even in a place where a bathroom seemed likely to be — so I decided to turn down another hallway, which led to a quiet area — thinking that I would have better luck in that direction — and so I wandered into a darker stretch of the building, and I continued searching doors for the appropriate emblem — but I only came across signs offering Dubbing, and Post-Production — and then, without forewarning, I saw Chomsky, standing in a shadowy recess in the wall — he was just standing there, facing away from the corridor, in towards a dense stack of cardboard boxes — they were empties that were waiting to be thrown out, I believe — but Chomsky was just tucked in there among them, alone in the dark recess, holding his glasses in his left hand — and with his posture somewhat bent — so I touched his sleeve, and he turned around rapidly, and said Oh — and then he emerged from the recess, while putting his glasses back on — and then he quickly gathered himself together, he became himself again — Here, he then said, while looking down the hallway — Here: I think what you may be looking for is over here — though when I heard the wavery tone in his voice a part of me dissolved — in silence I let him walk me on — and point out the door — very graciously — then he turned away when I went in — and then, when I was finished, there were no more paper towels by the sinks, so I couldn't dry my hands...

— We made it back to the hotel and arranged to jump on the first plane out — saying no more than functionalities to each other all the time, and comporting ourselves somewhat formally — I wanted to speak with him more substantially, of course, but I also wanted to honor his silence — because, I can tell you now, I was boiling — I was boiling about what had happened, I was just raging — his treatment, I thought, had been indefensible — un*think*ably rude — as we probably should have been able to foresee — but for a moment there, just for a moment, we thought that we had found a chink in the armor — we actually thought that we had been given an opportunity — a smidgen of a chance — but the structure, as always, is self-correcting — it has protected itself with layers of subsidiary defenses — ranks of backup SDI's — noise-gates against the dreaded biodiversity — some bigwig powerlunch producer cooks up an entire three-day prime-time TV mini-series just so he can scare up the right bone marrow for his son, who's been stricken with aplastic ane-mia—I heard the story the other day—and Chomsky can't even... — I mean, never once, not a *word* — not a fucking *fricative* — fucking media — fucking *communications* — but enough — enough of this — I mean, *enough*...

— In fact, that was exactly what I was thinking all through that time: *enough* — that was the word that kept chiming through my mind, for days after we had arrived back in Boston — the word that haunted me, that besieged me, relentlessly, seemingly compulsively — the word that was with me as I sat at my carrel in the library — and as I waited in supermarket check-out lines — and while I sat for long intervals at the unclothed kitchen table in my two-room Sommerville apartment — *enough*, I kept thinking — *enough* — *enough* of these internal contradictions — *enough* of the internal contradictions coursing through the Chomsky situ-ation — *and* of those that were knotting within me — *enough,* it was — *more* than enough — because seeing an instinct towards rightness being ignored, or denied, was an intolerable thing — because living with the terrible tension of being right, but irrelevant, was debilitating, corrosive — because witness-ing the freedoms of democracy being used as a license to war on democracy was just awful — and it all just left me *bursting* with rage, absolutely *unbundled*...

— And yet, and yet — and yet Chomsky, I knew, would just go back to his office and get back to work — the next day, I knew, he would be back at his desk, diligently writing ream after ream of reasoned argument — still pressing on, as if something had a chance of mattering — producing marrow for anyone who wanted it — and who had the resourcefulness to find it — because this was what Chomsky knew was right, and what had to be done — simply to persist, to continue —

in the wan, hideously outdated hope that rightness, that justice would eventually be acknowledged — that it *must* be acknowledged — and his passion, his magnificent passion, it seemed so much more solid than my own — solid and centered — and so deeply grounded in sources that were moral and intellectual — whereas my involvement, it was becoming evident, principally sprang from the emotions — and thus seemed so insubstantial — and, as I was beginning to fear, so fragile, and terribly perishable — fully as durable as gossamer — or, in other words, simply insufficient for the job — for what had to be done — and thus his excellence, I was coming to see, was also a measure of my weakness, of my insufficiency for the challenge — his incendiary glow was illuminating the fault lines and flimsiness of my involvement — beyond question, beyond comparison, his example showed me for what I was — with all of my shortcomings — for if he was the kernel sentence, then I was but a transform — and it was difficult, then, to see my model suddenly serving as a present lesson in my inadequacy, my derivativeness — because through him I could see that I was not a source, but a reflector — a reflection — a trick of light — and while I still adored Chomsky, adored him supremely, the thought then came that I also begrudged him, and even resented him, because I was not him — and could never become him — and this, I saw, was a difference, it was a distance that I did not know if I could bear or sustain — and so, then, I knew, riddled by these coarse thoughts, I knew that I had to put Chomsky past me — to make him part of the past — to establish another order of distance — in other words, to fight off the disease of proximity — because his principled excellence was too much of a burden — because the demands made by the fact of his existence were simply too difficult to support...

— And so, eleven days later, I was gone — I packed, and talked, and told, and took incompletes, and was gone — reducing two rooms of possessions to a few stuffed and taped cardboard boxes, strewn among heaped discards of what I had once thought central to my identity — but I had to go — I had to — Sommerville, Cambridge, they had both become uninhabitable to me — I resented their streets, when I walked

on them — I even resented the sound of the towns' names —
because, you see, I had become useless — yes: useless — not
only useless to Chomsky, but to myself — because, quite
simply, I had begun to doubt — yes: to doubt — and that
could not be abided — because I knew that once I had even
considered the possibility that the struggle was unwinnable,
or just not worth it, then I was already unfit for the struggle
— indeed, I had already been excluded from the ranks — for
the first breach, you see, is the conclusive one — that is to say,
we get only one chance — only one — in other words, as you
can well hear by now, they had won — against me, they had
won — *they had won* — and I was too tired to mount an
opposition — too tired for much of anything, for that matter... — so what to do? — where to go? — in which direction
to retreat? — because there are no choices left: where can
anyone go? — it's either the Procrustean bed or the centrifuge, take your pick — and I am not enamored of either
technology — no, not at all — this is not my way at all — and
so, here I am... — right here — keeping company with a
chaffinch — looking out a wooden window — unto trees —
standing by myself — listening, just listening — patiently
listening — and feeling like a nomad playing a game of
musical chairs — it's when I sit down that I am out...

    — And that, as they say, be that — though that, alas, be
me — I am my source, but I am my squandering — and that
be that — but what now, you may be wondering, for lil' ole
me? — what be going on? — and what, when, and wherefore
for the future? — well, we can't quite say, at the moment —
for the nonce, it's the same old nonsense — clearly my so-
journ in Emporia, and my stint at Apeiron, is transitory,
however much fun rifling filing cabinets can be — but still, we
all know it ain't gonna last — so I have my antennae up, and
my ear to the rail — one thing I've been considering, I'll have
you know, is, pace Rabelais, joining a Benedictine monastery,
or make that a nunnery — for they have some traditions that
I have come to think are mighty OK — such traditions as
humility, silence, and stewardship of the land — well, why
not? — and another alluring lure at the moment, I'll have you
know, something that I think would galvanize me egre-

giously, would be to go off somewhere and study the resonant, discombobulating work of Jung's most famous student — that being good ole Piaget — so that I can get to know something about stumblebum humanity before it is... — but let's hold back on completing that thought, shall we? — there'll be no obscenities in *this* interstate epistle...

— In fact, I would very much like to continue with my Piagettian plunge, which I began somewhat informally a few months ere I scooted Cambridge — but it's kinda tough to research the good researcher out here, I must say — and I should know, because I've been trying — a few weeks ago, in fact, soon after my glorious installation in this backwatery burg, I went a-hunting for some unprobed Piaget, because it's been a while since I've consulted anything new — so I drove over to the one bookshop in town, a place on the high street that closes for two hours at lunch and also stocks greeting cards and party fixings, but they, alack, had nothing — so the next Saturday, when I had some more time, I headed over to Grizzard to continue the search, but the general store there only had airport inventory — and the apparently preliterate Capron, where I went next, had no bookhandler at all — well, this was getting a bit vexing, I must say — most vexing indeed — and the situation wasn't helped when, the next Wednesday, I went into Lawrenceville, where I finally found a bookstore with a Psychology section, and then saw that its two shelves were 80% stocked with Self-Help — a subsequent outing to Roanoke Rapids turned up a Christian bookshop, and this, in fact, was well appointed—except for the fact that it had all of world fiction housed in one tiny cabinet, and arranged alphabetically by title...

— Finally, I realized that I would have to do what I had, since the outset of this Piagettian quest, balked at: essay an excursion to the Petersburg Mall — yes, I know — I know very well — but I was sure a few chains would have outlets there, so I managed to work up the nerve — I went on a sunny Tuesday evening, right after wrapping at Apeiron, and managed to find a parking spot relatively close — so close, in fact, that when I got out of my car, I couldn't even see the east and west ends of the mall's bi-level immensity — still, I marched forth — and as always, when I entered the place, I got that good old glandular transition-thrill: that unconscious physical perking up when you exchange the unruly for the orderly, the unplannable for the purposeful, and warm, gusty air for still, chilled, breathable crispness — all wrapped in a complementary security blanket of Muzak — I walked down the entrance corridor, and immediately passed a jewelry shop, a cigar store, a nut seller, and several other brightly windowed businesses — then I hit an intersection, where the mall's second floor lifted into view, atop a multi-angled courtyard of plastic benches, planters filled with sturdy shrubbery, an unflowing fountain, and refracted lights — meanwhile, throughout this orchestrated space, harmonious hundreds of people were milling, windowshopping, pushing strollers, and holding soda cans in round keep-'em-cool sleeves, while their abundant children, in large sneakers, straggled along or spirited about — and a piped-in rendition of Let It Be, performed by a high-cholesterol string ensemble, made the whole thing look like affectless, Nijinskian choreography — I then proceeded to the court's opposite side, where I found one of the mall's schematic maps, that black-backed circuit board from whose Candyland-colored rectangles and cross-referenced number system I managed to figure out that there were, in fact, two bookshops in residence — but you don't even have to ask: they were at opposite ends of the place — though, happily, both were on the first floor — and so I set out...

— At first I walked past a shoe store, a yogurt shop, J.C. Penney's, lots of women's clothing outlets, a funny-card-and-sexy-poster shop, several mannequinned haberdasheries, Nottebohm's pets, a little shed where engravings are made, and many more shoe joints — and then, they all kinda began to blend into a blur — nevertheless, people were entering shops, leaving shops, out on general patrol, and all was functioning smoothly — clearly, some folks had found their place — and amid the slightly disorienting vastness and variousness, the continual, nearly subliminal Muzak-track reminded me of the Islamic notion that one can never really get lost, because God is everywhere — forging ahead, I decided against sampling the fragrant trays of the California Cookie

Company, and easily passed up a stuffed baked potato, offered by a stand that was staffed, it seemed, entirely by children — then, before too long, I found Waldenbooks — its manicured presentability, all pastel shades and softness, immediately evoked table lamps and soft slippers — the store had a magazine rack along a wall up front, along with display tables sporting bestsellers standing on fanned pages — with red Sale signs in the shape of bookmarks taped to every tome in sight — also up front, droves of thematic and celebrity calendars slid around several wider tables, while a girlish cashier sat with a blank expression among the curvily-lettered paperback-promotional displays that cluttered her slightly raised counter — I strolled into the store and, against a wall towards shop-rear, found the Psychology section — happily, its few shelves weren't too bad, with a fair offering of Freud and Rollo May — but, alas, it was slim pickings on Piaget: just the Phillips primer and, pleasingly, Understanding Causality — and so I knew what was coming, I knew it all too well: I would have to make the long march back across the mall to the other bookshop — though while leaving the Waldenbooks I noticed that it had an entire wall filled with video games...

— Then, *shoop*, I was out again, and looking upon the appeased, presence-of-the-sacred procession of the mallfolk — from my position just outside the flow, the motley ambling drifters embodied an uncomfortable combination: they were both so familiar and so alien — but then, though, I was back in among them, negotiating my way, and the sequence recommenced: shoe stores, a camera shop, framed prints, Snooks', ladies' wear, candies and dried fruits, a home-electronics emporium called Unit 731—and I swear that I hadn't passed a one of these stores while walking in the opposite direction — then, however, I came across a lighting shop that had some interesting-looking floor lamps — tall bronze ones, all nice and swoopy — as it happens, I've been looking for something along these lines for my front room — so I decided to break from the shopping stream to investigate, when *boom*, I smacked hard right into something — and it really was a good jolt: it stunned my shoulder and chin and startled me terribly, bringing a kind of roaring to my ears — and the guy

I hit, a plaid-shirter of about 30, also got it hard: he was knocked back across a nearby plastic bench, and ended up sprawled among some adjacent potted shrubs — apparently he hadn't been looking either — so I went to him and hastened with my apologies and my please forgive me's, of course forgetting my hurt for his — but he was nice, and gentlemanly: he shook his head and waved his hand, then mumbled something conciliatory — still, I felt awful having clobbered him like that, so as the guy regrouped and brushed himself off I went and picked up his Walkman, which had been knocked off by the collision — happily for me, it still seemed to be in one piece — but to make sure it was still working, I brought the headset to my ear, and gave it a listen — whereupon I was astonished — I mean, *really* astonished — for I immediately heard that the Walkman was playing the same thing, the very same, as was on the malls' Muzak track — exactly the same recording, at exactly the same time — the two were as one — and I was just astonished — I mean, I put the Walkman to my ear and pulled it away, and then did this a few more times, and just heard the same thing, inside and out — the music was absolutely continuous, some syrupy well-known tune played by the same winds and strings, precisely in tandem — in other words, the dosages were identical — exo had commingled with endo — communion was complete — the spped bump had been erased — it could not be denied — so a little voice inside me gave a little *Yikes!*, before I handed the Walkman back to the guy and produced a few more burbled apologies — and then, gratefully, I was off — happy to be merging back into the crowd — walking a little dazedly, perhaps, and rubbing my shoulder a bit — and forgetting entirely about the floor lamp that I had seen — and who knows?: it may actually have happened...

    — *Other*wise, as they say, life trundles on — I flourish in spite of myself — here, there, anywhere — I still have trees to hear and songs to see — and, in fact, I see, just now, that the chaffinch aria, just outside, seems to have turned seriously sweeter than it had been — well Bravo, beaked songstress — but as for me, I manage to manage — although I'm not quite sure how I manage *that* — but, actually, enough about me —

or, should I say, enough about *I* — really, though, it's enough — *more* than enough — and I suspect I won't get any disagreements from you on *that* — because, while I have you on the line... — that is, inasmuch as you're here, I realize that this is quite an opportunity — yes it is, it is a rare and special one — because, while I've got you here, I must say that I've been wondering about you — yes I have — I have indeed — I've been wondering how you're doing — how you've been finding things — what's been, as they say, going on? — so tell me... — tell me what's been going on with you... — really, tell me — but hey: what's this silent treatment... — I mean, why this no go? — because, you know, you don't have to hold back any longer — really, you don't — I mean, all of that is over — all those days are gone — so really, now, you can finally let go — yeah: you — that's right, *you* — you holding this hot number in your little hands — so come on now, tell me — really, it's been a while, so I'd like to hear — I mean, don't worry about it, just lay it on down — so come on, tell me, let me hear... — hey: *come on*...

— Oh...y'know...; I'm OK...
— Yeah?...; you sure about that?...
— Yeah...; sure enough...
— Because...well, if you don't mind my saying so, I've heard better...
— Well...; I'm gettin' there, y'know...
— That's good, then...; that's good...; glad to hear it;
— Yeah, we're gettin' there...; you know...

From nowhere, a small sedan pulled up along our right-hand side and shoved past; evidently, it was in a hurry; reflexively, I tugged a little to the left, even though the speeding sedan was already showing bumper:

— I hear you, Archie then said;

We breezed down I-58, traveling along an embankment that left our eastbound half of the highway at least 25 feet higher than the road heading west; between the two paved strips, the slope of the grassy divider was so steep that a mountain goat wouldn't have been able to hold a comfortable footing; by then, dusktime was settling upon us, merging the tree banks that rimmed the highway into foggy darkness and

limiting visibility along the road ahead; I turned on my headlights, and they silhouetted the insect speckles that were
splotched across the windshield, pockmarking the forward
beams; so I squish-footed some detergent water out from the
engine—it took three good pumps to get the liquid up and
jetting—and hit the wipers; before too long, the bug remains
had been converted into the outline of an open book, pressed
flat against my windshield; it was a nice warm night:

— So how'd you like the fair?, Archie then said, placing
his palms against the dash in front of him and slowly
stretching his arms; he accompanied this with stretching
noises:

— Oh, it was OK, I said: didn't see too much of it,
actually, but it seemed OK; not really my cup of tea;

— Yeah, Archie said;

— There was that big Vasco da Gama's galleon that they
had there, that was OK, I said: all the reds and oranges that it
was painted, and the way it swung like that, way up, back and
forth, crazy...

— Yeah, Archie said, and yawned: it's kinda weird: first
they sell you the sausage rolls, then they invite you onto a
decathlon for the digestive tract;

In fact, I had only stopped into the fair to stretch my
legs; it had been a long day—I was up at 6:15, and out well
within the hour—all of which had been spent in driving,
except for a 20-minute layover for lunch; so when I saw the
sign for the fair—a sandwich board without a man sand-
wiched between its two halves—on the side of the highway,
I decided to investigate its red-lettered offer of Over 80
Attractions; the turnoff came about ten minutes later, after
which point I drove through about four miles of lowlands,
and past a continuing sequence of guide-signs that got more
worn-looking but less enthusiastic as they progressed (from
the early Fantastic Fun! to the final Just Keep Movin'); the
parking area was a greensward populated with lines of trucks,
cars, and RV's, and as I locked my car I could already hear
volleys of balloon bursts, gun shots, and disjoint music
coming from behind a course of trees; I walked towards the
sounds and, before long, came upon the outsprawling spread

of game-booths, all wrapped in a glaring, dark-orange hue; like a surreal Western town under siege from its own inhabitants, the fair held, in every direction, people shooting rifles, hurling projectiles, and participating in pointless noise, while other folks went into Horror Hotels or pressed up against small glass cages and finger-fed them coins; I strolled among the sound effects—whistles, sirens, bells—and the strings of visitors, going along a once-green walkway that had been abraded down to stony siltiness; eventually I went ahead and bought a cotton candy, when I came across a stand that didn't have a line; then I continued walking around; at one point, a contingent of heavy-metallers, in torn blackness and boots, drifted by, making fun of all the attractions; but then three of them suddenly grabbed pistols that were mounted on posts in one booth and began a mock-shootout, twisting the pistols around to riddle each other with invisible bullets; they laughed while doing this, but not after they had hastily abandoned their game; continuing on, I easily resisted the bumper cars, but a huge circling slide that must have been about 40 feet high did almost get me; eventually, though, I decided that I should limit my traveling to what I could accomplish in my car, and so headed back to it; I was doing a few squat-thrusts before getting in when Archie emerged from the trees and asked if I was heading anywhere near Suffolk; it was somewhat awkward, but I figured why not; he had a reasonable-sounding voice and was wearing a Ronnie Gilbert t-shirt, so I found myself, despite my inclinations, inviting him in:

— Incidentally, I then said, because the thought had just occurred to me: how'd you get over there?—to the fair, I mean;

An eighteen-wheeler grunted past us, on the left:

— Hitched, Archie said, from his now somewhat slumped-down position: made good time, too; the second ride got me to where I could walk the rest of the way;

— Mm, I said;

— Yeah, Archie said, and straightened up a bit: hitching's a good thing, all around;

— Hm, I said;

— Really, Archie said: it cuts down on gas, and you meet

all kinds of people, and the people really tend to open up
when they know they're never going to see you again;
    I laughed:
    — But it's true, Archie said: when you're hitching you
can get into some serious getting to it;
    — Hm, I said;
    — Yeah, he said: you know, they figure Why hold back?;
Where's the usual incentive?, and you can see they kind of
like it;
    — Mm, I said;
    — Really, he said: like one time, I got picked up around
here by this guy in an old Ford Econoline; it was white, and
he said it was a '75, and he had built up the rear part of the van
so that it was like a bedroom, with a mattress and a table and
things, so he could sleep in it; so I get in, and we're going, and
the guy just gets into all this shit about his dad, just right off:
he starts talking about how the old man used to beat up on
him for no reason at all, really slap him around and pull his
hair, and how his father used to call him a hundred-thou-
sand-dollar jerk, because that's what he heard it costs to raise
a kid—
    — Yow, I said;
    — Yeah, Archie said: really good stuff; and then the
guy told me that his father owned a taco franchise, and that
things got really bad at home when the franchise flopped;
then his father started attacking him for any kind of ridiculous nonsense, like once when he got caught using a buttertub
lid as a frisby—he got incredibly smacked around for that, he
said; and he got zapped for every single time he didn't ace a
test at school;
    — Hm, I said;
    — Yeah, really, Archie said, fidgeting a bit in his jeans:
but the guy told me that it was even worse for his sister, if you
can imagine it; she was also abused;
    — Mm, I said;
    — But she got over it, Archie said: at least apparently she
did; the guy told me that his sister found Jesus; she saw Jesus
in a phone booth;
    — A telephone booth?, I said, and broke into a laugh, but

then reined myself in;

— Listen, that's hitching, Archie said;

We sailed under the sign for the Courtland turnoff; immediately past it, posted much lower to the ground, were the area's informational glyphs, indicating a hospital, food services, sleeping possibilities, and information; the traffic was now relatively sparse, though the stars had not yet fully bloomed; still, the seeping darkness was growing dense, and was beginning to instill its usual mixture of immensity and intimacy; sadly, there wasn't much of a moon; I rolled my window up a bit:

— Yep, that's about the only reason I'd drive, Archie said, looking out his window: to pick up hitchers; I'd go around all the time just to do that;

— You're old enough to drive, though, aren't you?, I said; he looked around 24 or 25:

— Oh yeah, Archie said;

— So...

— So, I gave it up, he said, and took a breath: about, oh, two years ago; it always made me kind of jittery;

— Mm, I said;

— Yeah, Archie said, and looked out his window: I mean, with all the three-laners around here—y'know, what to do?; which one should you use...?

— Mm, I said;

— I mean, the right lane has all the cars entering into it, coming on the highway sometimes from a full stop, and the left is where everyone is really pumping gas, and it has all the high-speed passing; then in the center you have cars on both sides of you and, by necessity, all the crossing; so, you know, where to go?; which one makes sense?; so I figured hell, you know, with an attitude like that I'll probably cause the accident myself; better just to give the whole thing up;

— Hm, I said;

Though the road was empty, I pulled the car slightly to the left, then to the right, all the while remaining entirely within my lane; then I settled back where I had been, in lane center, and felt, somehow, more comfortable; then, however, I felt it was time to effect a liquid exchange, and decided to

stop at the next opportunity; but then I recalled seeing, before
the last exit, a sign proclaiming Last Facilities for 18 Miles; so
I skootched up in my seat and unclenched my left pants-leg,
which had tightened up around my thigh; then I settled back
into place:

— So, what'd you think of it?, I said;

— What's that?, Arch said;

— The fair, I said: how'd you like it...?

— Oh, you know, Arch said: not really my cup of tea
either;

— Mm, I said;

For the first time in several minutes, headlights appeared in my rearview mirror:

— So, if you don't mind my asking, why'd you go?, I
said: I mean, if—

— Why'd I go?, Archie said;

— Mm, I said;

— Hm, Arch said, and shifted in his seat: I went because
Erwin died;

— Mm, I said;

The headlights came up beside us and, after a period of
rushing noise, reemerged as parking lights:

— Who's Erwin?, I said;

— My gerbil, Arch said: my ex-gerbil;

— Mm, I said;

— Picked up some kind of distemper, about eight days
ago, Archie said: just got it from the air;

— Hm, I said: sorry;

— Yeah, Archie said: it was kinda rough; had him for
seven years;

— Mm;

— Had him forever, Arch said: since I was a kid, it seems;

— Mm, I said;

— And he was really cool, Arch said: really clever: he
would move from the palm to the back of my hand as I turned
it over, and he used to eat Orange Pekoe tea;

— Mm, I said: sounds like he was nice;

— Yeah, Archie said, and shifted his weight: I really miss
him; he meant a lot to me; I mean, I was really upset when

he died, amazingly so, when I came home and found him...
— Mm, I said;
— I mean, I was, like, *to*tally blitzed; I walked around
crying the entire night, and then couldn't get to work the
next day; I mean, this is *Er*win we're talking about, right?;
and even after I buried him it was bad; I put him in an old
Whitman's Sampler box that I found, and took him over to a
little brook near where I am, but afterward it was like I
couldn't forget about him; I couldn't let go; I mean, *no more
Erwin*...
— Mm...
— And this went on for *days*, Archie said: I was really
hurting for the guy, and it wasn't going away; I took two more
days off from work, and then when I got back it was like I
couldn't concentrate anyway, and the night times were like
*to*tally given over to him...; it was really fucking awful...
— Wow, I said;
— But then, you know, a few days ago—I think it was
Thursday—I began thinking, you know, *wait* a minute...just
wait a minute here; I mean, it's a gerbil, it's only a fucking
*ger*bil, let's keep some perspective on this...
— Mm, I said;
— And more than that, it's only one par*ti*cular gerbil; I
mean, what's the big deal here, with this one gerbil, with this
one animal?; you know, everything has to die, it happens a
zillion times a day, so why fucking kill yourself over one
arbitrary animal?; I mean, *real*ly...
— Yeah, but—
— I mean, he wasn't so drastically different from any
other gerbil, so what's the big deal?, Arch said: so then I began
thinking, you know, that I wasn't really hurting for *him*—for
Erwin, that is—but for *me*, because *I'm* feeling self-important;
and then it occurred to me that I've been buying my own
propaganda too much, that I've been hurting because I think
that *my* situation is special, because of my investing this
animal with something of *me*; and it all seemed so, I don't
know, so self-serving, so, you know, hierarchical...
— Hm;
— Yeah, he said: I mean the whole deal, it seemed to me,

was springing from my sense of centeredness—from my converting some arbitrary event into something with special significance; really, that was it, that really was it; and it just put another chill on the whole thing...

— Know what you mean; even so—

— But you know, I've been doing some reading about Relativity recently—that's Special Relativity, 1905—and Einstein understood a thing or two, and one of the primo postulates of Special Relativity is that there are no absolute centers, that no point can really be said to determine any others;

— Hm;

— But if you stop and think about it, that also means that *every* point has a claim to a kind of centeredness; in other words, now that every point is free of any larger architecture, any one point can claim itself as the center of everything, at least as validly as any other point can; so a really literal reading of Special Relativity lets you, for example, go back to geocentricism—to claiming that the universe really is spinning around the Earth; it's now perfectly justifiable; and the theory lets you go even further, to claiming that the entire cosmos is actually centered around *you*—

— No thanks—

— Yeah, really, Archie laughed: but the theory permits it: it's in the math, or something; but then I figured, you know, wait a minute, this can't be the case; I mean, who needs it?; it's a prescription for all kinds of bad shit—like, why vote?; I mean, this isn't, like, something that *I* want to live with—

— Mm;

— I mean, I don't want to *know* from that shit, in no shape or form; so then, the other day, I decided to put it to a test—that was the only way to check it: the scientific method, empirical evidence, go out and see for yourself; and that's when I thought of the fair;

— The fair?, I said;

— Yeah, Arch said: I thought there might be something useful there; so I hitched over this afternoon, and got in around 4:30; and then I just looked around a bit, at all the booths and stuff; and then I saw a ride, and decided that that was it; it was the one called the Spinning Tilt, over by the Ferris Wheel—you must have seen it; anyway, I waited in line and got my ticket, and then was led up a metal stairway and onto the ride itself: it's one of those rides that's like a huge spinning platter, maybe 80 feet across, with a wall running all the way around its perimeter; so I went up on this big disc, which has all these black lines radiating out from its center, like spokes, and a guy made me stand against a marked position along the outer wall; and after the guy had put people in every one of these positions along the wall, when the circle had been entirely inscribed with humans, the guy split and the ride began: something somewhere began to hum, and then the huge disc began turning; at first it stayed flat, and went very slowly; but then it began to pick up speed—and I'm, you know, moving around the circle with it, going around and around, just like little Antoine Doinel, going quicker and quicker; but Special Relativity says, you see, that another perfectly valid way of looking at this is that *I'm* stationary and it's the *world* that's moving, that everything is just spinning around immobile *me*—and I wanted to see if this could be the case; so the disc continues turning, and getting faster, and as I look out the fairgrounds are dissolving into blurry colors and streaks of light, and I begin to feel myself being pushed back against the ride's metal wall; and by then I'm getting a little nervous, you know, I'm feeling it in my throat, because it's already going really fast, and then all of a sudden the ride *really* takes off—I mean, it just gets faster and faster, unbelievably fast, and I can only see speckles and bleary smears of color and hear the racing of the engine; and then I close my eyes because they're tearing so much—and then I notice that it's becoming hard for me to move, and then that I really can't move at all—in fact I can hardly budge a muscle, I'm pressed back into nearly total paralysis against the wall; I mean, I can't even control my head, everything feels heavy and leaden—and then the ride begins to lift up on one side, the whole spinning disc begins to tilt, and so we're whipping around this raised circle up into the sky, going *way* up, not strapped in but just powerfully pinned into position, you even feel it in your jaw, and the whole thing is going unbelievably fast, and you have no idea what the fuck is going on—and then I forced myself, I forced myself to do it, to open my eyes, and I did it, I managed to do it, and all I could see was a teary streaking of lights and little bubbles of color before I had to close up again, to shut myself in; so it couldn't be, it couldn't be the case, there's no way that all this was moving around me, Einstein was wrong—

He lapsed into silence, then put an arm out to the dash, to brace himself; returning my eyes to the road, I thought it best just to leave him be for a moment; I even eased up on the gas a bit, to contribute what I might; still, the night shunted on, wrapping around us; I looked up ahead and saw that we . would soon be crossing a small suspension bridge, and I readied for it; it was nice and quiet without the radio on:

— So, Archie finally said, coming back: sorry…; I began to feel a little nausefied there, just by talking about it;

— No problem, I said;

— I've always had remarkable powers of self-empathy, if you know what I mean…

— Yeah, I said: sometimes feel the same way myself…

— Yeah, Arch said;

— If you know what I mean…

We both laughed:

— So that was it, that was my proof, Arch said: almost didn't live to tell it, but there it was; my story had been about Erwin;

— Mm, I said;

I picked up a little speed:

— So how about you?, Archie said, and cleared his throat;

— Sorry…?

— What brought you there?, he said: I mean, why'd you stop in, if you don't…

— Oh, I said: you know; just looking for a break;

— Yeah, Arch said;

— I've been driving for a couple of days, you know, so I thought I'd give the legs a stretch; maybe get some of that good fairgrounds food;

— Watch it, Arch said: I'm already feeling a little queasy
over here...

— Yeah, I said, and smiled: sorry...

— Hey, Archie then said, and tucked one leg up underneath himself: did you see that couple that was there, the ones
on the crutches?; kind of old folks...?

— Don't think so, I said;

— Yeah, Archie said: they were the best thing there; kind
of a human attraction...

— Hm, I said;

— Yeah, Arch said, and let his leg back down: they really
were kind of OK; I caught them just by accident, after I had
come off the ride, the Spinning Tilt;

— Mm, I said;

— Mm, Archie said: you know, I was kind of feeling like
shit at that point, and I needed to reassemble myself a little;
so I went over and sat on the steps of a skeeball booth that for
some reason was closed...you ever notice how nice those
booths smell?...anyways, I'm sitting there, waiting for my
innards to subside, and I happen to look into the midway and
there's this couple doing something really cool: they're a
couple of stocky little people, must have been about sixty, and
he's wearing an old-style fedora and she's in a fur coat; and
they're both handicapped in some way: both of them have
something the matter with their legs; so they've rigged this
system whereby they move by linking one of their arms and
using a single pair of crutches to hoist themselves forward—
that's together, in one movement, like a big swing; and it
worked, it worked really well, with the two of them between
the one pair of crutches: they took big lurches forward, and
really got where they were going, moving very quickly; I tell
you, it was pretty cool...

— Yeah, I said;

— Mm, Archie said: it was really something to see;

I checked the speedometer and saw that we were scratch-
ing 70; so I eased up on the gas a bit—not that there was any
real risk at that rate, cops always give you 5 mph's worth of
grace—but just because it felt better at that pace; it was a nice
night:

— So where you off to?, Archie said;

— Oh, I said: Virginia Beach;

— Yeah?, Arch said: I've got some family over there, a bunch of cousins; they're all musicians; if you're going to be hanging out for a while, I can probably get you a number or something;

— Nah, I said: you know, nice of you, but I won't be there too long; thanks, though;

— You got it, Archie said;

— Mm, I said;

— So what's bringing you there?, Archie said;

— Oh, I said: work; just for a little while;

— Mm, Arch said;

— They've got an Arts Center over there, I said: I'll be going in there;

— Hm, Arch said: never heard of it;

— Yeah, I said: there's a curator there I'm hoping to speak with; he's supposed to know his stuff; so...

— So you're doing research, Archie said;

— Kind of, I said: in a way;

— Sounds interesting;

— Not really, I said: it's mostly personal stuff; got to check something out;

— Mm, Arch said;

— Yeah, I said, and glanced down at my speedometer: my mother died a few months ago—

— Hm, Archie said: sorry to hear that;

— Yeah, well, thanks, I said: but it's OK, it wasn't too bad;

— Mm, Arch said;

— Anyway, she passed away back in March, and when she died I got this call from the Town Clerk's office, which, as you might imagine, was a little strange...

— Mm, Archie said;

— So then I had to get over to where she'd been living, to take care of things, which also wasn't too pleasant; and I also had to clean out her apartment, her three rooms, which had, you know, like sixty years of accumulations crammed into it; so I called in a service and we had a tag sale—just over one weekend, I didn't want it more than two days;

— Sure, Archie said;

— And we got rid of most everything, I said: even her bed, even her old-style nylons; then I got a liquidator just to haul everything else off;

— Mm, Arch said;

— And that was that, I said;

— Yeah, Arch said;

— An entire life sold off, I said: taken to term with that act;

— Hm, Arch said;

— Taken to term, I said;

— Mm, Arch said;

— But then, you know, a few days later, something came to me, I said: I mean, I knew something else had been kind of nudging me while this was going on, and finally, one night when I was back home, sitting in my living room, I remembered what it was: my mother used to have this, like, photo album that had originally belonged to her father—

— Oh yeah?, Archie said: really—?

— Mm, I said: but then, you know, after he died, we had it in our house; and I realized then that I hadn't seen it, that I hadn't come across it at all...

— Isn't that—

— I mean, I'm positive I didn't miss it when I was cleaning the place out, because I went through everything at least a couple of times, to make sure there wasn't any hidden money or something that my mother had stuffed away somewhere; so I'm sure I didn't just overlook it...

— Boy, Archie said;

— But I also can't imagine that she ever threw it away, or that it—I don't know—that it ever got destroyed, or anything like that: that's also impossible; it's just inconceivable...

— Yeah, Archie said, and exhaled hissily: it's rough, those kinds of situations...

— Mm, I said: it's, like, so *now* what...?

— Mm, Archie said: so do you have any family, any brothers or sisters who might have come in and—

— No, I said: no one; there's really no one else;

— So then maybe someone borrowed it, or maybe—

—Nah, I said: nothing like that; couldn't be; my mother didn't see too many people...

— Hm, Archie said;

— Mm, I said;

— So—I mean, you think it might be in Virginia Beach?, Archie said;

— Not really, I said: I mean, I'm sure it isn't; but, you know, I may be able to get some leads, or information, or...I don't know...

— Mm, Archie said, and turned to look out the window: so I suppose it just comes down to the same old story: why'd you wait so long...

— Yeah, I said: you're right...; you hit it...

— There we go, Archie said, and yawned;

We passed a dark station wagon that had a pair of upturned bicycles mounted, antler-like, upon its hood; then we drew up behind a large, huffing Snooks' delivery van; I accelerated to get past the monster, then slowed when I saw it signal for the next exit; soon, it veered away; beside me, Arch pulled one foot up on the seat; then he gave a good stretch, bending his torso back over the top of the head guard:

— But, you know, I then said, bringing my eyes back to follow the tug of the headlights: the other day I kind of realized that I *have* been looking for it...

— Yeah?, Arch said;

— Yeah, I said: even if I hadn't realized it, I have been looking, all along...

Arch said nothing;

— But somehow, you know, the whole thing would, I don't know, kind of slip my mind, I said: it would somehow get away...; I'd get distracted, or involved in other things...

— Mm, Arch said;

— Really, I said;

— Mm, Arch said, and yawned again: if you say so...

— *I* don't know, I said;

— So you've got to get past all that, he said: you can't just reduce it to a hunt, to an endless chase;

— No?, I said;

— Not at all, he said: it's not that at *all*;

— So tell me, I said;

— And it isn't just the violence and the pain, although of course there's enough of that to keep *everybody* happy...

— Really..., I said;

— I mean, you've got to keep the people coming back...

— *Really*, I said;

— What it's really about is survival, he said: the ability to persist;

— You think...?

— Definitely, he said: every film, if you think about it, is just a sequence of discrete smaller films, each of which retells essentially the same story;

— OK...

— That of the Coyote trying something, then killing himself;

— OK—

— They all replay the same microdrama of compulsive self-destruction, endlessly repeated;

— Of course;

— Certainly more *could* happen in these films, but of all the possible pathways to funniness, the Coyote favors just one;

— That's what makes him the Coyote;

— Precisely; moreover, the Coyote seems to retain nothing from blackout to blackout: after every scene he's right back at it again, intent on killing himself one more time; it's out of view finder, out of mind, for this guy: the boulder and the abyss teach him nothing; one frame later, he's forgotten everything;

— Funny;

— And he's none the wiser for his experience;

— Mm;

— So, OK, that's part of it, he said: but for me, the more significant thing is that, every time, the Coyote just comes back: the world somehow *allows* him another chance; he's always given another shot, as if he had not just killed himself; *that's* what matters in these films;

— Hm;

— You see the puff of dust, but he just comes back with another, identical story, and then it all begins again; and that's why I find these films literally miraculous: they're miracle plays, pathologically repeated, in which all the violence and destruction have very little to do with the central premise—this miraculous capacity for coming back;

— Got it;

— So rather than being about the Coyote's willful self-obliteration or Sisyphean failure, the films are actually narrating his resurrection—his ability to return, no matter what he does to himself; they're really tales of resurrection...

— Allegories of continuity;

— That too: our unknowable but assumed continuance; it's the same sort of denial or delusion that gave rise to the Christian drama;

— Mm;

— And, for that matter, to the Viconian myth, and to all the other theories of history's rhythm of return, be it Toynbee or Saint-Simon or Tertullian or Nietzsche, *any* of them...

— So despite all the pain and frustration, the films are actually rather optimistic, I said;

— Of course;

— Future-oriented;

— Even though the future is exactly the same as the past: a boulder blamming down on your head;

— Yeah, I said: though considering the alternative, it sounds pretty good to me;

— Mm, he said: but in some of the later Coyote films, if I remember, they replaced the great Warner Brothers orchestra with really cheesy canned music; I don't know if I'd want to come back for that;

— Not a chance, I said;

— There we go, he said: remember: the word Muzak comes from combining the words music and Kodak;

— Sorry—?

— That's the origin of the name, he said;

— Mm, I said: incidentally: I thought those things are known as Road Runner films...

— Generally, he said: I mean, I suppose...

— So—

— So that's just public relations, he said: they're obviously and patently about the Coyote;

— Yeah, I said: clearly...

— Incidentally, he said: speaking of resurrection...how do they know that Jesus was Jewish...?

— What's that?, I said: oh; oh...; how...?

— He lived at home until he was thirty, and the only reason he didn't go to law school was that he got nailed on his boards...

— Yeah, I said, and smiled: heard that one before;

— Oh, he said: sorry;

— No problem, I said: it's still good;

— Mm, he said: so then let's try anti-resurrection: did you hear the one about the self-destructing Honda Civic...?

— Yeah, I said: Jeez, that's rough...

— I mean, *Jesus*—I'm going to have to get back to campus before 7:30 tomorrow morning to make sure I don't get towed...

— Yeesh..., I said;

— And there's no playing around with security there, he said: I know one guy who ran out and saw his car in irons when he overslept by ten minutes...

— No one tougher than campus cops...

— It comes from a heightened sense of the value of the practical that they develop around there...

— So you have any idea what went wrong?, I said;

— You tell me, he said: I came out of the movie, just like everybody else, and got into my car, just like everybody else, and then just sat there pumping the gas and twisting the ignition while everybody else drove off and left me abandoned in the lot; it was kind of humiliating...

— Mm, I said: so tomorrow morning—

— I mean, it was just so bizarre: the thing was just dead, it had no life in it at all; and she had purred just fine on the way over from my place;

— Listen, I said: it happens...

— Maybe the car's become a pluralist, and is taking its

stand, he said: maybe it's come to think that the history of
Dead Blue Hondas has been suppressed on campus, their
culture and traditions and contributions to mainstream society...

— Could be;

— Especially after it saw how strongly speedbumps have
been embraced by the canon...

— OK, OK, I said;

— Yeah, he said: sorry...

— But tell me, I then said: you know, I'm going to be
heading back into Grand Junction tomorrow, and, you know,
if you need a ride...

— Really?, he said;

— Sure, I said;

— That would be great, he said;

— Sure, I said: I could get up a little early for you...

— Well great, man, thanks, he said: it would save me a
huge hassle;

— You got it;

— We can meet on the highway, where you drop me off;

— Sure enough;

— Well, great, he said: that would be terrific;

— No problem, I said: I'll be there;

— So you teach over at Mesa State?, he said;

— Me?, I said: no, not at all;

— Oh;

— No connection at all;

— Good, he said: cause for a while there I thought you
were this psychology prof that a friend of mine once had; her
description of the guy—physically—was kind of similar;

— No, I said: no connection;

— All the better, he said: she didn't quite cotton to him;
I mean, my friend's a nice girl—and a dead ringer for Cindy
Sherman, as it happens—but she said this prof was a real
Republican supremacist who liked to stand in front of the
class and impersonate Stan Laurel;

— Sounds lovely;

— Tell me about it;

— I'm just using the library, I said: doing some research;

— So you from Loma?, he said;

— Actually, from up near Minneapolis, I said: I'm only staying in Loma because all the hotels in Grand Junction are booked; there's some kind of storm-windows' industry conference, or something like that, going on;

— Yeah, he said: heard about it; you can't get a seat in a restaurant anywhere near campus;

— How about you?, I said;

— Sorry?, he said;

— You a student? I said;

— Yeah, he said: a junior; though I took a semester off last year, so I'm a little out of phase;

— So what you studying?, I said;

— Ways to adequately answer that question, he said;

— Sorry?, I said;

— Well, I seem to be a little late in declaring a major, he said: my faculty adviser said he's installing a hotline for when I make a decision...

— Yeah, I said: I remember faculty advisers...

— Actually, though, there may have been a breakthrough tonight;

— Oh yeah?, I said;

— Mm;

— So tell me, I said;

— Well, you know they had another film playing tonight—the one they showed after the Coyote film—and I decided I might as well stay around for it; and it was that early reggae movie The Harder They Come;

— I remember it, I said: I remember when it came out;

— Yeah, he said: you know:

> The harder they come
> The harder they fall
> One and all...

— Yeah, I said: it's a nice tune;

— And a good film, directed by a guy named Perry Henzel who no one's ever heard of again; in any event, the film, ya know, mahn—sorry: can't resist that amazing Jamaican accent when I get it in my head—any event, the film is set in the slums of Kingston, where they have these blocks and blocks of just un*bear*able shanties; I mean, they showed these *end*less rows of lean-tos and huts that are, like, made of slapped-together boards and corrugated tin, with nothing but ratty fabric for doors, and just piles and piles of garbage *ever*ywhere—the real eczema of the Earth; it was really a vision of the nightmare futuropolis—an entire town that looks like it's been pieced together from shit that someone's thrown out; but among all this horrific grubbiness, the local people are speaking with these *ama*zingly melodious accents, all singsongy and—

— I can imagine;

— Yeah: they have these voices that lilt *way* up and down; in fact, I think Henzel didn't use professional actors— except Jimmy Cliff, of course—in order to give the film some authenticity;

— Hm, I said;

— But the thing is, these people's accents are so thick that the movie is actually subtitled, to make the actors comprehensible—or at least it was in the print I saw; in other words, the people are speaking English, but at the same time they're also subtitled into their own language;

— Funny...

— And you know, at the end of the film, when I got out, and was walking across the parking lot, it just hit me...; and I thought *Hey*, you know, *Hey*: that's *it*; *that's* the answer; tell my faculty adviser he can go spelunking for the summer; I know what I want to do with my life: I want to translate English into English;

— Ha, I said;

— Yeah, he said;

— So why—

— Hey, watch out for that curve, he said;

— What's that?, I said;

— Look out for that curve;

— Where's—?

— There, he said, and pointed up ahead: right there; looks a little dangerous;

— Hm, I said;
— Hey look, he said;
— Yeah, I said: look at—
— Look at all that...
— Jeez, it's going on all through that area...
— But it probably comes around...
— Yeah; it curves, I'd think;
— It comes around—
— Actually—I mean, look—
— Yeah: *look*—
— But when she came around the corner of Chestnut sitting in the back of the Merle Norman convertible, just all pretty with her hair done up in a swirl and wearing her white chiffon dress, well I couldn't help myself, I just couldn't; so I pushed forward, I automatically just took a step forward to see better, to get closer to the curb so I could see her better— and I bunked into this woman who was there eating a fruit ice, this older woman; and she dropped it, the poor dear, the ice ended up on the sidewalk I'm sorry to say; I offered her another one, but I still felt bad, because I really must have given her a jostle—

— And then I saw this little skinny boy playing in the PS 44 band, and somehow he had been given the big bass drum to play, he had this huge round drum strapped straight out from his chest and, as all the trumpets were blaring away, he was booming at it with a big-headed stick; and then when the band stopped for a while near Stone Street, well the boy just bent forward and put the drum down on the pavement, and then just leaned down on top of it, to take a load off his shoulders; he must have been all exhausted, so he just went ahead and leaned on his drum, curving all around the drum-shell and holding onto it with his arms; but then, when the band started moving again he got stuck: his back wasn't strong enough to pick the bass drum up, so he couldn't move at all, he was stuck flailing on top of this big circle drum—

— And following were the fire trucks, one after the other, and they were so clean, not a fingerprint on them, they were so shiny, and the sun came pinging off their chrome and nozzles, right into your eyes, it made them water, but the sun was so high, it was nearly noontime, that I saw that all the people marching didn't have shadows, they had almost no shadows at all—

— And there were crowds all up and down East Main, and there were also people wandering all over Midtown Plaza, getting ice cream and sodas, they were walking all over, and I saw that they had put bow ties on all the faces in the Totem Pole in Midtown Plaza, every one had a bow, it was adorable—

— But then the Shriners went by, standing on the back of their truck, playing whiny flutes and horns and their leader whipping a huge curved sword around, making figure-eights in the air; and then I saw a truck with a big back hoe attached, hung with a banner from the Oak Growers Association, and then a car with a sign draped over its grille saying Crawford County Planning Board, and then—and then all the others just kept coming—

— Though of course the Ozark float was magnificent, just magnificent, with all the hyacinth and groundsel and hollyhock flowers all set out and draped on the flatbed in the form of a lovely front porch, and Anders Cosby and his wife sitting up there in rocking chairs limned with yarrow flowers, just rocking and smiling and waving so nicely, beneath a big bright yellow-and-red banner that said Doin' Great in '88; it was just magnificent, I thought it was easily the most beautiful float, easily number one—

— And then they had the Pony Express rider, with his mail sacks and his upturned hat, and I followed along with him, I just walked along as he went, though he looked a little frustrated at having to go so slow, and I followed with him as he rounded the corner and went down Exchange Street, and I saw they were laying a wreath at the War Memorial, all the men standing in black suits—

— Then the car with Puddenhead Wilson sitting on its roof went by, and he smiled and he waved at me, Puddenhead did, he smiled really big at me, and then the car passed and I saw this kid on the other side of Exchange, walking the other way—

— And then there was Jesse James, followed by the whole James Gang, walking down Exchange with their guns pulled and their rifles ready, all mean-looking and watching every way for lawmen but still, you know, kind of smiling; and then I saw this boy, walking the wrong way behind them—

— Walking right in front of all the people standing on the other curb, he didn't look at them, he didn't even seem to notice them, I saw him, kind of doubled into himself, walking in the opposite direction—

— And he just stormed past the Tom Sawyer car, just walking away in dark green pants, I saw him, crying his eyes out—

— But really bawling, just really heaving, the kind like where you feel it with him, I felt it with him—

— With his hands knotted together at his stomach, as if he was really grieving, I thought, or pressing himself together—

— And even when his crying was blotted out by the PS 38 band, even when there was all the trombones and the glockenspiels, you could still see it, I could see him—

— Just one of those gutting, body cries, all in the throat, his whole system hoarsing it out, just wrenching, I couldn't keep my eyes off him—

— Sure looked like it hurt, I'm sure of that—

— But where was he going, I was wondering, where was he —

— Because when the Snooks' float passed I couldn't see him any more—

— It's not that soil temperature is so critical a variable here, although it could conceivably provide some sort of distant correlation; listen—who knows?; still, I feel funny, even now, doing this: coming out here with my thermometer and dipping it into the soil; because people, you know, might say What is she—some kind of a nut?, taking the temperature of her own back yard?; but I love it, I love everything about it: the feel of the soil nudging under my knees, or the drifts of loamy fragrances coming from my planting area, or just seeing the white rectangles of the data cards poking up beside my cuttings—I love it, I love all of it; this is what a back yard's *for*, I'd think, so just leave me be; because I'm obviously on to

something here, with my lilacs: I've spoken to Greg, the owner
of The Flower Box over in Midtown Plaza, and he thinks so
too; I've given him a few examples to cultivate in their growth
chamber: it's temperature- *and* humidity-controlled, and it
has xenon arc lamps, and Greg said they have this special
mixture of chelated metals that they use in their pot cultures,
one that really gets plant processes cooking, so maybe they'll
be able to push the purple still further; still, even as it is, no
one around here has seen anything so dark, so rich: the
color is just gorgeous; in fact, it may be a first, a purple so
dark, though Greg doubts that it would qualify as a new
cultivar; whatever: I'm still hoping I'll be able to get it
included in the Lilac Festival next May—I would *love* that;
that I would really love; it has taken me eight generations to
get there, to produce such a color, and it's very exciting; but
I've been careful in my breeding, even meticulous; it's just a
question, really, of teasing the dominants out and tincturing
the recessives in; that's what it all boils down to—selecting
against the flower's ascendant tendencies and then letting
time perform its exquisite work; it's a living exchange,
leading towards beauty, one that traces its roots all the way
back to John Dunbar's first bringing lilacs to town nearly 100
years ago; he arrived here then, with his famous 20 varieties,
some of them having descended from Balkan Mountain
breeds brought over by early colonists; and now it has led to
this extraordinary purple...; I'd like to believe that Thomas
Hunt Morgan, and even Abbé Mendel, would be proud of my
amateur breeding work: pea plants, fruit flies—and now lilacs;
who knows where it will go: these two great streams, lilacs and
genetics, here converging, tradition entwining tradition...; I
tell you, the succession is exhilarating—
   —I will go up to him and ask him, just like that: I will just
go up and ask him; he gets off from the Gallery Cafe about
2:30, then he cuts down Prince Street to get over to Meigs, and
I'll be over there; I'll be cool, but I'll also let him know that
I'm *not* so cool: I will *use* my nervousness, I will channel it in
ways that will work for me; and the story is simple, it's
perfectly normal: I got these tickets for the concert with my
girlfriend Rina, but her brother went into the hospital so she

has to stay home with her grandfather, who lets you know he has to go to the bathroom by smacking his lips; and I think he'll like the fact that I asked him—he's that kind of guy; I *really* think he'll like it—I can see his monodimpled smile already; he'll respect me for it; I'll wear my yellow T, and I'll make myself speak slowly, and when I get to the corner, right at Prince, I'll make myself start thinking: OK, now, remember: you are not you; now you are someone else; just pretend that you are not you, and go to it—

— But if I were to sell my Speaking Dog, I could then put Calamity in its place; the mantle, then, might be a little unbalanced, with Calamity removed, but I suppose I could fill the gap with a photograph or something; and this is reasonable, this is OK: a good Speaking Dog sells for $600 these days, and no one in the world would care that I had let go of it, no one would even know; but, of course, *I* would feel the loss, *I* would know: there would be an emptiness to the room after my Speaking Dog was gone, there would be an invisible void, pulling my attention like gravity over to the sideboard where it had been; I would walk in and immediately sense it, the fact that something was missing, and I would list towards it, feeling this sucking absence...; yet, though, the simple fact remains that I need to have the refinishing done in the basement; I suppose I can't get around that any longer; I mean, I've put it off for too long already: it has really got to get done, and the $600 will just about cover the cost, according to the estimate; still, the way that dog wags his tail and flaps his mouth as the coin slips in—that has got to be my favorite Shepard Hardware piece, no question about it; for me, it's even up there with the best of J&E Stevens work, including Professor Pug Frog's Great Bicycle Feat; that one's just a simple manual displacement of a coin into an open basket—showy, but simple; for me, Shepard is still *the* underappreciated name in mechanical banks, although their Humpty Dumpty has been getting some attention recently (and though I will confess, under pressure, to an affection for some Stevens, especially during the period of, oh, Pig in a High Chair, or Bad Accident); for an old-timer at collecting, like me, I must say that what's been going on with prices of late gives me real mixed feelings; sure my stuff has gone up in value, but now I can hardly afford to pick up anything else; and now, no one ever actually puts anything in the banks, they're far too precious ever to be used; all anyone ever does is display the banks' workings with plastic poker chips or light washers; that's all there's left; the banks are now more valuable than what they contain; I mean, that's a situation that's been evident to me all along, but if you had said that to anyone back in the 1880's or so, when these things were being made, they would have laughed in your face; the banks were produced to protect what went in them, of course: that was their purpose— to harbor currency; but now we know better: now the container is the site of the worth; now people spend more than what they can cram into any of the banks just to buy the bank itself; (but, of course, most people now just buy the banks as investments, so they can eventually change the banks back into lucre and put that inside another bank;) but such is the way the market works, I suppose, and at least the worth of the banks has been recognized in some way; no longer are they merely sculpted, shuddering shells; it's all a question of scarcity, of course: no one was paying $2,000 for a Reclining Chinaman back when they were pumping them out like camcorders; but now there are so few left, so very few of any of them; I wince when I think about it, about how many were thoughtlessly discarded over the years; it was such a loss—an entire industry's worth gone; in their day they were underappreciated; now they're unaffordable; who could have foreseen it?; the container is more precious than its contents; it is both a miracle and a simple increase in wisdom—and this is hardly something, I dare say, that I can let some old refinishing interfere with; to remove myself from any of this, even once, is not worth it, especially for refinishing a damn basement; besides, I rarely go down there, and I wouldn't start to go down there even if it were more presentable; it's hardly charming downstairs, but I can live with it; I certainly can live with it—

— No, I told Alicyn, that's not it: I didn't register because I want to get what I want, or to direct our guests' generosity, it isn't *any*thing like that (and not, of course, because my Aunt works there—though it certainly didn't hurt her position); I know that some people think that registering is kind of goofy, but I registered at Lerner's for other reasons (though they *do* have some nice Wedgwood there; OK? —it's out); I decided to register because I though it was nice—that it was a nice part of the whole thing; I mean, when you get married, with all the ceremonies and rituals and stuff, and you have to certify it with the state, to get some official agency to make it legal, it's like you're inviting the public, everybody, into the marriage with you; or it's like you're writing it out for everyone to see, making a declaration that you're knitting into the larger community, and that's nice; the community gives us belonging, then we help keep the community going by publicly knitting into it; and so I thought that registering was kind of the same thing: publicly knitting into the business community, making public that we're part of it—our commercial life, which is also important; listen, what can you do: you get sentimental at times like this...; and besides, the Wedgwood at Lerner's is, well, *really* nice—

— And you know Tiny: we stop at the corner of Plymouth, and this old, old lady starts to struggle to get on the bus; so Tiny ducks under the bar and goes out to help her, like he always does; and the old lady's got plastic bags hanging from her arms, and her neck is bent like a buzzard's, and she moves incredibly slow, but Tiny just stays with her, holding her elbow and patiently guiding her in; and in the middle of this, some guy behind us gives a honk; so I turn to see, and it's just some big burgundy-colored Lincoln, but Tiny just lets the old woman take her time; and when finally the woman gets in and pays—it does take forever—and Tiny gets back into the driver's seat, just then the guy behind us honks again; but Tiny, then, just honks right back; and then he looks into the bus's rear-view mirror, and he smiles and says, to no one in particular: I've got a horn, too—

— *Already*, I said to the empty store, when I came out front and saw it; I mean, I only put the sign up on Monday, and there's already something; but, I suppose, this is what you've got to expect when you try something new; I mean, what do they know here of New York-style bagels?; you've

got to win them over first—that goes without saying; then, maybe, if you're lucky, you establish a niche; and if it works, and you become known, and you become *identified* with your niche, then you have an opportunity: you can open up a second store, maybe a third: they know your name; but don't expect miracles, and do expect a little resistance; but this— it must have happened when I went in the back, to sweep up; but who knows? —maybe it's been like this two days already; All Bagels Made By Hand, was the way I wrote the sign; so they take a magic marker and replace the 'H' with a 'Gl'; very funny...; but what do you expect—it wouldn't be the first time; so be it; but then again, there's always the possibility that this wouldn't be the worst thing for business...; listen— who's to say; still, I'll have to put the sign up a little higher next time, maybe over there above the refrigerator—
— *Damn*, I thought, when I opened the letter: *yeah*—the tightwads *finally* came through!; and you know that I went *straight* out to the Millrace to celebrate; fourteen months of haggling and writing proposals and getting all those interde- partmental approvals, and—and the fuckers finally put out!; God-*damn!*—I mean, I almost didn't be*lieve* it!; you know, Anthropology over at UM Rolla isn't exactly a leading light— its budget has got to be one-fifth of Chemistry's, one-*twentieth* of what they give to the computer center—so 2,000 greeners is a *major* victory; but how could they resist?; the outfitters, or their antecedents, have been working in these parts for centuries—it makes perfect sense to study them; they're virtually untouched, and so are perfect fodder for an Oral History; since the time of the First Americans, people around here have been in the business of providing river vehicles; it's a deeply traditional livelihood, with origins akin to relay stations and stage coaches but now mostly dedicated to tourist activity: they've gone from Osage traders bartering seed stocks to contemporary innertubers out on float trips, six-packs in tow; just by managing or supplying the craft— nowadays it's mostly canoes and rowboats—the outfitters bring together *so* much, a veritable infarct of binary opposi- tions: land and water, past and present, visitors and locals, movement and stasis, commerce and recreation, permanence

and transience—and who knows what else I'll find; when I discussed the possibility of studying outfitters with Professor D'Acierno, he agreed that they meet virtually all the criteria for qualifying as a High-Continuity Occupational Group—and their riparian traditions and practices are strung out right under our noses and we've never paid a whit of attention to them: these people are essentially entirely undocumented; so, while sitting there with the Professor in his office—well, I really thought I had pulled off a bit of a coup, if I may say so (and I continued to believe so, I'll add, even when the NEA's Oral History Project turned down my application for a matching grant); depending upon whom you talk to, there are about 35 full-fledged streams in southern Missouri; but I'm going to concentrate on the waterways in the Ozark-Ouachita Highlands, to keep the study local and specific: Curtois Creek, the Meramec River, Huzzah Creek, and maybe I'll get over to Mineral Fork or the Little Piney; I think these little, spindly streamers will leave lots of time for traditional ways, and lots of time for reflection, so they should be good; I've already spoken to the guy who runs the Misty Valley Canoe Rental, over in Steelville, and I know Joe Schiller of Joe's Canoes, in Leasburg, and they both seemed game, so I think things will work out; I hope to get started within a few weeks, after I wrap on another paper I have to write; the point, then, will be to get these people on tape as naturally and straightforwardly as possible, just to get them talking—about their lives, about their work, about themselves: let them be their own Rorschach tests; I'm going to use one of the Malinowki methods, which entails being as nonintrusive as possible: you don't want to Heisenberg your subjects into weirdness; and yet it's true, it's inevitable: the very presence of the tape recorder will throw the subjects off; it will unalterably prevent them from acting or talking as they do when the tape recorder *isn't* there; despite continued work on the problem, it's something that no ethnologist or anthropologist has been able to get around: unavoidably, you change what you're trying to study; the second you arrive, what you really want to capture is gone; it frustrates me sometimes, but such is the way that information mutates; more and more, the situation is being accepted by professionals as a given, and they also realize that no amount of interpretation can really rectify anything; but it's funny: just now, I have a friend at UM Rolla whose father works for a precious metals firm that has an office in St. Louis; his father goes to Japan about twice a year with his briefcase filled with bits of bullion, and he offered, the next time he goes, to bring me back one of those new digital tape recorders they have there; they're not entirely legal yet in the United States, thanks to pressures from commercial protectionists, but for an ethnologist they're a real boon: they promise absolutely permanent recordings of your work, with, I'm told, unthinkable fidelity; like CD's, they have insanely high signal-to-noise ratios, and are essentially hissless; well, of course I'd love to get one—it's clean permanence; but it's funny: it would seem that these two refinements of documentation and transcription are pushing in opposite directions: just when you can get perfectly accurate recordings of your work, it's becoming universally acknowledged that what you're recording isn't accurate at all; progress, in other words, means zooming in on an error, foregrounding experimental wobble; what we're finding is what we're missing; we're seeing ever more clearly that we're irremediably off; technological arrogance is proving the necessity of epistemological humility; well, as you can imagine, for someone in my field this is a little discomfiting; we used to be able to cloak our inaccuracies in innocence, but no longer; and now our displays of failure are perfect, and *permanent*—to which you can only say Hmmm...; still, you have to go on: to work as best you can with what's available, with what's possible; and then you just hope; is this denial or is it negative capability? —I couldn't tell you; so you just trundle on, hoping that maybe we, as receivers of information, have biologically-given decoder circuits that let us compensate for corrupted data, so that despite all the distortions—inadvertent, inevitable, or otherwise—we somehow can get a sense of what's going on, and something genuine gets through; because it does happen, every now and then: just think of Bartók and Kodály, early this century, tracking through the forests of Hungary and Rumania with their big-horned Edison phonograph to record Central European folk tunes; Bartók published nearly 2,000 of them, and, even mangled to fit into the formalisms of Western art-music notation, something of their authenticity comes through, if only an alluvial fan; you hear enough of it, I suppose, and somehow you get a sense—again, it's Heisenberg, sire of statistical man; it may not be plannable, it may not be provable, but something, you hope, communicates, and old Professor Popper is thus himself falsified; so, then, with your maps in your pocket and your DAT on your back, you get ready to go out and into it; and then you don't ask why, and you don't fixate on the hardships or the shortcomings: you just do it—

— Tomorrow let them be different, but today I want them the same; it is right for them, this first time, to be having the same meal—and not because it's less work for me, but because it is right; this is a beginning, but it is also a continuance, and so should be commemorated; I assume they will be eating together, on this first day—for where else will Tom go, if not to his father; so they may chide me when they come home tonight, they will say that I was lazy, or unthoughtful; but let them: they will understand, after I have explained; and they will be appreciative, after they understand; because I have my reasons, and they are good ones: I have not packed a lunch for Tom since he was in junior high school, and here I am doing it again; even folding the top of the bag, its brown neatness and crisp snap makes me proud; what I have done before I am doing again, and this is good; that means that what I did before was right, because here I am being asked to do it anew; and this is good pride, because it partakes of continuance; it affirms not me, but what I am a part of; today, Tom marks the fourth generation of our family to earn its keep within the same concern, inside its borders and walls; Greg and I had always assumed, and had always hoped, that Tom would follow in Greg's, and Greg's father's, and Greg's grandfather's footsteps, and here it has come to pass; and so we are proud; we had hoped, while Tom was growing, that he would sense, that he would know, that he had something in the world—something to do and something to belong to, and that he would feel affirmed by this;

now he, in turn, has affirmed our trust, and that is good; rightness has engendered rightness; we had hoped that he would grow up knowing that he could contribute to something greater than himself, and greater than us, and that this was, undeniably, good; many summers ago, I showed Tom, with something like this in mind, the cathedral in Beauvais, France; in high sun I held his hand as we, from Place Vérité, looked at the magnificent chancel—its arching buttresses and stained glass, the sculptured towers and magnificent tympanum of the north portal; sustained by faith and ambition that still stirs, this tallest of all Gothic cathedrals was given to us— across generations, across centuries it was built, set back but never silenced; uprushing, airy and magnificent, it was a summoning of excellence and time; and thus with only excellence and time, gray stone and rainbow glass were made to seem to leave the ground, to rise beyond earthbound proportions and become pure conception; so I let him look and I let him see, and here, today, I am rewarded—

— First position, of course, is probably OK: you have to assume they've machined *some* correctness into the bone; but beyond that it's got to be pretty rough: by third position, say, with your hand by the bell, the intonation has got to be turning slightly sour, and by seventh position, with your arm extended into regions where all fine distinguishing is lost— *forget* it, the instrument has got to be way off pitch; the slide itself is fraught with flaws and burrs (no matter how much valve oil you use), there are lip and embouchure fluctuations, and the only thing you've really got to guide your hand is the coarse workings of muscular memory; to me, in fact, it's astonishing that anything is listenably in tune on the trombone, and we've got *two* of us in the group...; boy, the bone: instrument of impossible perfection—although that's a thought I'd better keep to myself; I've got a gig tonight with the Nonet Minus One, over in Ozark Hall—their usual Memorial Day bash—and the last thing I need is for these ideas to creep into my boning: it could really throw me off; with a name like ours, the Nonet Minus One, I suppose we sound like we're some bizarre group playing backup tracks on records; but we're actually a pretty good Traddish-Dixieland band, covering a few corners of Bourbon Street, selected funeral stomps, things like that: spirited stuff; we aren't professionals, but we get the crowd moving, that's for sure; and even now, every time a clearing comes and I hear my horn rising above the clarinet, then sailing forth over Jake's trumpet and the rhythm section—*man*, you know, there it is: that's what it's all about; I just think I'm old Billy Watrous, and it is *so* sweet...; sure, I suppose I'm slightly out of tune, maybe terribly so—but then again, if you think about it, so is everybody else; any musician will tell you that: the violins with their fretless fingerboards, oboes with their weather-sensitive double reeds, pianos that've had their 88's banged on for a while—not a one of them will hit a true A-440; they're *all* slightly off, every one of them, all ensembles are studies in imprecision; but still, just ask anyone, musician or not: the people still listen; the crowd still gets on its feet; it can still sound *seriously* sweet—

— But there are a billion better things to do with the place, if you ask me, things that would really bring something new and different to town; in fact, for the longest time, I've had some ideas of my own: why not use the place to house an International Institute of Desserts, where they would collect and study and serve in a cozily decked out *Salon de Thé* all the sweet things they can find, all as part of a real research and consultancy group for—and here's their slogan—The Culminating Course; or, even better—a Museum of the Tonight Show, a genuine repository and archive; the house is big enough to hold it, they could easily get support from KSDK locally and NBC nationally, and maybe from Steve Allen and Jack Paar, and almost certainly from Johnny himself—he can't have much longer to go, so he's probably hungry for a tangible memorial, some enduring record (and how could it not be so: The Ed McMahon Lounge); attractions like these would have *thousands* of visitors, coming—even detouring— to Schroeder House from hundreds of miles off; oh, well...; these were the two ideas I sent in, one back some time last fall and the other just in April, but both of them received the same polite letter back from Ozark public relations: thank you, grateful, kept under consideration...; still, I sure wish they would make up their mind; in the last Aperture, they had an article about how Schroeder House was possibly going to be turned into what they called a home-video resource center, with display rooms and screening facilities and competitions and conferences—things like that; it sounded pretty far along, but they still said they'd like to receive suggestions about things to do with the place; so, why not—I'll keep working on it; what else are you going to do; and who knows—maybe I'll hit; and that would really be fun, if one of my ideas was chosen; in fact, it would be kinda amazing—

— Oop...hold on...just give me a second here...; there we go...; *there* we go...; good; mm; thanks...; I just had to touch up this one little area here, you see, just below the sill; they say these enamel-based paints are more weather resistant, that they'll stay good for much longer; so I figured I'd give them a shot, even though they're a couple of bucks more than the run-of-the-mill exterior stuff I've been using; listen, they look pretty good, it's a nice-looking powder blue, and what's a coupla bucks if they last like they say they will, and it's better than my kid saying the house looks like a sight for psoriasis...; so—OK, that's it for today, let me go now, the Cards are playing down in Houston in a few minutes, O'Neal's going against Darwin, I gotta get inside—

— But I was surprised to see what they've got in there now: as you walk in, on the left, they've added a little counter where you can get muffins and candy and sodas and stuff, really nicely laid out, all clean and orderly; just show them your employee card and, same as the film or anything else, the prices are at least 30% off; well, seeing this, you know, I was just so tickled; I mean, you tell me: where else can you get a can of Diet Coke for 35 cents in this world—

— And this new Buy-Day program they've set up in some departments—Dori told me they have it in accounting, and I heard they've brought it into some of the research sections—well, I like it; I like the whole idea of it; you work an extra 45 minutes a day for nine days, it can be in the morning or after five, it's up to you to choose, and then you can just take the tenth day off—so you can have a three-day weekend every other week; and that's great; the same amount of work gets done, but you save on the car, you save gas, it gives you a little extra boost looking forward to your free Friday or your free Monday—though I'm told some people actually take their day off in the *middle* of the week (well, some people are weird); regardless—I'm all for it; and when I asked Frank if Buy-Days were going to come to our department, he said that he's already seen a memo and that it's under consideration—

— But now I don't know where to lead him, where I should take him, what I should *do*...; for years, for seven years we've gone up Pullman and then turned on Aster and then came back via Steko, and he was good, he did everything just fine, in one of the same seven or eight places every time; but now he isn't right, I tell you, he's off; nothing happens; I keep him out, and I wait and wait, I keep him out longer, on Tuesday we went around twice; but nothing, and then during the night he does his dirt in the dining room, beside the door, though one time it was in a corner in the foyer; but Springers are clean, they're very clean animals, especially Jeremy, he's always been very clean, and then he didn't like it at all when I changed the route, when I tried to take him out along different blocks, when I tried to do *something*...; and I don't want to make him stay out in the yard all night, I can't do that, he would cry, I know it, he would cry, I would hate it, he would cry all night—

— So you need a minimum of one-third of an acre, that's for sure: I'm for it, I'm entirely for it, it'll insure the qualities of the neighborhood that we have always had and want to maintain here; new construction should be made to respect the characteristics of an area, we have enough of the tan townhouses in the inner loop all pressed on top of one another; a minimum of one-third of an acre, that's the absolute minimum, the ordinance should specify that—

— In theory, it is a good idea; that I can agree to; there are children in the neighborhood, young people, and they always need things to do: diversions for after school, a safe place to go—of course; exercise is always preferable to more television, and the playfield, I read, will be 56 acres, so it will be quite substantial; the most recent proposal, which I read about in the Republican & Chronicle, said that the playfield would have a baseball diamond, a jungle gym, and a few other games for climbing, chinning, and hanging; there'll also be a few basketball courts and, if I remember correctly, a few soccer goals, as well as some untended green, to be used for general play; it sounded like a handsome, capacious plan, nicely designed and considered; in fact, the proposal, I believe, was put together by the same architectural firm that did Irondequoit Mall, and that, of course, is very handsome; moreover, I also read, in the same newspaper story, that the project still has wide support—a sampling of public opinion indicated that; and that's understandable: the location is quite central—right at the corner of Ridgeway and Mount Read Boulevard—and, in addition to donating the land, the company has offered to foot the bill for the construction of the facilities, as well as to handle fees for daily on-site supervision; but of course: the Ozark people have always been good with things like this; but this is one thing that they must not do; I, for one, would be very uncomfortable about it; no, they must not do this—

— Because they are good about things like that: always reliable, always responsible, they take care of things and look out for their people's benefit; Mother Ozark is how people put it around here, and that's how I feel; I have a guardian, a protectress, someone who is concerned for me; when I wake up at night I can go back to sleep, knowing that; it keeps me warm; I'm not one of those people who has to go out and buy Sominex; I have security; and that's what I told my friend Julie; I said Where else are you going to find anything like that—because if there's a problem, any kind of problem, I'm sure the company will take care of it; that is something you can rely on, something sound; Julie should have listened—

— But they had the Juke box going and things looked like they were happening pretty good, if you know what I mean, there were people and they were hanging, if you follow me, so I decided to step on in; I mean, the State Street Bar is usually alright on Thursday nights, they have their Half-Price, Double-Kick Daiquiris until 10, so the population is usually feeling fairly friendly by the time I can get over there; so I stopped in and copped a Molsen's from Billy Velardi, who was subbing at the bar for Ron, and carved my way through the smoke over to the Juke, and then was *really* surprised to see that they had put in a box that plays CDs; well *damn*, I thought, will you look at that: things do move along; I mean, the machine had whole *albums* in there now, with all the tune titles typed out on cards, and the discs were, like, made of this *bright* bright silver, and really shiny; so I shed two quarters for some Hendrix and then rubbed the Juke's side as I moved along; and then I made my way back to the bar, and then waited standing when the song that was on ended, but it wasn't my Purple Haze that came up next, so I just sat on down, near one end of the bar; and then I saw Curt White sitting beside me, all amber from the light fixture over his head, and he was looking into the mirror on the other side of the bar but not seeing too much, if you know what I mean; I mean, I know Curt, and I know that he knows where to put them—he knows *exactly* where to put them; and so he tells me that he's doing well, really pretty well, but that his sister, Ginnie, is having grief with her kid—the kid's started in on Marlboros and she doesn't go for that at all; so now she has to quit to provide the right example, and it's proving tougher than she had thought; so I tell him I'll go by Ginnie's place to hold her hand while she's quitting—in exchange for all the cigarettes she's not smoking, of course; and Curt smiles and says Yeah; then he turns away and takes a sip from his tall glass; but then, you know, as I'm sitting there, I see that Curt has started to kind of rub his eyes, I mean he's really kind of kneading into them with the bottom of his hands while holding his elbows up on the bar; so I look for a while and then say Hey, man, you all right...?; but Curt just says Yeah, and then waves his hand in front of him; but then he starts back in again, rubbing himself, rubbing his eyes, so I say Hey, Curt —Come on, he cuts me off, and then he says Just the fucking smoke in here; Oh, I say, and wait a bit; but then when Curt turns to me and smiles, I see that both his eyes are really watery and *bright* bright red, really looking shimmery and *bad*; so I say Hey, man, come *on*...; but then Curt turns away from me and doesn't reply; so I say Hey, Curt, *come on*; and then, when he still doesn't reply, I say Listen: I've got some eye

drops on me if you need it, I've got some Murine here; but
then he turns around and looks at me square and says Listen,
man, it's OK...; and then we look at each other and then he
says Really, man—it's just a little irritation, OK?; I was waxing
my car after I got home, that's all...; and then he punches me
lightly on the shoulder and says OK...?; and I nod and wait
and then Curt smiles; and then he says: Now, what you
drinking?—
    — So I said What, you know, what do you mean?; and
then I said No, man, that's not it, it *isn't*, that isn't it *at all*—
    — Then put it this way: why should we bite the hand that
feeds us—that's what I want to know; you have a life, you
make a life for yourself, and that's it: goodbye; *goodbye*—
    — But what I know is that there would be no Isaura,
period, without them; they're our bread and butter; almost
everyone here benefits from them; it's a way of life with us—
    — There would be a lot of starving sons of bitches in this
town if them stacks weren't smoking; it's a damn fine town
to live in; I mean, the economy is good because them stacks
make money; they pay here on Tuesday, Wednesday, and
Thursday, because they can't haul that much money into
town on one day—
    — And listen: it's good, I mean it's *damn* good to have the
800-pound gorilla on your side for once in this life—
    — And remember: I don't feel that anything they have
there is any more dangerous than any of the other things
we're exposed to; everything you do these days, it's all bad for
your health; any way you look at it, Ozark is a great place to
work; we're required to wear safety clothing; there are very
strict safety programs; look—you have to have industry, so
you have to put up with certain things—
    — Oh, nonsense: they keep the place looking very nice;
they're entirely clean; they have a ballpark out in the back of
Ozark Park that they let people use; some of our scout troops
have their picnics there; because we know that whatever
happens, they're going to take care of it: of *course* it'll be taken
care of, removed and clean, as they always have done; I still
shop and drive my car and water my lawn same as always; I
don't see anything wrong at all—

— I am now 78 years old, and have lived at 808 Rand for 46 years; I raised five children here, three daughters and two sons, and I'm now awaiting my ninth grandchild; we're all fine, and I've been very happy with Ozark, and very, very happy with Rand Street—

— Then call me a traditionalist: you know, Show Me; I've been here all along, I grew up on Platt and then we moved to Emerson, and I want to tell you that I haven't seen nothing, not before or since; my life is here and my life is fine; I haven't missed a day of work in eight years; so if anything's happening it's happening to someone else, not to me; you know, with all the fracas it's sometimes good to just keep clear sight of your traditions; so OK then: Show Me—

— Yes, I go in every morning smiling—yes I do; I'm glad to be there, I'm happy to *have* it; think of what goes on there every day—all the products, all the services, going out all over the country and beyond, giving people a little of what they want in life—and just the fact that all of that can go on, every day, on such a scale, and despite the inevitable problems and breakdowns and whatever—well, you've got to be proud; just the pure efficiency of the operation, of getting all this detailed work done at what are really a very reasonable competitive prices—just for the efficiency of the thing, you've got to be impressed; and our efficiency would be crippled, we'd never get anything done—nothing, no thing—if we had to wait around to find out if things are safe—

— Because there is some risk in whatever you do; there's some risk even walking out the door; but you've got to accept it; in this field, risk comes with the territory; it's what you're paid for—it's why I'm given a check every week; why else do you think they pay me—

— Yes what else is the reason for all this, where else could it be going?; his reticence, his respectfulness, is almost reason enough for me to continue; because he said, from the outset, that he wouldn't do anything I didn't want; and he has resisted, he has been content not to continue, every step of the way; and this is respectful, and trusting, and I trust him, I trust him entirely, and trust, yes, should be rewarded; because in that hard chest, beneath the ripple of ribwork, lies trust, and the warmth of the cove of his neck is honest, and beautiful, and the warm tautness of the cords in his neck is wondrous and firm; he was calm and warm and caring when he first pressed upon me, taking his time, loving this, just this, our embraces, with my hand drifting down his back and up again, then down again and onto the softer firmness below; and he undulated, he gentled, as he floated atop me, our kisses were loving and enhancing, tongue-y and sweet, as my hands glistened up and down his hard, rippled sides; and he was so warmglowing and sweet that I pulled him to me with my legs, one around each of his, and I felt him, hard and hot on my belly; so I let him know, I let him know, I pushed him up towards me, and he slid up, and slowly, as if he didn't know, he slid up on his knees until the tops of his legs were astride my head; then I took him, and he rose up slightly, on his knees, his hard belly bending over my head, and I put my hands behind him, and gathered him to me, the yeasty scent, the briny taste, I attached myself to his heat; and I played with him; going away and coming back, going away and coming back, my tongue rubbing underneath, then around, then pressing him towards the side of my mouth, where my cheek felt him suddenly warm, then pushing him up against the roof of my mouth, for a singe of hotness; and it was good, it was sweet, his body was moving like a forest above me, grateful but not pressing; and we are together in this, we are mutualness, we are reciprocal, from him I have assurance, he is making no demands beyond those of trust, so I let him go, I let him go, and I push him down and further down, I take his hips and bring him down, and then I see his face, and make sure he sees me, and I let him know, I let him know, even though we don't have anything, we have nothing to protect us, and now we know; and I rise to him, just arching, to bring him to me, and he is there, and he lowers down, embracing me, and he is upon me, and he is with me, and he, yes, he is in me—

— Because this is the way it must be; I have clients, customers, and this is what they expect; this is how the world proceeds; I am to be courteous with them; I am to be pleasant; I can give them little tastes of things—this is what they *expect*; I must be grateful that they have found something to like in my cinnamon rolls, or my apple turnovers; if they want my sesame bread sliced, then I am pleased to put the loaf in the slicing machine and to wait for the rumble to finish, then to slip the waxed bag over the slices; and I must smile along with them when they look down into the case and smile at my strawberry shortcake, and when they expectantly hum; this is how life is lived, and I am to be glad for all of this—for *all* of it, and there is no room for any other emotions; I can think of no reasons for any other emotions here—

— Because shit, yeah, they've *always* been here, ever since there was an Isaura; Isaura *grew up* with the company, they put us on the *map*; when did they get going, or start up— *I* don't know, a hundred years ago?...yeah, that's it: 1880; for 108 years they've been the ocean for us fish, they've been the town and the town's been them; so they need us, because they *are* us, and so it's in their interest to look out for us; and there's no way that's gonna be allowed to change—

— All the evidence points in that direction; like that time when I fell, coming down the stairway in Building 53, they got me to the infirmary even though I kept telling them I wasn't hurt, and the nurse gave me coffee and put cold compresses on the swelling near my ankle which really wasn't anything—and then she called over to Ray and told him I could go home if I asked him to; and they let me go without a question when my kid got hit in the head with a softball at school, and the same for that day when I was feeling dizzy for a while; they're concerned, they're involved with their people: you always have that sense of support—

— I know it doesn't make a difference, but still I do it: after all the time it takes and all the snipping and the tearing out, what do you save—thirty dollars, maybe, over the course of an entire year?; now, I know this is hardly worth the effort, but nevertheless I stay with it; don't ask why: it's almost as if I feel I must, despite the obvious ruses; in fact, I remember once, some time ago, I was in Wegman's, and I had a 50-cent coupon for All just burning a hole in my hand; it was for the Giant Economy size, the one that's nearly 14 pounds; I hauled the huge box over the top of my cart, then felt something pull in my right arm, just above my elbow; it hurt quite a bit, but then I just heard myself thinking *Oh, come on*: you're saving *50 cents!* (though I didn't actually need detergent at the time); and then, when I got to check-out counter, I found out that they had raised the everyday price by 65 cents!; so there you have it; and still, I should add, I bought it anyway; it was already in my cart, and I had brought it all the way up to the register, and so be it; on the way out, though, while passing through the electric door, I just began to laugh about the whole business; it was really just a little giggle to myself, because it seemed so funny, I mean just so obvious, but then I ran into my neighbor Becky, who was on her way in; well, of course Becky asked me what was going on; this was soon after we had our episode, if I recall, and so she said that it was nice to hear someone laughing; so I explained what had happened, but I don't know, maybe I'm the only one who would find it so amusing, because Becky just looked at me and said that she had given up using coupons, and in fact that she had thrown a whole stack of them away just that week; so I just looked at her, you know, I just looked at her and really dressed her down; and then I said, Hey, you know, come on...; it's over; it's done; it's all over—

— Everywhere, you know, it was fucking everywhere last night; my friend Eddie, he was working late at the Riverview Cafe, so I went by and we did a doobie together in the kitchen; then I met Bill over at Big Boppers and we went out and smoked another bone out in the lot; the Bophouse was fucking empty, so Bill took me over to some friends of his over on Averill, there was a good guy there named Errol, and he had some XTC that he was sampling, and that we were all sampling before too fucking long, it was some good shit, and then Bill's friend Jimmy, this driver who lives over on University, then we caught him right before he started freebasing; and Jimmy was funny, he was really fucking funny, he was sucking on an Absolut after he had done the horse, and he looks up at us, with a big smile on him, he was all slacked down on his couch, and he looks up and says, slowly, with these big bright eyes and this big tooth smile, holding back laughing, he says Without chemicals, life itself would be impossible—

— On the contrary, I think—and not just now but even

back then, at the time; where would we have been with*out*
their help, is what I say; *that's* how it should be looked at; they
saw the situation, they recognized it promptly and assessed it
reasonably and then they acted in good faith; throughout,
they were genuinely concerned and very forthcoming, taking
charge of the situation and taking care of their obligations;
no, in every way they acted responsibly—

— In fact, if you remember, it was one of their own
people, it was actually an Ozark employee who discovered the
situation; I remember something like that he was leaving
work one evening, one evening just after Christmas, and he
smelled something in the air—

— I think they said he smelled solvents in the air—

— And then they traced it right away, I remember, they
traced it right to a pipeline running underneath West Ridge
Road—

— It was right between Woodside Street and Desmond
Street, I remember, that was where it happened, where it
burst, right between Woodside and Desmond underneath
West Ridge Road—

— It was a pipe that runs between Ozark's distilling
operation over in the west end of Ozark Park and its film-base
facility over on Oatman Avenue, if I remember—

— But come on, I mean, come on: it wasn't more than a
couple of hundred feet from PS 41—

— Not more than two hundred feet, I mean, only two
hundred feet—

— I mean an elementary school—*an elementary school*—

— And this was just one of twenty-two pipes that run
through there, if I remember correctly: I mean, there are
twenty-two of them—

— Almost immediately they came forth with a whole
host of responses: they threw money around left and right,
doing what they saw had to be done: they sent out that
mailing, which gave all the details, but which was something
they didn't have to do; and I remember they gave candy
apples to all the kids, they had them wrapped in ruby-colored
plastic and tied with ribbons, and one was left on every desk
for when the kids went back to school—

— Sixty people, I read, were used for the clean-up, working around the clock, day and night, scrubbing it up, which must have cost double or even triple overtime, when you get into 4 AM and like that; and the company offered to pay for sitters for the days when the kids were home, so their parents would know that they were being looked after—

— Even when they found that methyl chloride just becomes harmless—that it dissipates, I think they said, in closed areas—even then, they kept the school shut and kept the kids away for a third day; they were taking no chances; and then, they continued testing for three straight weeks, I remember, while classes were back, until they were sure—

— And they also did something else: they also dug what they called test wells, I remember, they drilled a dozen wells right there to test the water, the water below ground—

— And they also replaced, they said that they immediately replaced six of the twenty-two pipes that run under the ground there, I remember—

— Yes, I'm sure they were very concerned; the chemical is one that they use to make the film, so that's got to be something the company's going to take to heart; and they continued to be concerned; they called in an expert, the man who takes care of all of Crawford County, someone official, and he said, I remember, We can tell the people of Isaura that there is no reason for health concern; I remember reading that in the Republican & Chronicle; and right there in the paper he also said that the smell isn't necessarily anything to worry about, and that was also good to know—

— And then George Fobel, George Fobel himself came forward and said We are convinced that this situation has created no risk for Ozark employees or our neighbors, though we recognize and regret that it has caused anxiety and uncertainty; I saw that in the R&C—

— And then afterward, when Ozark offered those home-improvement loans to the people who lived near PS 41 at very, very good rates—what was it, 2%?, almost nothing—well, I don't think too many people took them up; it was thought unnecessary, I believe; everyone here understood that these things happen—sometimes something comes up; Ozark had done enough already, more than enough—

— Indeed, such systems, inlaced with free parameters, must inevitably face periodic stresses, or what I call inbuilt risks; such dynamic systems, linking uncountable components, human and mechanical, will unavoidably encounter elements unforeseen to design, and will then exhibit maladaptive responses to such variables; this occurs primarily because of what I call the interactive "tightness" engineered into the system—there is insufficient "give" or "looseness" built into system procedures, either for self-correction or for phasic compensation; the resulting response is characterized as an accident, though it is inevitable, and indeed, in a sense, predictable—

— And of course they immediately said—they *insisted*— that they were going to get to the heart of things, to tackle the problem at its source; they pledged a lot of money to clean up everything, and I remember they said that layoffs and whatnot would be kept to as few as possible; they were really very good about it—

— Then that idea they had, that development project— well I was touched, I was moved, at the way folks here just wouldn't let them go ahead; I mean, Meramec Caverns already gets lots of tourists—it's the largest cave formation in the world, for heaven's sake, and other people come to see it because it was where Jesse James hid, and because they have his hideout made up just like it was in the 1870's; and there's also the campground and the hayrides and all that in the park, enough for everyone; so, really, what more was needed?; but Ozark announced that they really wanted to build it up, to make it into some real tourist center or amusement park, they said it would benefit everyone in the county; I suppose some people liked the idea, especially up in Stanton, but this was right after the episode and so most folks here in Isaura just said Keep your money; Use it for yourself; You've got other things to think about just now, beyond building us up; and it was sweet, it was nice; I read an article about a petition that some people were circulating to that effect, to send to Ozark management, to say they've done enough for us, and I'm sorry I never got a chance to sign it; because I would have signed it,

I really would have—
— Though I knew they never would have accepted it, I made a proposal when the idea was first floated and I would still suggest the same thing now; they had come out of the episode successfully, with fine conscientiousness, so why shouldn't they be allowed to feel good about themselves; the Schroeder house is just down State Street from Ozark's main offices, and so the location would be perfect; as the site for a company museum or memorial hall I can think of none better; all they have now are those few display panels in the waiting area of the Executive Tower, which is obviously inadequate; a more appropriate tribute to Ozark's role in American life, and its position in the culture, would be a very welcome addition to town; and it would, no doubt, be very, very handsome, because the company knows how to do such things up, and in more ways then ever it would have been earned; sitting at home some evenings, these days, I still think of speaking with someone to see if we might overcome corporate modesty and bring the proposal to light—
— And there is *hard*-wired, and *hard* sell, and *hard* ball; and *hard*-bitten, and *hard* news, and *hard* knocks; and there is *hard* data, and *hard*nosed, and *hard* currency and—and I will continue with this 'til the end of the set: it keeps me going, it pushes me past fatigue—and so then *hard* core, and *hard* hitting...and...now...*hard*...*won!*...; *whew*—that was good; twelve good reps; now—*relax*...; you know, all these guys here, this whole bunch grinding away on the Nautilus, just doing this pulling and flexing, what can they expect beyond a minimal pump?; those seats and pulleys are too lazy, too *soft*; before long, if they're serious, they all come round to recognizing that there's no substitute for free weights—that's where the results are, pure and simple; when I was young, and I saw those monsters in Muscle Builder magazine—well, those guys were as big as linebackers, but *without padding*; just wearing *themselves* they were that big: plated, sculpted, they had made themselves *invincible*; then when I first got to the gym—my *first* gym, Gold's, on Ridge Road, back in '81—it all just seemed so far off; I looked at myself, at my skinny little slack-sack runtiness, and I wanted

to cry; so it took time, it took hours: day after day, month after month, year after year, isolating muscle groups, increasing resistance, achieving definition, keeping my diet under control—and *now* look: 48-inch chest, 21-inch bi's, 24 at the thighs; so *fuck you*, mirror: *I have won*; here I am; and it just took lots of *hard* work, and *hard*headedness, *hard* time and—

— And now I, too, can hardly sleep; oh, eventually I drift away, after taking a glass of handwarmed Courvoisier, which I feel as a vapor upon my face, just before turning in; but then I jolt awake at the slightest sound, and sit up, and am terrified, watchful; sometimes I can't tell if it was something I heard or something I dreamed; regardless, the effect is the same: I am fully awake, and anxious-listening for his distress; or, when I cannot sleep, I just lie there and spin noises out of silence, tweezing strands of sound from the night's nothingness; and, then, when inevitably I hear something, I get frightened, and immobilize myself even beyond crackling the pillowcase in my ear, listening with all of my resources for the confirmation that will send me running to him; often, in bed, I am reluctant to move, to wriggle in the slightest way at all, for fear of missing the beginning of one of his disturbances; other times, when it is very still and late, I begrudge my heart its gibbering interference; he has said that he dreams of planes with flaming wings, hurtling and falling; or sometimes he dreams of walls stretching and floors bending, giving way under his feet, furniture sliding, buildings collapsing; but I cannot get there, where these things are, where their frightfulness takes place; so after his kicking and swatting has summoned me to his room, all I can do is hold him, strongly, firm against my shoulder, and calm his gaspy crying by mobilizing other sounds—sounds such as It's OK...; it's OK...; it's over now...; it's gone...; it's not true—

— Aw, who the fuck talks like that, I says to him; but he don't hear, and then he just continues going on and on about it—*Jesus*, the way the damn guy keeps *yacking*; it's *enough* already, I says to him, you *made* your point—so a pipe burst near the school, what's the big deal?; be glad you weren't there when it happened—and he ain't got any kids neither; sometimes, when I'm out on the porch, I hear him through the window, going on about it on the phone to someone—I mean, the fucking guy's creating his own hardship: he's fucking *obsessed*; now he's saying he's gonna move to Albuquerque; how come you gave up on Grand Rapids?, I asks him; too cold, he says; forget it—next week it'll be the moon; listen, let him go; as it is, yesterday I didn't answer the bell when I saw him coming over; I mean, so what if he knew I was home—what of it?; maybe I was busy; maybe I fell asleep in front of the TV, OK?—

— So I suppose I will have to find something else to do; I mean, I have made a decision, and that is it; and I will stick to it: that's the way I work; jogging has been wonderful, and wonderfully enjoyable, for all these years—no question about that; but after so many years I have my knees to think about, and other stresses: I've already damaged the cartilage in my left knee once, and I also got shin splints, and I had to lay off for a few weeks during each of those times; it's a sport for younger men, I suppose, and that is it; I will simply have to learn to live without it; tomorrow, though, I'm going to buy an exercycle, and I hope I'll take to it; the way I figure, at least I'll be continuing with something, and I'll also have something to do at 5:30, when I get home; in fact, I'm kind of looking forward to seeing if my progress develops on the exercycle in the same way as it did on the road—if I go through the same kinds of what I called contractions, which were always a lot of fun; I mean, when I started jogging, doing that first little circuit up to Lily, then onto Clay, and then onto Magee Avenue, the whole thing was all of about half a mile; and when I reeled home those first few times I was *to*tally blitzed, really sweating and gasping and all collapsed on the kitchen chair; but then, you see, as I continued jogging, day after day, then the distance began to seem as if it were growing shorter—that is, physically shorter; and after a few weeks it almost began to feel like nothing, like nothing at all; and that's when I knew I could push the distance a little further; and so I went, initially, up to two-thirds of a mile, and then to the full mile; and then I took a leap up to two miles—I decided one day just to give it a try, and it didn't feel bad at all—and then to two-and-a-half, and then I pushed it to three—and at every length I knew it was time to go further when the circuit began to feel too short, too brief; in every stage the same thing happened: the distance began to contract, until it was no longer sufficient; I would be breezing by houses and intersections without even being aware of them, just thinking normal thoughts; and at the same time I would feel it less, even at the new distances, I would do my three miles and pull back in and still keep bouncing in the shower, with the water streaming over my hair and head...; but, eventually, I limited myself to three miles, because it was best; I read in Runner's World that three miles is a good limit for someone of my age and weight, so I kept it at that; it's best not to overdo it, I suppose, not to overdo anything; and so I won't overdo jogging itself; it isn't really a hardship for me to pack it in, and it's probably better all around that I just leave it go; it's just a question of recognizing one's limits, I suppose—of knowing, in everything, when to leave things go—

— Which is exactly it: it's enough already; I've had enough; I've heard about it, I know about it, and that's it: that's the situation, so what more do you want?; that's the way it is; listen—I'm on top of things, and I think the best thing is just to put it behind us—

— Ah—now: 9:30: Merv; now Merv; should I Pringles?; all the way to kitchen, all the way; then drink, too: good drink; Cranapple: nice, tart; but with a glass, and wash—then all the way back; all the way; hm...; vinyl warm; nice, warm; then ah *Tonight, on The*—

— It's been, what, nine months now?; that's a long time, that's enough time to have a sense; and there's been nothing, nothing bad at all; show me something if it's otherwise, but I don't think there's been a thing, nothing I would consider anything—

— But what do they know?: they aren't experts; why should anyone, why should *I* listen to what they're putting out; Mona isn't an expert; what the fuck does Mona know?; all kinds of things can be wrong with things, so she shouldn't be jumping to any conclusions; you've got to leave time to take everything into account before you can say anything reliable; and without that, they're just *proving* that they're guessing—that they don't know shit; so it's obvious: these people don't know what they're talking about—

— Listen: even the lab won't stand behind the results: that's what I heard; so there must be something inconclusive about the findings; the lab must recognize that the numbers they found or the quantities or whatever aren't realistic, so they can't say anything definite; that's science—those are its obligations, it's a question of proof; and if there is no proof, then they can't say anything; as a private lab, their reputation depends upon their producing solid results, so if they won't get behind them then you know the findings aren't persuasive; otherwise, they'd be out of business in about twenty minutes—

— But groundwater is filtered on the way up, as I understand it; it's naturally filtered by the layers of igneous or sedimentary rock, which provide natural barriers; sometimes it can take years for the water to pass through all the natural filtering strata that have been laid down for it, and the combined effect of all this purification is that all the adverse particulate matter is removed before it can do anyone any harm; it's a stunning system of natural protection—

— And all the way in, then, it's all treated, must be dozens of times, before it gets here; they've thought of everything, I reckon, to make sure there aren't any problems: that's what they're there for, that's what they *work* for; they make sure no gases get in along with the flow, and they clean it, they put fluoride in for your teeth, it's all sterilized, and who knows what else they do out there in those big plants; they have big machines to do all this; you never see no birds or twigs coming through the faucet, do you?; just think how big a reservoir is, but never a once I heard of anyone finding a feather in his mouth after he brushed his teeth—

— They should get the government to do these tests, the appropriate state or Federal agencies; anything else is irresponsible; the officials have the resources with which to do these kinds of studies, to make sure they've done *right*, so then you could put it past you; it's their *job*, for God's sake, that's what I'm paying my taxes for, exactly for that kind of assurance; otherwise, there are too many variables; there needs to be some final arbiter; it is irresponsible even to *think* of doing such tests without government participation, or at least their approval;   this is clearly the doing of people who haven't thought through the consequences of—

— Well, sure, if you take the sample right close to the plant, as I heard they did, then you're going to get some methyl chloride in with the mixings—that's to be expected; they *said* they use that stuff, didn't they?; so you've got to expect some traces of it if you go right nearby; there's always some little bit carried on folks' shoes or in their cuffs or such, and what else is going to happen with it; it isn't like any of that nuclear material that has to be so totally guarded that you can never touch it, where they all wear special protection uniforms and don't breathe and keep it all in sealed vaults; this methyl is a regular part of the process, in vats, open, just like that—

— Relax, will you?; you've got to remember that methyl chloride is naturally found in groundwater; it's a natural component of aquatic systems in this area, so there'll be a tiny quantity of it naturally occurring in every drop of water you use;   it's only one of thousands of these kinds of trace compounds, and they've always been with us and they always will, but in quantities that bring no significant effect; think of it this way: they've been with you for your entire life—in every cup of coffee you drink, on every chicken you wash, in every package of instant breakfast you make, and sitting in the cup you have on your night table all night long—but they've never done anything and never bothered anyone; it's like what I heard when I was in school: there are minuscule bits of St. Peter's body in every sip of tea you take; and all of these imperceptible fragments, all they do is give your tap water the sweet taste that you like and have come to expect—

— I like to buy oranges and bananas because they have that nice thick skin, and I also go for almost all unshelled nuts; but vegetables are real hard to deal with, because most of them, except maybe avocado, are just so *out* there; so I try to buy organic as much as possible, but the selection of organic veggies around here is really limited: there's Natural Approach over on Park, they're about the only shop around here that carries organic produce, although some of it tends to look awfully scrawny; but you've got to survive, you've got to eat, so I make sure to buy whatever I can without preservatives or added colors or raising agents or that junk; so that's what I do: I look, I research; I spend more time reading labels—

— And that was nice, that was good to hear: I was reading that the Isaura city council just passed a resolution, the whole town council got together on it, establishing once and for all that that damn methyl chloride isn't bad for you; their words were that it poses no threat to human health; and that means it's OK to relax, because it's safe; you can just forget about it, is what it means; because I was a little concerned there, for a while, I must say; my hands were sort of getting a little wrinkled there, you see, a little more than normal, right beneath the knuckles, and I didn't know what to make of it; I didn't know if I should use a cream or just leave it go, just do nothing—

— Because according to what I hear, the stuff is way down in what they call the aquifer, and then just the other day I heard that Ozark came out and said that any groundwater that's been affected by the methylene chloride is 20 to 30 feet below the surface—

— And then they said, I heard they said in an official statement that People just don't live down there, so there's no exposure—

— Ultimately, I now understand, the situation is safe; you need very high concentrations of methyl chloride to have anything to worry about, and it's just not there; as with everything, it's a question of exposure levels; if you take in too much salt it'll kill you; if you breathe too much *oxygen* it's also goodbye—

— Exactly, I mean ex*act*ly; I mean if the water is bad, the hell with it: everything else is bad—

— So you make your peace with the situation, and that's it; and then you just get your eye back on the ball; just yesterday, in fact, I decided to get around to repairing the outside stair by my kitchen door; it's just the one step below the door, but you kick it enough times over the years and the concrete starts to fall apart; so I decided just yesterday that the thing was looking ornery enough, all broken up and flaked, and that it was about time to get into action; now I'm not too good with fixing things like that, but I went over to Sears to try to get some supplies—in particular, a trowel—and overheard that they found two other chemicals in the source water, two new ones that they never knew were there; and I'm standing there holding the trowel by the handle sticking out of the bag and thinking What: what am I doing here—

— Though how they got there no one seems to know; maybe they come from cars, is one story I'm hearing, dripping from all the engines; though I also heard that they seep from the tar and macadam that they use on the roads; but from wherever it is they've got to find it, because—

— How bad can they be, I'm here to ask you; they sound like what we studied in high-school chemistry: they're acetone and methanol, simple substances, probably simple organic compounds, that's all; you can be glad they haven't got those unbelievably long, unpronounceable names like the real killers—

— Look here: it's all set out in black and white, clearly and simply, all what you need to know; it's in today's paper, in a special box, so you'd see; so, here—start here: here's what you want to see: ...Alarmism in any of its guises or expressions is entirely unjustified; fear can also be leaked into a community, with consequences that are, at the very least, unwanted and disruptive; indeed, overreaction to rumor will certainly hinder the more substantive efforts of research and discovery now under way by diverting attention and resources away from where they may be needed; in a world fraught with unknowns, the responses of our community—to concerns, it is wise to bear in mind, that are certainly temporary—should not be unknown; like the scientists and specialists at work on our behalf, we, too, must act responsibly; and we best can do this by heeding their advice and battling against undue alarm; otherwise, the consequences for Isaura—both social and economic—may become the foremost of our unknowns...—and that's where it ends; so you see, that's it; after I saw this I tore it out and stuck it up on my refrigerator, pinning it with a magnet, to make sure I'd have it—

— Sometimes, I see myself as resembling a water God; in parallel with the cycle of condensation, precipitation, and evaporation, I too channel moisture through an integrated system—my system—in ways that nourish and sustain it; there are inflows and permeations and outflows occurring through entirely natural rhythms, and I—*me*, the physical being—am the structuring essence that permits these natural rhythms to unfold; I lend to water essential characteristics that contribute to its worth as water, I let it realize itself, functionally, as water; now, I have been drinking this water for 20 years; I have been circulating it through me for all that time, through this constant cycling; but I have never had a problem; nor will I ever; my water does not comport itself in such ways—

— But it's preposterous on any level, that they'd let anything like this happen; think of the stakes, think of the consequences—they're clear enough, and I'm just one Joe living on Madison; Ozark's got hundreds of people working full time on safety concerns, people who are trained, who have degrees, who do nothing else but think about things like this; so it's impossible; they'd catch it; it would never happen—

— But more fundamentally, I maintain, the company would not *permit* it; it would *never* permit it—

— Oh, come *on...*; I mean, how much can there be?; they can't be there in immense quantities that just showed up all of a sudden; they've *always* been there; but then they go and isolate them and pick them apart from all the others, so of course they bring fear; they're out of context; they *are* scary when you look at them alone, all by themselves and separate, and then all magnified—you put ice cream under the microscope and it looks like a nightmare place; but in their raw state they're all part of the package, they're in a context that was designed to contain them and that naturally neutralizes their negative potentials; of course such safeguards exist: that's the reason for the world's hanging together; there's an equilibrium that takes care of them, and, by extension—

— Mona has always been a little flippo, and it's good to remember that; she was the one who was all up against widening Route 8 over near Berryman because it was going to cut too close to a pine stand there, she made that whole stink, and I remember when she wore that hat with the feather sticking up out of the band, all one winter; so realize who you're dealing with here—take her nature into consideration; so she says she can no longer keep quiet: well OK, speak your piece; nobody's stopping you; but then she goes and starts talking and one of the things she says is that she found some old surveyor's diagrams or something that show that the bedrock under town is saddle-shaped; and Jimmy's telling me this and I start laughing; and when I can stop laughing I say That's what she's got to say?; that's *it?*—

— But more important is the fact that, after all, the government wouldn't permit it; and I don't mean only town hall, but Jefferson City; now, they have their privileges, but they have their obligations; and first and foremost, I mean, first and foremost—

— I was sitting in the laundromat on Church Street, all by myself; I had dumped my family's two baskets' worth of wash into the machine, and was trying to leaf through a copy of Vogue that I had found on the folding table—or at least I thought it was Vogue: you know how magazines always change format these days, without saying a thing; in any event, someone had left this issue behind, or maybe the management had provided it—impossible to tell; it had an article—and a nice one, with some gorgeous shots—about Venice, but I just couldn't stay with it; rather, I was drifting among the familiar pleasant discomforts of the Elite Laundromat: the dusty-cottony scent of the dryers, underlying the livelier nasal prickling of detergent; the retreating line of the washing machines' porthole doors, revealing rocking and soapy-splashing and spinning; the clots of black lint, like decomposing insects, that lay among the scuffs on the white-gray floor; the panel of user instructions, which include every step you need to run the equipment but always manage to leave questions unanswered; the signs for the swap meets and moving sales that were stuck to the splotchy walls with dirty Scotch tape; now they say that methyl chloride is a carcinogen, that it causes cancer; that is now the word they use:

carcinogen; methyl chloride is a carcinogen; just the sound
of the word brings a clutching to my chest, a clutching that
feels as if it is perpetually falling through me; yet I never
actually feel what the word *means*, because when I try to grasp
the word's meaning, the word slips through me like a tomato
seed slipping through my fingers; and then, instead, I see an
image: a piece of tissue paper buckling inwards; that is what
I see; so I live with these falling movements, and these images,
I live with them presently and constantly; I live with them
and then work with other words; these are the words I work
with: it is now understood that something present and constant may kill every member of my family; it is now understood that something may kill every member of my family—
— But even so, what is the likelihood of that, I ask you:
how many people are ever really hit with it; one in a million?;
one in *two* million?; just think of those numbers—think of
them realistically, objectively—
— Then realize that it's principally a question of exposure, of units of intake relative to size, weight, and an array of
other variables, most of which are unknown and we don't
understand; so I keep a calm head; even the mice, rammed
through with floodtide quantities of DDT or whatnot don't all
develop difficulties; in fact very few of them—
— It's what you're born with: that's the determining
factor; the chances of catching anything at all are set by
genetics; either you've got good genes or you don't, and I
don't think anything else in the world makes a heck of a lot
of difference—
— But the whole question is still open, if you ask me;
where are the facts?; show me some solid information; all I
hear is galloping speculation, all of it unconfirmed, and I
know I'm not going to bother myself with hearsay—otherwise, you'd see me out in Highland Park with my head shaved,
still carrying a sign welcoming Kahotek; despite all the
scuttlebutt nothing concrete has yet been produced—and
when and if something concrete is produced I'm sure it will
serve to put the whole thing to rest; look at how the
Republican & Chronicle has handled things: with reason, and
hard objectivity—that should be your model; rightfully, the

R&C has said that it won't publish the alleged lab tests that started all the commotion because the lab won't come forward and let its name be used; so what does that tell you?; either there are facts or there aren't: in science there is no middle ground; who knows—maybe it was all a business ploy on the part of the lab, or a publicity gimmick: that's as least as likely as anything else; but after a while you've just got to face it: there's nothing there—

— Oh, no, no—*nonsense*; you're talking foolishness now; I've lived here my whole life and I don't have cancer—

— And there was Phisohex and microwaves and DC-10's, and you had your radial tires and cyclamates and your glow from the goddam color TV, and saccharine and paint chips and Pintos and Red Dye Number 2, and now it's tampons and stress and—and so forget it, just forget it, you hear what I'm saying?; they're all the same; they come, every one of them, and they all blow over—

— But it's through now, I suppose; I suppose I must recognize that I simply can't do it any more; perhaps I'll put another five dollars in with the card: maybe a larger check will distract her, and she won't notice anything missing—or if she does, she won't mind it so much; even so, it will be difficult for me to look at the left-hand side of the card, before it goes in the envelope—the left side will seem so naked!; but I hope she won't be sad—or think that I've forgotten!; oh, heavens, I hope she doesn't think that; that, I'm sure, would make her sad; but when she sees my handwriting—the little bit I have to do, because I have to put my name, I must at least do that— I hope she'll understand; I suspect she'll see that it isn't too easy for me to write any more; I'm sure that will come through; and it's all really too bad, because I have a good one this year; it's a nice one this year:

> Ten times ten is fifty
> Twice two is fifty-one
> And forty-nine is eighty
> And two, oh but we're done;
>
> Numbers can be numbing

Though some still do equate
And there's one equation I rejoice in:
Catherine is eight

Perhaps I could recite it to her on the phone—damn the cost
this once; it would be such a surprise—the call, and Marilyn
hurrying to get her to the phone, and my saying hello, then
the recognition, after which she'd probably give a little
squeal—my hands would be shaking from excitement for
a change; oh, I'm *sure* she'd like it—and, also, she'd be able
to hear that I'm not that old, at least not as old as the
handwriting in the card might make me out to seem; at her
age, granted, it's difficult to conceptualize; but at least after
receiving the call, and hearing my voice, she will get the
sense that my mind is clear, that what has taken hold of me
comes from something within me, but is not me; she will
learn, I hope, to distinguish between me and my body; she
will see, in fact, that my body is not me; she will see that, I'm
sure she will, and then she will understand that I am not that
old—
    —In the past, he seemed to like my lemon sandies better
than my shortbread—his smile would be brighter when he
stood up at his big wood desk to receive them; but now I'm
thinking maybe I'd better not bring anything at all; it will be
strange, that's for certain, to show up empty-handed after all
these years, but I just don't know what the right thing to do
is any more; still, I've got to see him, and he said I could come
and visit at 4:30 tomorrow afternoon; so I will be sorry to
disappoint him, but Father Curtin has got to get my mind off
these erroneous ideas—
    — But you're wrong, you see, you're wrong, I told him;
I made it clear to him from the get-go: Mona *did* ask the State
to test the groundwater, she went up to Jefferson City to see
the Department of Health, she made the trip all the way there
just to be able to speak in person, but they told her, in so many
words, they told her that the testing couldn't be done at an
individual's initiative—
    — Though it's been that way for some time, for quite
some time; not *all* the time since I got it, of course, the color

was nice and yellow when I first bought the machine; and the glasses and plates have always come out clean and fine, there hasn't been any problem there; but I'm glad that I generally don't have to open it when anyone is around, you see, because I'd be embarrassed, I'd feel real strange, if anyone saw how the insides of the dishwasher have got so dark, how they're so violet and dirty-looking—

— Now, I work in the classified department, you see, I take the ads down over the phone and send them into the composing room, for setting; I also explain the rates and take down the client's information for billing, and do some other needed stuff; but two other guys also work in my area, and the fact is that so many ads come in every day that you almost immediately lose track of what's gone in the system; so when Milt called me in and asked me to contact a client, I did it as a matter of course; I went back to my desk and called the client up, and explained to her that, as Milt told me, the ad didn't fit any of the rubrics we use—that we didn't have a section for it; and the client asked me what I meant, so I explained it again, and told her that inappropriate fits, which is what this was, happen every now and then; then I reassured her that we'd tear up her Visa slip so she wouldn't have to pay; so she said thank you and hung up, pleasantly enough; and I went into the system to void out the item, and then I saw that the ad concerned childhood leukemia, that known cases should contact a telephone number—

— And I'd be driving down Ridgeway Ave., you know, over by the turnoff onto 390, I'd be out doing some shopping or bringing in food, or I'd just be on my way home from work, and I'd see all the smokestacks scattered around Ozark Park, rising up over all the buildings and the piping and the conveyor systems all around the miles of the facility; and they looked so familiar, tapering up like that, just part of the landscape, so silent and familiar, always there, just reaching up and kissing the sky; they were part of the neighborhood, what you came to expect, and so they gave you a sense of things continuing, of industry, but industry in the other sense of the word—of work being done, with high organization, by lots of people all together; and you'd see the stacks' smoke,

pluming gently or drifting out, and then you could keep
driving, imagining all the things going on underneath them,
all the people working, as usual, harnessing their efforts
together; and you had the sense that the seeping smoke was
the sign that things were all right, that it meant prosperity—
   — Though the story I heard, someone was talking over
in the dry-cleaner's the other day, what I heard them say was
that 80% of the city water systems, which are used by 88% of
everybody all over Isaura, they all depend entirely on groundwater from the wells—
   — No, I don't usually read it, with all its stories of
custodial people getting married, or of departments surpass-
ing productivity goals, and all those notices of conferences or
engineers' kids winning scholarships and such; that's 85% of
what's printed in Aperture, and it all gets kinda old after a
while; but still I pick it up—force of habit doesn't let me leave
the plant without grabbing a copy when I see the new ones
stacked by the doors leading out to the parking lot; yet I've
got to tell you that the July issue had something about all
the stories that have been going around, and they said in
black and white that there is no link whatsoever between
chemicals used in the plant and any problems you may have
heard about or imagined; and I read that one, that's for sure,
I read that story—
   — And I saw they had this article with a specialist, a
guy named McCarston, who's independent of Ozark, and he
said that the level of fear and the reaction to the methylene
chloride was simply unwarranted—
   — Though I saw in Aperture that they spoke with a man
who's the head of the environmental affairs division of a big
chemical company, a company that's altogether separate
from Ozark, and he said, right there in black and white, he said
that there is no scientific evidence linking exposure to methylene chloride with any serious long-term health effects; and
he also said that there isn't any evidence that the health of
those who have been exposed to it is in any way different from
those with no exposure—
   — And so I kept reading; and then I saw, near the end,
that they said this, right here: that Ozark's vision of environ-

mental responsibility includes, in addition to fully complying with all governmental regulations, a commitment to respond to the concerns of our community; OK?—that's what they got right there—

— But it's gotten so that I don't do it any more: I used to be sure to get the comb out once a week, Lhasas are longhairs of course, and the care book said it had to be done, that it was like exercise for them, but now the comb totally fills up with hair, and the white hairs stick all over the side of the couch where I do him, and it's brown leather, and last time I found when I was holding him that a whole area on Pasha's leg had no hair at all, it was all gone, it was all raw pink and exposed, up there in the rear where it's tender, but he can't say anything, he can't do anything, he's just breathing normally, but I can see it, I see it right there, and I hug him and I don't know what the hell to do—

— And I'm looking through the R&C, you know, turning the pages, and I see they have an article about that playground they want to build over at Ridgeway and Mount Read; Ozark's come out in favor of it again, apparently they've put out some new proposals, and they even got a recommendation from some sociologist from, like, Harvard or somewhere, some guy who wrote something saying that having things like that in the community is good for the kids, that it's proven to make them do better in school and keep away from drugs and like that; and I wouldn't mind, you know, I live over on Mercer and it would be nice to have a hoop right around the corner, I'd go out and hang a few in there every now and then myself; and so I'm reading, you know, I'm reading the article—and then, I don't know, maybe my mind drifted away for a second, but then I click in, I click back into the article again, and I see that Fobel, Fobel himself, is saying that In spite of what you may have heard, we are very concerned about the environment; and I stop, I just stop dead when I see that, and I pull away from the article and I find myself thinking, Sure, George, sure: whatever you say—

— Because I've got to tell you, you know, there's another side to this; I mean, I heard on the radio yesterday, on an independent station with full freedom and no grudges to bear,

I heard Mayor Stockton say that there's not enough evidence to warrant any sense of panic—

— But at least, thank God, they're there for you; I mean, imagine if there wasn't anyone at all that you could go to— *then* where would you be; because it got that way a bit for me last week, I can tell you now, I got a little edgy, so I finally did something: I got information and called around, and finally found someone in the County Health Department who took the time to explain things, and he assured me that it was at worst a nuisance condition, but no serious danger; and that sounded good; I was able to function a little better; but imagine if I couldn't have found anybody, try to imagine what *that* would be like—

— And I'm standing in line with Richie in the cafeteria, and the woman behind the counter hands him what he asked for, a plate of pot roast and peas and mashed potatoes, and it all looks like it got caught in a long gray rain; and then Richie makes eye contact with Tony, who's in line in front of him, and smiles funnily at him and says E-G-D-S-L; well, I don't think too much about it, in fact I laugh along with them when they laugh, because, you know, it all seems funny, but then later on I bumped into Gene in the basement of Building 31; he was moving a desk over to Executive Tower, and he puts down his truck and begins telling me about how Bentley wants him to help paint a few offices starting next week; and you know Gene is such a pisser, he goes into this impersonation of Bentley with that real low, mucoid voice—*and if you would, uh, Gene, if you would*—and when Gene comes back and starts talking like himself he shrugs his shoulders and says the same thing to me, E-G-D-S-L; so I say, Hey, you know, what is that?, I heard it before; and he says You don't know?—everybody's got to die sooner or later—

— I had put out the crumb cake and the Lorna Doones, and all the cups and saucers and little plates just looked so nice, placed among the magazines that I leave on the coffee table; because it was good to see Susan, you know, she's got such a great sense of humor and she really keeps up with what's going on in the family; she's the one who keeps in touch with all the cousins; Listen, she once said to me: everyone complains that they haven't got time to talk, but they always manage to find the time when *they're* called, and it only takes two seconds to dial; that's Susan, she's always saying things like that; so when she comes down from Sullivan it's just so nice; so when she got here we were sitting in the living room and chatting, having coffee and just talking about what all the cousins are doing, like how Jimmy's doing in law school, and how Amy is handling being single again, when I hear the faucet go on in the kitchen and hear that Sandy, Susan's daughter, is filling a glass with water, to get something to drink; and I freeze, I just freeze, I stop talking and my muscles tense and I don't know if I should jump up or yell out to stop her, if I should run in there, or if I should just hope that it's all right and not upset the day—and I really don't know, I don't know what to do, because Sandy's six years old, she's only six years old—

— But thank God, you know, for the Republican & Chronicle, the way they stick to it; I'm glad when I see that they have these things; like today they're on top of it again, they have this article about an official Ozark spokesman, a man named Ronaldson, and look here: he said We do not believe that there is any health hazard or health risk to our community; we had to consider whether telling the residents about something that wouldn't harm them would nonetheless cause undue alarm; and that's good, you know, that's good that they have it like that—

— And today they have an article about some kind of panel brought together by Ozark, this panel of sixteen scientists who are studying the methylene chloride; and I saw that one of them, a Marvin Anderson, who's a toxicologist with the Air Force over at the Wright-Patterson base in Dayton, he said right here that I believe with methylene chloride the risks are overstated—

— Right: I read that this Air Force doctor came out and finally said common sense; he said that what the EPA does is disregard what we know about biology—

— They said that the methylene is not considered a known carcinogen because it doesn't cause cancer in all test animals; and then I read that this panel concluded that cancerous tumors and things that they find in mice and rats don't have much relevance to people getting tumors—

— And they looked good, you know, the little windows in the back door, I was glad I had finally gotten around to giving them a wipe, because they're kind of small and it's easy to get lazy and just ignore them; so I finally polished them up, all four of them in their nice diamond-shaped pattern; but while I was there, you know, I figured I'd also give the screen-door a wipe, because, you know, it also gets grubby; so I folded the rag against the end of my finger and damn if the screen didn't just give way when I touched it, like I was putting my finger through a slice of Muenster cheese—

— Oh how do you *think* she's going to support herself, how do you think, she's always got some wise-guy Johnny trailing after her, holding the door, putting his hand on the small of her back, and they don't stop with lighting her cigarette, and of course that's why she's doing all this, that's the real reason, because she was going around with someone who's an executive there, real Ozark brass, she was all crazy for him and hot and bothered and then he dropped her, he didn't want to have anything more to do with her, and I even heard he said she was crazy, that she was too pushy and crazy, and that's why she's doing all this, that's the real reason, to get back at him, she's so crazy that she quit her job to concentrate on getting back at him, you see how crazy that Mona is—

— I lifted my laundry bag onto the big metal scale, and the man sloshed it around a bit, to center it; then, after waiting for the needle to vibrate down and settle upon a number, he read the weight; then he went back behind his counter to write up the ticket; but when I gave him my address, he refused to take my bag; the man refused to accept my laundry; looking at me straight in the eye he just said Uh-uh: no way—

— That's right, no way; as President of the Isaura Homeowners Association, I am *not* going to take this lying down: because you see the com*plainers*, these *complainers* are destroying the peacefulness and harmony of the neighbor-hood over a boogie man that just does not *exist*—

— And you know I heard all that, I heard Doug Hasbro

saying those words just the other day; and then I heard some guy on the radio, some official spokesman, and he was saying that there's absolutely no evidence that ground or surface water ever left Ozark's property with contamination that exceeded legal limits; and so I—

— No, I should continue; I'm sure of it; I'm sure I should continue as if nothing had changed; I should go out there into the yard and just get the spiling board and clamp it on the next plank, because she can't sit up on her blocks forever; three years of dreaming and two years of working and now she's finally coming together, finally looking like something—my forty-two feet of river freedom, built plank by plank by plank; I remember lying on my bed for hours, just lost in dreams about her—about being out on her, and watching the buildings on the shorelines passing, and how the rocking water would feel, and the moving air; but now, to lie down near her, on the ground—because a rudder pintle needs to be bolted to the bottom of the stern post, and then I have to put my teak decking down, which will take days—I get to the back door of the house, and I look at her in my yard, all skeletal and immobilized, but just inches off the soil, and I just can't do it; I just can't do it; I feel an unease, a resistance in my abdomen and forearms; it's like they're trembling, and I can't do it, I cannot go out there, I can't, and I shut my door and stay inside—

— And I tell you when it got hot, it got worse—*really* worse; you'd take a shower and the steam would gather and then you'd smell the fumes; it was terrible; it was nauseating; you were *steeping* in it; and then I'd forget and make ice cubes with—

— The sense that something must be done, that something is demanding to be addressed—this sense always makes itself felt; it comes out, gradually, irresistibly, and cannot be stopped; and such is the case with the idea that we should establish an ordinance that new houses must be built on a minimum of two-fifths of an acre; it's an idea that I am wholeheartedly behind, that I'm altogether for—because it's right, it reflects common sense, and all of our needs for—

— Sitting on my rear porch these days, just idling

quietly, amid the hoses and bicycles and folded chairs, I occasionally close my eyes, or look over to the old, soil-blackened planters being stored in the porch's dirty corners, and am swept by such emotions of disbelief that I can barely move—disbelief that they would do this to us, under any circumstances, and that the state and local governments would allow them to do it even if they wanted to—

— And sometimes, after I get out of my car, and walk down my driveway to my front door, while instinctively flipping to the front-door key, I pause before I take my first step in; and I stand there and I think: I will be in there, in those rooms, for hours, nearly fourteen hours, moving and sitting and sleeping;   that is longer than any chemical worker remains in any factory—and *without* protection: without goggles, without respirators;   and I am afraid, I am terribly afraid—

— And this guy Ronaldson, in the paper, I saw him say in the paper that Residents are questioning our reputation, and we don't like it—

— And I went down to Florida, to visit my parents, because I hadn't seen them in several years, and all I was thinking when I was down there, all I could think, was that I hope the house burns down while I'm away—

— And now I hear that Lois Riggs has found something, that she's found some sort of document or something, and it says that Ozark has known about the chemicals since 1973—

— I mean, they're supposed to have known about all three of them, the methyl chloride and the acetone and the methanol—

— *Since 1973*, I heard: she says that Ozark has known all about all three of them, that they were found in the soil and the groundwater under Building 329 in Ozark Park, and that Ozark has admitted that the chemicals escaped during pipe breaks and leaks at Building 329—in other words, there were *many* pipe breaks and leaks—

— In other words, they've known perfectly well *for eight years* and they still haven't done anything about them, and now I heard that Lois has explained all this to Mona—

— And when I saw the letter my heart started jumping,

just knocking and jumping, right from when I pulled it from the letterbox, because I had no idea what it was going to say; I was scared, I tell you, I was afraid to open it, but then again it could have been something important, maybe something that was important to know, because the letter was labeled as coming from the Crawford County Health Department, and I didn't even know how they had gotten my name; so I went back in and sat at my desk and put my hand to my throat to calm my heart, and then I opened the letter and read that Isaura residents who were found removing foreign chemicals from the basements of their homes and putting them in the sewer system would be subject to legal action by the county, with fines beginning at $25 for each violation—

— He thought I was crazy! —he said he could give me the name of a good psychiatrist with an office in Davisville!; but I said Dr. Mazlin, *please*: this is *not* all in my head!; I mean, I'm sitting on the table in his office stripped down to my underwear and the rash is all over the insides of my arms and legs, and it's all on the tops of my feet, and I even have pustules in my damn *ears*—and he says I need psychiatric treatment!; so, you know, I just look at him and say Doctor, *Sir*: I know I'm not a specialist, but I'm also not crazy!: *look at me*—

— When you get right down to it, you'd be hard pressed to find any group of people who care as much about the environmental and economic well-being of Isaura as the people at Ozark (Advertisement)—

— But with all the advances in genetics, the progress in phenotypic reversal and recombinant DNA, you'd think they could find something, some gene-altered agent that could get in there, into the aquifer, and, I don't know—

— Why I look in there, why I open the envelope, because it's the same amount every week, down to the penny; but I suppose I can't resist: it still feels good to know that my check is really in there, a check with my name on it, to confirm its return yet again; or I suppose I want to make sure there aren't any problems with the check, that they didn't make any mistakes with the amount; so I crack open the envelope and along with my paycheck there's this slip of green paper, the same size as the check; and on this slip there's a note

from Bob Ross in Operations, who says that he is writing to
reassure us that Ozark, above all else, only wants to do the
right thing—
    — So I boil; I mean, I'm sure anything coming from the
tap is essentially fine, but you don't know what the hell can
get in there so I make sure to boil everything that has any
interior application: anything I cook with, anything I drink;
anything I use to wash the dishes or when I brush my teeth;
and I make sure not to open my mouth when I take a shower,
I keep it pinched closed, and only—*only*—breathe through my
nose—
    — So I hustled out to the concession stands when the
first period ended, but when I saw what they had done to the
prices I decided against getting anything—I mean, I'm not
100% sure, but it seemed to me that the hot dogs were at least
10 cents more than last season; I mean, I didn't need one that
badly, so I just went to the bathroom and that was it; then,
when I got back to the seats, everyone was up and stretching
or moving around a bit, and the trucks were out doing their
circles, their slow, snail-y dance planing down the ice, when
all of a sudden I hear a ruckus kicking up a few rows behind
me; and this woman wearing a parka, I didn't know who she
was, but she was just standing there fright-faced and fierce,
screaming at that girl whose name I think is Tonia, screaming
that Tonia was against Isaura, that she was obviously *against*
Isaura because she was doing some sort of something with
Mona, and that she obviously wanted to give Isaura a bad
name; and it was bad, with everyone looking at her like that,
it was very tense...; and Tonia, you know, that poor Tonia—
    — Where helpful, Ozark will, in the spirit of a good
neighbor, go beyond the requirements of the law (Advertisement)—
    — So what else could I do—I scrubbed; I scrubbed all the
hallways on the first floor, then I scrubbed my basement; I
used buckets and buckets of Ajax, and I kept washing and
rinsing out the brushes; down on my knees I scrubbed and
then I felt sick; then my hands, when I was laying down
afterwards, my hands felt like they were being crushed, and
then it spread, it spread into my feet and into my spine—

something *crushing*, like fire and pressure, as if I were literally being crushed; so I went to the Doctor's and I had steroid treatments and nothing helped; so I went back, I went to a specialist, and he didn't know what was wrong with me, he wouldn't give me anything, and now the crushing feeling is spreading to my hip and the doctors, these damn doctors, they're all afraid to open their mouths for fear of losing their license—

— And my neighbors are goddamn mad because I called the Health Department; but I only called because I had a few questions, I was just looking for a little information, but the Health Department couldn't tell me much and now my neighbors aren't talking to me—they see me on the street and they turn the other way; and I tell you it makes *me* mad as hell to see that, and furthermore I want to ask them how the hell they know, how the hell did *they* hear that I had called—

— So I don't say anything now, not a word; I mean, *no* one does, no one says a word to anyone; so I just do my work, just like always; for instance, I just finished a Kjeldahl of a peptide and that went well, although those are always fairly straightforward; and last week I did a gravimetric analysis of a chloride—it turned out to be AgCl—and that was a rush order, but I made the deadline easily, and that felt good; it's like Jim said: we're a small company, just a small lab; we don't have many other regular customers, and we should be glad they've chosen to work with us—to trust us; thus, we must trust them; in fact, Michael told me that, month to month, they account for between 60 and 70 percent of our billings— we always have results or samples being messengered to them across town; so it's like Jim said: we can't afford to lose them; we can't even *seem* to have done anything against them; and I appreciate his honesty, I really do—

— It's easy to hate a big chemical company (Advertisement)—

— And I see on the television this news report about something that happened in a town in Texas, where a train carrying wastes from a petrochemicals refinery crashed, and the train cars started to burn, sending fumes all over the town; and the anchorman says that it was like an eclipse, that parts of the town went dark, and some people put on their head-lights as they were running home or evacuating to an aban-doned Boy Scout camp four miles past the west end of the town; and already the local hospital was overwhelmed, there was a four-hour wait to be seen in the emergency room, and the TV anchorman is sitting against this backdrop of skulls and bones, all these skulls and bones are floating behind him at all different angles, and some of them are a little blurry or out of focus, and Billy, my son Billy, is sitting right in front of the TV watching all this, at age eight he's sitting there watching, without moving, without moving at all—

— And so finally they did something, they got off their asses and did something, that's what I heard while I stopped to fill up the Ford, that the State finally sent in the Department of Environmental Conservation to take water tests; you see, they did something, they have done something—

— So I feel guilty, I do, I am killing myself with guilt, because it was me: *I* talked my husband into buying this place; it was me, it was my idea, and because of my insistence we brought the kids here and poisoned them—

— There is far more chloroform in an ounce of tooth-paste than in 80,000 gallons of lake water (Advertisement)—

— But it was because of the State, because of what I read the State of Missouri said in the paper—

— That they weren't sure, that they didn't know the extent of the chemicals or if people had any reason to fear them, but with those things that Ozark's putting in the paper I just wanted to find out, to get *some*thing, so—

— I called Town Hall, I called over there, but as soon as the man on the phone heard what I was calling about he seemed to get mad, all sharp and impatient, and he wouldn't let me ask my questions and he cut me off and he said it was too technical for me to understand—

— But the main thing that always goes through my head is Can my kids have normal kids?; what is going to happen to them?; what is inside them, what are they carrying with them?; because it was me—*I* sent them outside every day to play, nobody knew, they never told us, and so I'm—

— Scared to become a grandfather: what will be born?;

do you ask your kids not to have kids, or do you tell them that I, that they may be—

— Tainted forever with something that may strike or may not strike or may wait another eight generations to surface? —but when I tried to deal with this, to pull this into a form that was in any way manageable, when I—

— Called the EPA's regional office in Kansas City, and finally got someone on the phone who would talk, the man said that he had files filled with other cases that were worse than how I was describing Isaura; and he said that the EPA didn't plan to investigate *any* of them, that they had no intentions for action of any kind, none at all—

— There are 150 different chemical substances in a potato; one of them is arsenic, a deadly poison (Advertisement)—

— And then he said that there's a high rate of cancer among my friends; that's what he said, and this is the County Health Commissioner talking, the top man himself, I saw him quoted in the Republican & Chronicle, but then he said, the County Health Commissioner said that it doesn't mean anything, that all the cancer among his friends means absolutely nothing at all—

— To do with her performance, because she was good, she was a good administrative assistant, Jim always was happy with her, and Lois was always proud to be the assistant to the Town Clerk, it was obvious that she liked her work, she was always happy here, she got along real well with everyone, you got the feeling that she regretted it when the end of the day came around; but then apparently Mona asked her to put in a call to KMOV in St. Louis, because she's got a brother-in-law who's a cameraman there, in their news center, and Lois went ahead and did it, she admits that she did it, but I don't think that's any reason—I *know* that isn't any reason to let her go, to *fire* her, to—

— Blame myself, but *I* did it, *I* wanted to, I thought it was right and natural and lovely, that it would forge and seal a closeness between us that could not otherwise be reached, and just the image of it was so beautiful, so tender, so *moving*, when I thought about it, his smallness and my giving, and my holding him to me, against me, and the tiny tugging, the essential giving—but what was I giving?, *what was I giving?; I have been drinking this water for 22 years so tell me what was I giving*—

— Because now they've changed the story, I heard that Ozark's changed the story about the number of—

— I heard that they had to change it—that someone found something and so they were forced to change the number—

— Because when it happened I remember they said it was only 600 gallons—

— I remember at first they said it was between 200 and 600 gallons—

— But then the next day I remember they came out and revised the amount of the chemical that had spilled near PS 41—

— Exactly: I read the very next day they came out and said that it had actually been 1300 gallons—

— Exactly—they changed it immediately; I remember they changed the amount of the methylene chloride that had burst from the pipe—

— Almost immediately afterward I remember they came out and said it had been 10,000 gallons—

— I mean first they went to 1300 and then they went to 10,000—

— And I mean *10,000 gallons*—10,000 gallons of methyl chloride right under the grounds of PS 41—

— And with all this changing, I mean with all this *changing*—

— Because now they say it was 60,000 gallons, I heard now they corrected themselves again and say it was as much as 60,000 gallons—

— And that the spill lasted for 27 hours before it was discovered, I mean—

— *27 hours*, I mean—

— And because of that the soil around the school has got high levels of toxic solvents, I heard they tested and they found the soil has toxics—

— And that 1300 gallons of the spilled chemicals got

into the Genesee River, I heard it flowed untreated directly into—

— And that one of the men they had working on the cleanup had to be rushed to Park Ridge Hospital, I heard that he burned his lungs when—

— I heard all he did was inhale some of the fumes coming from a part of Ozark Park and it inflamed his lungs—

— And I heard that Mona went to visit him—

— I heard she tried to get in to see the man in the hospital—

— Because he had been working in an area she can't get to, I understand they won't let her into Ozark Park—

— To continue with her tests, because as I understand it she's covered most of the area surrounding Ozark Park—

— I heard she's been testing every few blocks—

— She has this equipment and she's working with someone and I think she—

— Has been doing all those tests, and I heard that on the corner of Merrill Street and Lake Avenue—

— I heard that on the corner of Merrill and Lake she found methylene chloride in the air—

— She found the highest concentration of methylene chloride in the air right there, I heard—

— I mean she found 500 times more methylene chloride there than State guidelines allow—

— *500 times*, and I—

— *500 times*, and I just—

— *And I just live around the corner, on Ross*—

— But then the State, I heard the State stepped in—

— Exactly, I heard that the State is getting involved—

— I heard that in Jefferson City they announced—

— I heard they decided to raise the amount of methylene chloride that's legal to have in the air—

— It had been one part per billion, I heard, but now some State agency said it can go up to sixteen parts per billion—

— So what the State now wants, I heard, is to *raise* the permissible limits—

— I mean, they want to *raise* it—

— They want to raise it to *sixteen* parts per billion, and I—

— And Ozark, you know, Ozark has been arguing that
the State shouldn't do this, that they shouldn't change it like
that, but that the limit should be *two hundred* parts per billion,
and I—

— *Ozark wants to change the number to two hundred parts,
and I*—

— And it just seems endless, it just seems *endless*, and I—

— And I am in the middle of something that is everywhere and in every direction and in every thing—

— and without a past and without an end but with—

— a constancy and an everpresence and a sense that I,
that it—

— will never go away and will never *not* return in some
hidden form or some hidden way and I want it to just go away
and be forgotten and die itself and—

— *just go away, and I*—

— You can't sleep—everything just goes around and
around and you get up and it seems like you're going to fly off
and it's like this every night, every damn night and I—

— feel like I'm out on my boat in Irondequoit Bay, that
I'm hauling back on the mainsail fighting a killer wind, and
it's buffeting my face and whipping my clothes and I'm
reaching for the rigging and feeling it just burning through
my grip—

— and I hear the braying and the groaning wood and the
groaning metal and the shoving gusts keep whistling and
whipping—

— *and it does not stop and it does not pause and I*—

— and my burning hands are being *carried* and I am
being *pulled* and *being taken*—

— *and it is like, I mean it is exactly like someone shooting you
and then not having the decency to finish you off*—

— Friends; neighbors; good people of Isaura, he said:
members of our community; and then he looked up from his
speech and, I can still see it so clearly, he let his eyes slowly
encompass the audience, almost beatifically—

— And, yes, I do see quite a few familiar faces here this
evening, I remember he said: faces that I have lived and
worked and prayed with for over thirty years; faces that I

have sat on civic councils with; faces that have come to seem almost as reflections of my own—

— And then I exhaled when, finally, after a long pause, he said Welcome; welcome one and all—

— I have invited you all here to join me this evening because I need your support, I heard him say: I need your support in facing a challenge that has come to our community; yes, we have a challenge, but it is a challenge that, I tell you now, will soon go—

— But it is also a challenge that we must face together, I heard him say, as the photographer in front of the stage started clicking pictures from another angle: because, despite what some might maintain, it is a challenge unto all of us, together—

— Beside me, a man wearing green corduroy pants looked down to his lap and rubbed his long legs; two rows ahead, another man took off his painter's-style white cap; but I did not feel free to move, not even, as I wanted to, to crush the small paper cup that I had taken from the tables of Pepsi and Hi-C Orange that had been laid out by the doors into the auditorium; this was still, for me, a time of silence—

— And yet, friends, I ask you to consider the richness of the base we have for meeting this challenge, I heard him say: the strength that we share in summoning together our resources; we have traditions; we have continuity; we have singularity of purpose; what we want to achieve, I assure you we will—

— As you all well know, the Ozark Corporation employs nearly one-fifth of the entire labor force of the Isaura region, I heard him say: we are the city's largest employer and taxpayer by far, responsible for some 36% of Isaura's total real-estate levy; on the average, we give over fourteen million dollars to local educational institutions each year, and an additional five million to area charitable, community, and cultural organizations; we are the second-largest manufacturer and processor of film, photographic, and imaging products in the world—

— But as I am also sure you know, these are only statistics, mere numbers, I heard him say: what binds us, what gives us our bond, are the loyalties and sentiments that engender these numbers, the loyalties and sentiments that form their very foundation; and those loyalties and sentiments, I'm sure you will agree, outstrip the importance of any numbers, indeed cannot be quantified—

— This is why we wanted to meet with you tonight here in School 41, where our challenge originated some ten months ago, I heard him say: because it is also here that we will see that our situation need not only be viewed as a challenge, but as an opportunity; yes: as an opportunity to reaffirm the richness and durability of our bond—

— And there was a rustling throughout the auditorium, as if a finger had been drawn over taut saran; but before things settled down, I heard him go on, over the rustling: so I invite you, then, friends and neighbors: I invite you to join with me in reaffirming our bond—

— We have had a problem, Fobel's voice rang out, carrying above the microphone and directly into the crowd; and then I heard him say, I am sure I heard him say: but it is really no problem at all—

— For our problem, ultimately, is fear, I heard him say: and fear is what we must fight—fight it as we would any irrational force threatening to disrupt our peaceful and prosperous community; and this evening, with your help, I have but one objective: to replace fear, debilitating and irrational fear, with fact—

— Then, upon a flourish of his arms, I heard him say: so let me, then, introduce to you the Ozark Eight-Point Full Protection Plan—which is nothing less than a plan to free our community from the scourge of fear—

— Then, from behind him, up on stage, an assistant in a dark suit came forward with an easel and placed it down near the side of the stage; the easel held a stack of large, cream-shaded cards; the top card held the Ozark emblem and, if I remember correctly, the words, imprinted in large black letters, Eight Points Towards Full Protection—

— And then Fobel explained how Ozark had already pledged nothing less than 100 million dollars, to be spent over the next five years, towards cleaning up and preventing, as I heard him put it, any and all conditions that might give rise to community concern—

— And I saw that the new card said Our Pledge—

— And I saw that the next card said $100,000,000.00—

— And I heard him explain that Ozark Labs had already begun a program to replace, eliminate, or upgrade all one-thousand of their underground chemical-storage tanks, their full complement, even though all of them already met or surpassed industry standards both for safety and for longevity—

— And how, at the same time, they would be re-covering and re-insulating all of their disposal facilities, using special, hardened concretes and clays and, I think the card said, new alloys specifically designed by Japanese waste-management specialists for such purposes—

— And how Ozark was going to overhaul its entire smokestack system, including the construction of entirely new smokestacks near Lake and Oatman Avenues, a point that I just rejoiced to hear—

— And how this part of the program was going to reduce fugitive airborne emissions by one-third over the next three years, I heard him say, and by yet another one-third over the three years subsequently—

— And how Ozark was going to create what I think he called a subterranean migration barrier, to keep any and all groundwater from leaving the area of the tank farm near Building 115—

— And how they were going to install a comprehensive new air-monitoring system for the areas surrounding Ozark Park, I heard him say—

— And how Ozark was already implementing state-of-the-art technologies to run smoother, cleaner, and more efficiently, I heard him say—

— Including, I heard him say, a new carbon-based filtration system for all gaseous emissions from their film-base processors—

— As well as a closed-loop recycling operation that will recover more than 97% of all methylene chloride used, I heard him say—

— With an ultimate goal of reducing emissions of methylene chloride by a full 80 percent within five years, I heard him say—

— Indeed, I heard him say, Ozark has eight chemical engineers now working full-time on developing a groundbreaking new plastic base for photographic film that does not require methylene chloride as a solvent—

— One that would do away with it entirely, I heard him say—

— And the audience listened, and took it all in, remaining quiet, and hardly moving, not moving at all; and I saw that the man sitting next to me loosened his grip on his windbreaker, which he had been holding scrunched in his lap—

— And I heard a woman behind me say: Oh, thank God—

— In short, I hereby pledge to you to do everything in our power to reduce or eliminate all sources of concern, I heard Fobel say: not just the minimum that might be necessary, not just what is needed to get by, but the utmost that we can do to allay the concerns of our community—

— Furthermore, I heard him say, as an integral part of our community-assurance program, we will also be offering five-thousand dollars in home-improvement grants to homeowners in the area closest to Ozark Park, as defined as those blocks bounded by Ridge Road and Route 31—

— And we will also refinance existing mortgages in this area at below-market interest rates, I heard him say—

— And we have put together a package of interest-free loans to certain qualifying families, I heard him say—

— And if you are wondering why we are doing all this, I am here to tell you that our reasons are perfectly sound and clear, I heard him say—

— Because for us at Ozark, all of this is a sound investment, I heard him say: an investment in the long-term stability of our community—

— Because we are with you in this, I heard him say: we are a part of you—

— Indeed, we *are* you, I heard him say: there is no separation—

— Yes, friends and neighbors, today our message is stronger than ever, I heard him say: environmental responsibility is a fundamental Ozark value; and we are going to support that credo with concerted action—

— At Ozark, we are determined to be counted among the good stewards of the Earth, I heard him say—

— And I saw that the card then said Toward General Excellence—

— And then, I saw, Fobel took a pause; then he reached over and picked up a cup that had been beside his lectern, and took a sip—

— And I thought that what he had said sounded good, and responsible, and right—

— And I thought perhaps that I might clap, to show something, to break the ice—

— And I did, I started clapping, when I heard some other people had begun—

— But I held back, I checked myself, since it had died away so quickly—

— But then, when Fobel introduced the man from the County Health Department, I made my son stop fiddling with the coloring books that I had let him bring along; I just reached my hand down into his lap and stopped him from rattling the pages, and then pressed him into sitting upright so he would pay attention—

— But he was very timid, the health man who came in from Steelville; he took a while to get to the lectern at the center of the stage, and then he mumbled, and I could hear him breathing in the mike—

— And at first he gave his name and started right in to reading from his papers, I remember; but then he stopped, because he had forgotten to thank George Fobel for introducing him; but when he thanked Fobel and started reading again, he also gave his own name again—

— I think he said his name was Dr. Joe Nitzer, and that he was the county health director; and the auditorium became quiet, trying to hear him, his timid voice—

— And I heard him say As you know, for several months the State has directed air, water and soil specialists to study conditions in Isaura—

— The teams produced a comprehensive study, and I have recently had the chance to review the findings, I heard him say—

— And the first thing that must be established is this, I heard him say: that under all generally accepted metrics and standards, the statistical probability of disease arising from levels of exposure found in Isaura—

— Is so low as to be practically nonexistent, I heard him say—

— Practically nonexistent, I am sure were his words—

— In other words, I heard him say, still reading from his papers: there is, for most citizens, essentially no problem—

— There is really nothing to worry about, I heard him say—

— And when I heard that, when I heard him say that, I almost spurted out in tears—

— But I didn't, I held myself back, so I wouldn't make a damn fool of myself—

— And then I heard him say In particular, preliminary tests showed that, based on a weighted average of sixteen drill sites established equidistantly throughout the Isaura aquifer, water samples contained 49 parts per billion of methylene chloride—

— Which is slightly higher, it must be said, than the State guideline for lifetime exposure, I heard him say—

— But three-thousand times lower than the Federal occupational standard, I heard him say—

— And then I heard him say In addition, testing seemed to indicate the presence of an atypical subjacent plume—

— That might have temporarily inflated the findings, I heard him say—

— And I just sat there and was thinking What the hell's he talking about?—

— In other words, I think he was saying that what they found was worse than what it should have been—

— Which, if I understand him correctly—

— And then he read more, with other numbers and other qualifications, in a voice I could hardly make out—

— And then, all of a sudden, he folded away his papers, and I was wondering what he was doing—

— And he looked up, and I was wondering if that was it—

— He was finished, in other words, I believed that he was finished—

— And then George Fobel came back up and shook his hand and thanked him for coming, and then the photographer came back; but before the little guy was able to turn away, Fobel asked him—and here are his words—to give it to us straight, to explain the findings in layman's terms; and I was glad, I was glad he asked him to do that—

— And the County Doctor said Sure; I heard him say Sure, of course—

— And then he said that the numbers indicate, quite clearly, that the statistical likelihood of significant risk to any one person was essentially negligible; that is what I heard him say—

— He said everything was negligible, I heard him say—

— And, you know, I just thought—

— I just thought How could he?—

— And then George Fobel thanked him and, I saw, let him go back to his seat—

— And then Fobel introduced the next speaker, a much larger man, with thick gray hair, and I was surprised to see that this one went up to the podium without notes—

— He was a big, burly man, wearing a bow tie, and Fobel presented him as a medical expert with the State; I think he said that the man was chief of the State health survey, and that he had come all the way from Jefferson City to be with us—

— And he was a doctor too, I'm sure I caught that, on the faculty of Lincoln University and affiliated with some hospital up there—

— And he just talked, he just went up to the microphone and talked without any papers, while holding his glasses in his right hand and gesturing with them; and he seemed like he knew what he was saying, I thought, he knew just exactly what he was talking about—

— In fact, he seemed real friendly, as if he were just

having a conversation; I felt as if he was really talking to me—
— And in a nice low voice he said Friends; people of Isaura; fellow citizens of Missouri; I am here to tell you that you have nothing to fear; and I thought he spoke very nicely and openly—
— And he said that for the last several months he had been asked to serve as a consultant to the Epidemiology Division of the Missouri Department of Public Health, one of whose current projects was Isaura, I heard him say—
— He had spent weeks assessing data collected from a broad range of sources, I heard him say, reams of information systematically gathered from local hospitals, clinics—
— Doctors, nursing homes, and other health-care providers, I heard him say—
— And he had also exhaustively analyzed the findings of the blood-test program that had been sponsored by the medical section of the Ozark corporation, I heard him say—
— Which, I heard him say, had been expertly run—
— And then I heard him say And based on a rigorous review of this information, all of which met the highest epidemiological standards, I can assure you that all the findings are negative—
— *Negative?*, and I grabbed my armrests with both hands; but what about—*so why doesn't*—
— And I was wondering how the hell everyone was taking it so calmly—
— But then, but then I realized—
— There is no evidence whatsoever of unusual health problems in the community, I heard him say—
— All blood serum levels for suspected chemicals were normal to low-normal, I heard him say—
— And, based upon all available information, representing all customary matrices for epidemiological investigation, mortality rates for Isaura Township, including its several outlying satellites, are within expected statistical limits, I heard him say—
— Likewise for aggregate rates of illness, I heard him say—
— That is to say, epidemiological norms would lead us to

expect an average of two childhood cancer cases in a community conforming to Isaura's demographical profile, I heard him say—
— But occasionally clusters of cancer do occur, I heard him say—
— So the slight local elevation probably represents a chance finding, I heard him say—
— Indeed, that is almost certain, I heard him say—
— So, to conclude, then, I heard him say—
— To put all of this in a form that should put your minds to rest, I heard him say—
— After using all of the most powerful epidemiological models at our disposal, I heard him say—
— We just can't find any health problems, I heard him say—
— And I heard that, and, you know—
— I heard it, and—
— And I thought: Thank God—
— I thought: *Thank God*—
— And I thought: *My God*—
— None of the findings, and none of the numbers, are anything other than absolutely normal, I heard him say—
— You have my word on that, I heard him say—
— And a report I have prepared on Isaura, containing and analyzing all of our significant findings, is available for your inspection, I heard him say—
— Actually, I had been hoping to have copies of this report to distribute tonight, I heard him say—
— But, unfortunately, I didn't have time to get to our Xerox center in Jefferson, I heard him say—
— So whoever would like to take a look at my copy can come forward at the end of tonight's assembly, I heard him say: or, you can put your name and address on a piece of paper and we'll send you one—
— And by then George Fobel was next to him, shaking his hand, and thanking him, and saying something to him that I couldn't hear—
— And one more thing, I then heard the nice-sounding man say: just one more thing—

— On behalf of the State of Missouri, I have been asked to convey our appreciation for the forthrightness and generosity with which the people at Ozark have responded to the current situation, I heard him say—

— To commend them for their responsibility in addressing the needs of our citizens and our economy, I heard him say—

— Ozark has committed here to being a model corporate citizen, I heard him say: this company is way ahead in terms of environmental initiatives—

— And then I saw that the photographer was by the lectern again, with his extra lenses hanging around his neck, and entirely ignoring the applause—

— And then I saw George Fobel walk the State guy back to his seat near the end of the table—

— They were talking and smiling, I saw—

— Then Fobel went back to the microphone at center and, I saw, took a drink of something, from a paper cup—

— A paper cup that was bigger than the ones they had laid out on the tables for us, I thought—

— The cup, I assumed, had been on the podium all along—

— Now, I heard him say: now, friends—

— He had his hands on both sides of the podium, I saw—

— I'm sure you have some questions that you'd care to ask us, I heard him say—

— So, in a few moments, we are going to open the floor to you, I heard him say: and we would encourage anyone who has questions or concerns to come forth; we invite everyone to participate, because we believe that free speech and open debate are the prerequisites to understanding—

— And that, fundamentally, is what we are here for, I heard him say: to foster understanding—

— To help dispel any uncertainties or fears that may remain, I heard him say—

— My colleagues here and I, as well as Doctors Nitzman and Tarrou, are all available for your questions, I heard him say: we will tell you if we do *not* know something, and we'll give it to you straight when we do—

— Because in the same way that we know that we—all of us, together—are bigger than this, I heard him say—

— I am also certain that, with your support and participation, we—our amity, our community—will prosper, and, indeed, will last longer than the petroglyphs over in Washington State Park, I heard him say—

— And then, two men appeared from the left of the stage and carried a tall podium to the front of the auditorium's center aisle; they placed it down gently and then adjusted its legs until it stood without wobbling; and I was thinking that one of them was that new custodian who came over from Building 68—

— And then one of them scurried back and attached a microphone to the holder at the top of the talk-stand; and I saw that he wound the cord around the mike holder a few times before plugging it into an outlet right at the front of the stage—

— But people held back, you know, they sat there and waited, before a few people finally stood and made their way to the aisle; then a woman two seats to my right got up and excused herself and slid past me, and I looked and saw that some of the people who had been standing in the back of the auditorium were also making their way forward—

— And when I looked around and saw all the people filling the seats, and standing shoulder to shoulder along the sides of the auditorium, and peering around the columns, and all the people crammed in the back, sometimes three deep, just so many of them—

— I wondered where everyone was, why the entire *town* wasn't here, how *anyone* could have stayed away—

— And I looked and I saw that some of the people lining up to speak at the podium were carrying slips of paper in their hands, little notes to themselves—

— And George Fobel was just waiting there behind the podium on stage, smiling at everybody; and I heard him say Welcome, everybody, that's OK: everybody can have a chance, everybody is welcome—

— And there were still people joining the line when he said All right, then; so I looked up front and saw him say OK, let's get started; you can address your question to anyone you wish—

— Though I couldn't see who the first questioner was, because the person standing behind her was a heavy-set man in a pea coat, and he was in the way; but then I heard a woman's voice, a little shaky-sounding voice coming over the PA system; and the voice said Yes: what I want to know is will it get worse—

— And George Fobel smiled and then he laughed a little and he said I'll take this one; and then I heard him say First, Ma'am, if I may say so, your question is predicated on a faulty supposition; your question implies that things are bad to begin with, and they most certainly are not—

— All of the experts who have spoken here before you this evening have confirmed that, I heard him say—

— Further, as I outlined earlier, we are renovating or replacing virtually the entirety of our waste-management sequence, outfitting every phase of processing with state-of-the-art technology, I heard him say—

— Triple-reinforced compacted-clay pits—each of which will be supported by two separate leachate collection zones—scrubbers, deoxidizers, high-pressure thermolysis—we will have it all, I heard him say: it will be a staggering system of waste neutralization; therefore, I'm sure I speak for all of us here in assuring you that you will never have any cause for concern—

— And you can count on that, I heard him say: it will be the last word in community safety—

— Thank you, I heard the woman say—

— And thank you, I heard Fobel say, and he adjusted the little boutonniere he always wears in his lapel: Yes, sir—

— Yes, Mr. Fobel, I have a question, I heard the next man say: Sir, you described a program of home-improvement grants before, for five thousand dollars for people who live between Ozark Park and Ridge Road; well, my question is, I live on Hiett Road, which is just two blocks past Ridge, and I don't think that those two blocks should...well, I know that my aluminum siding—

— Sir, I heard Fobel cut in: sir, thank you for your

question, because it is a good one; in fact, it is an important one—

— You know, I heard him say: we have been aware all along of the inherent difficulty of establishing boundaries for some of the administrative decisions that we make, for the boundaries may, to some, seem arbitrary or exclusionistic—

— Yet, after long and serious reflection, we can find no alternative in some situations to establishing boundaries, and have therefore always tried to be generous in the ones we declared, I heard him say: nevertheless, we are aware that individual exceptions occur, and must be taken into consideration; so if you'll drop me a line, to my office, briefly setting out the nature of your concerns, we'll be sure to give it our fullest attention—

— Thank you, sir, I heard the man say: thank you—

— And he turned away from the head of the line, and I saw that he was scrunching his cap up in his hands—

— And I saw that two other people left the line, as well, after that question—

— But then the next man on line put forth the next question; and I think he said flat out that he wanted to address it to the County health man—

— And then the little guy who spoke, the mumbling one, he looked up from his place at the long table and I remember he said Uh, that's OK—

— And he put his hand on the small microphone in front of him, I saw—

— And so the man in line said, I think he started off by saying Thank you; and then he said You told us all about the methyl chloride, but I think a lot of us are wondering about the other chemicals they found down there—

— Could you tell us some more about them, I'm sure he said—

— All the other chemicals, I think he said—

— And the mumbly man, the little mumbler, I heard him say Yes, certainly, I can do that—

— Then he flipped through his notebook and, when he found what he wanted, I heard him say From all of the test sites, a total of twelve chemicals and five heavy metals were found—

— Though in no more than trace quantities, I heard him say—

— And then I heard him say That is to say, these chemicals, although present in detectable concentrations—

— But let me say, let me just say right here, I heard George Fobel say—

— If you'll permit me to elaborate, I heard Fobel say—

— You know, chemicals such as these, and at these levels, are present naturally in all consolidated-rock aquifers such as ours, I heard him say—

— Especially those composed of carbonate rock such as limestone and dolomite, as is ours, I heard him say—

— All of which may sound a little technical, I heard him say—

— But what it all means is, it's OK, I heard him say—

— That is, based on all the evidence and expert opinion, we do not believe there is any health hazard or health risk to our community from any of these elements, I heard him say—

— Yes, I then heard the little mumbler say: that's correct—

— But how about the story that you've known about all these chemicals for something like eight years, I heard the next man on line say—

— That's a damn long time, I heard the man say—

— Yes, that is a considerable quantity of time, I heard George Fobel say: and your question is a good one—

— But during this time, while we were indeed aware of the existence of these chemicals, I heard him say—

— We did not believe that they had traveled beyond the boundaries of our property, I heard him say—

— There was no reason, no indication, to believe that substantial migration was occurring, I heard him say—

— That is, we had our containment and reprocessing systems in place, I heard him say: and we—

— But if I, if I could just say something here, the man sitting at Fobel's left side then said, and I saw that he had his hand on his microphone—

— That is, if I might just add a thought here, I heard him say—

— And then he identified himself, he gave his name, I think, and he said he was some sort of Ozark Senior Vice President—

— And he spoke very calmly, and very confidently, I'd say—

— And then he said You know, years ago, many companies weren't aware of the hazards of these wastes, I heard him say—

— And we, too, were not aware of all of them at the time, I heard him say—

— That is, I heard him say: we knew about the existence of these chemicals, of course—we were using or producing them—but we never—

— If I may, John, if I may just add one thing here, George Fobel then said, and then I heard him cough—

— If you would, John, I think a good way to look at the situation would be like this, I heard him say—

— You know, under State and Federal regulations in effect during the 1970's and continuing through today, we were not obligated to notify State officials about these aspects of our operations, I heard him say—

— There were no laws that required it, I heard him say—

— We were in perfect compliance with existing State and Federal disclosure standards, I heard him say: and I'm sure Dr. Tarrou will back me up on this—

— That is correct, I heard the Government man—the big one, with the gray hair and bow tie—say from his end of the table: our regulations were clear as regards to documentation and notification—

— And, indeed, after thoroughgoing research into this issue, we could find no legal basis for mandatory disclosure of any such activities, I heard him say—

— Occurring as they did on private property, I heard him say—

— Indeed, for many years we had no review structures in place for such information, I heard him say—

— There will be no judiciary action on that count, I heard him say—

— In fact, it may interest you to know that Ozark has, since its founding, participated in what are now known as environmental practices without there having been a legal need to do so, I heard Fobel say—

— More than 60 years ago, we began extensive source reduction and recycling efforts, I heard him say: and we have continued to expand this program until, today, we recycle more than 4.2 billion pounds of materials per annum—

— Indeed, today all the investments we make and the decisions we pursue reflect an increasingly clear commitment to environmental responsibility, I heard Fobel say: and every year finds us doing more to protect the environment, and doing it better, with a heightened sense of urgency—

— And then this woman, this really fat woman, wearing these wide, scooping jeans and this ripply shirt that looked like parachute folds, she went up to the stand; but she was so small that the man behind her had to unhook the microphone and bring it down to her, and I also saw that she was reading from a piece of paper—

— And I heard her say Good evening; my name is Alma Walker, and I have been living with my husband and my four sons on Old Well Road for twenty-four years; before that, I lived in Isaura since the age of eight; now, I would like to know how you could let this happen—

— And George Fobel, you know, George Fobel just jumped on that; he leaned forward on his lectern so much that it moved and squeaked, and then I heard him cut in with Ma'am?; Mrs. Walker?; you will pardon me for saying this but I don't think that's entirely fair—

— You see, you are presuming a guilt on our part that is simply not sustainable, and are presenting to us as a fait accompli something that simply does not exist, I heard him say—

— We have acted entirely within the boundaries of the law, yet you persist in clinging to rumors that we have done something wrong, I heard him say—

— In other words, you are continuing with the dangerous course of responding to *fear* and not to *fact*, I heard him say—

— And then I heard him say Ma'am, you and everyone else in here must realize that chemicals are an integral by-product of our industrial society, and represent by-products of the daily life of every citizen of that society—

— In other words, of every single one of *you*, I heard him say—

— In everything you do, and in everything you see, there is an inescapable base in chemicals, I heard him say—

— They are in what we produce and in what you buy, I heard him say—

— Therefore, the situation that exists is societal in scope, and the mechanisms for responding to it must reflect its societal nature, I heard him say—

— So there is no getting around the fact that all of us— *all* of us—are in this together, I heard him say—

— And if we, at Ozark, are to respond wisely, and properly, to events as they unfold, then you must support the process by responding wisely and properly as well, I heard him say—

— But then I saw that the next man on line, the one behind the fat woman, he took the microphone from her and said But at Love Canal—

— This is *not* Love Canal, Fobel then said and smacked the top of his lectern: there is *no* equivalent between that situation and ours, I heard him say—

— At Love Canal, the Hooker Chemical Corporation was found guilty of *monstrous* violations of the law, I heard him say—

— For years, for *decades*, those people were found guilty of the most flagrant abuses of public health, I heard him say—

— Of dumping chemicals almost indis*crim*inately, with *no* regard for public health and safety, I heard him say—

— In *immense* quantities, *tens* of *thousands* of leaking barrels, I heard him say—

— For that was their business, I heard him say—

— Explicitly and specifically, the manufacture of chemicals, I heard him say—

— Moreover, Hooker was engaged in the manufacture of chemicals of extraordinary virulence and toxicity, I heard him say—

— Real and known killers, I heard him say—

— Chemicals that have *nothing* to do with the kinds of substances we are dealing with here, I heard him say—

— I mean, people in Isaura hear methylene chloride and they immediately become unhinged, I heard him say—

— You freak out, I heard him say—

— When, in fact—and Dr. Nitzman will back me up on this—nothing has *ever* been concretely established about methylene chloride's health consequences for people, I heard him say—

— That is, after long and repeated study, it has *never* definitively been shown to be a human carcinogen, I heard him say—

— Indeed, it may interest some of you to hear that methylene chloride, the very same methylene chloride, I heard him say—

— Is a major component of aerosol hair spray, I heard him say: and in this commonly-used form, methylene chloride is present in concentrations of up to thirty-one times *higher* than anything that has *ever* been found within Ozark Park, or in the adjoining neighborhoods—

— And it may further interest some of you to hear that methylene chloride, our very own methylene chloride, I heard him say—

— Is used by the Norelco Corporation in the manufacture of filters for its successful Clean Water Machine, I heard him say—

— In other words, methylene chloride is used in this product to *clean* water, I heard him say: to make it *pure*—

— To *cleanse* drinking water of impurities and thereby protect people from contamination, I heard him say—

— And these machines and filters have been very successful, I heard him say: they have been very successful indeed—

— With sales well into the hundreds of thousands of units, I heard him say—

— Ah, George, George, if you would, I then heard another voice say—

— And I saw that down at the other end of the table, a man who had kept quiet all along began to speak: George, maybe I could come in with something here—

— And then I heard him identify himself as another Ozark official, as a member of the board of trustees; and he certainly looked the part, all dressed in cufflinks and a nice navy-blue suit—

— And I heard him say You know, I happen to have in front of me something that may be able to make a meaningful contribution to our discussion tonight—

— And so I listened, and I looked, but all he was doing was sitting there with his elbows on the table, and his arms angled around a small pile of documents—

— And it is this, I then heard him say; and then he slowly reached and grabbed a paper cup that was near him—

— Yes, this, I heard him say: a cup of water, taken from a normal sink in the boys' room here not forty minutes ago—

— In other words, this is good Isaura tap water, I heard him say: fresh from a faucet just like all the ones you have at home—

— And then he held the cup up to the light and looked at it for a good few seconds; and then he took the cup and, I saw it clearly, slowly brought it to his lips, and drank it all down—

— Now, that's pure, I then heard him say, when he had finished drinking: there's nothing in there—

— And the auditorium, you know, was quiet for a moment after he did that; and I was thinking, you know, that I was glad he made that gesture—

— But then this woman, you know, a somewhat younger woman, I saw that she came to the microphone, and she leaned right up to it, directly, and she spoke into it directly—

— And I saw she had some papers in her hand—

— And I heard her say Dr. Nitzer, you spoke earlier about the quantity of methylene chloride that Missouri has established as legally permissible in its potable water, which you put at forty parts per billion—

— And the one who mumbled, the little man sitting at the table who mumbled, I heard him say Yes: that's correct—

— But then I heard the young woman say But in both Vermont and Washington States, the legal limit is only *twenty* parts per billion—

— And then someone, some man in the back of the auditorium, he screamed out *Can* it, Mona; and I saw that most of the people sitting near me turned to look at him—

— And then I heard another man yell out *Go get a job*—

— But the young woman stood her ground; I mean, despite all the people turning around and buzzing and bickering, I saw that she just stood there looking George Fobel in the eye—

— And I don't know why he put up with her, with the way she was disturbing the meeting, with all the people talking and disputing; but he stood very calmly at the lectern and said Yes, that is true—

— And Mona, that damn Mona dressed all in black, I don't think she was ready for that, for that direct an answer—

— But she was staring at him, I saw she was just staring at him—

— And then George Fobel continued, and I saw that he kept his cool—

— And I heard him say Yes, there are variations in all sorts of state indices—

— But for all we know, the limits established by the Missouri Department of Public Health are six times too *high*, I heard him say—

— Indeed, I look at the Missouri DPH's track record and notice that it habitually errs on the side of safety, I heard him say—

— *That's* it, *George*, I heard somebody call out—

— For example, if you had looked elsewhere on your list, you would have seen that New Mexico permits levels of up to *sixty-five* parts per billion, I heard Fobel say—

— So where does that leave us, Mona, when standards are thusly variable, I heard him say, just going on coolly above all the talking—

— What we must aim for—our absolute standard, if you will—is to comply with what the Governmental bodies with jurisdiction in our community have established for us, I heard him say: that is what we must obey—

— But that's *ridiculous*, I heard the girl say: you know that; compliance isn't the same thing as safety; you can kill with impunity as long as you comply—

— Exactly...*say it!*, I heard—

— And then there was a lot more jeering and catcalls, and there was whistling, everywhere, from all over the auditorium; but I saw that Fobel, holding his hands up to try to get things calm, only backed down when the official from Jefferson City got up—

— Miss...miss...if you *please*, I heard the man in the bow tie say, the tall man who had spoken before—

— And then I heard the taller man say, after the auditorium had begun to quiet down, The standards promulgated by the State of Missouri have undergone the most severe review and scrutiny, by a panel of medical experts in accordance with national guidelines—

— These decisions are not arbitrary, or politically motivated, I heard him say: they are determined by the necessity of establishing action thresholds so that our society can continue to function—

— And their one goal, their *sovereign* goal, is to protect the well-being of our citizenry, I heard him say: that is what the guidelines are *for*—

— Hear, hear, I then heard George Fobel say: they are guidelines for *safety*, not for maximum allowable license—

— Therefore, these are the standards to which we adhere, I heard Fobel say: they represent *our* law; and so, through adhering to them, we have comported ourselves, *by definition*, as a responsible corporate citizen—

— And then I heard the young woman say But don't you—

— But don't you think you should let someone else take their turn at the microphone?, I heard Fobel say—

— But I just have—, I heard the young woman say—

— You can always get back in line, I heard Fobel say—

— Yes, I heard the next woman say: I've heard you saying all those things about the chemicals in the water supply, and all those tiny amounts and stuff, so many parts per billion, but my question is, is that dangerous or isn't it?—

— Yeah...*Yeah!*, I heard—

— That's *right!*, I heard—

— *Please*, people, *please*, I heard Fobel say: *please* try to control yourselves, so we can have a civilized exchange of information—

— *Aw*—, I heard—

— Now, Ma'am, I heard Fobel say: before I answer your question, I think it's important that we establish a sense of some of the realities of modern life—

— *Tell* us, George, I heard—

— And by that, I mean to put the notion of risk into a context that is in some way meaningful, I heard him say—

— Because it is important to bear in mind that virtually everything entails some level of risk, I heard him say—

— *Tell* us something, George!, I heard—

— For instance, I heard Fobel say: we recently commissioned a risk-exposure projection; and at current levels for all the chemicals *combined* that were observed in the township's aquifer, we would expect, for persons drinking two liters of water per day, 1.6 cancer deaths for every 100,000 people exposed over a 70-year lifetime—

— So what are you going to do about it!, I heard someone scream—

— But remember this, just remember *this*, I then heard Fobel say: over the same 70-year lifetime, motor vehicle accidents will claim the lives of nearly eighteen-*hun*dred of every 100,000 people, and smoking just one pack of cigarettes per day will kill *four thousand* of the 100,000 from respiratory cancer *alone*—

— Put it *away*, George!, I heard—

— But that's a risk *we* take, our*selves,* I heard—

— *Hey—come on*, I heard—

— *Please*, people—*please*, I then heard Fobel say—

— *Please*, I heard Fobel then speak out: nevertheless, these figures put the absolutely *minu*scule, insi*gnifi*cant risk

posed by the trace compounds into its proper perspective—
— So, Ma'am, to return to your question, I then heard
Fobel say: there is risk present, as there is in almost everything;
but in relation to other, universally accepted risks, the risk
from the trace substances is virtually nonexistent—
— *Yeah*, I heard: but it's a risk *you* make for *us*—
— Listen, *listen*, I heard the man from the State cut in: the
fact of the matter is that if you people were seriously interested in reducing your exposure to risk, you could do far
more than any corporate board or legislative council ever
could—
— Aw, *shit*, I heard—
— For *instance*, I heard him say: national actuarial data
reveal that the number of deaths per annum from cardiovascular disease is more than *212%* of what it is from malignan-
cies—over *twice* as high; but cardiovascular disease, it is a
known fact, directly correlates with diet—
— So think about that, I heard him say: and then *keep*
thinking about it the next time you reach for your *potato
chips*—
— *Fuck you!*, I heard someone call out—
— Right, right, you can't tolerate *that*, I heard the man
from the State say: because you have decided that that is an
acceptable risk, although it is *thousands of times greater* than
any risk posed by Isaura's water sources—
— So the problem here, the *real* problem, is that you are
responding to your *own* perceptions and decisions, and not to
the *facts* as they *exist*, I heard him say—
— *Exactly*, I heard a man sitting at the other end of the
stage say: but risk doesn't exist in *perception*, but in the *world*—
— And while *you* are only concerned with the former, *we*
must pay attention to the *latter*, I heard this man continue—
— For instance, I heard him go on: there is no question
that, here and now, with conditions as they stand, you are
facing a greater chance of water pollution from your own
septic tanks than from anything that makes it past the Ozark
Corporation's waste-management systems—
— Yet that is something that you *refuse* to let yourself
acknowledge in any way *at all*, I heard him say—

— *Bullshit,* I heard someone say: that's *bullshit*—

— You're crazy!, I then heard: you're fucking *crazy!*—

— The other opposite of freedom is *power!*, I heard—

— *Let the man talk,* I then heard—

— And then Fobel, George Fobel, he got up again and raised his arms and tried to quiet things down; and I heard him say, amid all the noise, People...; people...; *please...*—

— *Please* let us try to proceed with some order and civility, I heard him say: because if we don't, if you don't—

— And there was talking and arguing and buzzing from every corner of the hall, and even some people laughing, and I was turning all around in my seat to look—

— And then I heard a voice from way in the back yell *You said you wanted to listen to us*—

— *Yeah,* I heard: *yeah!: you said you*—

— *So listen to us,* I heard: *listen to what we're*—

— And then I heard *People*—

— And then I heard from the stage *People, please*—

— And then I saw a man from the stage take the mike, and hold it to his face, and open his eyes wide—

— And say real strong and loud People...*people...,* I heard him say: we're not suffering from too *little* democracy here, but too *much*—

— And then I—

— But finally, then, finally the next woman in line went up to the podium, I heard her voice over the PA, it was quieter, and the auditorium quieted down a bit when she began—

— And I heard her say Yes; my name is Jeanette Baylog, and I live on Riga Street—

— *Riga?;* but where—I mean which one—

— Maybe the yellow—maybe that little house in by the cul-de-sac where I—

— I am with the Ozark Heritage branch of the Missouri Winegrowers' Association, and I have been asked to pose the following question to all of you, I heard the woman say: given the delicate chemistry that supports every aspect of quality viniculture, can you guarantee us, who are already experiencing adverse effects from the increased development of the

Potosi and Viburnum lead mines, that our vineyards will not be additionally stressed by your—

— Now Ma'am, I then heard George Fobel say, and I saw he was pursing and releasing his lips: once again, and for what I hope will be the last time—

— You know, George, I then heard another man say, halfway down the table: George, I must say that it's coming to the point where I can't believe what I'm hearing here—

— And he identified himself as an Ozark director of products research, and I heard him say You know, it's occurred to me that what's going on here is a kind of chemical McCarthyism—an absolute return to the McCarthy mentality—

— And then I heard the Ozark man say From where I'm sitting, it's obvious that these chemicals are just being attacked indiscriminately, that their reputation is being *ruined* without anyone actually resorting to *facts*—

— Oh yeah?, I then heard someone say: *Oh yeah?*—

— *Hey,* come *on,* I heard from the stage: *people, please,* just pipe *down* now—

— But get this straight, I then heard the man say: get this straight; we think methylene chloride is a very important symbol; if we were to lose on this issue, it would mean that the American public has been taken back a couple of hundred years to an era of witch hunting, only this time the witches are chemicals, not people—

—So *that* is the importance of this issue, I heard the man say: it certainly has nothing to do with Ozark Laboratories, or methylene chloride—

— But then the audience just surged up in sound, with everyone talking and complaining and bickering, and I heard people calling out *Nonsense!* and *Liars!* and *Just listen to yourself, will ya*—

— And I saw this woman sitting next to me, with gray hair all done in waves like from a salon, and she was wearing a windbreaker and a plaid shirt, and she was sitting there with her hand up to her face, she was crying—

— And I heard somebody scream *Sure—where all YOU guys live up in*—

— And then this other man at the table, a man who hadn't spoken before, I heard him start in and say You know, you people should also consider *your* role in all this—

— You fucking *crazy?*, I heard—

— That's right, *your* role, I heard him say—

— I mean, we're only *in* this business because of the demand from *consumers*, I heard him say: we're only producing things that people actively *want*—

— *Bullshit!*, I heard—

— They want *killers?*, I heard—

— *Yes*, that's *right*, I heard him say: it's a demand expressed by the whole *country* for our products, by the whole *world*; and it's a demand from *you, too*—a demand to be paid a competitive wage in an industry where the competition is *fierce* and the regulation *incessant*—

— *You fuckin' crazy?*, I heard, and—

— *Who you telling that to?*, I heard: *who do you think you're talking to?*, and—

— *I am not an externality!*, I heard—

— It's OK, Mike, I then heard Fobel say: Mike, it's OK—

— Come on, Mike, just leave it go, I heard him say—

— And, you know, one of the policemen in the hall, one of the policemen by the door, I saw that he uncrossed his arms—

— And the State doctor, the big man with the glasses, he banged his fist on the table a couple of times, real loud, and he took off his glasses; and I looked at him and the noise came down a bit and then he began speaking into his microphone—

— You know, people, I heard him say: you know, you are all just acting like spoiled children—just like spoiled *children* when they hear answers they don't like—

— *Right*, I heard the man in the blue suit say: when you don't hear simple *consolations* or *solutions*, when we try to act re*spon*sibly and give you a *real* sense of—

— *You're not saying anything!*, I heard—

— *You're just spewing the same old shit!*, I heard—

— *It's not what WE don't want to hear, it's what YOU don't say!*, I heard—

— *All right, then—all right!*, I heard George Fobel then

say: *all right!*—

— If *that's* what you want, then we'll *tell* you all the things we're *not* saying, I heard him say—

— And I saw that Fobel was glistening, he was standing up there holding his microphone in one hand and leaning his other hand on the lectern, and he was glistening—

— Yes, we *will* tell you then, I heard him say—

— We will tell you how we have sixteen people working full-time on the paperwork requirements of regulation, I heard him say—

— *Damn them too*, I heard—

— *Township* regulations, *State* regulations, *Federal* regulations, I heard him say: regulations for storage and regulations for transport; regulations on bleed restrictions and safe containment and heat resistance and substance adherence—

— And then the regulations to make sure we comply with all the *regulations*, I heard him say—

— And then we'll tell you about Marshall Photo, I heard him say: remember them?, up in Lansing?, one of our chief competitors?—the company that, after 34 years of business, went under because, as they themselves put it, of excessive *regulation*—

— Because they couldn't write a memo without having to file six *compliance* reports, I heard him say—

— And we will tell you about how this episode of ours is coming at a point in our 101-year history when gross revenues, for the first time *ever*, have begun *declining*, I heard him say: and how our third-quarter earnings are down 18.8% from third quarter 1980—

— And we will tell you about a Dun & Bradstreet survey that was just released, I heard him say: and about how this survey found that over 10,100 American businesses had closed by mid-August of this year, representing an increase of over 41% from the same period *last* year—

— And how mortgage interest rates are now expected to go up to 17%, I heard him say: a situation that has brought nationwide housing starts so low that it has only been this bad three times since 1948—

—And how from April through mid-September of this

year, the Dow Jones has dropped more than 17%, I heard him say: it has fallen more than *160 points*—more than *half* of which came in the month following the President's new tax and budget reductions—

— And how the prime rate now stands at a near-record 20.5%, I heard him say—

— And how many economic experts fear a rekindling of double-digit *inflation*, I heard him say—

— *OK?, OK?*, I heard him say: how's *that* for what we're not saying—

— And then you can put that together with what we *are* saying, I heard: how in the middle of all this we are embarking upon a waste-control and community-assistance program of *monumental* proportions, entailing millions and millions of dollars expended for *your* benefit—

— A program that, according to *all* questioned consultants and experts, is *not* needed, I heard—

— For which there exists *no* legal requirement, I heard—

— Think about that!, I heard: we will be spending *over one-hundred million dollars* on a program of reconstruction and renovation just so *you* can *sleep* at night—

— A *massive* program, I heard: comprehensive and *massive*—

— Because we feel we must be *responsive* to you, and to your *needs*, even to your *psychological* needs, *no matter how groundless or irrational they may be*—

— Still, *we* feel that we must take all this into account—that it is part of our responsibility—

— Even though it is *not* legally required, I heard—

— But don't you think this is *costing* us—that it's *hurting* us?—

— Don't you think that all this is going to make things even *tougher* for us up on State Street than they *already are?*, I heard—

— That is to say, just because we didn't *tell* you about our new directive to reuse computer paper as scrap pads, does that mean that we aren't instituting cost-cutting measures *wherever we can?*—

— Just because we haven't wanted to disquiet you with

public announcements about switching from paper to Styrofoam cups in our cafeterias because they are marginally less expensive, does that mean that we aren't facing real financial hardships *right now?*—

— Because *we are*: things are *tough* for us now—

— Nevertheless, we are committing *over one-hundred million dollars* to further protect *your* safety—

— Now, we don't want to *bankrupt* ourselves on this—

— We don't want to go into *bankruptcy*—

— We don't think there's one person in this whole auditorium who would be in favor of *that*—

— No, *you* don't want that *either*—

— Because there is no way to *imagine* what that would mean—

— So if we are to minimize the inevitable losses of jobs that are going to result from our current crisis—

— From our dedication to safety—

— And from this downturn in the economy—

— *And* the burden of excess regulation—

— Then we are going to have to count on *you* for support—

— For *understanding*—

— For pitching in and doing what *you can*—

— For *all* of us—

— For otherwise, there will have to be the inevitable cutbacks in our labor force—

— There will *have* to be—

— It will be *inevitable*—

— And we can't guarantee *how many* will go—

— Or else Ozark Labs, despite its history here, Ozark Labs will have to go elsewhere—

— We will be forced to move—

— To relocate our corporate headquarters and principal operations—

— To pull out!—

— And maybe just leave a small administrative force—

— Just shut the shop up!—

— Because if we can't stay, we can't stay—

— Despite our 101 years here—

— If we cannot continue to do business in this area then we cannot continue to do business in this area—

— It is as simple as that—

— In fact, we have already begun speaking with a few other cities throughout the Mid-West that would be very pleased to receive our presence—

— They would be very pleased *indeed*—

— And they have *said* so—

— In so many words—

— Some have already begun to offer tax abatements and other incentives—

— Des Moines has offered to subsidize the construction of an entire 8-square-mile industrial park—

— And Dr. Tarrou here, who works closely with officials in Jefferson City, will certainly be able to confirm all this for you—

— Yes, that's true—

— Ozark Labs has communicated to the State Department of Commerce that the company has been investigating alternate business venues—

— That can be confirmed—

— So OK, then, OK, Fobel said—

— There you have it—

— Right there—

— And that's just a *taste* of the things we haven't wanted to tell you—

— Just a *sampling* of them—

— Just the *beginning*—

— And now we trust you understand just *why*—

— Just why we *refrain* from saying some things—

— Some *important* things—

— It is because we do not want to sow discord—

— To spread unnecessary *alarm*—

— This is precisely what we do *not* want to do—

— Because we are in this together—

— *All* of us, *together*—

— And so we must *work* together—

— We must work *hard* together—

— To preserve what we have—

— To keep on growing—
— To sustain our *traditions*—
— To keep what we have from *falling asunder*—
— Because there are risks—
— There are dangers—
— We are facing unpredictable hazards—
— And it is *you* who will ultimately bear the burden of surrendering to these unpredictable hazards—
— And it is *your* lives, and *your* livelihoods, that will suffer as a result of internal dissension—
— And it is only through increased and ceaseless vigilance that we can *ward off* these dangers—
— And that is it—
— That is it!—
— *That is it!*—

...When I press it together it holds for a while; but then—without warning, without sound—it just gives way; then, without warning, my throat is cold, and I feel the chill air trickling all the way down to the skin above my stomach; the last time the snap gave way was over on Aster Street, as I was stepping over a snow mound at curbside, crossing to Avis: I was lifting up, stepping over the blackened snow, when all of a sudden my throat flashes cold, as if cold electricity has come to my throat and neck and chest; immediately I pull back onto the curb; then I take off my gloves and try to press the snap back together—it's much too small to battle with gloves on; so I press the snap together, and it gives, and I press the snap together, and it gives, and all the while my fingers are cold and my throat is exposed and is cold; then, finally, when I do something right, and the snap stays, I am reluctant to move, for I know what the least joggle will likely cause to happen; that is why I don't want to move; I can see, of course, what has gone wrong with the snap, I can bend the chin-flap up to my eyes and just look at it; the male side, the little bulb, is fine; it is as it has always been; but the female side, the little ridged circle, has worn away; one arc of the circle has flared up into a little wave; so the snap, with the slightest move, just comes apart; it automatically gives; and that is it; every time the snap just gives way; it doesn't pop, it just loosens; the grip is just no longer there—

— While the output from the cable box feeds into the VCR's input jack, and the VCR's out line feeds into the TV; that's how the diagram says it's supposed to go, I think; but I don't get it—this video player, the Magnavox 800Y, is supposed to let you tape one show at the same time as you're watching another program; that's why I bought it, to have that flexibility, but I can't see how this configuration of cables would permit it; I don't think the cable box splits signals, so I thought I would try switching to a different channel on the cassette recorder, to see if that might reroute the line, or somehow divided the input; so I picked up a remote control, but, because I now have three remote controls for the system, I ended up changing the channel on the television, because I had used the wrong control; so then there was a different picture on the TV, but it wasn't either of the two I wanted, so I manually changed the channel on the VCR and then saw that the program didn't change at all—it was the same transmission; but I realized what I had done, so I changed the station on the television by hand and saw the screen fill with snow and begin to roar; so I shut the whole thing down, all of it, all three components, and went around and gathered up all the plastic bags and the Styrofoam and put it back into the VCR box, so I could throw it out; but there it was, on the carton, among the advertised features—Watch and Tape Different Programs at the Same Time; it was also in the manual, with instructions and sequential letters and line diagrams to assist you; but I don't know—I can't do it, I can't figure it out; there must be something in all these inputs and outputs that will permit this to work, something between the inputs and outputs, or some way different inputs can be made to go in parallel, because it's not what I want, I can't get this arrangement to run right; I can't even see how it *could* work: with all the in-jacks and out-jacks and all the remote controls, it's a little confusing, and the diagrams don't seem to accord with the equipment, and—

— There must be some modification made: this time I must make sure to do it; Mr. Archer will just have to understand, or to be made to understand, if it is necessary; but how to do it?; should I just do it, and wait to see if he says something, or should I say something to him first—with my eyes down, then bringing them up to meet his, so he will get a sense of how difficult this is for me; oh, I don't know; each approach entails risk, that is sure; I was stunned at how quickly Mrs. Culhane gave me a quizzical eye, the very first time I tried some modification: she had come in last Wednesday afternoon, as usual, for her half-pound of Orange Pekoe, and just then I decided that I could no longer afford to put it off, that I simply had to institute the new policy; so I filled the bag with precisely half a pound of tea, the scale-needle was very nearly exact, and by the time I had taken the bag from the scale and folded closed its top she was looking at me discordantly; that was not a smile, but an eye at an angle; but what can I do?; I cannot go on being overgenerous; I had hoped that after these last few years of making sure I did well by my customers, of helping them in the way that I could, that they would understand; I have been grateful for their continued patronage, but the way things are now I have simply got to think of ways of cutting back; the problem is, of course, that my customers have gotten used to my generosity, they have come to expect it; but it is not, as I had planned to say to Mrs. Culhane when she came in on Wednesday, it is not as if I am now trying to cheat you: now I am just giving you the *correct* amount; as it is, I had hoped that my customers would see that I've started staying open late Thursday evenings, and that I've cut Leonard down to afternoons and Saturdays; but in this business there aren't many other possible modifications; I do not want to take in coffee, because the scent ruins the tea; that's why there are so few of us: along with Perch's in Copenhagen and another store in Amsterdam, we're about the only pure-tea people left, at least in the West, and it's known that specialization is particularly fragile in slow times; even the winter months didn't do too much this year; so I have little choice; I must think of imposing some austerity; but Mr. Archer—he has been coming in Friday evenings, right about 6:15, for a pound of Lapsang Suchong almost since we opened, for nearly eighteen years; no one else has been with me for so long; and Mr. Archer—I know that Mr. Archer has a watchful eye, a very watchful eye; that Mr. Archer—he has such a watchful eye—

— I can go out, of course; in fact I should: I've been in all day; but Roy Rogers has gone up to $3.49 for the large roast beef sandwich with cheese, though that sauce is nice and salty; but why spend the money?: with tax and a Pepsi it's nearly five dollars, and I can use that to do the laundry and be ahead for today; and they have that special on tonight about date rape, I can see that; but what have I got—I don't know, there's that chicken from yesterday, and I can finish the hamburger rolls before they're too hard; but I really should go out, to break things up a little—though I'd have to change, I couldn't go out in this; though if I went to the movies, I think Beetlejuice is still around, then I probably could wear what I have on: I only go from the car right into the movie's darkness, so no one would see how wrinkled this blouse is, even the collar; the lines are usually short in the middle of the week, so no one would notice except maybe at the tickets; but the movie's even more expensive than Roy Rogers, and it's a little chilly tonight, and I'd miss the special on date rape; but I don't really *want* chicken, and maybe I should get out, and maybe even changing clothes would be good for me, though the TV is free, and why bother getting all dressed just for nothing; though if I do the laundry tomorrow I can throw this blouse in with another day of wear, and tomorrow Beetlejuice will still be playing, and I wouldn't have to miss the date rape special, and maybe it'll be warmer, and the hamburger rolls will be really bad by then; and the chicken too, it might be bad by tomorrow, I might have to throw it out; but I don't think I want any more of the chicken, so why *not* throw it out, though Roy Rogers is expensive, and that on top of the movie, as long as I'm out—

— Though when I got there she was baking crullers; she was standing at the counter in the kitchen, and she didn't even turn around when I walked into the room; she just continued spooning water into an aluminum mixing bowl; then she set the timer on the stove; Ma, I said: come on— we've got to go; but she just continued fiddling with the bowls, and then she opened a package of margarine, and then she dusted the cutting board with flour; Ma, I said: Ma; then she opened a cupboard and looked into it and took out a tiny bottle; Ma, I said: it's already almost time: we'll be late; then I felt warmth coming from the stove, so I went over and twisted the knob to shut it off; Ma, I said: come on, we'll be late; This is something new, she said: got oat bran in it; still, during all of this time I had not seen her face; But Ma, I said: the appointment's for 11:30; she picked up one of the deeper bowls and began to stir it with a spoon, metal scraping muted metal as she held the bowl against the side of her stomach; then she turned on the faucet, then turned it off; still, I had not seen her face; Ma, I said: it's only a general check-up; she put the bowl down on the counter, then opened and closed a side cupboard, then took another spoon out of the rattly drawer—

— But you could be anyone, the woman said: it doesn't matter what you tell me, you could be anyone at all; so I said OK, then, let's both hang up and you can call me back and you'll see it's the right number; you'll see that it's my number in my house, I'll be right here and answer it; but she said Don't you see: you could be anyone calling from that number; and I said I know, because I knew, I knew this all along; so I said Forgive me, but this is crazy, it's my own number that I'm asking you for; and she said We're sorry, but we can't give unlisted numbers out to anyone, not at all, unless you come in with proper identification; and I said I know, because I knew; still I said But as I told you, I seem to have lost or misplaced or maybe threw out the notice with the new number, and so I have no other way of knowing; so she said As I said, you can either come in with proper identification and we'll give the number to you, or I suppose you can wait for the first bill to arrive and see it printed there; but I didn't *want* to go in to the phone company, I thought; I hate those places, with the endless lines that people always cut and the smudged chairs in the waiting area; I just couldn't go there, I thought, though I could hear from the woman's voice on the phone that there was no point in asking to speak to her superior; the superior would just say the same thing, definitely, she wouldn't even hear me, or really talk to me, what was I to them; they aren't concerned about things like this, and that is it; ; so I thought maybe I would wait for the first bill, maybe that would be the best way, the only way, and then this woman came to my door—

— And that Roy, man, always cracking the whip, just cracking the whip, telling me I got to bring those boxes out to the gate for the 4 o'clock pick-up when he knows that all the resodding I'm doing around the plaza, which *he* gave me to do, is going to take all day, and he said he wanted it finished by five; and then him making fun of my shoes, saying they look almost as old as I am, and looking down at them, and his now always saying that I'm showing my age, I'm showing my age, even if he is just teasing, then Jack once hearing and calling out That's right old-timer, and smiling and going off; so what do they expect, tell me what do they expect, maybe I am slipping, I know I'm slipping, so Roy calls and says when you coming back, and I tell him when I can, when I can, so then Roy waits a few weeks, he waits a few weeks before he calls again, and he says they got to lay down the fertilizer, they need it for the front lawn, he says the lawn is waiting for me to do it; but I hear his voice and I don't want to go in, I can't go in, they can get someone else to do it, they know that, they understand that, they'll fire me if I go in, so I can't go in, I don't want to, I can't—

— Imagine why, because I was just sitting on my divan,
with the TV on, the 6 o'clock news, in the semidarkness, and
I was just bending over to unlace my espadrilles, so I could
relax and stretch out, when I felt something, this kind of sharp
tick, it was almost as if I *heard* something happen, so I put my
hand up to my face, and pressed my nose, and on my knuckle
I saw blood, I could clearly make it out in the light that
remained, a darkish shiny stain on the top of my knuckle, so
I tilted my head back and stepped around the coffee table and
ran to the bathroom, and I turned on the light and in the
mirror I could see that my nose was bleeding, that there was
dark red in there, and dark red dipping out a little from the
nostril, and I had no idea how it happened, or why it
happened, so I got cotton, and I ran the faucet, and I didn't
know what to do about it, if I should call a doctor, or call
Marion, because it just started, it began all by itself, I didn't
touch it, I didn't do anything, it just started all by itself, and
I don't know why or what from or what it means, whether it's
an indication of something and I should go to the hospital,
just not take any chances and get to the hospital, and I lean
against the wall and worry and don't know what to do when
I hear something and I step out of the bathroom and see that
there's a woman at my door—
— Though in the beginning, he wrote, in earliest in-
fancy, the child knows neither self nor world as distinct or
differentiated entities; the infant experiences only a fluid
melange of feelings, stimuli, and perceptions, in an unbroken,
constantly modulating field of *presence*; the sensory con-
tinuum is a timeless, boundary-less drifting in oneness, with
a complete lack of self/world differentiation; but during the
fourth substage of what he called the sensory-motor period—
that is, from eight to twelve months of age—self and world
become progressively differentiated: simultaneously, the child
experiences a centrifugal process whereby external reality is
gradually objectified and a centripetal process of burgeoning
self-awareness; *self* and *other* come into being, and the infant
learns he is a thing apart from his external environment;
further, whereas until then the world had seemed centered on
the infant's own body, now the personal equivalent of a

Copernican revolution takes place: the infant's own body is no longer the center, but becomes an object among other objects; thus, after living an infantile sameness of self and world, the child learns that the self is a thing apart from the world—analogous, historically, to the Greeks' discovery of mind as something separate from nature—and that the self is a thing apart from all other, equally displaced, selves; thus, first comes the fall into distance, into universal distance: between self and world, and between self and all other selves; after knowing only undifferentiated oneness, something far more deeply interfused, the child then establishes the sense of here and not-here, here and *away*; but it is only later—in the fifth substage of the sensory-motor period, between twelve and eighteen months of age—that the child obtains what Piaget called a sense of object permanency; in other words, it is only at this juncture that the child learns that things *endure* when they are no longer in the child's perceptual field; the child becomes, then, in Piagettian terms, a *conserver*; so it is, after all, just a question of sequence: the child first develops the sense of "elsewhere," but only later matures into an understanding that unseen objects continue to exist; apartness precedes persistence; and so the child has—just briefly, terribly briefly—a treacherous interval, a tiny curb of incomprehension, just before the development of object permanency; for in this interval distance is experienced as negation: things can go "away," but then they no longer exist; there is distance, but without continuity; a mechanism for denial precedes the comprehension of duration; alternately said, the illusion of "away" becomes, for an evanescent moment, persuasively real, before "away" itself goes away; and so the child, the temporarily unknowing child—I cry, how can I not cry, for the unknowing child, when distance is negation—

— But she came in, you know, I let the woman in, and although she was relatively young I must say she was very courteous, she was so pleasant and friendly that I didn't think twice about letting her in; she was wearing a lavender blouse with a pattern of scattered circles on it, and a simple dark skirt, and her hair was set up in a nice wave, and she had this lovely, lowish-toned voice—

— And she measured her words, she spoke very thought-fully, so I just invited her over to sit on the couch; I didn't know her, of course, I had never met her before; in fact, she said that she was new to town, that she had just moved into Isaura four months ago, in February, during the winter—

— She liked it here, she said, she liked what she called the unhurriedness of the town; and she also said that she was glad to find a house that she could afford, one that was big enough for her and her son; she said that her house was big enough for the two of them to get away from each other when it was necessary, when they needed to feel territorial, is how she put it; and that was kind of funny, the way she said it; so I ventured, you know, I asked her directly—because, after all, she was in my house, and she seemed to be speaking freely— I asked her if she was married, and she said No, I've outgrown that—

— And she said that she had been going around for a couple of days, when she could find time, in a few residential neighborhoods like Brighton, Greece, and Ozark Park; she said she made herself work up the nerve to ring a house's doorbell whenever she saw a light; and then she thanked me again—at first, she had thanked me just for inviting her in; but this time she thanked me for speaking with her, because some people didn't care to talk, she said; and so, then, I thanked her—

— And she turned down coffee and turned down a piece of my fresh spice cake, because she said she didn't want to impose; I said But it's no bother at all, but she just thanked me again and said that she really just wanted to talk—

— That was why she hadn't sent out a mailing, she said; she said that she just wanted to talk, I heard her say, that she wanted to listen and to hear—

— Because one day about a month ago, she said, she hadn't been able to find a shopping cart in front of Wegman's, so she walked around to the back of the supermarket to look for one, and she saw a white-and-gray cat collapsed alongside the market's air-conditioning unit, lying stiffly on the ground with its back to the metal cube; and I think she was right when she said that this seemed unusual, because cats, in general, hide themselves when they are hurting, they usually try to spend their last moments in seclusion, in quiet and solitude—

— But of course she didn't think too much about it, she said, although the sight made her sad; and then she said she also didn't make too much of a story she heard maybe a week later, over at the Spring House restaurant, where she's the hostess: there were two couples waiting at the bar for their table, she said, and they were talking; and one man began saying how his daughter had come home from school and said that a farmer's boy had brought in a pig for show-and-tell that had three ears; it was a living, functioning animal, I heard my visitor say, but then she said that she became too busy with seating and with checking reservations at the restaurant to pay the story too much mind—

— Then, just a few weeks ago, she said, her son's gerbil died; it had been his prize pet, almost his boon companion, I think she said; she had bought the gerbil for her son several years ago, she said, right around the time of what she called her retirement from marriage; the gerbil had always been fine, and had weathered their move from Springfield back in February without a hitch; her ex has a soda distributorship in Springfield, she said; but then, suddenly, the gerbil just expired, she said, right in her son's hands; and the kid, apparently, was devastated by this; he really took it to heart, she said, he cried his eyes out for three days straight—

— And to begin with, she said, her son didn't want to let go of the gerbil; he put the gerbil in his cage and kept on replacing the food and changing the water in the hanging bottle; she watched this for a while and then couldn't bear much more of it, she said, so she told her son that she would buy him another gerbil; so they took the first gerbil and buried him in their back yard, in a Campbell's Chicken & Stars soup can filled with cotton; this was three days after Memorial Day, I think she said, and her son was still really crying; but by the next day, after the burial, her son had calmed down, and he told her that he didn't want another gerbil, that there could only be one Erwin—

— Of course, she said, she began talking about the incident, about her son and his gerbil, when she was at work, mostly to people sitting or waiting at the bar when it was slow; the episode had gotten to her more than she had thought, I was touched to hear her say, and she needed to work it out of her system; and as she told the story to different people, she said, as she repeated it over the course of a few days, she began to wonder if maybe there was something between her son's gerbil and those animal things that had happened before; and one evening, when it was slow, she mentioned this to a man in a black jacket who was sitting at a cocktail table in the corner of the lounge; he had asked her to bring him a Tom Collins; and she also talked a little, she said, to a couple that was at the bar, waiting for a third party—

— Though when her boss told her, later that same night, that she should be keeping her mind on her work, she told me that at first she agreed; and I must say I agree with him, with her boss: she was in a place of business—

— And I told her that, too—

— I said, You should be glad you *have* a job, these days—

— That's what I told her—

— But what did she want me to say or do, is what I was wondering; I had invited her in, and I was listening to her in my own living room, but what did she want from *me*, I kept on thinking; what do you expect me to do about what you're saying, I sat there thinking—

— And I go into the den, and at the far end of the couch, there is my father, watching TV; and I hear the clear voices, and the studio laughter, and I ask him, You want me to turn the lights on?; No, he says, it's all right; So how about the lamp?, I say; but when he just keeps watching I don't know what to do; so I say, I read it isn't good for your eyes to watch like this, in the dark; and when he just keeps watching, without replying, I look at the orange and chalky-yellow radiance patching over his face; it makes him look moister, and more creased; then, without warning, he gets up and walks past me, then continues through the living room; and all throughout, there is only light from an outside street lamp coming into the house, through the living room window, silvering one side of him; then he continues into the kitchen, where there is only the throw from the refrigerator, dousing

the whole bending front of him; and after he walks back through the living room, only lit from outside, he goes back into the den and over to the end of the couch; there, he sits and settles back in; then he looks at the television again, his brow dimming as he gets caught up in it; even in the darkness, I can see that he has gotten nothing from the refrigerator—
— I knew it; we *all* knew it; the gig wasn't happening; from the outset the band was a little off, a little dodgy; we just weren't finding the pocket, and no matter how hard I laid into the backbeat with my snare drum no one really seemed to lock in; not that anyone in the audience seemed to mind—they were all dancing like there was no tomorrow—but *we* knew: we were playing notes, but not making music; that sense of ensemble, of a single organism breathing as one, just wasn't there; and it was obvious that we all felt bad about it: we stayed away from each other during the breaks, going off to grab something to eat or drink on our own; I spent most of my break time alone at the bar, and I should point out that this almost never happens; then, after the gig was through, after we had wrapped with Don't Go Way, Nobody, our traditional and much-loved finale, Jake, of all people—the guy who's the most light-hearted of all of us—Jake himself came over and started grousing; he had split a few high notes, he said, and had flubbed an entrance, and now he thought that talking about these totally inconsequential mistakes would defuse them; I tried to make him feel better by pointing out that I wasn't exactly thrilled when my bass-drum pedal fell apart during Skeleton Jangle; it was one of those nights, we both agreed: we hadn't kicked off the summer very well; but then Jake just went on, doing all this talking about how the group just didn't feel anchored, that we were drifting, that we sounded—as he described it—thin; and then he surprised me: after taking a moment to look at the last few stragglers leaving the hall, he said that maybe the way to deal with the situation would be to bring in a guitarist; a good, hollow-body Rickenbacker going four to the bar would make all the difference, he said: it would center us, it would give us back our center; and I just said Y'know, *wait* a minute; and Jake said Aw, it would be all right; and I said Oh, come on, Jake: that

is *not* going to fly with too many people around here; and
Jake sheepishly said C'mon, man, it's been enough time...;
and I looked at him, I just looked at him in his brown leather
jacket, and then I said You know, the whole idea was to
remember, to leave a marker, even an absent one; and Jake
looked down and said Yeah...I suppose...; and then he turned
his case on end and sat down on it, and I could see that he
was already feeling a little bad about asking the question; so
I decided to try and lighten the moment for him, and, for
that matter, for me; so I said Besides, how about the name?;
you ever think of that?; we're so established by now as the
Nonet Minus One that, if we went ahead and added somebody, we'd have to call ourselves the Ozark Nonet Minus
One *Plus* One; and that, you know, would never work; and
Jake laughed and he waved at me and said Yeah; and then
he got up, and it was obviously over; he took his trumpet
case and left; and I was glad it was over; I must say, I was
glad—

— And you know I'm hearing this, I'm standing in line
at the Genesee Pharmacy hearing these people talk, and I can't
believe it; I'm standing there thinking I can't be*lieve* this; of
course, I didn't want to butt into the conversation, to intrude
or say anything, but I just couldn't believe it; and then I was
so distracted that I forgot to have my money ready when—

— I was overcome by disbelief; it surrounded me, and
made my atmosphere prickle and go dense as soon as I hung
up; and I just had to sit down, on my divan in my living room,
amid my plants and my end tables and piano and lamps,
because this heaviness, this stormcloud of disbelief, it—

— Shouldn't have been there, present, with me; in other
words, it was not over; that's what kept jutting into my mind:
it's not over; *it's not*—...; I had thought, of course, like
everyone else, I had thought—

— That the episode was through, that it had been dealt
with, and would not return; I had thought—

— That it was just a thing of the past, that it wasn't going
to come back; but now, I hear—

— And I can't believe it: I really cannot believe it; for the
life of me I cannot believe—

— That they seem to have found something, I have heard—

— Something has been found; it's what people are saying; there hasn't been anything yet in the Republican & Chronicle but I—

— Heard something, while I was—

— Helping my son replace the chain on his bike, in our back yard, just yesterday; the day before, my son had gone for a ride down to Seneca Park and had had to walk most of the way home, up over the hill; so the bike—a Raleigh three-speeder, which I bought for him last summer—was pitched up on its back, resting on its seat and handlebars; its pedals and kickstand were all sticking up, like insect legs, and we had some newspaper with us, for wiping; Jason was clicking oil onto the front gears, while I, kneeling, was turning the bike's pedal with my right hand and guiding the chain back into place with my left; and as I was about to finish laying the chain around the front gear's big circle, I stopped and grabbed Jason and hugged him to me, oily fingers be God-damned; seven years ago, in the middle of everything, my son came down with what they called chronic Eustachian catarrhis, a long-term clogging of the ears; he was only three years old then, and the condition would not go away; for months it dragged on, all throughout one summer and fall, for so long that one ENT man said that Jason might lose his hearing; we saw at least six doctors, and all of them said they couldn't explain it, especially since the problem had taken root in both ears; it was idiopathic, they said; and Jason was too young to do much to oppose it, beyond accepting antihistamines; I remember thinking, at that time, that if Jason comes through this, if he comes through this healthy and sound, I will remember, for the rest of my life, the priority of everything; and I do, now, I remember: I remember the priority of everything—

— So now I am there and I am not there; I sit, and I carry on a conversation in my office, and although I seem present and fine, inwardly I am not there, because if someone, now, is saying something—

— If something has to be said, now, after all this time, if

something is actually emerging, then I know, then you have to know that—
— There is a document: that's what I heard; someone has found some sort of document; somehow something has emerged; it has surfaced—
— Some kind of a letter, if I understand correctly: some letter or interoffice memo; that's all I heard: there is some kind of interoffice memo—
— And I hear this and I start thinking, What is my child thinking?; now, for the first time, I need to know what my child is thinking; for what are his or her thoughts if not my own—though purified, and stripped of inessentials; that, for me, had been a reason to have a child: to be able to think again, but anew, afresh, displaced; after all, it is called *conception*; until now, I haven't wanted to communicate with my child through anything even approximating language; all through my first months of pregnancy, I was glad to dispense with literal meaning, to free myself from the restrictions of verbal significance; then I could just listen, and hear what my child—my self—was telling me without words; and there was much that I heard; but no longer: now I want to hear what my child would like to say—what he or she would *want* to say; in an excess of significance I had waited 5 years before agreeing to conceive, following the California Organic Growers' Association guidelines for reconversion of soil; it was foolish, I knew all along, but I needed it: I needed some objective metric; now, again, I need some objective metric: I want to know what my child is thinking; I can no longer rely on an absence of meaning: I have been betrayed by silence and interpretation; now I want to know what my child is thinking; I am terrified of unmeaning—
— Because it was something I had been looking forward to—to getting away for a while; I mean, I know Key West is supposed to be a cauldron in June, but I really needed to take some time away and I didn't want to wait any longer; so I packed appropriately—nothing beyond t-shirts and shorts—and decided to give it a go; and, in fact, it was beautiful down there, sunny and sparkling and everything in bloom; I didn't feel the heat too badly at all, and I did whatever I wanted, lots

of gamefishing and snorkeling—one afternoon I went snorkeling for lobster—and I even got up to Key Vaca to take a look at the manatees; one day, in fact, about a week into my stay, I went out on one of those drift boats they have off Key West—they're big, broadbeamed things—and angled for grouper near the offshore reefs and crevices; I was sitting on the boat just enjoying the water and gabbing with some nice folks from Laramie, Wyoming, when I decided I couldn't stand not having a beer any longer; so I got up to get one—and then saw my red Cardinals' cap loft out onto the water; apparently my beer-urge was a little, shall we say, overenthusiastic, and I had managed to spring up in just the wrong way; so I stood there and watched the cap slowly settle under the water's ripples, and then went to commemorate it at the canteen; within about an hour, though, back outside, the sun was getting a bit heavy for me, so when we came back to port I drove into Old Town to pick up something else to put on my head, preferably just one of those green plastic-visor things; and as I was waiting in my rental car for the light to turn, at the corner where Duval meets Simonton, all of a sudden George Fobel, our old George Fobel, pulls up beside me, in a big burgundy-brown Mercedes convertible; and he looked good, I can tell you that, all tan and rested, and then I remembered that he has a retirement home down there; and although he looked over to my car and smiled, I'm sure he didn't recognize me; I mean he was friendly, he nodded his head, but he didn't recognize me—

— Exactly: I'm hearing all this stuff, too, I'm hearing it, just like everybody else, but after you hear it all you wonder what they're really saying; I know they had some something or other way back when, I heard something about it, and I'm sure this'll just be the same; it'll be no big problem, and they'll fix it; it'll be like fixing a water main that breaks—

— And I don't know what it is or where it's from or who's printing it—I've never heard of this Citizens' Reclamation Committee, and they don't give an address or any credentials or any explanatory background, I don't even know how long they've been around—

— But it just showed up in the mailbox today, along with

the rest of the junk, addressed to Resident—and I wasn't sure if it was right, if I was the one who was supposed to get it—

— Because Resident, you know, is usually just junk, and I wasn't even going to read it—

— And then there was a thunderclap in my heart, I swear it, just this thunderclap that was loud and decisive and—

— When I read it, I mean, when I finally decided to read it, and—

— It said that Ozark had toxic chemicals, I read, the company had toxic chemicals—

— 66 poisonous chemicals, I read, chemicals that were known to be poisonous—

— On their property, I read: Ozark had these chemicals actually located on their property—

— And that they had had them for quite some time, I read, at least several *years*—

— And that they had taken them *in*, I read, that these were chemicals from outside that Ozark had *brought in*—

— And that they were storing them, is what I read, as best as anybody could tell Ozark was just storing them—

— And I couldn't believe it, you know, what I was reading, I didn't know *whether* to believe it—

— Because I couldn't understand why, or what for, what the reason could be—

— And I just couldn't figure it out, what it was saying: why would Ozark be dealing with chemicals that they didn't even use, what would they need them for?; I don't know, and it doesn't seem that anyone knows—

— The County Health Director, up in Steelville, even he said There are a substantial number of unknowns; I read that they got to him—

— A Dr. Lipkin, the Crawford County Health chief; and despite the fact that they showed him the memorandum they found, they said that they gave him a copy of it, he still wouldn't commit to saying anything more than that; so I don't know if I should start worrying again and put the tarpaulin back on the Buick or just forget about it and go about my business—

— Because even though they gave an Ozark official a

copy of it, I read that they showed him the official document they found that is printed on his own company's letterhead, the Ozark spokesman said, he's quoted as saying I feel really bad that we have never been able to convince you people that there is nothing wrong—

— *You people*, the newsletter then put, in italics: Now we can be more than *you people*, I read; and they went on to say how the Citizens' Reclamation Committee was going to give us, the people of Isaura, a voice, a presence—

— All that kind of thing that you always read; I mean, I read about what *they're* going to do and what *we're* going to do, and after a while, you know, you just think you've heard it all already—

— And they said they were going to continue working and to continue digging and to continue keeping us informed; and I was thinking My God, how large *is* this group—

— And I saw that they gave a number where you could call, if you wanted to help them out: In any way, on any day, is how they put it—

— But, you know, I didn't have a pencil handy, I wasn't at my desk, so I didn't take it down—

— Although they said that they were still looking for a place in which to base their operations; and I thought, you know, that it would be perfect, just perfect, if they could somehow get to use Schroeder House—

— And so now they're going to start all that testing again, going around and doing, I don't know, doing some kind of damn researching—

— At least you *hope* they will; I mean they've got to, they've got to start again, I'm sure they will, even though I never really saw them doing any testing last time—

— But I don't get it: is this the same thing, the same as last time, wasn't it taken care of—

— Because they spent all that money, I remember, those millions, it cost them so much—

— And then all the problems, all the difficulties, I remember, they were gone—

— They dealt with it, and successfully, I think, it was all taken care of—

— Everything was taken care of, I think; so it must be something different now, something new—

— Which they'll also take care of, I'm sure—

— Because they *have* to: I'm sure they will take care of it—

— Because it was becoming obvious that he needed some professional care; I mean, we had tried long enough to work with the condition, and I simply didn't want to wait any longer; so that same morning I took him to the internist I had used when he had the mumps a few years ago, when he was four; and I had Matthew tell him, I had Matthew tell the internist in his own words about the headaches he was having, how they seemed to float around the top of his head and also behind his forehead, and how they would get so bad that they made him nauseous, and about how his eyes sometimes felt like they were burning; and so Dr. Barron took him in his room with the paper-covered examination table and did some tests, shining light beams into his eyes, performing reflex checks, having him touch his fingertips together in mid-air with his arms extended, and some other things; and then, as Matthew was dressing, the Doctor asked me to come into his office; and there he told me that he couldn't find any evident source for the disorders, so he was referring us to a specialist, a neurologist; and immediately, you know, immediately I said Well, you hear what they're saying; I mean do you think this could have anything to do with the water?; and the Doctor, sitting in his own office, the Doctor said that he didn't really know; so I said Well, don't you have any opinion, any idea?; and the Doctor, sitting there in his own office, I mean a medical doctor in his own place, he said that he wasn't terribly inclined to take risks with lawsuits, so he wouldn't say so even if he knew—

— So I called Town Hall, you know, immediately—

— I called Town Hall—

— And I got through to this woman, though she wouldn't give me her name—

— Even though I asked her for her name—

— I asked her nicely—

— And before I could finish with what I was—

— Before I could even get started—

— I was told that there was no information available at this time—

— And when I finally got through, when someone finally picked up, and a woman said Yes—

— And I could hear that she—

— And I heard, just from the tone of—

— They told me that they had seen the newsletter, so I—

— They told me they had seen it; and when I—

— But they didn't think there was any reason for concern; so I thanked him—

— So I called over to Berryman, the Town Hall there, seeing as how they're so close that they might have known something—

— And thinking that maybe I could get through—

— And I was right, they did know about it, they already knew—

— And I called over to Berryman, the Town Hall, and they told me that the best they knew, there was nothing to worry about—

— And the woman over there told me that she had also been calling the Isaura Town Hall, all morning, she said, and couldn't get through; so I thanked her—

— And I tried the Police—

— I called over to the Isaura Police Station, up on East Main—

— Because I didn't know what to do, so I called the Police—

— *I called the Police—*

— And I was sitting here, in my kitchen, thinking My eyes...my vision...*my eyes...*—all those times I was practicing calligraphy and the characters were fading and dissolving on me, and all those times at night when I would turn on the light in the front bathroom and couldn't see the handle of the shower door—

— And last week when I was walking down Augustine Street coming home from work, and I got so dizzy that I had to sit down on the curb and I couldn't say anything in my defense when that girl on the bicycle stopped behind me, she stopped and looked—

— And this dragginess, this damn dragginess—I'm sitting here wondering, after all this time, *after all this time*—

— And how I act with my husband, the way I snap at him, the way I just fly off at him about absolutely nothing, about his staying late at Marty's, *I* know it's nothing—

— And now those people close to Ozark Park are going to get paid off again, I'm sure of it: thousands of dollars that's supposed to go into their homes...*right*—

— Because all along, all long I've been wondering, I have been wondering all along: *asthma*...: where the hell did Jerry get asthma—

— Home improvements that I know *I'm* gonna end up paying for; where else is it going to come from?—because you know it's got to come from somewhere—

— And when I would come home, when I finally got there, after work, that's when, finally, I felt I could relax; in the foyer I'd flip off my shoes, and then feel the transition to dense, friendly carpet; I'd see the stairway leading upwards and away, and the hallway leading to the kitchen, and a silent voice within me, after registering these things, would exhale *it is all still there*; and then, as I stepped into the hallway, and my living-room furniture fanned into view, my bones would finally unclench; now I arrive and see the unlit hallway, with the edges of the picture frames dwindling towards the kitchen, and I tense; now I do not want to enter; now I do not want to take off my jacket and drape it on the chair, and I flinch at the thought of putting my shopping down; I cannot put my shopping down; even in my refrigerator, on the wire shelves, where it is bright and cold, I do not want to put my shopping down—

— Though maybe this time they'll expand the designated area; they'll have to, they'll have to do more, they'll have to go beyond what they did last time, because those houses have already been taken care of, they've already received their share, and so I—

— Stay here, and spend all my time—all my time—thinking of ways to get out; this is my home, these are my rooms and walls; but now all I want is to leave; I spent all last night thinking about possibilities of leaving, just lost in chasing means of getting away, sitting there oblivious to the television chiming and flashing across my living room: I could sell the Buick and use the money to live on while I reestablished myself somewhere else—maybe Chicago: I've always wanted to go to Chicago; or I could move into Jonathan's room at my sister's in Oakland, while he's at Northwestern; or I could look up that guy who said he owned a restaurant in Taos, and take up his offer to be a waitress; or I could...; and I listen to myself, I sit there and I listen to myself; and I witness the images of myself doing all these things and I feel the urgency behind their abandon and I realize that this is all I can do: all I can do is listen to myself; that is all; all I can do is sit here and listen to myself—

— And then, only then, after everything was already made, it was only then that it came to me: it was only after I had shaken the colander until it no longer sprinkled, and had taken it away from the sink; and after I had tonged the wet spaghetti onto the plates, and had adjusted the three slippery mounds to make them equal in size; and after I had spooned on the Puttanesca sauce from the pot on the front burner, and had sprinkled on parsley, and had picked up the plates, and was holding onto the plates, ready to bring them out—it was then, only then, while standing in the kitchen holding onto the prepared plates, it was only then that—

— I went down Aisle 3—cereals, condiments, and cooking oil—and got the Kretschmer Wheat Germ I was looking for, the 20-ounce bottle; and I was glad to find it—they're often out of that size; then I pushed the cart past the low refrigerators filled with chicken parts at the rear of the store and swung up Aisle 6—cookies and crackers—for my Lorna Doones; I also grabbed a package of Vienna Cremes while I was in the neighborhood—why not?; then I continued on to the last aisle, where the space sweeps open and they have the large display tables of produce; and I turned the corner and I looked around, and then I stopped dead: I just held onto my cart and couldn't move, immobile amid the pyramids of apples and grapefruit and the ranks of radishes and carrots, all the varicolored produce in the expansive space; it was as if a low and powerful chord had been struck on a piano, and I felt as if everything had slowed and was moving through a cloggy, sticky liquid that made everything draggy, and sagging, and dulled people's steps, and muffled machine sounds, and added blurry barriers and impassable distance; and all I was thinking, all I was thinking, was that it all still looks exactly the same—

— But then I saw—

— Then I saw that it wasn't—

— I saw that it wasn't the same, it wasn't—

— Though the style was the same, I saw that it wasn't the same—

— I saw that it was another one—

— Already!, I thought: another *already*—

— And I was almost afraid to look, I will admit: I almost didn't want to see it—

— I did not want it to be there—

— With the same type and lettering, I saw, and the same two folds—

— And I did not want to open it—

— And when I opened it up, there it was, right there on the first page—

— Unmistakably, unarguably, it was right there, I saw it with my own eyes, reproduced from a piece of corporate stationery—

— Should the water-quality control regulatory agencies become aware of the fact that we percolate our wastes, they could justifiably close down our entire operation, I read—

— And I read it, of course, and I felt, immediately, I felt—

— In my eyes and in my head and, I don't know, going all the way down to the ends of my fingers—

— I felt this, I don't know, I felt this—

— And I didn't know what to make of it—

— What did it mean, I wondered: what is it actually saying—

— And they got to a Senator, I read, a State Senator in Jefferson City—

— They spoke to Lloyd Masterson, I read, over in Jefferson City—

— And I read he said You know, you can panic people

with things like that—
— And I read he said he doesn't want to see people screaming in the streets—
— That's all he said, I read; the newsletter said he wouldn't say anything more than just that—
— And when they asked him more questions, I read, he said he was due in a meeting and would call them back—
— And then they couldn't get him on the phone again, I read; when they called, his secretary would always say he was away from his desk—
— But when they finally got to him, I read, when they called him at *home*, he said In our opinion, the Ozark Corporation has acted responsibly from beginning to end—
— And then he got mad, I read, he got really mad, the Ozark public relations man actually began yelling at them for calling him at home—
— And so they replied Why, where's the difference?, I read: that's where you reach *us*, that's where you attack *us*—
— And I read that he yelled But don't you think I live here too?—
— And I read he yelled So if you have to have a comment right now, call someone from management; I only make statements when I'm at work—
— And he screamed *I'm not at work at home*, I read—
— And then he hung up, I read, there was a click and the line went dead—
— *This is one of our neighbors*, I then read—
— A model employee of Good Samaritan, Inc., I then read—
— But for the grace of God there goes every one of us, I read—
— And then, on the back, I saw they repeated their appeal—
— The people who put out the mailing made another appeal, I read—
— The CRC needs things, I read—
— The CRC needs volunteers, supplies, card tables, lighting fixtures, corkboards, portable radios, a Xerox machine, IBM-compatible PC's, filing cabinets, multi-lined

phones, spirit, ideas, guidance, decorations, someone who knows how to fix a Sun Microsystems laser printer, I read—
 — I read they're just a small group—
 — But most of all we need space for our headquarters, I read—
 — And space for general meetings, I read—
 — Please get in touch, I read—
 — We'd love to hear from any of you out there in the mortal majority, I read—
 — Who would like to take a stand based on this association, I read—
 — Because without you we are nothing, I read—
 — And then, I saw, they put those last words again, in capital letters—
 — And I read it, you know, I read the whole thing twice—
 — And I saved it, I folded it away in the letter slot of my desk—
 — I made sure to keep it—
 — And I was wondering what the big deal was about—
 — I mean, Ozark is a company, and they have to make money; it's as simple as that; what do these people expect—
 — I mean, what do they want to do here?—
 — I mean, who *are* these people?—
 — I mean, who needs them?—
 — I don't need them; who needs them?—
 — I mean, *I* certainly don't need them—
 — And I, you know, I just hope that they don't send any more of those newsletters—
 — I really wouldn't care to see any more—
 — Because tomorrow, I'm sure, tomorrow I'm not going to want to go to the mailbox; I'm not going to want to open my mailbox—
 — I'm not even comfortable that they have my address—
 — I mean, what do they think they're doing here, aren't they aware of what people will think?—
 — Am I the only one who has thought about the repercussions of all this?—
 — I mean, when I go into Rolla, to work at Memoryville—
I do maintenance on the classic cars they got there, like before

and after show runs and such—when I go there, and they all
know I'm from here, I mean—
   — I mean, they might not want to shake my hand—
   — They might want, I don't know, to stay away from
me—
   — At Jenny's, I mean, no one is going to want to taste
my applesauce cake—
   — Because in the corner, in the corner there, I always see
it's dirty—
   — Because when I open the screen door I always notice,
in the corner, that something seems to come in—
   — Some little clump of dirt, or something, or a leaf, a
piece of a leaf, I always see it there—
   — So I put on rubber gloves and get it, and clean it—
   — Though these gloves are only normal gloves, I mean
they're only normal gloves to wash dishes with—
   — So I use a sponge, I get in there with a sponge—
   — I put on my rubber gloves and also use a sponge—
   — But then what?, do I throw away the sponge?—
   — Can I reuse the sponge?—
   — Though I have to wash it if I want to reuse it, I have
to make sure that I wash it—
   — But how do I wash it—what can I use to rinse it off,
where is there—
   — Where is there anything that I can use to—
   — So I have to keep my gloves on while washing, keep
them on until the end, until everything, until everything is
finished—
   — I have to make sure that I have my gloves on and
never, and never—
   — But when I took them off one time, one time in the
hallway—
   — When I took them off in the foyer, when I was finished cleaning, when I was exhausted from scrubbing—
   — And I took them off, unthinking, in the kitchen, I took
them off—
   — And the blood on my hands, on the heels of both
hands where I had been pressing—
   — *I was bleeding*—

— *I had blood on my hands*—
— And stinging, I was stinging—
— But I couldn't wash them, how could, where could I wash them—
— *How could I wash the blood on my hands*—
— Still, I still shower—
— I do nothing else, but I have to shower—
— But quickly, I only shower quickly—
— But now I bathe—
— I have given up showering, which I loved so much, in the morning, the hot wet steaming and streaming and you're all waking and—
— Now I bathe—
— No, I still shower, but I give my kids baths—
— I make sure that my kids only take baths—
— I give them quick baths—
— Though the last time I took a bath I couldn't stand sitting in it, I got so edgy; so how can I, how can I—
— So I boil; I boil everything—
— Not for me, but for my kids, I boil—
— I boil everything, I boil everything that we—
— But even boiling, even boiling, how do I know, how do I know that—
— Why should I even think that—
— Why should I even think—
— I mean, what is there to accomplish by thinking?—
— I mean, I can do nothing, I can accomplish nothing by thinking—
— Nothing will change, nothing will get better if I—
— Nothing will become any clearer if I—
— Except fear; except that; when I think I fear—
— I mean, my thoughts have become fear—
— I only bring fear—
— I am only fear—
— What I am left with is fear—
— For my husband, who I—
— I do fear for him—
— Will he, who is fragile, be able to endure this?; and so I fear—

— Will he, who has to go out every day—I fear—

— He must go outside, and speak to people, and deal with people, *many* people; and I know that he knows, that he is constantly aware—

— From his window at work, he can see Building 115, where they have all those tanks containing solvents; he is right next to it, a hundred feet away, right in the Ozark plant—and he has been at that same spot for 18 years!; and I know what this is doing to him, I see what it is doing to him, when he comes home, when he can't say anything—

— When he has to work among it all and not say anything, to anyone there; and I know how he feels; I know what he feels—

— Because when he comes home, and I see him—

— And I can say nothing to him, nothing that would make a difference—

— Though I have been waiting for him, I have been waiting all day for him—

— And when I hear that he comes in, and goes upstairs to change, and doesn't say anything—

— And I still can say nothing—

— Because there is nothing that I can say—

— What *can* I say, beyond that I have been waiting for him all day—

— Yes, I have been waiting all day in here, at home, while he was able to escape—

— To go to work and get away, while I—

— While I have been stuck in here *all day*—

— And lived with this and dealt with this, knowing that I was moving around in it and stewing in it and could not get away—

— While he could go out the door in the morning and get away from it, even for a few hours; and I—

— *And I can never get away*—

— Finally, yesterday, at night, after dinner, when we were in the living room, I said something—

— I had to say something—

— Inadvertently, without thinking, I had a lapse and opened my mouth—

— And I snapped at him, I jumped at him, I just flew off in a rage at him—

— And I regretted it instantly, immediately, when I realized what I had done; I mean, afterwards I just wanted to kick myself; *but how was I to know...*; it happened when I was at my sister's place, last Wednesday, working up on the second floor; you see, a few years ago I installed a fairly elaborate track-lighting system in my den, down in the basement, with faders and swivel-mounts and a few other showy features; it extends from above the bar all the way down to where I have my aquarium, employing eight separate lamps along the way; and I remember that my sister—her name is Nina—paid me a few compliments about the system when, eventually, she saw it; in fact, I was pleased that she had even noticed it, and so was especially touched by her kind words; then, a couple of weeks ago, I got a call from her, and she mentioned that her husband—his name is Darryl— had decided to move all his exercise equipment up to a room on the second floor of their house, and had thought that track lighting might provide the best sort of illumination; the room is relatively small, she explained, and only has one smallish window off in a corner; with a track system, they reasoned, they could keep the light indirect and gentle, and have maximum flexibility for adjusting the bulbs so as not to glare off the floor-to-ceiling mirrors Darryl had mounted across all four of the room's walls; well, she didn't even have to ask: I was glad to be able to help them out, and immediately offered my services; I don't see them nearly enough, and so welcomed the chance to spend some extended and non-formal time with them—seeing people at weddings, and such, just isn't the same thing, at least for me; so I finally got over there last Wednesday and, after a nice lunch out on the patio—sandwiches on Italian bread—I got to work; we easily agreed on where the tracks should go, and then it became a fairly straightforward installation, significantly smaller than the one down in my basement; but it was only later, when I was up on the ladder, stapling a fixture's electrical cord to the ceiling, that I became appropriately impressed by what Darryl had put together for his work-outs: the room had a long, low bench, apparently designed for benchpresses, jutting from one mirrored wall, alongside a backless, leather-covered seat, which I believe is used for certain kinds of curls; there was also a wide rack supporting lots of long barbell bars, and there were stacks of massively heavy-looking discs, and a second rack hung with free weights; several ribbed, no-slip floor mats, jet black, were spread around the room's perimeter, and a small clipboard, holding a slight stack of lined forms, lay in one corner; Darryl was sitting on the benchpress bench, apparently fixing one of the clamps that keeps the weights from sliding off the barbell bar, when, at one point, I had to move my ladder; I had stapled as far as I could reach from my first position, and so had to move, under the drooping cord, closer to the wall; (I also saw that stapling the cord into where the wall meets the ceiling, to make the cord invisible, was going to be a little tricky, due to the mirror running all the way up; but I decided to keep my apprehensions to myself;) so I climbed down the ladder and repositioned it, just as Nina came in carrying some free weights up from the basement— she could only manage two at a time, one in each hand; she brought the free weights over to Darryl, who showed her where they went on the rack; then she came over to see how I was doing; I finished my next staple and looked down to her, and then saw that she was brushing the carpet with her foot— she was only in stockings; I asked her what was up, and she said that she thought she had stepped on something; and, in fact, she had: she bent down and picked up a thumbtack, whose flat end had been painted white; I recognized it immediately; Oh, I said: sorry about that; and then I explained that I had found the tack up in the ceiling when I had been installing the fixture and had pulled it out; It must have fallen off the top of my ladder when I moved, I said; but then I saw that Nina was just standing there looking at the tack, flipping it around in her hand and touching its point with the tip of her index finger; still looking downwards, she brushed some hair from her face, then hooked it behind her ear; It's from his mobile, she then said, slowly, still looking at the tack: it must have been from Jeremy's mobile—at which point Darryl shot up from his bench, threw down the weight-clamp he had been working on—it bounced into the middle of the room—and stormed out, turning Nina around as he pushed past her; she fretted for a second, then ran into the hall after him; *Darryl*, I then heard: *Hey, Darryl*...come on now...; but then I heard a door slam, and then there was silence; about ten seconds later, Nina came back into the weight room—slowly, with her head down—and apologized to me, in faltering language, for what she called her husband's rudeness; she was still looking downward; from my position on the ladder, I could see, in the mirror behind her, that she was holding her right hand behind her back, and that it was squeezed into a fist; I came down from the ladder and pulled her to me; she pressed her face into my shoulder; I put my arms around her; I felt, and heard, that she was fighting tears; *Oh him*, she then said: *him*...; and I said It's all right, Nina, it'll be OK...; I stroked her hair; and then she said I'm sorry— really, I'm sorry; and then she looked up at me with shimmering eyes, and then looked away, and put her hand to her temple; Please forgive me, she then said: forgive *us*; Darryl told me, he's told me several times, that when we're in the house he never wants to hear Jeremy's name—

— And I just thought—

— And I just thought, *you*...—

— You thoughtless shit, I thought—

— You selfish pig, I thought—

— You stubborn shit, I thought—

— With your insisting, your just demanding and *insisting*, as I remember you did—

— With your doing all that sly suggesting, all that little *suggesting*, like I remember you did—

— For just broaching the subject, which I remember you did—

— That we move here, that we come here in the first place; I remember when you said it—

— That I should give up my job at the—

— That I listen to your scheme for—

— That I should follow you in order to—

— That I come with you—

— To this house; and I—

— This damn cursed house, in which I—

— Will never forgive you, for even suggesting it; no matter what I say or appear or let on—

— I will never forgive you—

— And I lie there at night, until three or four in the morning, and I think of what you said—

— And I think of what you did—

— And I think of you—

— In your room, across the hallway, with the door closed; are you sleeping?, or can't you sleep too?; and I—

— And I will never forgive you—

— Because I am here, and you are there—

— And that is both too close and too distant; and I fear—

— And I fear that—

— I fear—

— Because I have seen it—

— Because I have understood it—

— Because I have seen it and, for the first time, it seems, I have understood it—

— And it is clear, it is unmistakable; all I had to do was look at it—

— I just had to take it out of the mailbox and unfold it and look at it—

— Because they just let it speak for itself; and I saw it—

— Because I saw the company logo—

— And I saw the company letterhead—

— And I read, highlighted in the middle of the page: Recently, water from our waste pond percolated into the yard of a neighbor's house—

— And I read, just below that: His dog got in it, licked himself and died—

— And I read, after that: Our laboratory records indicate that we are slowly contaminating all of the wells in our area—

— And I read, just after that: And two of our own wells are contaminated to the point of being toxic to animals and humans—

— And I read, below that: THIS IS A TIMEBOMB THAT WE MUST DEFUSE—

— And I saw, below that, a signature, by someone named

Ellison, some engineer or something—

— And below that, near the bottom of the page, I saw that four lines had been added, in different type—

— Citizens' Reclamation Committee, I saw—

— Carol Daren, Group Coordinator, I saw afterwards—

— Without you we are nothing, I saw on the next line, in capitals—

— And then I saw there was a telephone number—

— And that was all there was, I realized; just the one page—

— Just the one folded, stapled and stamped page, I realized—

— That was all they had sent this time, I realized—

— Though the next day—quickly!—I saw they had an article in the Republican & Chronicle—

— An article about the letter, I saw, a good-sized article—

— And I read it immediately, even before I had my coffee, this article on page 8—

— And it talked about an Ozark Corporation memorandum that had been obtained by an ad-hoc advocacy group, I read, and how it had been circulated through the parts of Isaura closest to Ozark Park—

— And how the memorandum referred to apparent lapses in Ozark's waste-management program, I read—

— But apparently it isn't so, I read—

— An Ozark vice president came right out and addressed the situation, I read—

— He said that the company had investigated and addressed the concerns set out in the letter months ago, I read, back when the letter was written, and that the letter was found to be inaccurate and alarmist even then—

— The letter had to do with a past situation that was short-term and localized, I read—

— And that there was no reason to worry at this time, I read—

— He said This quote-unquote timebomb is a dud, I read—

— But this woman, this woman working with the advocacy group, she didn't seem to believe that, I thought—

— Though she refused to say how she got the memorandum; they asked her and she wouldn't say a word, I read—

— Though the Ozark man came out and admitted that with an organization as large as Ozark, small, temporary problems are bound to crop up every now and then, I read—

— And that such small situations can even be considered inevitable, I read—

— Even with our state-of-the-art waste-management program, perfection is elusive, I read the Ozark man said—

— And he also mentioned that Ozark is currently dedicating some $18 million per year to waste-related concerns, I read—

— Even so, that woman said that she had sent copies of the memorandum to the Crawford County Health Department and to the Missouri Department of Public Health and to the local EPA, I read—

— And she was waiting for their response, I read—

— And then someone from the Chamber of Commerce spoke, I read, a spokesman from there, and he said that the Chamber was distressed by the document—

— He said they were deeply distressed, I read—

— That such a document was circulated in an alarmist and incendiary manner, I read, without proper research and verification and sensitivity to its potential consequences—

— Ozark has been good to us, to all of us, I read—

— Without them, most of us wouldn't even be here, I read—

— And it is most distressing to contemplate the possible consequences of such irresponsible actions on the local economy, I read—

— In particular on the labor force, I read—

— No one here wants to lose any more jobs, I read—

— And then the article said something about the CRC, I remember, about the group that that woman is working for—

— And I read how they're a small group, working out of a room in the basement of the building where one of the women lives—

— And how they were currently putting together a plan

to raise money for their postage costs, I read—
— And you read all this and you think I can't fucking believe it, I can't fucking believe what these people are trying to get away with—
— I mean, what do they think they're trying to do?—
— I mean, can't they see what's going on out there?—
— *Everybody's* struggling; I mean, why try to make things *worse*—
— I really can't believe these people—
— But eventually, you know, it subsided, everything subsided, and I went back into the living room and sat down; but then, almost immediately, it came on again, almost immediately, and I ran back and this time I didn't make it, I vomited all over the sink, all over one side, and some went on the floor and the back wall—
— And there I was, holding on to the banister, and my elbows, and my shoulders, and my knees were all shaking, I was holding on with both hands and I was shaking—
— And I became aware then, when I turned down the television, that it was back—because I had almost forgotten, I had actually almost forgotten over the course of six or seven years what it was like; but it was the same, it was the same thing, in my ears, the same ringing, the same steely ringing—
— And when I went into the kitchen—
— And when I was turning onto Atkinson Street, driving to work—
— When I came downstairs—
— And I turned on the radio—
— I heard it on the radio—
— I heard that the EPA was getting involved—
— I heard that the local EPA was going to conduct what they called a water-quality survey of the entire township—
— In response to a document that they had found, I heard—
— I heard they were going all over town—
— *I heard the Government was getting involved*—
— And I find myself thinking, you know, this can't go on, I can't go on—
— What are they going to find, I find myself thinking—

— And I'm thinking Who the hell knows what they're going to find—

— And I'm thinking, you know, it's time that something got done, something concrete; let them look: I want them to look—

— But whatever happens, I hope they don't find anything—

— I hope they don't—

— I hope to God, I just hope to God—

— Because it's been hard enough already, I know—

— It has been so hard, and I—

— For months, for years now, and I—

— It has already been *years*, and I—

— And this is going to make it impossible, I'm sure now it is going to be impossible—

— As it is, I hardly see anyone—

— For two years now, I haven't seen anybody at all—

— I haven't gotten together with anyone for *years*—

— And I'm willing to come down, to lower what I want—

— I'm willing to compromise—

— I'm willing to make all kinds of concessions—

— I mean, I'll accept almost anything by now—

— As it is, I'm already down by over 35%—

— Four years ago I started at 84,900—

— And then I brought it down to an even 79—

— And I'm sitting with it at 59—

— I would take *any*thing by now, and this for a good split-level on Malden Street—

— Because I'm not one of those people who can just walk away—

— I mean, I don't just want to walk away from it—

— I can't absorb that kind of a loss—

— I can't *possibly* do it—

— And I had been hoping, it had always been my plan to send my son to college on what I got from this—

— I had been planning to retire on this—

— But now the real-estate agents don't even want to fill out fact sheets for any more houses; they laugh at you; the last time I tried to list—

— And with prices going up so much everywhere else, I can't even think about buying—

— I can't even afford to rent something else—

— But why should we move somewhere else?; I mean, we'd just be walking into the next town that has it; the problem is everywhere; how would we know we're not moving into the same nightmare elsewhere?; all towns are alike—

— Even so, I can't even kid myself that I *can* do anything, with that ordinance they passed last year—

— That ordinance that you can't put a For Sale sign up on your lawn, I mean—

— You can't even make your own case; you can't get heard; you can't even take an independent shot; I mean—

— I don't want no $500 fine—

— I mean, I don't care that the City Council thinks there are too many houses up for sale; I don't care that they think For Sale signs look like flags of surrender; I want a fair shot—

— That is all I want—

— Listen: I pay my taxes; what do I pay my taxes for—

— And now, now I hear the Department of Health is getting involved—

— The Missouri Department of Health, I heard on the radio, is—

— The State Health Department is coming in to do a study, I heard; they're going to study—

— They're going to be going around looking through hospital records and going to doctors, I heard—

— And I'm sure they must know something or have heard something or I don't know—

— Because they must already be certain that something is wrong before they start any such I don't know—

— And just *damn* them and *damn* them and I just want to *God damn them*—

— And I don't believe it, I just cannot believe it—

— I mean you see it and you just can't believe it—

— In the paper, in the R&C, I just turned the page—

— And I was almost struck breathless—

— It took up the entire page, and I—

— An entire page of the R&C, and I—

— And this, I thought, this is what the Chamber of Commerce is spending its money on—

— WE'RE PUTTING IN A GOOD WORD FOR OZARK, I read, in *huge* letters, letters that took up half the page—

— HOORAY!, I saw they put, just beneath it—

— We believe we speak for the entire Isaura business community when we salute you today, Ozark, I read below that, in smaller letters—

— For all the good you do, I saw after that—

— Hooray for you!, I saw it ended—

— And below that, they had a list of all the big banks and department stores and other big companies in Isaura that had sponsored the ad, and of course I know every one of their names—

— And I saw this, and I thought: Yeah; it's about time—

— *Yeah*; I mean Ozark is a world-class concern, a powerhouse, and we should damn well remember that, and be glad we're part of it; listen: you're either part of the steamroller or you're part of the pavement; so get *with* it—

— And you see all this and you read it and, I mean, you can't believe it—

— I just tore up from my chair and threw the whole paper away—

— I mean, you see this and you think How stupid do they take us to be—

— I mean, do they actually think we can't figure it out—

— *Do they really think that we don't know*, I mean—

— I have eyes and I have ears—

— I mean, what can they be thinking of—

— I mean, what could they have ever been thinking of—

— Because, I mean, what this woman was saying—

— What I heard she was saying—

— That she had obtained this interoffice memorandum, and I—

— And she insisted, I heard her insisting that it was genuine—

— She refused to tell the interviewer where she got it, because he asked her, but I had no doubt from the tone of her voice that she knew it was authentic—

— Absolutely, I heard her say: beyond question—

— But the interviewer, I heard, he remained calm, he continued to speak easily, he was a real professional—

— Even as I heard him say Do you know what this means—

— And the woman, the reasonable-sounding woman, I heard her say I certainly know what this *seems* to mean—

— It's right here, I heard her say, right here in the third paragraph—

— Where the memo is going on and on about the depressed earnings reported in the second quarter, I heard her say—

— And about how their principal fiber supplier in Brazil had just been fined for regulatory difficulties with their export license, I heard her say—

— And about how all this was happening just when they were beginning to dedicate substantial capital resources to their new waste-management program, I heard her say—

— With its strong negative impact on workforce deployment and earnings, I heard her say—

— And then here it is, I heard her say—

— Here it is, I heard—

— Therefore, one option might be to put our new waste-control systems to some productive use, I heard her read—

— And then the memo goes on to another discussion, I heard her say—

— Now this, I heard her say, this one sentence—

— In conjunction with another document we obtained several weeks ago, I heard her say—

— Which seemingly listed an inventory of chemicals that Ozark, as best we can tell, does not use, I heard her say—

— Well, it paints a most alarming picture, I heard her say—

— Explain for us why, I heard the interviewer say—

— Because what this would seem to indicate, I heard her say—

— What it would seem to indicate is that Ozark has been accepting refuse from other sources, I heard her say—

— Actually taking in other companies' wastes, I heard her say—

— In other words, I heard the interviewer say—

— In other words, I heard the woman cut in, it seems that Ozark may be trying to recoup some of the investment it made in waste-management equipment by processing toxics for other companies—

— Or, as it says here, putting their system to quote-unquote some productive use, I heard her say—

— And as you can see from the date of this memorandum, conceivably they have been doing this since August of 1982, I heard her say—

— In other words, from less than a year after when the last local toxic scare subsided, I heard her say—

— What you're saying then, I heard the KTUI interviewer say, is that conceivably, for nearly six years—

— For nearly six years we have been living in a toxic dump that we had no idea existed, I heard the woman say—

— And I heard this, and I drove past the YMCA on Monroe Street—

— And I looked at my dishes arrayed in the drying rack—

— And I made my turn at the corner of Union and Weld—

— And I saw the blind's falling cord bending around the radiator cabinet—

— And I thought of the padlocks and keys we store in the cupboard above the refrigerator—

— And I passed the Strong Museum, with its fine lawns—

— And I looked at the row of catcher's and outfielder's mitts hanging from the garage beam—

— And at the Stop sign I looked down Alexander Street—

— And I saw the pillows plumped in the corners of the living-room couch—

— So then what are we to make of this, I heard the announcer say—

— Assuming that the situation you describe is true, what kind of response would be appropriate, I heard the announcer say: what should we—

— There is only one thing, I heard the woman say—

— There is really only one, I heard—

— We must organize, I heard her say—

— We must organize, I heard her say—

— We will not dignify the scurrilous charges recently leveled by some ragtag band of alarmists and opportunists with a reply, I read—

— For they are as empty of reason as they are of any basis in fact, I read—

— We will only reaffirm our commitment to working together—with our people, with our community and with others, in order to build on our accomplishments, I read—

— To make sure we continue to grow, I read—

— Just in the same way as we have for the last 108 years, I read—

— And we will also reaffirm that our commitment to environmental protection is active, ongoing and strong, I read—

— And then I read that Ozark has recently produced a video about some the environmental and safety programs in place within the company—

— And, you know, I just folded away the paper—

— I forcibly pushed away the paper—

— I shoved the newspaper, all buckled and unfolded, across the table, away from me—

— But what do they expect us to do?, I mean, what are we supposed to do?—

— I mean, the EPA, I heard on the radio that the EPA has announced that it wants to conduct more tests, it is coming back to conduct more tests—

— It wants to test the water again, I understand that they feel they have to test everything again—

— Because the first tests were inconclusive; I heard they thought that the first tests didn't reveal what they were looking for—

— From sixteen sites, I heard them say; they said they took soil and water samples from Rand Street and Malden, and also from Jones Square and Alliance Park and Straub Road and—

— And now they say those results were flawed, I heard,

they're saying that the findings, when they got them back to the laboratory—

— Somehow the samples got contaminated, I heard them say, they think it happened during transport back to where they were being processed—

— *Again*: they say *again*; they say they have to test *again*; but when, I mean, when did they first do it, when did they originally—

— And now the Crawford County Health Department is getting involved, I heard, now the *County* health people are coming in—

— *Now the Health Department...*; and I—

— And I heard that and I—

— And I can feel my skin, my whole skin turning cold and tautening up cold and—

— Now the State thinks it's too much for them; I heard that the State agency now feels they've got so much to do on this that they have to contact the County to assist them—

— And that the State and the County would coordinate their findings and pool resources, and on the radio I heard that they may streamline billing procedures between them so it goes smoothly and there aren't any unnecessary—

— So now they'll be going through my medical records and my records at the hospital, twice I was at Genesee hospital with my bladder and now they are going to look at everything and every little detail and they are going to know everything and even things that I don't know, that Dr. Feldman doesn't tell me and that they never tell you at the hospital and they will see all my results *they will know all my results*—

— And there will be questionnaires, I heard more than likely they will come in the mail; and they say you should fill them out, that you *have* to fill them out, but I would not know what to put, I wouldn't know what they would want, so then they said maybe they will have people coming to the door, there will be someone at the door and they will have papers and questions and I would not know what to say; so when the door rings, when there's someone at the door, I won't want to answer the door, and I don't want that, I don't want to avoid the door, the same way that now, already now, I don't, in the morning, every single morning, I don't want to get the mail—

— And who can know what kind of hell I am taking in, what they are putting out and that inescapably I am taking in, because the DEC, the State Department of Environmental Conservation, they wouldn't undertake a study if there was no cause for concern, if they weren't already tipped off about—

— What they called *the growing concern* over the Ozark Corporation, I heard the newsman call it that on the radio, on KMOX, he was reading the news and he led the roundup at 6 o'clock with Ozark, even before the national news or the campaign, he made it come first—

— But who's going to be in charge of all this, I want to know: who's going to coordinate all these groups that are coming and doing studies, and when they start, and what they do, and who they do it to, because if they want us to co-operate I want to know what I'm doing is for, and to what end, and if it will make a difference, and who is going to be seeing anything I—

— And when there'll be some findings, some results, and when will anyone hear, and when will they start, because I no longer sit out on my porch, and when I sit in my hot dark muggy living room with no breeze I don't know what I am supposed to do, how I am supposed to comport or restrict myself when they start or until they finish—

— But now, I understand, the DEC already *has* a report, I heard that the DEC already has a report about Ozark and spills that goes back *for six years*—

— On the radio, they said that the DEC already knows all the details about Ozark's chemical spills, I heard they already have a file on that, and that the file goes back to 1982 and has continued all along—

— So what were they doing with—?, I mean *why the hell didn't they*—

— But then an Ozark man said that these were just minor incidents, just small mistakes that have to happen, minor leaks and accidents that I heard they cleaned up quickly every time—

— Except for a few incidents where they said that trespassers had illegally dumped chemicals on their property; I mean Ozark said trespassers did it, without their knowing—

— *They said that trespassers did it,* and I mean—

— But even then, as soon as anything was discovered they cleaned it up, I heard the Ozark man say—

— And that it should be borne in mind that it was Ozark itself that gave the report to the DEC, that it was a report that they themselves had prepared and submitted to the DEC; so I think they were claiming, I think Ozark was implying—

— They took the posture that they had nothing to hide; I heard the man say, quite explicitly, that they have been open and forthcoming, and entirely up front when it comes to compliance—

— But then the newsman said that the report that Ozark was talking about, the one they said they had submitted on their own, he said it had been prepared because of some sort of Federal requirement passed in 1986, dealing with the public's right to know—and so, and so you don't, you can't, I mean *you can't ever those damn—*

— And I am now fucking doing three packs a day, easily that, sometimes more, three fucking packs, and sometimes when it's late and I'm still staring at the glaring green computer screen and my eyes are clouding and hurting and my neck gets that sore crick down by the top of my backbone, I break off the cigarettes' fucking filters and just go direct; I hate it—my throat burns and my fingers reek, and I cough up this cordy shit in the fucking soot-stinking morning and—

— I know and I know and I just can't stop, I just can't stop myself, even when I'm not hungry—especially when I'm not hungry: it's like a trembling, a clamor inside me, a welling from my chest and in my throat and it's like I dissolve into it, into this inner welling—and my objections and my reason are both overridden and neutralized, even though I am aware of what is going on; but I just must do it, I must have something, and I do not let myself hear the voice inside me urging *don't—just don't,* and I swoop up from where I am and blindly swoop into the kitchen and anything, I just take anything—

— Because I am an axle: that is how I feel: I am an axle whirling and suspended and stretched out and jolting to every pebble in the pothole road—

— Because I know and I do not know—

— Because I understand and I cannot understand—

— Because I see what they are doing and I cannot believe what they are doing—

— Because this strategizing is intolerable: because I am tired and this incessant strategizing is intolerable—

— And I cannot believe what this has come to—

— I cannot believe—

— Even the headline, just seeing the headline: I saw it and I thought, am I the only one who just cannot believe—

— Am I the only one who cannot believe—

— IT'S OAK VS. OZARK, I saw across the top of the page—

— All in big letters, I saw, across the sixth page—

— Group Will Use Tree to Sue Company, I saw—

— And I thought: has it really come to this?—

— And I thought: *now what?*—what new duplicity has been concocted—

— Because this woman, this woman from over on Wheatland Street, I read she's going to initiate a lawsuit against the company on behalf of an oak tree in her back yard—

— And that she has already applied to the court to establish a guardianship for the tree, I read—

— She wants to be named its legal guardian, I read, either her or the CRC, where she volunteers—

— Because she believes the damn tree is endangered, I read—

— Not only its safety, I read she said, but its entire life—

— I mean—I mean *they're having a tree sue the company*—

— It's the tree that, when I was a girl, kept my family from having a swimming pool, I read the woman said: it's right in the middle of my back yard, and we would have needed to cut the tree down to make room for the pool—

— But my father couldn't bring himself to do that, I read she said—

— And I mean—

— I mean aren't they aware how this makes them look?—
— Because the attorney, I read the attorney from Ozark
got right in and said that there are no legal grounds for
anything even approximating what they're trying to do—
— I mean, what do they think they're trying to do?—
— Objects such as trees cannot have legal guardians, I
read the lawyer said: nor do such objects have the defensible
rights implied in such an association—
— We will deal with this situation appropriately, I read
an Ozark spokesman said—
— By ignoring it, I read he said—
— Of course they will, I mean *of course—*
— Ultimately, we view it as a somewhat sad stunt, I read
that the Ozark man said: simply the latest in what seems to be
an unending series of broadsides perpetrated by people following an agenda that is clearly counterproductive for just
about everyone—
— Of course it's a stunt—what else would it be?, I read
another CRC woman said—
— But at this point what else can we do?, I read she said—
— The simple fact is that we must galvanize public
attention in some way, I heard her say: we have to obtain some
measure of national attention, and we have to do something—*anything*—to mobilize local support—
— Besides: why not?, I heard her say: the issue we're
raising is at the frontier of modern legal thinking; why
shouldn't trees or brooks have legal rights—
— Why shouldn't natural objects be accorded protec-
tions just by virtue of their existence, I heard her say—
— It's an idea that's been around for at least 15 years,
I heard her say: none of this is new; just because trees
and forests don't have a voice, that they can't speak, it
doesn't mean that we should be able to do anything we want
to them, and that there shouldn't be mechanisms for them
to obtain legal redress for crimes or offenses committed
against them—
— Lots of abstract or non-human or even inanimate
things have been acknowledged as having legal rights, I heard
her say: trusts, estates, universities, Subchapter R partner-

ships—all are the possessors of rights, and there are always lawyers who will speak for them—

— Even corporations, I heard her say: even townships, or nations—

— All of these are abstractions that we've come to invest with legal rights, I heard her say: we refer to them as *it*, and think of them as *persons* or *citizens* for many statutory and constitutional purposes—

— Even though for jurists working before the granting of such rights, such ideas seemed discordant and preposterous, I heard her say—

— Remember, in the past, and not so long ago, even certain *people* were deemed not to have some fundamental rights, I heard her say: slaves are the obvious example, but if you go back far enough there were times when women, children, the insane, and Native Americans were legally treated more like objects or things than as persons—

— And for the people of those times, to confer rights on such quote-unquote subordinate entities also seemed ludicrous, and even unthinkable, I heard her say: precisely because until a rightless thing receives its rights, we cannot perceive it except as a *thing*—as something to be used and controlled by the persons who already hold rights—

— So here's a chance for us to be in the vanguard, to respond with something new, I heard Carol say: what we're proposing is the natural next extension; it represents an inevitable progression in our thinking—

— But when the interviewer for KTUI suggested that the fight would be an uphill battle, I heard the woman reply: All the better; we need something that will be conspicuous and controversial—

— We need to make our case known, I heard her say: I mean, for the rest of the world Isaura is the middle of nowhere; we *have* to get noticed; and at the same time, we will be prosecuting a conventional class-action suit—

— After so many similar cases, we're fighting a strong national habituation to our kind of situation, I heard her say: people get tired of hearing the same story over and over again; so, for us, any kind of shocker can't hurt; and, frankly, we must do something to counter the level of local apathy, which is, in fact, incredible—

— And I thought—

— I mean, it's almost as if our community is experiencing some kind of mass Stockholm syndrome, I heard her say: you know, it's like they've fallen in dependent love with their own captors—

— And I thought—

— And I just thought—

— And I thought, *you*—

— That's why we're so very grateful and indebted to you for this time on your show, I heard the woman say: this kind of communication is essential to our efforts—

— Of course we've written letters to the editor of the R&C—*lots* of them—and we've submitted editorials, I heard her say: but the R&C hasn't published a one of them—

— It was the same way with the display we set up two Sundays ago in Crossroads Park, I heard her say—

— I mean, we had placards and photographs of sick animals and three tables of leaflets and information, I heard her say—

— A half-a-dozen of us CRC volunteers were out there for over eight hours, I heard her say—

— Not a word about it, I heard—

— And quite a few people stopped by, too, I heard her say—

— Not one word, I heard—

— Not a chance, I think—

— Not a fucking chance, I think—

— I don't think there's a single fucking chance—

— It isn't going to do anything at all, I think, I know it isn't going to do anything at all—

— It will do more harm than good, I think—

— I'm sure it will do more harm than good—

— To make us ridiculous like this, I mean, to use a stunt to make us fucking ridiculous—

— I mean, what is this shit with a tree—

— I mean, what are they trying to do with a *tree*—

— I mean, why should anyone care about a—

— I mean, *who the fuck cares about her tree?*—

— It's just a tree, I mean, *it's just a fucking tree*—

— I mean, it's not like that other one—

— Not like that other tree, I mean—

— That tree that got poisoned, I mean—

— That tree down in Texas, I mean—

— The one that was, like, the oldest tree in Texas, I mean—

— And that guy came along and poisoned it, I remember he tried to kill it—

— He spilled poison on the oldest tree in Texas, I remember, this huge old tree in Austin, Texas—

— Because he wanted to impress some girl, I remember—

— He wanted to avenge something on some girl, I remember—

— He was a drifter, I remember, and he poured some kind of herbicide on the oldest tree in Austin, in Texas—

— He tried to kill the oldest tree in Texas!, I remember—

— But her tree, I mean, this *woman's* tree—

— In her *back yard*, I mean—

— A tree in a woman's *back yard*, I mean—

— I mean, who the fuck—

— I mean, who the fuck cares—

— I mean, who the fuck cares about—

— I mean, do you think anyone gives a fuck—

— When they don't even care, I mean—

— I mean, when they don't even—

— When they don't even let you speak your piece, I mean—

— I mean, when you call and they don't even—

— I mean, *I* called and—

— I got off my ass and called—

— I was terrified, and I called—

— I called the regional office of the EPA—

— I got information, and they referred me into Kansas City, Kansas, where they have the regional office of the EPA—

— And I called—

— I called the DEC—

— In Jefferson City, I called the DEC—

— I was so upset that I called the Department of Health—

— I sat down and called the Department of Health in Jefferson City—

— In Steelville, I got the number of the County Health Department in Steelville—

— I called over to the Crawford County Health Department—

— And I went straight to someone who would know something: I called Washington—

— I called the Centers for Disease Control in Washington—

— I called the EPA in Washington—

— I was referred to something called the National Institute of Environmental Health Sciences, in Washington—

— And I got through—

— I finally got through—

— I mean finally, finally I got through—

— And he said he wasn't aware of the problem; I mean—

— He said his office wasn't aware of the problem, I mean—

— She said the matter was under investigation, I mean—

— He told me the situation was still under investigation, and I mean—

— He said he wasn't at liberty to say, and I mean—

— He said that he couldn't say, and I mean—

— He said he could say nothing, and I mean—

— She said she couldn't say anything, and I—

— But he said he understood there was no reason for panic, and I—

— And she said I might try calling over to the Bureau of Health—

— And he said I should call the Department of Environmental Conservation—

— And I called, you know, I called immediately—

— I called Town Hall—

— I called Town Hall, and they said something—

— I mean, finally someone said something—

— I mean, finally they admitted that they had done tests—

— When I asked them they said yes, tests have been done—

— They said that they had tested the water for bacteria, and that there was none, so the water was safe; and I, you know, I—

— And I heard this, I listened to this, and I, you know—

— I couldn't believe it—

— I could not believe it—

— What they were saying, you know, I couldn't—

— Those miserable, I mean, those miserable—

— It was impossible, I mean it was fucking impossible—

— I couldn't fucking believe it—

— I couldn't, I mean, you couldn't fucking *believe* it—

— But there it was; I mean it was fucking unbelievable, but there it was—

— On page one, we have reproduced, in its entirety, an Ozark Corporation invoice, I read—

— A signed invoice acknowledging receipt, in August 1984, of delivery of a chemical, I read—

— Some 8,000 pounds of a chemical, I read—

— A chemical known as C-56, or Hexa, for short, I read—

— But whose full name is Hexachlorocyclopentadiene, I read—

— As is entered on the invoice, I read—

— As best we can determine, Hexa is not utilized in any aspect of any phase of any of Ozark's production operations, I read—

— By our reliable research, Ozark has no use for this chemical at all, I read—

— Yet it has been described as among the most deadly compounds ever synthesized, I read—

— Capable of causing damage to every organ in the body, I read—

— A compound that, in gas form, has an established threshold exposure limit ten times more stringent than phosgene nerve gas, I read—

— Hexa is acutely toxic by ingestion, inhalation, or skin absorption, I read—

— Rats exposed to hexa for four hours all died within

two days, I read—
   — After showing severe hemorrhaging of the lungs and hydrothorax, I read—
   — Specifically, hexa is a chlorinated hydrocarbon, I read—
   — Used as a chemical intermediate in making dyes, plastics, fungicides and pesticides, I read—
   — Including both Mirex and Kepone, I read—
   — Both of which are now banned, I read—
   — According to our research, the US Army rejected employing hexa as a nerve gas in World War II because of potential uncontrollable dangers associated with its use, I read—
   — But the Ozark Corporation has apparently been bringing this substance into our community, I read—
   — They have been bringing it into our community, I read—
   — For reasons that are at best unclear, and, at the very least, inexplicably and massively unsafe, I read—
   — As always, we have attempted to contact officials at the company, I read—
   — And, as always, their offices accepted our calls, I read—
   — But then the officials never called back, I read—
   — And our certified letters have been accepted and signed for, and then not responded to, I read—
   — Finally, we tried calling Ozark's warehouse manager—the man who signed the invoice—at home, I read—
   — But all we got was his answering machine, I read—
   — Six calls in a row, I read—
   — While the company that shipped the hexa, Vessico Chemical, I read—
   — Has been out of business, as best we can determine, for about two years, I read—
   — Nevertheless, we have forwarded copies of the invoice to appropriate county, state, and federal regulatory agencies, I read—
   — But we will not stop, I read—
   — We will continue our fight, I read—

— We will continue to fight for *you*, I read—
— Because please get this straight, I read—
— Our company, our benefactor, our good father, has been needlessly exposing us to one of the deadliest chemicals known on Earth, I read—
— Because they believe they can make money by doing so, I read—
— Please think about this, I read—
— *Please think about what this means*, I read—
— And then join us, I read—
— Join us on Friday, July 8, at 8 PM, in Oatman Auditorium, I read—
— To make our plans, I read—
— To consider and plan what we can do, I read—
— What we can do *together*, I read—
— *Please come to our meeting*, I read—
— Because everything we do depends on your support, I read—
— We do not want to use persuasive skills, or strategies, or snazzy phrases to lure you into coming, I read—
— Because we believe it is unnecessary, and condescending, and cynical, and abusive, I read—
— We will just say it straight, I read—
— You must come to the meeting, I read—
— You must join with us, I read—
— And if you want to know why, I read—
— Why your one presence is needed, I read—
— Think of the hexa, I read—
— Just think of the hexa, I read—
— Where scientific studies say that one part per *billion* is unthinkably dangerous, I read—
— That is what *one* can do!, I read—
— Friends and neighbors—*Wake up!*, I read—
— And I just sat there—
— You know, I just sat there—
— And I thought—
— And I thought *you fucks*—
— You miserable fucks, I thought—
— You miserable mother*fuckers*, I thought—

— *Fuck you!*, I thought: fuck you—

— Just *fuck* them, I mean, *fuck* them—

— Fuck them where they *live*, I thought, and fuck them for everything they do—

— I mean *all* of them, fucking *all* of them, they should *all* get a fucking *life sentence*—

— *Fuck them—fuck* that fucking Carol and I mean her fucking—

— *Word has come from Washington that an investigator for the House Committee on Interstate and Foreign Commerce has discovered unrevealed EPA data*, I heard on television—

— *EPA data that had been transmitted to the Missouri Department of Public Health six weeks ago*, I saw on television—

— *Data that the chemical hexachlorocyclopentadiene, also known as hexa or C-56, has been found in a test well drilled in Isaura's Edgerton Park*, I heard on the news—

— *With levels of up to 4,800 parts per billion*, I heard on Channel 5—

— *Nearly 5,000 times the EPA-established risk-criteria level*, I heard on TV—

— *A chemist at the EPA's Kansas City regional laboratory has confirmed these test results, and has told the KMOV news team that he was, quote, shocked by the findings*, I heard—

— *In Jefferson City, David P. Alanson, deputy commissioner of medical services for Missouri, claimed that the results had not previously been brought to his attention, or to the attention of other responsible State officials*, I heard on Channel 4—

— *I will personally look into the reasons for the delay*, I heard—

— *I can say now that I don't believe it's coming from our property*, I heard an Ozark plant manager say on Channel 2—

— *It's impossible that it's ours; we do not use C-56 and we have never used C-56*, I heard an Ozark man say—

— *In a joint letter issued just hours after the disclosure, Dr. Karen N. Ball, Crawford County's acting health director, and Nancy J. Pim, the State health director of the Division of Environmental Health Assessment, said that the limited data gathered so far do not show any obvious impact or health concern*, I heard on Channel 4—

— *At present, we see no evidence of any special health hazard requiring immediate action,* I heard on Channel 4—

— *Jon Larmen, director of the EPA's Hazardous Waste Assessment Program, said that a direct link to the Ozark hazardous waste disposal facilities apparently has not been established,* I heard on TV—

— *There is no health problem, no health hazard, this has been our contention from the start—Anders H. Cosby, Chairman, the Ozark Corporation,* I saw on Channel 4—

— *Our waste-containment procedures meet or surpass all current disposal standards—Rob Loast, Ozark official,* I saw—

— *There is no need for fright or panic; I just want to make that clear—Albert Butsen, Missouri Department of Environmental Conservation,* I saw on Channel 5—

— *Albert Butsen, of the Missouri DEC, gave the KTVI news room a letter from a medical group called Doctors for Facts that said No chemical is hazardous if we consume it or are exposed to it in small enough amounts,* I saw on Channel 2—

— *We recognize our obligation to be forthcoming and thorough in sharing information with the public—Phil Semper, Ozark vice chairman,* I saw—

— *We believe in full disclosure—Phillip Semper, Vice Chairman, Ozark Corporation,* I saw on KMOV—

— *If there is a health hazard out there, it's very subtle and very small—Dr. Jason Lipkin, Crawford County Health Director,* I saw—

— *Ozark is a good corporate citizen—Thomas C. Horling, Commissioner, Missouri Department of Environmental Conservation,* I saw—

— *Company spokesmen said that recent complaints about the local water's smell and taste were solely the result of small amounts of manganese, iron and sulfides in Isaura's well water, and insisted that it is perfectly safe to drink,* I heard—

— *We've got to be sure we are not poisoned—Robert Isaacs, State Attorney General,* I saw on Channel 2—

— *We have to be sure our children are not being poisoned—Robert Isaacs, Missouri State Attorney General,* I saw on SDK—

— So far, there is no hard evidence of health damage from any Ozark chemicals, I read the next day, the very next day, in the R&C—

— Enough is as good as a feast, I tried to teach my son; it was my little refrain, for a boy with an appetite; I would say it to him every time I had to rein him in at the table: enough is as good as a feast; even when we would go to Aunt Lillian's and she would make him something special—her cheddar cheese tarts, which look so beautifully caramel-y, and which lift so easily out of their little aluminum pie tins—even then, I would stop him at one-and-a-half of the tarts; enough is as good as a feast, I would say, and he would hold back; but today, when I found him in the kitchen, sitting up on the counter with the door to the cupboard open, I did not glower; I did not say anything, even though he had guilty eyes; I simply walked over and picked him up and stroked his back, then brought him to the table and put him in his chair; then, while he was sitting in place, I went back to the cupboard and got him what he was after: a box of Good 'n Plenty's, his favorite; I brought it back to the table, opened it, and sat with him as he went through the whole sugar-and-licorice box; then, when he had finished, I went back to the cupboard and got him another—

— And the first thing I did, of course, was that I called: I looked in the book, then I called information, and I got a number for the EPA; then I dialed and I got someone and I explained my question, and I was passed to someone else and I explained again; happily, this person heard me out; and then she said that she's been instructed that she can't say anything other than the fact that they're aware of what's going on—

— And when I came out of the dry cleaner's, holding my shirts up in their streaming plastic, and walked out into the Marketplace's parking lot, I heard something and then saw there was this fight going on, halfway down the lot, right next to a big blue station wagon; I mean these two guys were pummeling each other, just pushing and grabbing and really hitting—

— *In Isaura, a task force assembled by the town's Office of Consumer Affairs and headed by Beverly Prager, a cancer researcher at the Wilson Health Center, released the results of a telephone*

survey of over 1100 of the community's residents, I saw on Channel 4—
— *The document reported that nine of the sixteen children born to the study group from 1983 through June of this year had birth defects: one child was born deaf, three were born with serious heart defects, five have mental impairment and six suffered from severe kidney disorders,* I heard—
— *The document concluded that women in Isaura have a 56 percent chance of giving birth to malformed children, and advised area women not to get pregnant,* I saw—
— *The survey also noted the story of one woman who had had two normal pregnancies and healthy children before moving with her family into Isaura; thereafter she suffered six consecutive miscarriages and then gave birth to a child that was severely deformed,* I heard on TVI—
— *Dr. Karen N. Ball, Assistant Deputy Health Director for Crawford County, said from her office in Steelville that the study's, quote, limited nature made it impossible to determine with certitude if the findings were caused or contributed to by effluents from local industry,* I heard—
— *Dr. Karen N. Ball, the Assistant Deputy Health Director of Crawford County, spoke against the value of the survey, saying Further study would be useful,* I saw—
— *State health officials criticized the report, saying in a written statement that it is, quote, inconclusive, lacks depth and needs considerably more testing and analysis,* I saw on Channel 5—
— *When you're dealing with statistics and numbers of this nature, there's a lot of room for interpretation and explanation; there could be other risk factors that could greatly contribute to, weaken, or actually enhance what we're seeing now—for example, alcohol exposure, prior exposure to hepatitis, smoking, exposure to other chemicals, or history of gall bladder disease—Sharon C. Edelman, Vice President of Environmental, Health and Safety Affairs for Hansom Chemicals, Englewood, NJ,* I saw—
— *A new report just in from the Environmental Protection Agency has disclosed that wells in Isaura Township are showing high concentrations of potentially dangerous organic contaminants, in addition to the chemical C-56 or hexa recently discovered in area*

water sources, I saw—

— *The carcinogenic industrial solvent tetrachloroethylene has been found in a residential well on Isaura's Glide Street at levels determined by the EPA of 2,400 parts per billion, or 10,000 times in excess of the maximum level found acceptable by the agency,* I heard—

— *Along with 41 parts per billion of the toxic contaminant chlorobenzene, which is also on the National Priority Pollutants Consent Decree List,* I saw—

— *State health officials, in a statement issued in Jefferson City several hours after the EPA disclosure, said that the unusual amounts of these chemicals, quote, appear to be associated with the presence of household products,* I saw—

— *At a press conference called today in Ozark's Executive Headquarters on State Street, Rob Loast, Director of Site Operations at Ozark Park, said that calling the chemicals a leak or a spill is, quote, a misnomer,* I saw on Channel 2—

— *The material in the ground has been there more than 50 years; we're really not looking at this as a spill—Rob Loast, Director of Site Operations for Ozark Park,* I saw—

— *Ozark officials said today that the company has dug hundreds of wells in recent years to monitor and test groundwater quality at and around Ozark Park, and that lab analyses of area groundwater and consultants' reports are currently being studied,* I saw—

— *The hydrogeologic environment is at present attenuating any migrating contaminants to a level minimizing any health or environmental impact—Vernon Duke, Ozark official,* I heard—

— *It is our judgment that the problem we're talking about is not a health hazard—Rob Loast, Director of Site Operations, Ozark Park,* I saw—

— *Live with us from Washington is David Wall, Director of the National Institute of Environmental Health Sciences; Mr. Hall—,* I saw on KMOV—

— *We don't have the appropriate tools or even the appropriate background with scientific knowledge to evaluate these problems,* I saw him say—

— *Scientists probably don't even know what the short-term effect of half to a third of each of these chemicals found in residential water supplies have on laboratory animals,* I heard on Channel 9—

  — *Without this basic knowledge, assessing the immediate effect on people is almost impossible,* I saw—

  — *We have even less understanding of what each chemical may do over a long period of time,* I heard on KETC—

  — *Albert Butsen, the Missouri Department of Environmental Conservation official in charge of overseeing Ozark's compliance with state environmental regulations, declined comment on the EPA disclosure, pending a review by state, county and town officials,* I saw—

  — *Yes, this has been a disconcerting period for the company because this whole episode has called into question our reputation and integrity—Anders H. Cosby, Chairman, Ozark Industries,* I saw—

  — *At this point, what we would most like is to have this all resolved and behind us—James Blaspher, Ozark Spokesman,* I saw—

  — I was sitting in my breakfast nook, dabbed by the late-day light that was sprinkling through the shrub-tops bunched just outside the window; it was a quiet moment, for myself and for some good aromatic tea; braced by this opulent quietness, I reached out and fingertip-touched the edges of my breakfast table; and soon I found myself stirred by its massiness and rectangular bulk, the cool planed fineness of its lacquered darkwood, its perfect flatness and four-legged heft and the way its corners were thoughtfully rounded; it was, I thought, just so *present*—and yet it expressed its profound presence through attributes that were exquisitely non-assertive; indeed, it was this play of pure presence and exquisite non-assertiveness that lent the table its value; and again I reached a hand out, and ran it down one of the table's tapering legs, when my daughter, Jaquie, sidled up—she had been playing in the den—and put her hand on my knee, and told me I should have another child—

  — *In Jefferson City, the Missouri Department of Public Health released the results of its recent epidemiological screening of 211 residents of the township of Isaura,* I saw—

  — *Test results just published by the Missouri Department of*

Public Health revealed that all 211 people had been directly exposed to the chemical hexa, or C-56, and that the chemical was now circulating in their blood, I saw—

— Department of Public Health spokesmen said, however, that the study did not reveal, quote, a medical syndrome, or group of symptoms, which can be related to C-56, I saw on Channel 2—

— The trace amounts of C-56 found in subjects' blood do not have any clinical significance—Harmon Almond, Department of Public Health, I saw—

— So far, we have found no real difference in the health status of those exposed and those not exposed, and we have no reason to believe that any will be found—Harmon Almond, Missouri Department of Public Health, I saw on SDK—

— Health risk is speculative: there's a big difference between that and health effects, and that's what we're still waiting to learn—Karen Ball, MD, Assistant Deputy Health Director for Crawford County, I saw on Channel 11—

— The Ozark Corporation today published the results of what it called a rigorous and thoroughgoing study of the health of its work force, I saw on Channel 9—

— The study, signed by a team of Ozark physicians and scientists, found, quote, no significant excesses of deaths due to cancer or cardiovascular disease among Ozark Park workers, I saw on Channel 5—

— The study is OK on its face, but it doesn't say anything at all about the animal data—Richard J. Schwinger, Deputy Director of the Food & Drug Administration's Center for Food Safety and Applied Nutrition, I saw on Channel 4—

— Also today, the Ozark Corporation acknowledged that it was reviewing a recent Missouri Department of Health study that found elevated rates of pancreatic cancer among women living near the company's Ozark Park site, I heard on Channel 2—

— A new study commissioned by the Environmental Protection Agency has for the first time investigated the state of the genetic material of Isaura Township residents, I saw—

— The results of the study were released at a press conference held today by Barbara Bloom, a deputy EPA administrator, I saw—

— The study, conducted by Dr. Dante Pucciani, a cytogeneticist with the Biogenetics Corporation in Houston, found that 12 of

the 36 residents tested had, quote, increased frequencies of cells
with chromosome breaks, I saw—

— *It appears that chemical exposures in Isaura may be*
responsible for much of the apparent increase in the observed
cytogenetic aberrations and that residents are at an increased risk
of neoplastic disease, of having spontaneous abortions and of
having children with birth defects—Dr. Dante Pucciani, head of
Study, I saw—

— *But later today a State of Missouri scientific panel,*
organized by Governor Stockton, declared that the Pucciani study
was, quote, literally impossible to interpret and cannot be taken
seriously as a piece of sound epidemiological research, I saw—

— *Such a poorly designed epidemiological investigation*
should not have been launched in the first place, the panel said, I
saw—

— *With so much at stake for the residents involved, the panel*
said, to have set up experiments that lead to public conclusions of
such magnitude, without prior review of the protocol by qualified
uninvolved peer scientists, and without any after-the-fact, indepen-
dent review by competent scientists before release of the results, was
a disservice to the citizens most intimately concerned, I saw—

— *The findings are totally, absolutely and emphatically*
incorrect—Dr. Geoff Barron, Missouri Department of Health, I
saw—

— *The Environmental Protection Agency today reversed its*
own opinion on the recent, so-called Pucciani study of genetic
defects among Isaura residents, I saw—

— *A study that the Agency itself had commissioned,* I saw—

— *An EPA review panel, chaired by Dr. David Wall, director*
of the National Institute of Environmental Health Sciences, criti-
cized the Pucciani study, saying that it had no control group, used
a sample population that was too numerically small to be statisti-
cally meaningful, and had other faults that should have disquali-
fied it from bearing the EPA's imprimatur, I saw—

— *The EPA said that its own study, quote, provided an*
inadequate basis for any scientific or medical inferences from the
data, even of a preliminary nature, concerning exposure to mu-
tagenic substances by residents in Isaura, I saw—

— *I apologize for the poor performance on the part of my*

agency—Thomas C. Horling, EPA, I saw—

— *A new survey released today by the Missouri Department of Health shows that women between ages 30 and 34 residing within a half-mile radius of the Ozark Park section of Isaura have a miscarriage rate nearly four times higher than normal,* I saw on TV—

— *Although the survey concluded that there is, quote, no evidence for higher cancer rates associated with residence near Ozark Park in comparison with the entire state of Missouri outside St. Louis,* I saw—

— And I stood there, you know, I stood there in my living room looking at the television and I thought: whatever's in there is in us now—

— Shit: as far as I'm concerned, a lot of these so-called environmentalists are a bunch of bloody elitists who don't want the view from the kitchen window messed up—

— *New findings from Isaura show that the toxic and probably carcinogenic compound hexachlorocyclopentadiene, also known as hexa or C-56, has been found in water sources serving parts of that residential community in concentrations up to 12,000 parts per billion,* I saw—

— *Or nearly three times greater than the concentrations that recently sent State and Federal health and environmental study teams, including the EPA, swooping into the Missouri township,* I saw—

— *The results have been confirmed by chemists working at the EPA's Atlanta laboratory, one of whom said he was, quote, shocked by the findings,* I saw—

— *Contacted for comment, David P. Alan, Deputy Commissioner of Medical Services of the State of Missouri, said he could not believe it when he was told,* I saw—

— *They must have misplaced the decimal point—David P. Alan, Missouri Deputy Commissioner of Medical Services,* I saw—

— *Reversing its previous position, the Ozark photographic corporation, which is based in Isaura, acknowledged in a statement today that it does use the chemical C-56 in some of its imaging and processing procedures,* I saw—

— *Yes, we have some uses for C-56, which is a common industrial compound—Dr. William H. Lufton, Senior Vice Presi-*

dent for Corporate Relations, I saw—
    — Yes, we use C-56, although for reasons that must remain a trade secret—Anders H. Cosby, Chairman of Ozark Industries, I saw—
    — Nevertheless, it goes without saying that we have never had the chemical brought in purely for purposes of disposal, I saw—
    — We continue to believe that the presence of chemicals in the aquifer and bedrock poses no health hazard—Rick Polito, Unit Director for Water and Solid Waste Technology, Ozark Corporation, I saw—
    — It's intolerable; it's outrageous; this is as much a disaster as a flood or a tornado: we need aid from the federal government— Carol Daren, local activist, I saw—
    — Come on: what's going to happen?; I mean, we live two miles from Ozark Park; nothing could happen to us—
    — In Washington, a spokesman for the Water Resources Division of the United States Geological Survey has issued a warning about water quality in the Ozark Park section of Isaura, I saw—
    — Dr. J.E. Kennedy, Chief Hydrologist with the USGS, issued the announcement that, quote, A clear and immediate threat to local water supplies in Isaura does exist, I saw—
    — Responding to the USGS warning, Dr. Karen N. Ball, Assistant Deputy Health Director for Crawford County, urged caution, saying that the findings were preliminary and the testing not complete, I saw—
    — With the available information, it is not possible to demonstrate with certainty that unsafe levels of contamination do or do not exist; there remains a need to demonstrate more unequivocally that affected sections of Isaura are safe now and over the long term for human habitation—The Office of Technology Assessment, Washington, D.C., I saw—
    — We really have no idea what we're dealing with—Dr. Karen Ball, Crawford County Assistant Deputy Health Director, I saw—
    — Thomas Horling, Assistant Administrator of the EPA's water and water-management programs, today condemned the inconsistent information being presented to the public concerning the Isaura contamination scare, I saw—

— *I think our behavior in this instance is deserving of criticism—Dr. Thomas Horling, the Environmental Protection Agency, Washington, D.C.,* I saw—

— *In Isaura today, the town, already reeling from repeated threats of chemical contamination of local water supplies, was rocked by the news of a 14-year-old girl's suicide,* I saw—

— *Junior high school student Jolie Nevelson took her own life today with an overdose of sleeping pills, reportedly fearing that she would develop cancer,* I saw—

— *In the same way that members of eight of the twelve families living on her block had already developed the disease,* I saw—

— *Reached at Park Ridge Hospital today, the girl's distraught mother said that Jolie had become terrified of developing breast cancer, or a cancer that would make her unable to bear children,* I saw—

— *She worried that she would be unable to have a normal marriage—Ruth Nevelson, Mother,* I saw—

— *Today: findings of the deadly chemical hexa reach 19,000 parts per billion in residential water wells in the besieged city of Isaura,* I saw—

— *In Jefferson City this afternoon, Dr. Robert Malen, the Missouri Commissioner of Health, called a press conference to detail the state's position on developments in Isaura,* I saw—

— *A State Health Department study has found a slight increase in risk for spontaneous abortions among all residents of Isaura—Dr. Robert Malen, Commissioner of Health,* I saw—

— *But his later pronouncements were more sweeping,* I saw—

— *Discharges from the Ozark Park manufacturing plant constitute a public nuisance and an extremely serious threat and danger to the health, safety and welfare of those working at the plant, living near it or exposed to the conditions emanating from it—Dr. Robert Malen, Commissioner of Health,* I saw—

— *Ozark officials responded cautiously,* I saw—

— *We have a problem, we're not denying it, and we're working with all parties in trying to deal with it in the most responsible way—William H. Lufton, Senior Vice President for Corporate Relations,* I saw—

— *We want to do the right thing, and we will—Anders H.*

Cosby, Chairman, I saw—
— There may be things out there; we don't know—John L. Lehman, Vice President, I saw—
— Considering the circumstances, however, I would certainly say that the company has made an honest effort to try to communicate as best it can, in a very complex situation with an awful lot of different constituencies and an awful lot of different participants—Rob Ronalds, Ozark spokesman, I saw—
— In Jefferson City today, the Missouri State Supreme Court issued a cease and desist order against the Ozark photographic corporation to prevent further discharges of chemical wastes from its main plant in the city of Isaura, I saw—
— The order also set out a five-month compliance schedule for the company, during which the Isaura facility will have to submit a plan to State and Federal officials to concretely determine the extent of local chemical contamination, I saw—
— And to complete a survey of the plant itself for chemical contamination, and to remove all of its contaminated soil to a secure landfill, I saw—
— The company will also be obliged to seal all of its chemical treatment and storage areas to prevent further groundwater contamination, to submit a report detailing the extent of groundwater pollution and to make a comprehensive recommendation for a program of remedial action, I saw—
— And I thought—
— And I just thought—
— I am disappointed that the public reacts so intensely and emotionally about hazardous wastes and ignores such things as air pollution; often the same chemicals are involved; the public outcry over the air in St. Louis should be enormous, more so than over hexa—Ren Lafson, Director, Missouri Department of Natural Resources, I saw—
— In Washington today, the United States Department of Justice, in conjunction with the State of Missouri, filed a civil suit against the beleaguered Ozark photographic corporation in Isaura for its alleged noncompliance with Federal and State health and safety standards, demanding $30 million in penalties and $15 million for emergency reparations and cleanup, I saw—
— In addition, the Department of Justice announced that it

will begin a criminal investigation into Ozark's alleged violations
of interstate regulations concerning transportation of hazardous
substances, I saw—
— And again, I—
— And *again*, I—
— And again, *again*, this is something that I, for the life
of me—
— *This is something that I cannot believe*—
— I mean, it's like a nightmare, only the nightmare is
real, and it's our own land and it's destroyed for all time—
— I mean, it is *inconceivable*—
— I mean, the layoffs will be—
— *It's official: In Washington at noon today, the Environ-*
mental Protection Agency issued a press statement ordering all
individuals and families residing within a two-mile radius of the
Ozark Corporation photographic plant in the besieged city of Isaura
to be permanently evacuated from their homes; the Agency, quote,
strongly recommends that affected parties leave immediately or as
quickly as is practicably possible, but in no case later than by
Tuesday, August 16; the Federal Disaster Assistance Administra-
tion announced that it will pay all costs for temporary accommo-
dations needed and secured by evacuees, while a consortium of
Federal and Missouri State agencies, led by the Federal Emergency
Management Agency, will oversee the relocation of the affected
population and guarantee the fair market purchase value of all
relinquished homes, I saw—
— *The EPA later issued guidelines to residents of Isaura's*
two-mile contamination zone, to be followed without exception
during the eight-day period preceding mandatory evacuation: to
refrain from using well water for any human contact; to refrain
from consuming any and all fruits and vegetables produced in
backyard gardens; to refrain from entering area basements or
underground storage facilities, I saw—
— *The Missouri Department of Public Health today sent*
eighteen trucks carrying uncontaminated water to affected neigh-
borhoods in the besieged city of Isaura, and over 80 buses have been
brought in at State expense to wait along the streets of Isaura's
downtown area in case of emergency and cardigan and cardigan
not finished but I must, I must, of course, I must, so much, so

much work and mixing console, my mixing console, and of
course the brooch, I must my brooch, my mother's cameo the
cameo she for so long, for so many years, for so many so many
damn around her neck every holiday every wedding every
time anyone, when anyone would come, would visit, and I
can't, I cannot, and my Pinkerton, the badge, my damn badge,
which he gave, which I have got to take my Pinkerton badge
my Burkhard, of course Burkhard, I of course my newspaper,
at least, at least that, the newspaper, from my birthday, from
I, from *the* paper from *the* day, which he, which I, and which
my father's, my father's, my that I, that I just, and my lease,
I should, to know, I to have, I to have and keep, but where *my
damn lease*, and the Issa, my Issa, the book, exquisite little
ricepaper that I, that I cannot *and where is her sweater, where
is her* which was so, which was *so*, which so tiny, so very
small, that I, that I and even my scarf, my long wafting
wonderful, my long pale pink sheer I mean I, I cannot,
without, I cannot without, of course I cannot, of course not
never without, I can't, *I can't* and the saw, I my circular, good
heavy Black & Decker I saved for, so hard, I can't, I mean I
shouldn't can't, I should not even think about I and Kenwood, I my FM/cassette Kenwood, should I, but, but how,
and even the .44, even that, but should I, but should, should
I even the Late Quartets, even just CD of Juilliard, Late
Quartets, the Late, how can I without, I just a CD, I just a
Scooter Pie, but should I, no can't no be, should I, how can I
these tapes, all reel-to-reel, all the old no shouldn't, mustn't
of course shouldn't, just shouldn't, shouldn't even my clothing, my own clothing, my shoes, I shouldn't even take my
own shirts, my I nice, my I Polo, I should I just leave, just leave
back, and my sneakers, I with tread shouldn't, I shouldn't, I
shouldn't even take the shenai, dear shenai, my own dear I
where I breathed, where I through air, I shouldn't I even touch
it again, I shouldn't even take out of the box to goodbye, *I
shouldn't even touch it again* and the Physica, and even the
car, my car, how can, I mean, how can I, I should just, I
shouldn't even take my car *I shouldn't even take the Civic*
and pocketbook, my own, my with me for years, *for years, I
cannot even take my own pocketbook* I cannot touch I cannot

take, I must not, I must not even think, I cannot even take, so then what, then *what*, what then do I, do I do, do I just, do I just drop, do I just abandon, do I just *leave* do I just *leave* and *abandon*, and leave, leave everything, throw everything, just throw everything *just throw my entire* just *out*, physically *out*, just put them, physically take them and put them but where?, put them where?, *where can they be put?*, where is *where is out?*, where is *bother*, it's not, not even worth the bother *it is not worth the bother* where difference why bother throwing anything out?, it is already, it is *already it has already been done, everything is already everything is already out*, everything, every tiny corner and scintilla, definitively and forever, all definitively and forever, and *forever*, and *forever*, so just go, just go *out*, just get out, just hide in time and get out and become other, pretend there *is* other and hope to be able to return but to know that no return is possible and that it will never be possible, and to refuse to say goodbye because this cannot be goodbye, I cannot let myself believe that it is goodbye, but in saying this I also know that it is goodbye, that it definitively it is forever goodbye it cannot be otherwise and that the only return that will be possible will be the return that determines that returning is no longer possible, and so there is only turning, all that remains is wandering and turning, just going and *quickly* and turning, turning and *quickly* and turning and going and turning down Holmes Road and then down Somerworth Drive and then down Ridge to get to 390, and turning down Holyoke to get to Bonesteel to get over to 104 and then to get on 390, and turning down Emerson to get to Lee and then heading west on 31, and turning down Margold and down Flower City and then down Lake and over to Gorsline to get onto 104 going east just flowing, full flowing, inexorable flowing irreversible flowing, slow erratic mournful hesitant but flowing unstoppably flowing, flowing away from Norbert Street and Hammond Street and Bryan, and away from Curtis Street and St. Martin's Way and Johnson and Colin, and past Milford Street and Albemarle Street and Chesterton Road and Auburn and Towngate and Esquire, and past Birr and Castleford and State and past o dear God that poor little Stephanie, that pitiable little Stephanie, how that dear poor suffered, born faulty, born mangled, with a cleft palate and a bad ear, a deformed ear, and then o God I heard that soon her eardrums collapsed, her eardrums just disintegrated, and her heart was bad and her teeth were deformed and I will never, God I will never forget poor Stephanie Schroeder past Ridgecrest Road and Seneca Parkway and Rodessa, and up past Britton and past Elmgrove and past and in waves, the cars, the people, the families now as waves, disjoint, disparate, differently propagating differently routing but waves, finally waves, the cars the people the families now waves, unarguably waves, but waves out, waves away, waves that will refract and dissipate and scatter, waves that are bending and flowing and coursing, waves that are bending around what is flowing in, flowing back, flowing back in, the inflowing waves of government trucks and government equipment and leased equipment, of reinforcing equipment and removing equipment and transporting equipment and protective gear, of low-risk specialists and high-risk workers and high-risk workers, and then someone finally someone showed up, finally damn finally someone finally showed up, the cipher running for vice-president showed up, someone finally deigned to show up, but the someone he only stood in an insulating suit and walked around and looked around for five minutes, he walked into one rear area and behind one fence and that was it, he only drove in for five minutes with all his cars and guards and that was it, that was all, it was only a photo opportunity, that was it, it was nothing, there was nothing, nothing but in time there were others, there began others, there began other arriving, over time other arriving, just arriving, arriving and flowing in, streaming in, arriving, from limitless sources unknown and known: letters, sealed letters, flowing in and truck-taken in and transported in, letters from all, from all the state, from all the nation, the continent, the scatterling all, streaming and fluttering in, flowing in, letters addressed to an address, to a particular address, to an address on Wheatland Street, letters streaming in by the dozens then by the hundreds then by countless quantities, fluttering in in countless continuous arcs of fluttering white, in fluttering arcs streaming in, streaming in from every direction, continuous arcs of fluttering white streaming through the air and into an address on Wheatland Street, to a tree at an address on Wheatland Street, from wherever they came they were addressed to a tree on Wheatland Street, and when eventually they were opened, when some of the letters were opened, all the letters, all read like confessionals, they seemed confessionals, an abundant and endless outpouring of confessionals, an outpouring that kept coming, and streaming, just streaming in, the letters, just streaming in, and so the cry went out, the cry went up No more letters, please no more letters to the tree on Wheatland Street, but still they came, still they came, winging in, fluttering in, fluttering in arcs in, great bending continuous discontinuous arcs of fluttering letters, so finally the letters were returned, they had them returned, they were returned to sender, the announcement came that they did not know what to do with all the letters, that they could not handle all the letters, so the letters were being returned, all returned, but the letters, the letters just kept coming, endlessly coming, they kept arcing and fluttering in, but then the arcing white-trail letters came fluttering in with just one address, with just one address and no return address, but with just the one address on Wheatland Street, they only bore one address, and so the inflowing letters piled and flooded and massed, they poured and fluttered and stacked and massed, bearing just the one address and a stamp and a postmark, that was all, flowing and blurring in bearing only a stamp and the one address and the varied postmarks of the trauma-kindred towns of Rehoboth and Yellow Creek and Institute, and of Williamstown and Acton and Midland and Waterford, and of Friendly Hills, and of Pittsfield, and of Glen Cove and Lathrop and Coventry and Aurora, and of Hicksville, and of Texas City and Mead and Darrow and Granite and Nash and Point Pleasant, and of Corrigan, and of Montague, and of Charlotte and Youngsville and Byron and Agana and Alsea and Hopewell and Ambler and Pittston and Canton and Bayou Sorrel, and of Model City, and of Elizabeth and Mosco Mills and Pichens and Albuquerque and Kernersville and Medon and Belmont and Lebanon and Winnebago and White Springs and Chester and Denny, and of Camden, and of Shakopee, and of Dundalk, and of Toone, and of Stringfellow, and of Orleans, and of Allendale, and of Gray, and of Mount Vernon, and of Wilsonville and Bedforf and Taft, and of Beatty, and of Arlington, and of Hemlock, and of Southington and Philadelphia and Hodgenville, and of Waynesboro, and of Attleboro and Little Elk Valley and Edison and Shepardsville and Columbia and Sheffield and Howell and Friendswood and Deerfield and Newark and Briggs and Old Bridge and Yerington and Charles City and Saltville and Forks of Salmon, and of Syracuse and Allentown and Beaumont and Kimball and Emelle and Coeur D'Alene and Kingsport and Riverside and Lincoln and Geneva and Lima and Globe and Greenville and Youngstown and Ponca City, and of Sellersburg, and of Batesville, and of Barnwell and of Maui, and of Bridgeport, and of New Bedford, and of Escondido, and of Mio, and of Harriman, and of Lansdale, and of Bethpage, and of Hanford, and of Jackson Township, and of Criner, and of Wawayanda, and of Erie, and of Seymour and Livingston, and of Saint Louis Park and Patterson, and of Rancho Cordova and Waverly and Somerville and Joliet and Basile and Triana and Detroit and Cabazon and Lowel and Perham and Montebello and Farmington and Syosset and Richland and Perth Amboy and New Bedford and Donara and South Brunswick and Puyallup, and of Plainfield, and of West Nyack, and of Fort Meade, and of Staten Island, and of West Covina, and of Verona and Miami and West Valley and Kokomo and Islip and Holtsville and Tuscaloosa and Wallkill and Goshen and Kearny and Pleasant Plains and Eddy Stone and Humacao and Warwick and Centralia and Roosevelt but by then the letters no longer had letters, they no longer held letters, the letters were empty and vacant and were only envelopes, thin light rattly white paper envelopes containing air and nothing, only air and nothing, but still sealed and still stamped and still sent, and they came fluttering in just as envelopes, the letters were only envelopes, and the letters that were not in the envelopes said Race of Samsons Race of Samsons where else could this end?, where else could this go but here—to this sub-banal recounting of cliché upon cliché, of sub-banal cliché reinventing itself but still cliché, where else could it end but here—at the *away*, the definitive *away*, the conclusive *away*, for this is our classicism, our contemporary classicism, this is our willed determinism and sought-after structure, the nostalgic dynamism that strumpets fractal consciousness, that totals the holomovement, that goes beyond the Encompassing, beyond the reaches of distributed memory and even beyond these exercises in extended empathy, bringing to crib death even the babies satisfactorily born, putting to rest even the catcalls of misplaced Millenarianism, and the other letters, all the other letters that were not there said Where are the new crusaders? and Who could imagine such betrayal? and Where are the new crusaders? and Tell me now of jackals and betrayers and Where you will die I will die and *Where are the new crusaders?* but by then the signals were faint, the sounds and the signals were flickering and faint, yes, the signals were flickering out, flickering into the amassing regathering, into the conclusive regathering where physics becomes math becomes psychology becomes biology, yes flickering and lost to the definitive regathering, the comforting regathering into continuity, into continuousness, into abundance, into that abundance that is silently and invisibly working on every variation, into full and enfolding abundance, into the extreme abundance of silence, yes into its opulent abundance, its sweet unity and opulence, this definitive regathering into willed abundance, into the sweet abundance of silence, of unity and silence, yes this definitive reclamation, this grand extreme regathering and reclamation into silence, for where else could this go but silence, yes silence: silence. Silen